(1179)

YEAR
of the
MONKEY

Ronald Argo

Simon and Schuster
New York London Toronto Sydney Tokyo

Simon and Schuster
Simon & Schuster Building
Rockefeller Center
1230 Avenue of the Americas
New York, New York 10020

SIMON AND SCHUSTER and colophon are registered trademarks
of Simon & Schuster Inc.

Designed by Irving Perkins Associates
Manufactured in the United States of America

1   3   5   7   9   10   8   6   4   2

Library of Congress Cataloging in Publication Data
Argo, Ronald.
Year of the monkey.

1. Vietnamese Conflict, 1961–1975—Fiction. I. Title.
PS3551.R418Y4 1989   813′.54   88-35638

ISBN 0-671-66360-7

Excerpt from "The Way of Tet" reprinted from *The Prairie Schooner*
by permission of the University of Nebraska Press. Copyright ©
1988 by the University of Nebraska Press.

to
Mary E Anderson

Year of the monkey, year of the human wave,
the people smuggled weapons in caskets through the city
in long processions undisturbed
and buried them in Saigon graveyards . . .
Tomorrow blood would run in every province
Tomorrow people would rise from tunnels everywhere
and resurrect something ancient from inside them . . .
in a wave that arrives
after a thousand years of grief
at their hearts.

—Bruce Weigl
from "The Way of Tet"

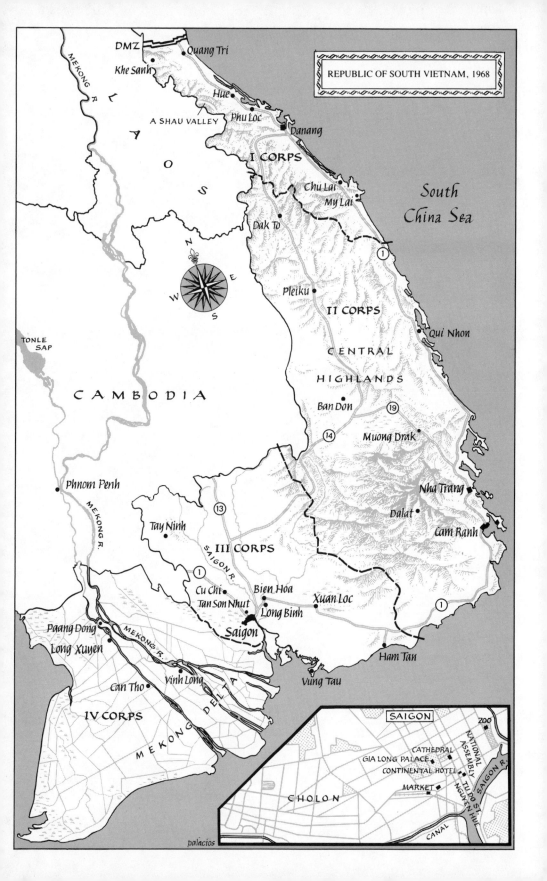

REPUBLIC OF SOUTH VIETNAM, 1968

DMZ
Quang Tri
Khe Sanh
Hue
A SHAU VALLEY
Phu Loc
Danang
I CORPS
Chu Lai
My Lai
Dak To
Pleiku
II CORPS
Qui Nhon
CENTRAL
HIGHLANDS
Ban Don
Muong Drak
Nha Trang
Dalat
Cam Ranh
Tay Ninh
III CORPS
Cu Chi
Bien Hoa
Tan Son Nhut
Xuan Loc
Long Binh
Saigon
Ham Tan
Paang Dong
Long Xuyen
Can Tho
Vinh Long
Vung Tau
IV CORPS
MEKONG DELTA

LAOS
CAMBODIA
TONLE SAP
Phnom Penh
MEKONG R.
SAIGON R.
South China Sea

SAIGON
ZOO
CATHEDRAL
NATIONAL ASSEMBLY
GIA LONG PALACE
CONTINENTAL HOTEL
MARKET
TU DO ST
NGUYEN HUE
SAIGON R.
CHOLON
CANAL

palacios

Chapter

I

The window in his cell looked out on a closed-in yard of pines and ivy. The view reminded him of the courtyard in the New Orleans hotel where he and Ann had stayed on their honeymoon, its slender airy trees stretching for sunlight beyond two tiers of balconies, and water softly gurgling, like a love song, in the mossy fountains. The honeymoon courtyard had ornate wrought-iron tables with glass tops where they brunched, chilled in the late-morning shadows. Here, behind a high, entombing brick wall, there was a single redwood picnic table sequestered in a cluster of dark timber. And the falling water was rain, the showers of spring. That he thought of the New Orleans courtyard was odd, for this yard had neither flowers nor open verandas nor lovers.

The smoke falling from his nostrils climbed along the window pane, blurring the view in a translucent blue softness.

Payne turned from the window and called down the hallway. Keys rattled and a voice replied, "Right there," followed by the click of boots sounding along the polished corridor. It surprised him how quickly Hansen responded. His was a civility out of character for an MP.

"Going out in the rain again?" Hansen asked good-naturedly, unlocking the door. His cheerfulness too was inappropriate; it contradicted his job. "Won't help your cold none, you know."

The guard walked Payne down the corridor and unlocked the

9

outer door, complaining that he looked sick and ought to go to the infirmary. "You don't need to go out in no rain, man," he said again, as though they were buddies.

Payne turned up his collar and held it as if he were stepping into a blizzard. "I know," he said.

The rains had come early, cold droplets hurled to earth with fierce, impatient anger, as though Payne were being reminded and assured his ordeal was not yet over.

The downpour pelted his lips and eyelids, cooling the flame on his skin. The cold had gone deep in his chest.

He walked straight-legged under the soiled sky without the crutches. The hip was getting better, for he was able now to maneuver longer at a normal gait before the wire-pulls bent him in a knot. Prolonged or fast walking heated the metal, often pulling so sharply he would cry out. The doctors said the discomfort might last a year or more, he'd have to adjust, use a crutch. But Payne couldn't get used to the crutches, and only at his lawyer's insistence did he use them in the courtroom.

He knew that being outside with a fever was foolish; yet the rain had a way of soothing and clarifying things, like therapy, reminding him who and where he was and that he was still alive when he too should have been dead. The rain reminded him of Willingham. So he walked in it, hating it and thankful for it.

When the pain became unbearable, he went in and took a hot shower and later met with his lawyer, who showed up unannounced. The court had appointed Captain Lowe, and Payne had accepted him after their initial talk; the lawyer had been responsive and seemed sincere. The case was not a career builder, but Lowe worked diligently, putting out an effort beyond Payne's expectations. He was matter-of-fact and did not try to delude his client with false hope.

Lowe had a long neck with a high, egglike Adam's apple that bobbed when he concentrated or talked, an adolescent quirk he seemed unaware of; and he constantly blinked his eyes. The eye blinking was an unquieting habit that made him look nervous and unsure of himself in the courtroom.

The lawyer had come to clear up some details.

"You got an Article 15 you didn't tell me about," he said accusingly. "It cites habitual tardiness to company formations when you were at Polk. What about it?"

"I'd forgotten about that," Payne said wearily. "My top sergeant wanted my ass."

"Why?"

"Because I kept putting in paperwork to delay my orders. He didn't like paperwork."

"What was the reason for a delay?"

Payne sneered at him. "What the fuck reason do you think? I didn't particularly want to go. Did you?" He knew the lawyer hadn't done a tour.

Lowe was used to tolerating outbursts from the accused. His Adam's apple and eyelashes fluttered as he waited for an answer.

"All right," Payne relented. "My brother was in the navy, in the Gulf of Tonkin at that particular time. I thought I might have a shot under the clause that eliminates brothers from serving at the same time. But that didn't work since it wasn't a declared war. Then my mother had to have an operation and I tried on those grounds. I was the only one to look after her. But Top thought I was just fucking off."

"The Article 15 says habitual tardiness."

Payne sneezed into a handkerchief and yelped from the resultant pain in his gut. "I was late to one fucking formation. I had to pull extra duty for a weekend, no big deal. He was a hard-nosed bastard."

The lawyer blinked disappointedly. "Look, Russell, I'm trying to build a character case. How do you think it would look if they were to bring this thing up now without my knowing about it? Is there anything else on your record I should know about?"

Payne moaned from the burning in his sinuses. He grinned ironically. "Yeah, sure. Two Purple Hearts and a shitload of commendations."

"I meant negative. I know about those." The lawyer sighed easily. "Now listen to me. I'm going to put you on the stand and a lot of what the court decides will depend on the way you present yourself. If you come off flip, they're going to take a hard line. I can guarantee that."

Payne looked sourly at him. He got up and walked around the chair. "I'd say they've already taken a hard line, wouldn't you?" he said through his teeth. "You think it matters how I conduct myself? They're going to burn me and we both know it." He spoke levelly, knowing his anger was misplaced with the lawyer.

Lowe scowled. "Don't presume judgment. It's not a clear-cut case and they're human, capable of being influenced by an honest display of remorse. . . ."

"Remorse means I'm guilty."

The lawyer shook his head hopelessly. "Let's face it, there's a ton of evidence that says you are. We have to concentrate on the reason you did it; that's all we've got to go on."

Lowe snapped his briefcase shut. "You look like hell, Russell. I want you to get some rest over the weekend. Monday's it."

Payne was escorted back to the detention barracks. The cell had a soft bunk and an overstuffed easy chair with padded armrests that smelled of the sweat of men before him. Overhead was a light he could switch on or off at will. There was a desk with a screw-down lamp similar to the crane-necked lamp he'd had in the hootch. The cell had the same general dimensions as his hootch.

He peered through the rain-forked window glass into the growing darkness outside where the city's glow haloed the high wall. It was the sudden burst of buzzing yard lights that started the reel—the burning huts and Willingham under the tree, sprawled there as if sleeping peacefully amid the shouting, the screams, indifferent to the paroxysm of close-quartered combat. The reel had played in his mind so many times now it had become as familiar as looking into a mirror.

He sank into the armchair and began concentrating on numbers, counting like an ethered patient, until the reel finally ended.

Before he drifted into sleep Pruett called out across the hallway. "Hey, Payne. You busy, man?"

Payne lifted himself tiredly out of the chair and went to the door. Pruett was across and up a cell from him, peering through the peephole window with a fist white-knuckling the bar. His eyes were opened wide and angled sideways so that he had the look of insanity. Pruett was supposed to have left for Leavenworth days ago, to do twenty years for killing an ARVN officer. He was nineteen.

"I got some angel food in the mail I'll trade you for your dessert," Pruett said. "Where you been anyways, man? You there, Payne?"

Payne spoke in a deadpan so Pruett would not get excited and start kicking the door. "Strolling. Talking with Lowe."

"What'd he have to say?"

"Told me to lay off the booze and women and grass."

Pruett laughed and kicked the door. "Hey, yeah. Maybe I ought to do the same. But, no shit, what does he think your chances are for dismissal, did he talk about that?"

Payne had a hand inside his fatigues, unconsciously tracing the ridges of scars. Because the area was still sensitive to the touch and aggravated easily in starched greens, he wore silk underwear. "He doesn't know."

"He's fucking with you, man."

"He's okay."

"Oh yeah? Then how come he won't bring up the business about that colonel selling them gook bodies? Huh? Fucking racket, man."

"It's not relevant."

"The fuck you say it ain't relevant." Pruett violently kicked the door and Payne told him to knock it off. He was sorry he'd ever told Pruett about it. Pruett had a hot temper and seemed to enjoy getting worked up.

"You got the royal shaft, Payne. You ought to of been ribboned for what you done. I mean nobody in the bush would've got sent up for wasting his buddy. Nobody ever wasted a buddy, and I don't give a good goddamn if he was a grunt *or* a fucking REMF; it just never happened, man. Just goes to show you how fucked—"

"All right, Pruett."

Pruett was quiet for a moment, then said, "You want to play some backgammon?"

He and Pruett were the only prisoners on the floor. The day he arrived Pruett told him what he'd done, and he in turn had wanted to know Payne's story. Pruett's had been a clear case of premeditation and it bothered Payne that he enjoyed killing the man.

"The fucking ARVNs were supposed to guard part of the perimeter," he had said, animated and livid. "That's all they had to do. We was out doing seek and delete, doing their fucking job, and all they had to do was pull guard. Then one evening this motherfucking gook lieutenant pulled his men in because it was raining and he didn't want them to get their fucking uniforms wet. That's when we was attacked —just then, just like Charlie fucking knew there was going to be an opening in the line. We lost eight on accounta what that ARVN done. I had a close buddy that was one of 'em. The gook cried to the old man that he was sorry, but he done it again three days later, the same goddamn thing. They just gave him a hand slap and said it was okay, could happen to anybody. So I decided to waste him. I got him in the night, just like a fucking slope woulda done. Side of his own command post. He knew it was me, I made sure that he knew. You shoulda seen the surprise on his face when he saw my intent. I stuck him under the ribs, then I stuck him in the carotid. If I'd a done the job right and cut off his head, I'd a got by with it cause he coulda never identified me. But fuck the consequences, man, I'd do it again."

Payne envied the transparent simplicity of Pruett's action and the fact that even now, months later, he had no moral compunction about it. But he wondered how Pruett would feel years from now, when the agony of his hatred tempered, or whether he would ever get over it. Payne didn't hold Pruett in contempt for what he had done; Pruett wasn't to blame. It was the Nam, the way it had of sucking you in so deep that you lost track of right and wrong, to where you didn't care what happened. It was the Nam that made you say, "Fuck the consequences, man."

"I've got to sleep for a while, Pruett. Maybe tomorrow."

"You can have the angel food anyways, man, cause I hate the shit."

Payne drew the curtain over the door slot and again reclined in the soft chair with his case folder on his lap. He lit a cigarette and lightly rubbed his thumb along the smooth surface of the Zippo. The smoke burned his nostrils and he breathed it through his mouth. He skimmed over the pages of documents. There were the reports of the army investigators, several dossiers, sworn interrogation statements and affidavits and depositions taken from witnesses and other officials, and the charges. The English language could be cruel and the wording of the charges made him out a monster:

Specification: On 6 January 1968, at about 2000 hours in an unmapped hamlet used as a North Vietnamese Army encampment in the province of Tay Ninh approximately two kilometers from the Cambodian border, Specialist 4 Russell Henry Payne of Headquarters and Headquarters Company, Saigon Support Command, Long Binh, Vietnam, did commit assault upon Corporal Daryll Willingham by shooting him in or about the head with a pistol of unknown caliber and did thereby intentionally inflict fatal bodily harm to him. . . . Specification: . . . that Specialist Payne, by not attempting to defend a senior officer in grave danger of his life, did willfully neglect and therefore contribute to murder in the brutal death of Lt. Colonel Rupert Shellhammer. . . . Specification: . . . that Specialist Payne demonstrated blatant negligence amounting to acquiescence in the deaths of four enlisted personnel of the Army of the Republic of Vietnam and furthermore of the systematic murdering of thirteen Asiatic refugees. . . . To the specifications, charges of one count of murder, and two counts of willful neglect resulting in murder.

There had been no deal to reduce any of the charges as there might have been if, as Lowe reluctantly admitted, the death of an American colonel had not been involved. Consequently, the charges had not been altered since the preliminary hearing at Long Binh. The lawyer was hopeful he could get the murder charge reduced to willful manslaughter. He was unsure what he could do with the other charges. He would not even speculate on the possibility of dismissal or acquittal without any supporting evidence. As to how much real time Payne might do, the lawyer mutely threw up his hands, as if it were anyone's guess.

At the change of guard Hansen stopped by his cell with an amber-colored bottle. "It's codeine," he said, pushing wide the door and assuming a stance that under the naked light made him the metallic, menacing figure he was supposed to be. "I got it for myself but you need it worse. Here, have some."

Payne swallowed a slug and lay back down on the bunk.

This was Hansen's first assignment out of MP school and getting it had been a stroke of luck, which Hansen resented. He didn't complain about the job, but he was disappointed his request for Nam duty had not yet come through. His interest in the war zone seemed undaunted by his contact with men who had cracked over there and gone off the deep end, committing some kind of violent criminal act, men who did not want to be bothered by a shiny-faced guard asking naive questions. But Payne didn't belittle him and Hansen threw questions at him whenever he had the chance.

"Hey, these of you in the Nam?" he asked, stepping to the desk.

Payne lifted himself on an elbow.

"Mind if I take a look?"

Payne shrugged. "Nothing interesting, but go ahead."

Hansen picked up a handful of the pictures. Most of them were extra six-by-eights Payne had printed up for his personal use, photos of peasants and villages and a few of the sights in Saigon he'd wanted to remember. Some of his belongings had been sent home and Ann had brought him the photos.

"Shit, you must have had some wild times getting to go anywhere you wanted to. Who's this one of, man? Fucking beautiful."

Payne leaned over to look. "Girl I knew, a Montagnard."

"Shit," Hansen said, stretching the word out. "Your babysan? Looks about twelve. I guess the women are all pretty tight, huh, being so little. Is it true that you can tie their nipples in knots?"

The guard had no idea who the girl was or what she meant to Payne, and Payne might have reproached him for it, assumed that condescending attitude you would assume with a new man arriving in-country, just because he was a cherry. But Payne was ingratiated with Hansen's childlike spontaneity; he didn't pretend to know any more about the Nam than the rumors he'd heard, and he didn't mind asking. It was his being himself that Payne liked; it was a quality that reminded him of Willingham.

Payne grinned off the side of his face. "It's true. But don't try it with the Chinese. They'll want to tie your pecker in a knot."

The guard's big arms shook when he laughed. He stopped flipping pictures and said, "Hey, fuck. Look at you, man. This one of them Russian AK-47s you've got, ain't it? Way I hear it, 47's about the best souvenir you could ask for. How'd you get it?"

Payne shrugged and pillowed his head with his arm. His eyelids were already growing heavy from the drug; he hadn't eaten since breakfast.

Hansen persisted. "You get it in a firefight? Was that it?"

"Naw. Traded some potatoes for it, with another Indian. Friend I used to smoke opium with," Payne said tiredly. "Called himself Tieng-of-the-Two-Faces."

"What the fuck kind of name is that?"

"Crazy, huh," Payne drawled. He didn't elaborate.

"I wish my orders would hurry up and come through," the guard said. "I'm ready to get on over there."

Payne regarded him kindly. "Yeah, I guess you have to go, find out for yourself. . . . Listen, Hansen, I need to get some shut-eye. Thanks for the medicine."

Hansen stiffened into an MP again and jangled keys. "Sure. I'll crank the heat up before I take off."

"Don't. I sleep better when it's cold."

The guard shrugged his broad shoulders and said goodnight. Payne was out before the clicking of his boots faded.

By breakfast the fever had gone, and despite the increased rumbling in his chest he felt better. When notified of Ann's arrival, he took a double swallow of codeine and met her in the visiting room. She was dressed in a summer cotton print of brown and beige, colors that heightened the glow on her skin. Her presence gave warmth and color to the drafty gray room.

Her hair was damp with rainwater and she stood by the window brushing it out. Turning as he entered, she went through the motions of smiling and moving forward to hug him, slightly parting her lips, waiting for his kiss.

"I've got a cold," he said, kissing her under the ear. His hands slid along the full length of her bare arms. Her skin was warm and inviting to the touch, and she didn't wince at the coldness of his hands.

Ann assumed a maternal frown and put the back of her hand to his forehead. "Is it the malaria? Have they given you anything?"

"I'm okay. How was Mother when she left?"

Ann sat down in a straight-back chair and crossed her legs. The sleeveless dress looked good on her. With her strong shoulders and slender hips, almost anything she wore flattered her. Payne had never heard her fuss about the way she looked or what she wore; she seemed never to give it a thought. She was especially desirable in cotton print.

"It wasn't easy being with her," she said, averting her eyes. "I think she just won't let herself accept what's happened. And you really can't blame her."

She lifted her eyes as far up as his chin. "I don't want to hurt you, Russ, or make things worse for you right now. I know it must be terrible what you're going through. But I'm having trouble understanding it too. Whatever happened to you that could have caused you to shoot somebody you say was your friend is . . . it just doesn't make any sense. It's hard to accept."

Payne sat down in front of her and leaned forward, touching her hands. His skin was pallid but still darkly tanned, and her hands in his were the mere ghosts of hands.

Losing Ann was not the hardest part; that had seemed inevitable for some time, and Payne had already accepted that she would leave him. It came almost as a relief, for now he would not have the burden of trying to make her see that it wasn't he who was to blame for killing a friend but rather the circumstances. Circumstances that were impossible to make sense of.

"Do you remember me writing you a long time ago how I was going to make a lot of money, and then had to write you later that the scheme backfired?"

The tenseness on her face eased slightly and Ann grinned reflectively, saying she remembered.

"And that I was always telling you how easy I had it, that I couldn't be in less danger anywhere else?"

He waited till she nodded. "Remember before I left how solid we were? Nothing was going to come between us. It's hard to imagine back then, isn't it? So much has happened since. Back then we were so . . . so young. I don't know. I guess what I'm saying, Ann, is that we're not the same two people we were before."

"I know," she said distantly, as though to confirm that their differences had become too vast to work out. "You're not the same man I married, I know that. But neither am I. We—" She hesitated. He thought she was about to get on her antiwar platform again.

He stood behind her and squeezed her shoulders. He couldn't keep his hands off her. He kept thinking of her in bed with Rand and the thought made him want her more. He stroked her hair and she didn't resist.

"But how could it happen, Russ? I have to understand. Don't you see? If you can't make me understand, I don't know what's going to happen with us."

"I know it's hard, Annie. I don't understand myself. The only thing I can tell you is I don't believe I did the wrong thing. I want you to know that."

Her head dropped and he thought she was crying. "I want to think so, Russ. Believe me, I do. But how can I? How can anyone?"

Chapter

2

The final game of the World Series had been broadcast this morning, at the same time it was played later in the day yesterday back in the world. Since baseball is not a morning sport, the game was aired again this evening, one full day after the live performance, to give Vietnam a semblance of normalcy.

Payne didn't feel any sense of normalcy listening to yesterday's game; Vietnam already knew the Cardinals had won it and he had already lost the twenty he'd foolishly bet Cowboy on the Red Sox. But he was plugged into his portable Sony anyway, feet propped on the top of his desk, a can of beer from which he periodically chug-a-lugged safely concealed under the desk. Except for the secretary's occasional peck-and-check on her typewriter keys, the office was quiet; everyone had left early to catch the rerun on television.

Sportswriters had unanimously picked St. Louis, some saying the Cardinals would sweep Boston and others predicting five games, six at most; the Sox, they agreed, didn't stand a chance in hell against the incredibly hot Cardinals. But the Series had achieved something of spectacular proportions when Boston came back to tie St. Louis at three to take it to the final game. Regardless of the outcome, the Red Sox had already elevated the '67 Series into the stuff of myth, and it seemed to Payne that this gave Boston the impetus to win and he took Cowboy on.

The pundits had called a seventh game "inconceivable," and

19

when it happened, they changed their tune, pontificating that Boston had achieved the "impossible dream." The last year Boston had won a World Series was 1918, the year the United States won its first world war.

In retrospect Payne knew he should not have made the bet; it was foolish taking a chance on something you knew very little about. He had paid no attention to the playoffs; he didn't know the Sox had just survived one of the fiercest struggles in AL pennant race history and that they were a haggard team going into the Series. In the seventh game they had to start ace pitcher Jim Lonborg with only two days' rest, and he came out pitching them up in the batters' faces, allowing six runs to score before drive-'em-till-they-drop manager Dick Williams mercifully walked to the mound in the sixth. Even Carl Yastrzemski's triple-crown bat turned to rubber and couldn't pull the Sox out of the six-run deficit.

Payne made it through the fifth inning before jerking the earpiece and dumping the radio into a drawer. When you know your team has been beat, he decided rationally, why endure the agony? Get the hell out of it. The money was the hard part; other than a propensity to root for the underdog, he had no fan's tie to the Red Sox. But on a Spec 4's salary after spousal allotment was taken out, losing twenty bucks meant sharply altering his spending habits for the next couple of weeks. Payne liked to challenge himself, but this stupidity had taught him a small lesson: know something about what you're getting into before you fucking do it.

The secretary read his sour mood and looked at him as though she might cry. He smiled benignly, appreciative of her support.

"You berry sad dog, Lussell," she said, beginning to tidy up her desk for the day. "What matter you?"

"Shows, huh? Guess it's that I didn't get a letter again."

"You wife no undah-sand. She spoil," Lai Sin said frowning.

"Yeah, she ought to be spanked."

"You want me write you wife, tell her you write you husband or he get Saigon girlfriend?"

Payne laughed. "That would do it all right."

He finished off the lukewarm beer, hook-shot the can into the wastebasket across the room, and made himself busy with the stack of hometown news releases in his In basket, not in the mood to think about home. That Ann had not written in twenty-one days was a great deal more discouraging than losing his drinking and gambling money, and if he started on the business of her anemic correspondence, he knew it would lead to worse thoughts.

He was writing a piece on a trooper from San Francisco whose information sheet said he had danced in Balanchine's *Jewels,* embellishing the article to make enough inches that it might get picked up by the dailies back in the world, when Lai Sin suddenly shrieked. This wasn't especially unusual, since Lai Sin startled easily; the sudden whoomp of a helicopter or Cowboy cranking up his radio would set her off; even the lieutenant's officious pacing could get her going. But Payne had never gotten used to her shrieks, and his eyes shot her way and saw her walking her chair back against the wall, staring in wide-eyed horror at the man standing in the doorway.

Payne had to think her discomposure this time was not unjustified. He too was taken back at the sight of the man, the way he stood framed in the doorway, cool and mean and ready for anything. His hands pressing the framework, as though he could push down the walls if he wanted, made him seem larger than he really was. It was the weariness in his eyes that let him down.

Payne narrowed his eyes, studying him. He wore rumpled jungle utilities, boots cracked and caked with red mud, a limp boonie hat that had "Die High" scrawled across the front in black ink. You didn't see many guys like him at Long Binh. He was out of his element. You could see he didn't belong here; he belonged to the jungle, the way a prisoner belongs to his cell.

"What can I do for you?" Payne said guardedly.

The man cocked his head and glared at Payne. He was tall and had an athlete's build and a rugged angular face with a long chin. The chin was thrust arrogantly forward; he was grinding a wad of gum. His face was deeply tanned, with creases of thin, milk-white lines at the corners from months of squinting in the sun. You had to imagine him without the stubble and grime to see he had a handsome face.

When he didn't respond, Payne sneered self-consciously, "Who are you? You lost?"

Peeling bubble gum off his chin, the soldier stepped forward, regarding Payne curiously, still ignoring the questions. His eyes left Payne to survey the office, skipping quickly from one thing to another as if disbelieving what he saw. The office was equipped like any Stateside Public Information Office with metal desks, electric typewriters, multilined telephones, ceiling fans, bookcases, a private room for the officer in charge.

Finally he shook his head and said, "In-fucking-credible. A fucking refrigerator."

He brushed aside the bush hat and manufactured a grin that lifted the hardness off his face. His hair was a dusty sun-bleached blond and curly, wildly exceeding regulation length. There were zigzagging lines of infected scratches on the backs of his hands and forearms up to the rolls of his sleeves; his unit patch had been removed.

"Shit, you guys have got the life of fucking Riley here, no doubt about it," he said easily and foot-pushed his duffle bag next to an unused desk. "I'll take this one," he added.

He fell heavily in the chair behind the desk and swung side to side a couple of times going through drawers.

"Where'd you plan to take it to?" Payne said. "You from supply?"

The grin broadened. "Wiseass. Guess it comes natural with the job to ask a bunch of questions," the man said. "That what you people call yourselves, reporters?"

He spoke in the same easy tone, looking not at Payne now but at the secretary's short-skirted legs, which she held tightly together. It was time for Lai Sin to leave if she was to make the six o'clock shuttle to Cholon.

Fidgeting under his stare, Lai Sin slipped her legs inside the desk cavity and turned to Payne for help. She did this silently with her eyes. Payne winked, fixing a smile, and told her she could leave.

The blond man watched with apparent disinterest as she gathered her stuff and traipsed quietly out of the office, freshening the air with a faint aroma of roses. Hers was the classy walk of the Vietnamese gentry.

"Journalist," Payne said. "So what are you?"

The dying sun streaked through the blinds, casting oblique shadows across the slumping soldier so that he appeared trapped inside the wall behind him. He shifted his eyes furtively, almost as if he wasn't sure of himself and was cloaking his uncertainty with a sullen placidity. His eyes in the sunlight were the color of blue steel.

"New guy on the block," he said, stretching and cracking his knuckles. "Any beer in that thing?"

Payne eyed him doubtfully; he wasn't a journalist or a clerk of any kind. He was strictly the outdoor type, a bushbeater. "I hadn't heard we were getting a new body," Payne said. "Let me see your orders."

"Any beer in that refer?" the man repeated tiredly. "It's been a long hot day, man. I could use a beer."

There was a genuineness in his tone that caused Payne to relent. "Nothing but sodas and cranberry juice. The lieutenant's, he's up-tight. You really been assigned here?"

"That's right. I really have."

"Well, where the hell did you come from then?" Payne was lean-ing over his typewriter, his thoughts racing with a mix of nervous curiousity and dread. "We usually get notified in advance when a new body's coming."

"You need a reservation or something? I was transferred. Hap-pens all the time. What do they call you?"

Payne told him his name.

"Tell you what, Payne. You lay off the third degree, direct me to the nearest bar and maybe a place to crash for the night, and I'll underwrite the beverages. And I ain't talking about fucking cranberry juice. Rumor has it you can get cold beer at Long Binh any fucking time. How 'bout it?"

Having lost his bar money and already resigned to a dry night, Payne grinned with idiotic delight. "You got it, man. Your choice, domestic or imported. Just one other question."

"Shoot."

"What do they call you?"

"Willie," he was told, short for Willingham, and after the fourth round of imported Moosehead at the clubhouse the new man drew a line. "Just so long as you don't make it Willie Peter or Willie Boy. Let's get that straight here and now. I hate being called Willie Boy."

"All right," Payne said in a higher-pitched voice than he meant to use. He was getting drunk and defensive.

Payne learned a few more things about him in the span of half a dozen beers. The guy had been transferred from 5th Special Forces Group of the 1st Special Forces out of Nha Trang, an outfit Payne knew about only from what he had read in military publications; 5th Special Forces was the home of the Green Berets, about the toughest and tightest group of motherfuckers in the Nam. The 5th was com-posed of guerrilla strike forces which pulled counterintelligence and secretive joint-allied operations, the kind of jungle-version cloak-and-dagger warfare higher would puff up with pride referring to, as if the fate of the war could be determined solely by Special Forces.

Willingham wouldn't talk about his outfit; he said only that he had been transferred yesterday, just like that, but he wouldn't give a reason. That he had six months left did not seem to bother him one way or the other. Payne figured it was because he had gotten out of the real war and would spend the rest of his tour in the safe confines of Long Binh.

Willingham talked freely, even amiably, about his background before the Nam. He came from Huntington Beach, California, and produced a snapshot of his girlfriend, Becky, a cherub-faced blonde in a skimpy bikini posing angularly to show off her curves and long hair. She was hugging the outside mirror of a jeep. "Mine and the old man's Baja machine. Bitchin'," Willingham said of the jeep, as if the girl were nothing more than an accessory to it. "CJ-7 with a high-performance 289 Mustang engine. Did the modifications ourselves."

He said he had been accepted into prelaw at UCLA, planning to follow in the footsteps of his father, a corporate lawyer, but got this wild hair and joined up instead. "I decided, fuck it," he said. "You can get educated anytime, but you can't go to a fucking war anytime." He shook his head miserably. "Goddamn beanbrain. Shows you what I fucking know. How about another cerveza?"

He had hunted bighorn sheep in the mountains of Baja California with his old man since he was ten and had brought in a marlin off Cabo San Lucas weighing 423 pounds. Not the biggest but it beat his old man's record of 300-something. He claimed to love baseball, a diehard Dodger Blue fan, but didn't even know the World Series was over or who had played in it. "You're shitting me," Payne said.

"Fucking world bullshit. Who won it?"

He had a horse's grin and offered it unsparingly, talking and joking about times back in the world, the crazy chances he'd taken on excursions with his father and surfing rock breakers at a beach he called Wipe Out, as if it were a ski chute; a fucking rich kid. He didn't consider himself especially attractive but admitted without any sign of vanity that the women must have thought so since they always seemed to be around, and he half grinned, half grimaced in mental reflection of their apparent abundance. "Can't help it, man. I'm just a born sucker for the chicks," he said. He was nineteen years old.

But when Payne came around with questions about his previous outfit, Willingham became cagey and dour, brushing him off with terse noncommittals, as though he had already divorced his thoughts from that part of his tour, as if the last six months were too dark to talk about or even remember.

A few of Payne's buddies dropped by to say howdy, wanting to shoot the shit, sheepishly eyeballing the grunt with him; Willingham made an imposing figure in his Die High boonie hat and tattered utilities reeking of cordite and jungle; among the preened and starched troops at the clubhouse he was as alien as the enemy himself. Haughtily, Payne said that he was the new guy and left it at that. Willingham appeared put out every time someone came over, turning his back, making it clear he didn't want to talk.

From the moment they'd walked in, Payne was keenly aware of who he was with and it made him feel a special kind of power, an invulnerability. But it was also an uncomfortable feeling, even frightening, being with a man whose presence testified to the fact that there really was a war going on outside the gates of Long Binh. His presence, Payne realized, announced danger.

"It must have been rough with Special Forces," Payne said, pressing to learn more. "What's your MOS?"

"You tell me. Whatever they call this PIO bullshit."

"I mean what was it before?"

You could see he was getting annoyed; a guy with a quick temper. "A specialty," he said patronizingly, letting his eyes wander. "Nothing I can use here."

"I thought you Special Forces dudes wore berets?"

Willingham measured him glancingly, drumming fingers on the bar as if deciding whether to tell Payne to get fucked or hit him with a beer bottle. "Not all us dudes."

"See much action?"

At length Willingham said, "Nothing I'd fucking write home about, man. Okay? You want to drop it?" and then changed his tone just like that. "So what are your women like down here?" He searched out the club's dim interior as if he expected to find women stationed at the bar or shooting pool.

Payne didn't feel like obliging him with an answer; he lit a smoke and leaned back pressing the cold sweaty bottle of beer against his face and neck.

Willingham didn't seem to notice the stares he was drawing. Soldiers drifting in took a second look at him, went about their business, then sought him out with stealthy sidelong glances, as if not knowing quite what to make of him but not anxious to find out. It wasn't just his looking like a grunt that drew attention; he acted like one, the obdurate, easy way he carried himself, as if he had been through it all and nothing else could ever affect him. But something affected him; you could tell he was hurting inside, the way he clammed up and wouldn't talk, as though he was haunted by some terrible thing he couldn't shake or hide from no matter where he went.

Payne watched him play with a ballpoint pen, unconsciously clicking the point in and out; it seemed a nervous habit.

"Nice pen, a graduation present or something?" Payne asked. The pen looked like one of those that comes in a set, gold-plated.

Willingham stopped flicking the pen and stared at it, testing its weight. "Buddy of mine gave it to me."

"Oh yeah?"

"Used to write nature poems, a regular Walt Whitman," Willingham said. "Definitely insane."

Payne sucked his beer and cigarette. "Doesn't sound weird. Lots of guys write poems. I write poems."

He pointed the beer bottle at a huge, shirtless man shooting pool. "Now that guy there's insane. Motor pool, pure fucking crazy," he said slurring his words. "I wouldn't go messing with him."

Willingham glanced at the man. "Bad, huh?"

"Yeah. Drowned a dog in a barrel of oil on a dollar bet. Well, maybe it was two bucks, but what's the difference? He also emptied a clip at his bunker relief," Payne added. "Which isn't so crazy, I guess, when you think about it. Got him permanently out of guard duty."

"He waste the guy?"

"Nah. Couldn't aim straight, I guess."

"That don't make him crazy. Probably just loaded and freaked." Beer dribbled down Willingham's chin to the tangled web of hair high on his chest. He raked the back of his hand across his mouth, raising a grin. He sliced a little stretch of air with the gold-plated pen. "This guy was definitely crazy. Lassiter, real superstitious type. He got cold feet one time before a crawl, said it didn't feel right, and gave me the pen to hold for luck."

"What's a crawl?"

"Tunnels," Willingham said. "He was our gopher, a true-blue volunteer."

"The guy volunteered?"

"Told you, insane. He wrote poems about trees. Had some clever things to say about roots being the most important part of the tree, the part you couldn't see. Crazy as a yo-yo, but very sensitive and smart."

"So did he?"

"Did he what?"

"You know, come out of the tunnel."

"Yeah, sure. Came out smiling with the gook ear between his teeth and popping his jaw no different than usual. Completely deaf; useless for the next hour." Willingham chuckled. "Then he wanted me to keep the pen because he *did* come out. Had great night vision. We called him Eyeball."

"Shit," said Payne. "The guy is crazy."

"Nah, not anymore," Willingham said. "He's dead."

He put the pen away and said he was going to take a piss and was gone, leaving Payne suddenly lost in a void. Payne slumped on the bar stool, trying to imagine how it would be, what you would be thinking, crawling down a small dark hole in the earth knowing the enemy was down there. You'd have to depend on more than instinct to survive; you'd have to know what to expect, and the only way to know what to expect would be from experience. But how did you get the experience without doing it first? What if you got stuck twenty feet down and discovered your gun was trapped under your body and there he was, Charlie, laughing at you with his yellow eyes; or hit some kind of booby you hadn't run across before, a den of vipers in your face, something like that? Who in their right fucking mind would volunteer to do that?

Payne wondered if he could do it, if he had the courage to kill a man. He had never even gotten mad enough at anyone to ball up his fist and hit him; there were times growing up in the South when he had backed off rather than fight, and he had never really been tested to know if he was just smart or afraid. He could have gone to AIT and been a foot soldier pounding the bush as easily as he'd gotten the quirk MOS of a journalist. He knew he'd been just plain lucky, and he was thankful as hell he would never have to know if he did have what it took.

It was six-thirty, and the club began to fill with supper traffic. Philadelphia subs was the special tonight, a favorite in the company. The clubhouse was one of those bennies Payne at first appreciated but by now took for granted, like everyone else; it was a place where you could have a change from the well-balanced messhall food, watch a movie, shoot pool, relax after work. The clubhouse was nothing spectacular; its hull was a rickety composite of plywood sheets and corrugated tin. Stacked sandbags kept it from falling apart. But it was furnished nicely with a regulation pool table that had live bumpers and good felt, an authentic L-shaped bar with leather padding, a large barroom mirror plastered with pinups that glowed under strung ornamental lights like a shrine. At the far end of the connecting patio was a ten-foot movie screen. Like a neighborhood bar, it was familiar and comfortable.

"Fill me in on this PIO business," said Willingham, taking his place again. "I mean do you sit on your ass all day or do they let you get off post?"

"Shit," said Payne. "You can go all kinds of places. We got field units spread out all over the bottom half of the country to do articles on. All kinds of bullshit things to get you out of here. I get around some," he said, modulating his voice to sound cool. "You know how to use a typewriter, or take a picture?"

Willingham found humor in that and laughed openly, exposing against his burnt face a row of luminous white teeth. "You call them grip and grins, right? That what I'll be doing?"

"We'll find something for you to do, don't worry about it." Payne didn't fully comprehend the sense of intimidation he felt, or that looking at the veteran soldier was an embarrassing reminder of what he was not.

"So what about the women?" Willingham said, holding a lop-sided grin.

"Sure we got women. You think this's the fucking boonies or something," Payne said loosely, nearly drunk on his empty stomach.

He caught the attention of the soldier tending bar and asked what flick was showing tonight. The soldier had a baby skin with a swab of peach fuzz over his lip, a bright-eyed kid probably no older than Willingham, but a lot younger-looking.

He talked on the move, adroitly distributing the eight bottles of longneck beer carried between his fingers. The kid was practiced at his job. "Double-O-Seven," he said. "The one with Pussy Galore, I think."

The place would be packed before eight, in a state of pandemonium by nine, closed by the MPs by nine-thirty. Payne didn't want any part of it; he was ready to leave now.

Willingham said to the bartender, "You have a movie every night?"

"Every night. Usually a different one," the kid shouted from the other end of the bar. *"Bonnie and Clyde* tomorrow, back by popular demand."

"Need a reservation for *that* too?" Willingham said to Payne and banged his bottle against the table like a rowdy drunk. "Fuck me. You people've got style—cold beer, refrigerators, a fucking pool table. Next thing you'll be telling me is you got television in your hootches. Welcome to the rear."

"It's not the fucking Riviera," growled Payne. "C'mon, I'll take you to a place a guy like you would like, if it's women you want. Chinese," he added with an air of cockiness.

"Chinese?" Willingham said amusedly, and as an afterthought, as if thinking to himself, said, "They must come from Saigon."

"Doubt they're smuggled in from fucking China," Payne snarled. He was growing increasingly fond of the new guy for allowing him the opportunity to make this sort of sarcastic remark. The guy didn't even take it personally.

Willingham passed his eyes around the growing crowd of short-haired, showered troops. "Probably be a good idea to make a move. Half the fucking guys in here look like they want to hear a bedtime story. A couple look like they're ready for a piece of my ass. Your crazy dog killer, for one."

He looked at Payne sympathetically. "Strange place. You people must get awfully bored around here."

Chapter

3

China Village was located off MacArthur Highway in the section of Long Binh known unofficially as the East Side Stretch, headquarters for half a dozen commands. It was here the post commander kept his thoroughbred racing horses on a thirty-acre spread behind his quarters. A year ago the Stretch was barren lowland desert where dust twisters roamed freely and vultures lulled away their days riding heat thermals and going hungry.

The place wasn't far, two clicks from the clubhouse. As they walked alongside the highway, Payne filled Willingham in on his new command. "Used to be the 506th Quartermaster Depot before the buildup started. Then it outgrew itself and they expanded it and called it Saigon Support Command. It was in Saigon then, down by Tan Son Nhut on Plantation Road. You been to Saigon?"

"Nope, not yet."

"You will now. I'll take you next time I go; you'll need to see the operation anyway."

"What goes on?"

"I put the paper to bed," said Payne. "That's right, I'm the editor, the number one honcho."

"I am impressed."

"Usually takes me about three days, one at MACV with the paper and two for R&R on the town. That's just between us, though. The lieutenant thinks it takes that long."

"Sounds like a real winner, your OIC."

"Ninety-day wonder. You'll love him."

"No doubt about it, a man that drinks cranberry juice."

"He bowls too," Payne said, grinning. "Wouldn't hurt to say something nice about his trophy when you meet him."

"Make a good first impression, huh?"

"Something like that."

Payne was enjoying the guy's sarcasm. He imagined the lieutenant's expression upon first seeing the new man; his boyish face would go blank and he'd stammer for something to say, trying to figure out what in hell he was going to do with a ratty grunt in his section, a section where dress conformity and the ministering of PR were fundamental to the job. The thought gave Payne something to look forward to tomorrow.

"Anyway," he continued, "the command moved to Long Binh because there was no place to billet all the fresh bodies pouring in, so they moved up here. That was last year. It's a big goddamn outfit, let me tell you. Thirty thousand and growing fast, largest depot in the world. Saigon Support keeps half the country rock-and-rollin'. Munitions, toothpaste, prophylactics, you name it. The motto is if a soldier uses it, SSC supplies it. Everything you guys get in the bush is compliments of SSC. Bet you didn't know that, did you?"

"No shit, everything? That include the dysentery?"

Payne stopped to dig a pebble out of his boot. He was panting from the pace Willingham had set. Other than an occasional jeep or truck the unlit road was deserted. A high half-moon bathed the ground in a blue-white glow, casting their bouncing shadows on the pavement in front of them. The stars shone bright and twinkled in a vaulted black sky, the Dippers clear and so bright they haloed. There was a clarity about the night sky here that took Payne back to his childhood, reviving fond memories of lying in the grass and making up stories of life in other places, exotic horror tales that scared his playmates. He was good at making up horror stories because, like scary movies, he never thought of them as real.

"I had a buddy die over here," he said offhandedly, recalling his closest childhood friend, a gullible boy named Junior Cotton— always scared to tears in the dark. "Fucking joined the marines. I knew him practically all my life."

"That all, just one?"

"It's not exactly the same as someone you didn't know before the Nam. It's different when you knew the guy that long. We were blood brothers, did all kinds of shit together."

"You get to know a guy real quick in the bush; real quick and real good," Willingham said. "You just lose one buddy, that don't mean shit."

"The hell it doesn't," Payne said.

"Not when you don't see the guy take it, not if you aren't there to see the life leave his body, the fight to live go slack in his face. There is a difference."

"Yeah," Payne said with an effort. He had to concede the point; it would make a difference if you were there when a buddy died. But that didn't mean the death of a friend you'd known all your life was any less meaningful or painful to bear.

"Where that light is up ahead, that's the place," Payne said.

The light was a flashing red and blue neon above the door of a squat cinder-block structure with no windows. The money and imagination had gone into the double doors, which were padded in fake buttoned-down leather, and into the neon, an outline in blue of a palm tree on a tiny island in a red sea.

Payne didn't make it with a whore. The new man did, with a Filipino going by the name of Rosebud. Willingham got a kick out of the name, said it reminded him of his grandmother who used to get after him for pinching her rosebuds before they had a chance to bloom. He told the girl his grandmother would scold him, then give him cookies, and that little anecdote turned the Filipino on. Payne wondered if he had made it up.

The lounge was segregated from the eating area by colorful Japanese shoji screens and tall plastic plants. Blue velvet dominated the decor; even the air seemed blue. Overhead fans churned slowly and you could hear them squeak between the change of records on the Wurlitzer. Business in the lounge was slow, and only five or six girls were working the place tonight. Willingham's Filipino was the best-looking one.

Payne slouched at the bar. He ate a bowl of pretzels for his supper and ran a tab of Chivas and soda while the new man and the Filipino were in the back. A heavily perfumed Vietnamese girl in a miniskirt propped herself next to him, sipping the tea Willingham had paid for. She'd tried but Payne wouldn't take, and now she was giving him the cold shoulder, jaded but hanging around him to save face. The place depressed him tonight.

"Why you no like me? I beautiful girl Hong Kong," the Viet said, looking off. "Plenty GI like me."

Payne forced a smile. "It's not that, honey. You're very beautiful and real sexy."

"You have other girlfriend," the whore said petulantly. "I be you girlfriend for one night. I show you numbah one time. Nobody know. Other girlfriend—" And she flipped a hand as if to forever dismiss the existence and memory of any other girlfriend.

Payne dropped the smile.

"You buy me one more tea." Her tone was now demanding, which irritated Payne. He was about to say something nasty when she suddenly hiked herself up, smoothing her skirt, her interest abruptly shifting to the front door. Fresh meat had walked in.

"You go 'way now, come back when you want girl," she said and bounded off to beat out another girl who primped herself quickly to welcome the man, an officer. Officers were prime rib, whereas EMs were anything from T-bone to hash. Payne was hamburger, a grade under ground round. Payne's whore won the sprint and she led the officer like a blind man to a half-moon booth with a blue glass candle on it.

Someone cranked up the volume for "House of the Rising Sun," and then Chuck Berry came on to do "Mabellene" and got Payne melancholy.

His foot automatically kept time with the beat, but it was a lousy song to listen to waiting on a guy to finish with a whore while your thoughts raced eight thousand miles away to the arms of your wife.

They had danced themselves into putty with Chuck Berry, he and Ann. The parties they'd gone to before the army, the year Payne had gone to college, where he met Ann. He even thought of it as their song. But now it seemed old, disposed to nostalgia, as if their courtship had become nothing more than pages in a scrapbook, washed out and brittle around the edges.

It was with ill-humored self-pity he thought of that time, how long ago it now seemed. They had been married less than a year when he got his orders and had to leave her, not even enough time to work out the kinks and get into a routine the way married people do, and now he could hardly visualize her. The fucking Nam was to blame for that.

It had turned her against him. Back then, Vietnam didn't seem to mean much to Ann one way or another; but she changed when he was called up for induction. He had gone over her objections; she pleaded with him to resist, run away to Mexico. "You've got to stand up for what you believe in," she had argued. "At least you'll stay alive. Don't go, Russ, please." He admired the vociferousness of her budding opposition to the draft and later to the war; it demonstrated her strength of character. That was something Payne felt he didn't have, strength of character. But he had given no more consideration to running away than he would to robbing a bank. It wasn't the way he was brought up. You did what you were supposed to do; there were rules you had to follow even if they were wrong, and he obeyed his orders.

And this was what it had gotten him, a wife who was becoming one of those radicals, actually protesting against the war, while Payne did his duty and tried to stay faithful, diligent in his effort to hold to the notion that you got tough and stuck it out through hard times like these, supporting each other. He considered this experience, the separation, a test of their love and devotion and he was determined to pass the test.

Payne indulged himself in more self-pity, glumly moving his lips to the chorus of "Mabellene," the only part of the tongue-twisting song he could keep up with. . . . *"Mabellene, why caint you be true? Oh, Mabellene, why caint you be true? You've started back doin' the things you used to do. . . ."*

And he was misty by the time Willingham slipped on the stool next to him, his blond hair a disheveled mess of curls from tiny fingers of passion, his countenance satiated and youthful. "Think I'm in love," he said sprightly, lapsing for the moment into the true role of an undaunted teenager. "Don't they have any Beach Boys on that box?"

Payne looked at him with a long face.

Willingham had started for the jukebox but stopped. "Well, shit, man. You're the one that didn't want the chick. I offered to cover expenses."

"I think she's screwing another guy," Payne said, his voice almost catching.

"Aww. You're jealous of a gook cunt. This housecat life has definitely screwed you people up."

"Naw. My wife, I'm talking about my wife, man. I think she's screwing a buddy of mine, a guy I asked to look after her."

"And Jody done rolled the bones. Some buddy."

Willingham sighed, relenting, and assumed Payne's slumped posture, folding his arms on the bar top. "Hey, man, there's a lot of bad shit a guy can think about if he lets himself. It doesn't mean it's true, though. What makes you think it?"

"I don't know, it's just a feeling."

Payne shook his head dismissingly. He didn't know for a fact she was sleeping with Rand; it was a hunch he'd made into a notion because of the lack of intimacy in Ann's letters, when she took the time to write him, which wasn't very often anymore. But maybe Willingham was right, maybe he was making too much of it. "I think she's becoming a fucking hippie, too."

Willingham grinned and took a long breath as if he wanted to say something smartass but held off. He ordered himself a beer and Payne another Scotch.

"You don't have to buy me any more," Payne said. "I ought to be shitfaced by now anyway."

"You are shitfaced, but don't worry about it. That was the deal."

Payne noticed a purplish scar running along the hairline of Willingham's shiny face and asked about it. "What's that from, some bush bitch?"

Willingham touched the slightly puckered scar as though he had forgotten it was there. "Just a birthmark; everybody's got some kind of flaw."

"Yeah. You can't tell it, but one of my legs is shorter than the other," Payne said. "An inch more and I'd've been an exempt gimp."

Willingham's grin was sardonic. "Pretty much exempt anyway," he said.

Payne took the remark as another putdown. "I can't fucking help it if I'm a lucky dude."

"I'm the fucking lucky one, man," Willingham said bitterly, as if he meant to be ironic. "Luck's a thing you can't depend on. Not in the Nam. It's more like fate."

"Well, my luck ain't been so good lately," Payne said, just to be saying something.

The officer who had been seized by Payne's whore suddenly appeared behind them. He wore pressed khakis and stood with both arms akimbo, gathering himself up as if to address a formation. "Gentlemen," Payne imagined him starting, but he wasn't interested in both of them; he was looking hard at Willingham.

"I heard the remark you made about the girl, Corporal," he said softly. "I don't know what your problem is, but in this establishment, and any other for that matter, we don't refer to the Vietnamese people with that kind of vulgarity. Now, I want you to march over to that table and apologize."

Willingham made a throaty sound and smirked.

"I mean business."

Willingham grinned off the side of his face and swung around, passing his eyes from the officer to the girl in the shadows. "You can't be serious."

The officer was working himself into a rage. He stepped closer. Any closer and they would have touched noses. "I'm goddamn serious, Corporal. Now you get your ass over there right now."

"Back the fuck off," Willingham said evenly and turned his back to him.

Sure as hell, Payne thought, the new guy was going to get him into trouble already. "We were just talking, sir," said Payne, interceding. "You know, shooting the shit. We didn't mean anything by it."

The captain kept his eyes on Willingham's back. "The girl demands an apology."

"I'll do it," Payne said and walked over to the table where the whore he had rejected gave him her best bitch's grin. He said, "I know you've heard of General Wheeler. I'm on his staff, and one word from me and you won't fucking be working this post again. You think you can understand that, cunt?"

The whore shut her eyes to show she got his meaning. Payne sighed and added, "You did better than me anyway, why be nasty about it?"

She turned to stare at the seat padding, and Payne walked.

The captain was demanding Willingham's name and outfit, trying hard to keep his voice contained.

Willingham was facing him again. "Planning to make life hard for me, huh. Go ahead, see if I give a shit. Name's Willington. Unit's the 506th, right here in the Stretch. I'm a regular here."

The officer had actually taken a pad and pen out of his khakis and started writing the information down. And as he did, Willingham accommodated him by thrusting his shirt pocket forward, his fingers cleverly concealing the last three letters on the name tag.

"Your commanding officer will hear from me personally about your insubordination *and* your appearance," he barked, tight-lipped and red-faced. He was practiced at barking. "You'll be a private in a week, that I can guarantee."

Willingham shrugged carelessly, and the officer went back to his booth in the corner. Willingham frowned at Payne. "That how you stand up for a guy in a situation?"

The question was backed by disappointment or hurt, and it took Payne by surprise. "Well, what the hell was I supposed to do, let you get us both busted, for nothing? I don't know how it works where you come from, but around here you don't pull that kind of shit and expect to get away with it."

Willingham grinned. "Oh yeah? Didn't I have the asshole going?"

"I guess you did at that," Payne admitted. "The 506th, that was pretty good," he said. "Think he caught your real name?"

"Who gives a fuck. What'd you say to the gook?"

"Nothing." Payne chugged his drink. "We ought to split."

Willingham didn't have any problem with that.

They took a shortcut back to the company area, strolling along Pershing Avenue past dark office buildings that in the moonlight took on the uniform shape of boxcars. The two-lane was deserted and there were no street lights. Before the headlights caught them, it had slipped Payne's mind that curfew had been moved up an hour, the result of last weekend's flair of rioting—bored soul brothers looking for some fun.

"This way," he said and dashed between two darkened buildings. Willingham followed about five meters behind.

The MP jeep stopped where they had left the street and combed the gray buildings with a searchlight. The spotlight went out after a paltry attempt to locate them, then the jeep took off.

"They saw us," Willingham said. "Why'd they leave?"

Payne walked on, keeping to the sidewalks leading through the complex of office buildings. "We're white. They're white."

"It makes a difference?"

"It makes a difference."

"Fuck me," said Willingham. "You sure got some weird psychology around here."

"Not really. The blacks like to post turfs here and there, defy you to step across. Sometimes they like to step across just to liven things up a little."

"Ridiculous," Willingham snorted. "Bloods I know aren't any different than anybody else, just grunts doing a job."

"Well, here it's called boredom."

Heading across an open field, Willingham again fell back and hesitated. He wanted to know what the chances were of land mines. Payne laughingly said none, and they continued on, arriving back at the company area without getting their legs blown off, and crawled inside the bunker where Payne earlier had stowed Willingham's duffle. Payne lit a Sterno and dug under a sandbag and drew out his stash, a regular-looking package of Marlboros inside a Band-Aid tin. "You guys from the boonies do indulge, don't you?"

"Been known."

The hootch bunkers had been divvied up into individual smoke chambers. Everyone had access to a bunker; it was the only place you could get a little privacy. Guards didn't poke around after hours, since they too used the bunkers. They were fine bunkers, encased in forged steel and reinforced with four tiers of clay-filled bags. The short L-shaped anterior blocked light and low voices from carrying outside. If a bunker was used regularly the rat count stayed down. Payne shared this bunker with his cubemate and another man, both heads, so he never had a problem with the rats.

Payne stretched out on a bench and stared at the low ceiling; he let the smoke trail effortlessly from his nostrils. The potent weed was heavy and hot in the lungs and made his eyes water. He passed the smoke to Willingham. "Finest in the land, they say."

Willingham sputtered smoke and agreed with a bob of the head. He unbuttoned his shirt and pulled it aside. His chest paled against the dark V line of his neck. Where he came from they didn't take their shirts off. Payne had an even tan down to his belt line, cultivated on weekends at poolside.

"Those cuts are infected, man," Payne said. "You ought to get something for them."

Willingham looked his arms over, then squeezed both his hands into tight fists. The pressure caused pus to discharge from the scratches on his hands. He used a handkerchief to clean it off. "Guess you're right; I usually don't have to do that till morning."

"You get scratched up bivouacking?"

Willingham chuckled thinly. "Bivouacking? Yeah, I guess you could call it that."

"So, how many dinks you do? Got any souvenirs?" Payne asked, trying for the cool vernacular of grunt talk. He sounded awkward and frowned in self-disgust at the pretension.

Willingham leaned back, letting his body go slack, and squeezed his eyes. "This shit is definitely righteous," he said thickly, fighting his exhaustion.

He gave Payne a lazy sidelong glance and worked up a dog-tired grin. "Don't give up, do you?" he said languidly, appearing on the verge of giving in.

"Shit, man," Payne said. "We're going to be working together."

"Looks like you're going to be a royal pain in the ass, what it looks like—but I'm not bitching. Look, we'll get along a lot better if you just get off my case. Can you do that? Give me a little adjustment time?"

"All right," Payne said. "Sure."

He sank back and closed himself up, drawing in his legs. Maybe the guy hadn't fought at all and just wanted to give Payne the impression he had; guys from the bush could be like that, wearing the mystique like a flag when half of them never even shot at Charlie. But Payne knew that wasn't true of this guy. He was not putting him on; he just wasn't talking. Willingham had something to hide.

"You ever get in-coming here, infiltration?" Willingham said. "I mean, I don't have a weapon and I'd like to know if it's safe to go to sleep tonight."

He had stretched out. His frame was longer than the bench, his boots sagging heavily off the end.

"Fuck of a lot safer than Detroit," Payne said. He shoveled the duffle into the secondary catacomb and told Willingham there was an empty bunk in the hootch if he didn't mind the smell of monkey.

"Monkey?" said Willingham, raising himself on an elbow. "Shit. Our RTO had a monkey story. Guy we call Jesus. Squirrelly little fucker."

"Oh yeah?" Payne said.

"I got to admit this is good smoke."

"Laced with opium. What about this guy Jesus?"

Willingham smiled in private thought. He sat up and drew his legs underneath him, arching his back along the curve of the sandbag wall. "Jesus had this Chinese fable he used to tell every time we'd come across water, a stream, even cratered pools, anything with water. You'd have to hear it from him to appreciate it."

Payne stretched his legs. "I always liked fables. My mother had some good ones she'd save for stormy nights."

"Well, it ain't storming tonight."

"You ain't my mother, either," Payne said. "But let me hear it anyway."

Willingham let out a short sigh, with a nod and a half grin. "He's just a little fuck who likes to talk big, something like James Cagney. He was from Alabama, so he had this hick twang too, a lot worse than yours. Imagine Cagney with a lobotomy and you've got Jesus. He'd say there was this here monkey and this fish that got caught in the Mekong River. The river was a raging flood, see, and this here monkey, being nimble like monkeys are, sprung out of the current, but the fish didn't. The monkey thought the fish was gonna drown. He didn't stop to think that water was where a fucking fish lives."

Willingham had to stop to laugh.

"But this here monkey had good intentions. Thought he was destined to do good. He roped his tail on a tree limb overhanging the river and swooped down and caught the fish. Very agile this here monkey—he always said it like that, 'This here monkey.' But the fish was pissed. The fish fucking lived in the water, see. And the monkey, which was generous—I mean he took a big chance swinging down like that into a fucking flood. The monkey couldn't believe the fish didn't have no gratitude. The monkey thought he'd saved the fish's life, man.

"Anyway. This here monkey turned out to be the laughingstock 'cause he didn't save no life. The fish died. He *killed* the goddamn fish."

The joint had dwindled to a roach. Willingham sucked it down to millimeter size and flipped it off, spraying the sagging wall with tiny quick-dying cinders. "And then Jesus would say seriously, 'A fish caint live out of water. But this here big, dumb monkey didn't know that, see.'"

Payne lost part of the story somewhere in the telling because he was busy tracing the function of his kidneys. This dope did that to you. He figured it was the opium. "That the guy's real name, Jesus—Hay-soose?"

"Naw, his bush name."

Payne started to ask if this guy Jesus had died too, but he decided Willingham would just get pissed again. "What's an RTO?" he said instead. He sat up quickly, bumping his head. "Shh. You hear that?"

Willingham lifted his eyes halfway.

"Sounds like a cat on the bunker," Payne said.

"You got good hearing."

"Maybe it's Charlie."

Payne crawled slowly on his hands and knees and shoved his upper body through the opening. The outside air smelled humid, like approaching rain. He pulled himself back inside. "Nothing."

"The smoke," said Willingham. "This shit is in-fucking-credible. But you're just a little weird, Payne, you know that?"

"Huh?" Payne said. Then it registered: "Oh. I got it. What I mean is Charlie, the monkey I was talking about."

"*I* was talking about a monkey," said Willingham.

"Yeah, right. Well, so was I."

"What monkey?"

"Charlie, for Christ's sake."

"That the monkey's name? Charlie?"

"Yeah."

Willingham coughed a laugh. "Fuck me."

"How come you keep saying that?"

"Saying what?" Willingham said irritably.

"Fuck me. I don't get it. Doesn't make any sense."

Willingham shook his head dismally, then pulled the limp boonie hat over his eyes. "The RTO's the guy that lugs around the radio. Every unit's got one. Base camp likes to call you early to see how you slept, if you had your regulation bowel movement, stuff like that. This monkey your mascot or what?"

"I think she's dead," Payne said. "I had a dog like that once—Bowzer."

Willingham's chortle put a bounce in the soft part of his stomach.

"That was his fucking name. All right? The dog got sick when my brother left to join the navy and just disappeared. I figured he was heartbroken and went off to die."

"Sounds just awful."

Payne frowned. "He was in the family a long time. You get attached."

"What's the deal on this monkey?"

Payne waited for a meandering cockroach to find the shadow of his uplifted boot. He rotated the tip of a cigarette in the Sterno flame and puffed it to life. The cockroach zigzagged at a frantic pace and, sure enough, halted under the boot, safe in the shadow. Payne hesitated a moment, gave it a chance before snuffing it because it was too easy.

"Nobody's seen her in a month or so," he said, referring to the monkey called Charlie. "She went crazy after Smith got it. You awake?"

Willingham lifted the drooping brim of his hat to expose one eye and Payne said, "You're not going to believe this," and told him about Charlie without getting sidetracked on his kidneys or his liver or heart.

It was Smith, the medic, he told him, who found the monkey half dead on one of his flyouts. He brought it back to the hootch and nursed it back to health. The men in the hootch thought that was nice of Smith until lice began to spread from bed to bed and the odor ate through the incense. Then signs began to appear on the wall of Smith's cubicle: "This cube condemned," "Off limits to Humans," "Monkey Lover!" Smith got the message and took the animal away.

A week later she reappeared. Smith thought that was something, a monkey that could find its way back to one barracks out of three hundred. He was overjoyed. He named the animal Charlie and put her on a diet of almonds and potatoes. He called a hootch meeting to see if it was all right with the other men to keep the monkey, since she was now well but still weak. He did the right thing asking communal approval, and the men said okay. Nothing wrong with having a mascot called Charlie.

Smith began training Charlie and soon he had her doing somersaults at his command. He claimed her blood, like his, was Rh-negative, a point he seemed proud of. Charlie sat on his shoulder like a bird and picked at Smith's ear with deft, agile fingers.

Payne said Smith told him he could understand Charlie's chirps and could communicate with her, that she was on the same evolutionary level as highland Montagnards, among whom Smith had spent part of his tour. He had a girlfriend in a village up around Dalat and kept snapshots of her tacked to his wall. "Charlie is just as sensitive and responsive as my babysan was," he exclaimed. He was enthralled by the possibilities of his theory. "When this fuckin war's over, Russell, they ought to do a study. I mean it."

Smith was a rotund man, too large and slow to be a medic. The men in the hootch called him Baby Huey because of his unwieldy gait. His legs would not support his weight when he came in stoned and the men in their cubicles would poise themselves, thinking it was another black gang raiding the hootch.

Sometimes Smith was called out on special medevac and when he didn't return from his last flyout, the men draped his wall in black crepe paper and adorned it with items Smith would have appreciated. Someone hung a toy huey copter, another pinned up a mainliner syringe. Payne threw in a blowup he had made from one of Smith's scrapbook pictures, a shot of Charlie on the back of one of the mamasan's dogs. It was a good candid shot: the dog was trying to throw Charlie and she had one tiny hand clutching the dog's ear and the other flung over her head rodeo style, but held femininely, like a woman extending her hand in formal greeting.

The monkey's temperament changed without Smith around. She hung out under his old bunk as if in mourning and when someone tried to coax her out to play she would turn mad and puncture the arm with her razorlike teeth. It became her habit, after circling and plopping down on her old convalescent pad, to bite her tail. Terrible caterwauls rang through the hootch in the dead of night, then a sad howl would issue from the cubicle. Someone had to clean up the blood smears the next morning to keep the rats out. Soon the lice and fleas were in the covers again.

It was then that Sergeant Ortega, who worked at the armory, formed a squad and set booby traps around the hootch and in the bunker where Charlie left her droppings. Some of the traps were rigged with explosive caps and the men were briefed as to where they had been set and how to avoid setting them off. A week later a charge was tripped and rat remains were found, but no monkey parts. Rats could not have activated the trap, Ortega said, even if a pack of them had chewed on the trip wire; rats just couldn't do that. The incident remained a mystery.

Charlie was sly. She continued to slip in under the cover of night and howl miserably. Ortega refused to allow a trap in the cube where Smith had slept. He said it would be a bad omen to tamper with the place of the dead. "We put the hurt on that animal, man, she come back from the dead and put a fuckin hex on our fuckin lives."

The flame off the Sterno flickered dimly, causing the close shadows to waver as though the drooping sandbags were filled with gelatin. Payne was getting seasick from it. He stirred the canned mixture with a stick. It sputtered brightly and then died down again.

"The last time we saw her, her tail was festered and she looked like shit," Payne said. "The fruit I left in her bunker rotted. But everybody was glad when she quit coming around. They all have the same crazy idea that Smith bought it because he went on that flyout tired from taking care of his monkey, that Charlie was somehow responsible for him getting zeroed. But I got to agree, she did cause a lot of problems. You ready to crash?"

Willingham's boots hung off the bench like two huge rocks; they made a clunking sound when he tapped them together. "You people sure have got a shitload of superstition down here," he said and snorted. "What kind of caps did this guy use in his rigs?"

"I don't know, claymore or something like that."

"Wasn't that. He wasn't using the right stuff," said Willingham.

"How do you know?"

"Popular Mechanics," he said.

"C'mon. You can bunk out on Smith's bed. It's getting late."

Willingham rolled to an upright position. "That the only available bunk?"

"Unless some dude's out for the duration, in a gutter or somewhere."

"No, thanks. I'll crash here."

Payne worked the stiffness out of his legs. "Suit yourself."

Chapter

4

Payne stuck his head inside the lieutenant's office a few minutes after eight in the morning and said, "Everyone present or accounted for, sir."

Lieutenant Finn sat in a swivel chair with his feet propped on the typewriter slab of the desk, wearing his thick short-distance glasses and reading *Rolling Stone*. He squinted over the top of the magazine in an effort to focus Payne, questioning him with furrowed brows and surprised parted lips. The magnifying glasses gave him a bug-eyed look even when he squinted.

"The meeting," Payne said. "It was to start at eight, remember?"

"I thought I'd said O-eight-thirty."

Payne shook his head pleasantly. "Your memo says eight."

The lieutenant closed the magazine, taking a moment to admire the cover photo, which featured a busty Janis Joplin with her legs thrown apart, looking wild and sexy on a fiery psychedelic stage. "All right, I'll be right there. Anyone not present?"

"Langley. He's still on R&R. A new body arrived yesterday, a transfer. Guy named Willingham."

"Why wasn't I informed? What's he do?"

"Beats hell out of me. But I doubt it's been any kind of desk job, judging from his appearance. Wait'll you see him."

The lieutenant grinned. "Needs a little spit-shining, huh?"

"You said it, sir. But he's okay."

The lieutenant was sweating. The air conditioner in his office blew warm air.

"All right. Tell the men I'll be out in five minutes."

Payne shut the door behind him and grinned triumphantly at the faces around the room. He strode over to Sergeant Sterr's desk and snatched the two bills Sterr waved listlessly in the air, then collected from Cowboy. He'd suckered them into betting on Finn's punctuality.

"You guys ought to know him better than that," Payne said smugly and stuffed the cash in his contingency-fund can. He had built the contingency up to eleven or twelve dollars now, and four more bucks helped lighten his loss on the Series. He would tap the contingency fund only when absolutely necessary, if he ever had a bad run at poker, say; it was sacred money.

Lai Sin had Thermo-Faxed the lieutenant's memo and put a copy in each man's In basket yesterday. Memos weren't necessary for a section with only five men including the officer in charge, but Finn liked to have them distributed about; such things made him feel in control. Finn was an officer first and foremost and beyond that a mix of whiz-kid hard rocker. In college he played keyboard in a group calling itself the Do-Wa-La Do-Wa's, which he claimed was the hottest band at Northwestern University, booked every weekend. He also earned his keep on the contract-bridge circuit. He was an ROTC officer.

The lieutenant emerged from his office ten minutes later, posing himself after General Patton. At five-six and 140 in combat boots, he was the smallest man in the section. He was twenty-three, but his severely cropped red hair and the explosion of zits that plagued him in humid weather made him look boyish. On first impression you would judge him incapable of leadership. But he performed adequately and was a conscientious OIC who looked after his men.

He took a quick head count and sat on the edge of Lai Sin's desk, offering her a small perfunctory grin. "This won't affect you, sugar."

Lai Sin took the hint and gingerly walked her chair back, stood, and smoothed out her skirt. She covered her typewriter and shut and locked the middle desk drawer and scrutinized the desk top for anything that might be out of place, making a ceremony of it. She didn't get much work done, but she was tidy and Finn liked that about her.

"I go now," she announced, martyrlike, as if her job had been rudely terminated, and departed hurriedly to escape Cowboy's lip-smacking gaze. Cowboy was always after her for a date, and Payne invariably had to fend him off her. She had come to look to Payne as her protector against his and any other American's crude advances.

Cowboy grunted wolfishly as she breezed past him swaying her hips. Lai Sin liked to tease him when Payne was around.

"Listen up, men," Finn said, clearing his throat officiously. He had his head thrown back now and was leaking a little water at the edges of his eyes because of his contact lenses. "Where's the new man?" he asked Payne.

Payne shrugged. "Processing, I suppose."

"Well, never mind. Sergeant, were you alerted we were getting a new man?"

"First I heard, sir." Sterr used both hands to hold his coffee cup but still couldn't keep it steady. The copy of *Stars & Stripes* spread out on his desk was splotched with coffee stains. "Want me to check with the orderly room?"

"Never mind that now," Finn said. He wanted to play with a pimple that was ready. "First item. I want you men to know that command is pleased with our coverage in last quarter's issues of the paper. General Wheeler is going to present the office with our second meritorious citation at the awards ceremony next week. I want to be the first to commend you on a job well done."

He played with Lai Sin's letter opener to keep his hands away from the pimple. "Now. Item two. As you know, MACV called a special briefing of all support group information heads day before yesterday. I won't bore you with all the sundry details at this time, because the whole thing was rather vague. Suffice it to say, policy changes have come down the chain which are going to put a huge demand on us to expand our coverage. The bottom line is they want a blitz on pacification." He paused a moment to look at their faces.

"I know you men have spent a lot of time on the articles you've been working on for the magazine, but most of them aren't about pacification. So all of it's going to have to go on hold right now. Sorry about that, but that's the way it is. Our directive is to concentrate on the pacification effort. At least the brass could agree on that point."

He took a copy of *Time* magazine off the media shelf of the bookcase and tossed it at Payne. Payne had already seen the issue.

The cover pictured a bird's-eye panorama of antiwar demonstrators packed around the Lincoln Memorial, waving banners and placards, doing the fun things protesters did. Payne morosely scrutinized the cover in an effort to make out the tiny figure of his wife among the throng of people. It was impossible with the naked eye. She had been there with the new crowd she was running with. "You can see me," she had written on a postcard in her excited scribble. "I'm right behind that huge poster of LBJ on the left, the one that says 'War Criminal' on it. See me?" Using a magnifying glass he had found her cheerful face, arms splayed in the air, showing off her tits in a T-shirt in Washington in October. Wasn't it cold there in October?

"The war is escalating on two fronts now," Finn continued. "MACV's worried these riots and demonstrations back home may severely damage the war effort. So they've concocted this new public relations campaign to try and make the country sympathetic to our commitment here by emphasizing how we're helping the Vietnamese to help themselves."

"Good luck," said Cowboy.

Scowling, Payne roughly flipped the page and ran down the magazine's contents column to the book reviews, which listed *The Confessions of Nat Turner* and *Rosemary's Baby,* and turned to page sixty-three. Both titles sounded exciting.

"Just pass it on, Payne," Finn said and waited until he did. "The whole thing's further complicated because the top brass is split on whether pacification will get results. As you can guess, it puts all PIO people in a no-win situation. We're supposed to be operating a house organ for a support command, not a vehicle for Vietnam's social and political problems," he said, letting his irritability get him sidetracked. "At any rate, we are going to be focusing on civil affairs. We're to get with the people connected with the CORDS program, and I'm afraid you'll have to do some traveling with advisory teams."

"What's that?" Cowboy said.

"CORDS is a joint operation with the Saigon government to get rid of the VC infrastructure," Sterr said before the lieutenant could answer. Sterr knew about those things. "It's to help get the people in the countryside organized, building them villages and roads and shit. You ought to know that, Cowboy."

"The hell. What do I know? I'm a draftee."

Sterr rummaged through his desk and took out a fat communications pamphlet and held it open with a trembling hand and read: "'Civic Operations and Revolutionary Development Support, combining the Office of Civil Operations with the republic's revolutionary development cadre.' The project includes—get this—personnel not only from MACV but the State Department, the CIA, the USIA, AID, and the fucking White House. Pretty big operation. Started up earlier this year I believe, didn't it, Lieutenant?"

With no apparent pretense or presumption Sterr could make the lieutenant feel that he was in charge. Sterr's demeanor with people was his forte, his strength. After fourteen years he should have been a grade or two higher than staff sergeant; had his affair with booze been less than interminable, he might even have made top sergeant by now, for he knew how to work the system, how to glide. He even had the looks of a first sergeant, thick wiry eyebrows capable of both intimidation and understanding, the lumpy jaw of a Slav. About his eyes was the unassuming maturity of a man who had been around. It was because of Sterr that the office ran smoothly, which earned him the lieutenant's respect and a certain admiration from the lower EM, who in turn covered for him when he went on a binge. Payne thought of Sterr as a coach, when in truth the sergeant came closer to being a surrogate of the father Payne did not have.

Finn confirmed with an appreciative nod. "It's a big operation, all right, Sergeant. Command wants us to show what the army is doing for the Vietnamese people, to project an image of us working side by side with them. Which reminds me, in future articles we will no longer be referring to pacification as winning the hearts and minds of these people. That's out. From now on you are to use phrases such as 'develop community spirit' or something equivalent. They want profiles on our troops working with the locals building schools and bridges and medical dispensaries. Things like that. The paper's not a problem, but this puts the pressure on us to meet the magazine's deadline. We'll have thirty or forty pages to fill with new copy. So we've got to get in gear on this thing. I know you must have some questions."

The lieutenant waited, and when no one asked a question he crossed the floor and opened the refrigerator. "Sergeant, would you mind picking up some more juice next time you're at the PX? Maybe something different this time, tomato juice maybe."

"How 'bout beer?" Cowboy suggested.

"I'll head over there right now if you're done," Sterr offered. "Be back in thirty minutes."

Saturday was a regular workday, and Sterr always made it in. But Stateside he'd gotten used to free Saturdays and hadn't changed his habit of Friday-night inebriety just for Nam duty. He showed up reeking of too much whiskey and cigar butts, drank his coffee, and somehow managed to get lost without being missed. You could find him recovering at poolside or sweating himself back in shape at the NCO gym. Then, around two in the afternoon, he would drift back in with a couple of six-packs tucked under each arm, which would go in the refrigerator for anyone who was working and felt like a cold beer on a hot Saturday afternoon. Saturday afternoons the lieutenant had his bowling league.

"All right, Sergeant, go ahead. The other matter I have doesn't involve you."

Sterr put on his cap, adjusted the dark glasses on his purple-splotched nose, and left, giving Payne a wink to verify cold beer later on.

Finn went to a window and rested an arm on the sill and glanced cursorily at the squad going through a drill and ceremony exercise in the quadrangle outside.

"I realize you two probably feel you've earned some easy time," he said in a concerned voice. "But we have a big job ahead of us and I need your cooperation now more than ever. I want to be assured that I can count on it."

"Sure," said Payne, uncharacteristically quick to volunteer himself before he knew the specifics of what the lieutenant was after. He assumed he meant field work, and Payne realized he was anxious to get into the countryside again; maybe the new man had something to do with it.

"I knew I could count on you," Finn said. At that instant he dropped his guard and a hand shot to the pimple, a pair of deft fingers squeezing. He grinned like a schoolboy.

"How about you, Meyer?" he said to Cowboy, whose name was Meyer. "Can I count on your cooperation too?"

"You're the lieutenant," Cowboy said. "All you have to do is give the orders, right?"

It was a nasty thing to say. That Finn himself would not go off post had long been a standing joke. He feared for his life even driving the fifteen miles into Saigon and would make the trip, as he had day before yesterday, only when directly ordered. The joke originated four months ago when he flew to Vinh Long with Payne. He'd gotten word weeks before that his contract-bridge partner was stationed down there and wanted to look him up but was fearful of making the trip by himself. He had been a nervous wreck prior to leaving. It showed, and everyone teased him about it. As soon as they deboarded at the airfield, Finn got lost. Payne made a halfhearted attempt to find him, but he didn't try very hard and gave up his search the next day; it was embarrassing for a Spec 4 having to ask around after a dufus redheaded second lieutenant. When he returned to Long Binh two days after Payne, he was haggard and short-tempered. He wouldn't say what had happened to him or even if he had located his friend, and the incident was never mentioned in his presence again. After that Finn always had a tight schedule, which kept him on post.

"That's right, Meyer. I'm the lieutenant," Finn snarled. "Which brings me to the other thing I want to talk to you about. Dress code. I don't know what kind of company your first sergeant is operating, but at your duty station you are going to start dressing according to regulations. That includes regulation haircuts and polished boots. And belts. We *will* wear belts."

He motioned them over to the window. Payne rose lazily from his chair and tucked in his shirttail. The platoon parading under the hot morning sun was a spiffy SSC drill team composed of hand-picked troops, a collection of like-sized, virile boys who made outstanding models for public relations brochures. The SSC team was one of several on display at parade ceremonies when dignitaries visited the Stretch. The men wore khakis and white spats, the brass on their uniforms catching the sun like a sea of gold mirrors. They twirled rifles with nimble hands.

"Feast your eyes on those men," the lieutenant said, "and ask yourselves if they do justice to the uniform. Now, you see that man malingering over there in the general's palms? See him? Unless we take some corrective action, pretty soon you'll start looking like that. Which I most definitely will not allow."

The man under the palms had his hands in the pockets of loose-fitting, dingy fatigues, leaning casually against a tree with one foot crossing the other, watching the show as if amused. Bleached curly hair bulged under a drooping boonie hat that hugged his head like wet burlap. Payne grinned and almost blurted something out loud.

"Faggots," said Cowboy.

"Strack faggots," Finn said, loosening up. "Anyway, you get my point. We represent PIO, which means we have an image to project, just like that drill team."

Payne watched the man in the cluster of palms hike up his pants and march deliberately past the drill team with eyes right, kicking up his boots like a Czar's soldier. He headed toward the entrance in the quadrangle that led to the office. Payne returned to his desk and leaned back with hands behind his head and waited.

When Willingham came through the door a moment later, the lieutenant was still going strong, giving an old speech on moral conduct, pointing out how the men should lay off teasing and flirting with Lai Sin. "These are very religious people and especially her and we have to treat them with respect."

"Like hell," Willingham interjected from the doorway. "They'd sell their ancestors' souls for a pipeload of opium." He grinned at Payne.

"Who are you?" Finn said, disconcerted.

"Name's Willingham, Lieutenant. Got orders assigning me to this outfit. If it's an inconvenient time, I can come back next week."

He looked even grubbier today, as if he had spent a week in a trench. Payne thought he might have been in the showers or at the infirmary when he didn't find him earlier in the bunker. He had the boonie hat crumpled in the hand at his side now and stood at a quasi-attention stance with his eroded boots together, smiling congenially at the lieutenant. Mockery was written all over his posture.

"Well, come on in, Willingham." Finn seemed eager. Contrary to Payne's prediction, the lieutenant didn't drop his chin or stammer. "You're not interrupting anything," the lieutenant went on. "Matter of fact you might find this useful. We were just having a little discussion on personal hygiene and conduct, both of which you appear to be in need of. Have a seat."

Willingham didn't lose the smile. "It's nice to get a warm welcome to your new outfit," he said and took a seat behind the desk he'd gone through yesterday. He sat with his hands folded on the desk top. Payne grinned at him and nodded.

"Let's see your papers," ordered Finn.

Willingham kept his hands poised on the desk top. "I believe it's

SOP for the company commander to forward reassignment orders to the section OIC."

Finn drew back. "I stand corrected," he said and put his hands on his hips.

"Sir," said Payne, "why don't I get Willingham oriented, introduce him around."

The lieutenant grimaced. "Not looking like that!" He said to Willingham, "What's your MOS?"

"Whatever's required. What do you need?"

"No. I mean, what was your prior MOS?"

"Your basic eleven bananas. Which I assume won't cut it around here."

Now the lieutenant seemed stifled, at a loss for what to say next. "Well, do you have any basic office skills," he managed, "any writing background or experience in photography?"

"Whatever you want me to do, I'll do. I'm versatile. You name it, take pictures, write stories, stand tall around the brass. Just so long as I'm not a clerk."

"Now that's the kind of enthusiasm I like to see," Finn said, and Payne could not tell if he was being facetious or sincere. "You can start by getting over to supply and outfitted in some new fatigues, a haircut. Then report back here after you get squared away. Meyer. Go down to the lounge and tell the secretary the meeting's over."

The telephone rang. The lieutenant said, "I'll get it," and went into his office and shut the door.

"Catch you later," Cowboy said, moving papers around on Sterr's desk. "Where's the keys to the jeep?"

"The sarge took them," Payne said. "You can find him at the NCO club. But have the jeep back by noon. I've got to run it over to the motor pool this afternoon for servicing."

"Damn lifer can't even huff it that far."

"By noon, right?"

Cowboy cocked and fired a finger at Payne. "I hear you. You gonna have it back by tonight? I promised this hot little slant-eye at the Feathered Fingers I'd take her out for a little whoop-tee-do tonight. And I need wheels."

"Feathered Fingers?" Willingham said. "Fuck me."

"A dive," said Payne.

"The hell. Cleanest cunt on post," Cowboy retorted.

Payne sighed. He introduced them, telling Willingham that Cowboy was the resident expert on women and leisure activity. "A man of discerning taste. Still a virgin at his age, must be twenty. But he takes good pictures."

"The fuck you say."

Willingham extended a hand. "Call me Willie."

"Just because you don't ever get laid, don't mean others don't," said Cowboy, shaking hands. Addressing Willingham, he said, "Payne's got this ballbuster wife makes him toe the line. Guy's a real do-gooder. Always plays it safe, by the rules."

Payne grinned. "You'd know; you got my twenty bucks. Cowboy's from Arizona. Used to shoot whiskey bottles from the hands of drunk Indians. He can catch a mongoose barehanded. And if you believe that, don't play poker with him. He's a great bluffer."

"On guard duty," Cowboy said proudly. "Caught one of them little fuckers before it could get to the wire."

"No shit?" said Willingham. "You can pop a goose if you're fast, but I never heard of anyone ever catching one, not even with a trip device. How'd you do it?"

Payne didn't know whether he was kidding or not, stringing Cowboy along to nail him.

Cowboy didn't seem to think he was being kidded. He hiked up to his full length, a glitter in his chestnut eyes. He narrowed his eyes and hesitated, as if he didn't want to give a secret away, then relented. "Shit. It was easy. I used a white flare. Has to be white phosphorus. That's the only kind bright enough to hypnotize 'em. You gotta hold it out in front of you so they don't see what's back of the light and creep up slow. Then grab it quick behind the head like you would pick up a cat on the attack. But wear your earplugs. You ever hear a mongoose bark, you know why. Fucking deafen you, man. Plus they got teeth like piranha."

He glanced at Payne with a hopeless look. "It's real dangerous. Takes a lot of balls and patience. I wouldn't go advising anybody to try it if they don't know anything about the nature of rodents."

Willingham laughed easily. "I can dig it, man. We'll do it some night. Now, tell me about your hotshot LT."

Abruptly the lieutenant opened his door, as if he'd heard the reference. He called Payne in. Cowboy walked the new man outside, whispering buddylike to him the comments the lieutenant had made about him in the general's palm garden.

"Close the door," Finn said. The pimple was now mutilated, a glistening blood-red spot. "Some captain from G-5 phoned and wants to see you immediately. He's in General Wheeler's offices waiting."

"What's he want?" Payne asked.

"I don't know what he wants, it was an order," Finn said disgustedly. "He wouldn't say when I asked. He asked a few things about you."

"Like what?"

"Personal performance. Do you do a good job, do you complain. Hell, I don't know why anyone would be asking that kind of stuff. Unless maybe they're going to reassign you—now that we've got a new man. Damn."

Finn seemed to be taking the thought seriously, as though he really did think he might lose Payne, and was working himself into a panic figuring out who would replace him as editor.

"Probably just something to do with this pacification thing, an article maybe," Payne said reassuringly, trying to settle him before he did go into a panic. "Don't worry, sir. I'm yours."

Finn dabbed his bloody cheek with a lens tissue. "I didn't want to mention this in front of the men yet," he said. "It's a little premature. But I might as well tell you now. I'm considering letting you go to Tokyo with the magazine. You've done a good job editing the paper and you deserve it. I know you want to go."

Payne could hardly believe what he was hearing. A week in Tokyo, a longtime fantasy come true? He tried to compose himself, hold down the excitement. "You serious, sir? Weren't you going?"

"You're the one for the job, Payne," Finn said, proving he could be a magnanimous person. "But I'll expect you to bust your ass in the meantime in return—and bring me back some expensive sake."

Payne left the lieutenant's office on a cloud. Tokyo. The fantasy had originated in the small, windowless back office of his father's furniture store where Payne would go after school and sit in a deep, musky armchair, thumbing through the pages of *National Geographic* and having a six-cent Coke with peanuts in the bottle. His father was a giant thin shadow of a man in Payne's memory, who wore a spy's gray raincoat. But in the back office his father was always in a white shirt, and it was there he took Payne to the faraway places of the mysterious Orient, to Singapore, Rangoon, Shanghai, Hong Kong, Tokyo. Traders and scalawags and pirates on the high seas, typhoons and great dragons that rose from the sea.

But Tokyo was the place his father loved most, that most allured Payne as well. He had a snapshot he would show Payne of himself in Tokyo with a group of his army buddies with their arms hugging small women in colorful dresses, everyone caught in laughter. They were on a brightly lit night street coming at you. "In Tokyo there are golden temples and great dragons that got turned to stone so people like us could look at them," his father had said. "The biggest ships in the world sail there with stacks of treasures." Payne imagined it a place of adventure and romance, of serene botanical gardens with lily ponds underfoot that were stocked with huge venerable speckled goldfish. Marble wing-tipped palaces and golden pavilions, bathhouse geishas, and quaint, clean-lined rooms. He imagined dancing on the neon street where his father had been. The impressions were murals painted in Payne's imagination, and the images remained long after his father's death.

He didn't quite comprehend why he was so attracted to that city more than the other mystical places of the Orient; it couldn't have been solely the memories of his father's stories with his buddies in the bars and baths of Tokyo and how he would laugh telling them; maybe it was because they were stories joining them in confidence, stories his mother was not allowed to hear.

Payne walked across the quadrangle and was met at the general's secretary's desk by a captain whose name tag identified him as Burns. He showed Payne into the XO's plush office. The XO wasn't there.

"Sit. Take a load off, Specialist." He had a friendly smile. "Damned hot, isn't it?"

Payne agreed with a nod.

"Hot enough to make you want to leave this country, get an early out?"

"I wouldn't object."

"Well, maybe we can do something about it. How would you like that?"

The thought hit him, and Payne said nervously, "Is something wrong at home? Is it my mother?"

The captain calmly lifted a hand. "Nothing like that. Tell me, what do you think of our effort here? I mean about this fucking war in general?"

Payne sat uncomfortably in the soft chair. He shrugged and studied the man. Burns was a short, stout man whose round face and lack of eyebrows made him appear very youthful, almost pubescent. A contrastingly stiff upper lip was marred by a scar that ran from its apex upward into a nostril like a harelip. That he didn't have a mustache brought attention to the disfigured lip.

"Do you think we're doing the wrong thing?" the officer persisted. "Feel ambivalent about being here, anything like that?"

"I didn't join, if that's what you mean. I was drafted but I'm not complaining. I guess it's the right thing."

"I believe you're married, practically a newlywed. You don't feel being here's disrupted your life that much?"

"Yeah," Payne said quickly, then added, "but I wasn't going to avoid the draft. It's the law."

Somehow he felt guilty, as if he were lying, even though he wasn't. "Why are you asking me these things, sir? Is there some question about my job, about my loyalty?"

Burns smiled, very relaxed. "To some extent, yes. You've kept your nose clean, your record indicates as much. By all accounts you've done an outstanding job."

He withdrew from his shirt pocket a Sherlock Holmes pipe and a leather tobacco pouch and started packing the pipe while looking at papers in an open folder on the desk. Then he came forward in the XO's chair.

"The confidential you filed back in June," he said. "Seems you turned in three of our troops for destroying property at a village outside Can Tho in the delta. It's not every soldier who'd report that kind of infraction against his own men. Especially when it's only the property of peasants we're talking about. You seem to be conscientious of the Vietnamese people. Any particular reason for that, a girlfriend perhaps?"

"I've got nothing against them," Payne said, his voice turning defensive. "Those guys didn't have any reason to shoot that buffalo. Some old papasan was out there begging them on his knees. They were just showing off. That's why I reported it."

"Says they were shooting birds off the animal's back," the captain said. He seemed amused. He shut the folder and leaned back.

"And you still maintain it was your obligation to report them?"

"I didn't think of it as an obligation, but, yeah, if that's the way you want to put it. Was I supposed to just forget it?"

Burns shrugged, which meant nothing one way or the other to Payne, then put the folder in an attaché case. "Records don't always tell the story. I'm simply trying to get a feel for the man behind the record, which is the reason for these fucking crazyass questions I'm throwing at you."

He was talking down to Payne, a lowly enlisted man, trying to get on his level, and it smacked of pretension. It gave Payne an edge.

"Well, have you?" he said. "Gotten a feel for me?"

After firing the pipe, Burns turned to the window air conditioner behind him and depressed the vent button.

"Feel free to smoke," he said and went on in the same breath, "A man has been transferred to your section. Willingham. Have you met him yet?"

So that's what this is about, Payne thought, the episode with the officer at China Village. He grimaced openly. It would probably shoot to hell the trip to Tokyo.

"Look, sir. If this is about last night, that officer was way out of line. Willingham was minding his own business; so was I."

Burns stretched his flawed lip into a tight grin. "You're ahead of me. That one hasn't come to my attention yet. But we'll forget it. You were out with Willingham, so you've talked. Good."

"Yeah. I got him bunked down for the night. I guess he'll get assigned a hootch today."

There was a moment of silence in which Burns tapped the bowl of his pipe and stared at Payne. Payne stared at the captain's harelip.

"I like the way you skate around the question without answering, Specialist. That should be an asset for the job you're going to do," Burns said, still speaking easily. "But right now I would like a straightforward answer. What do you know of Corporal Willingham, his previous duty?"

Payne fidgeted in the chair; it registered that he'd better be careful what he said and he spoke deliberately. "I asked him about it, out of curiosity," he said. "I mean you're just naturally interested in a guy that's been in the field. But all he would tell me is that he was with Special Forces. He wouldn't even tell me what his MOS is. He didn't want to talk about it. He got pissed when I asked him."

This seemed to satisfy Captain Burns. "He didn't give you any indication why he was transferred to Long Binh?"

"No, sir. He didn't seem to know, or care. What kind of job are you talking about?"

"One that's a privilege. One you've been selected for," Burns said, like a recruiter. He leaned back and lifted a boot to the edge of the desk and adjusted the elasticized band in his pants leg. "Let me fill you in. I'm not with civil affairs, as your lieutenant thinks. I'm with the CID, but it's easier all the way around to identify myself as a civil affairs officer. That way less questions are asked."

Lowering the boot, he rested his arms on the desk top. "We're conducting an investigation on the activities of Corporal Willingham's previous commander, a lieutenant colonel named Shellhammer. Willingham has no knowledge of the investigation, and it's just as well he think his reassignment was a bureaucratic fuckup, sending him to a unit that has no slot for an infantryman."

"The CID?" said Payne.

"That's right. It's a criminal investigation. Willingham was part of an unauthorized outfit that took orders directly from Colonel Shellhammer. A small unit, five men." Captain Burns looked at Payne's eyes as he talked. "Understand that by its nature this investigation requires secrecy, and that you are bound to keep what I say to yourself. You understand that?"

Payne nodded.

"Fine. We know that each of these men was personally selected by Shellhammer himself, apparently as a result of their proven capabilities under fire and their varying individual expertise. It was a unit of tough, battle-tested men—gung-ho grunts, you could say. But we have reason to believe Colonel Shellhammer was using the squad for illegal purposes, for his own profit."

Payne thought back on what Willingham had freely offered on his own, about the tunnel-rat poet and the guy called Jesus, and how little he had said about himself, his "expertise" or his previous activities. Payne couldn't figure why Willingham would have told him about these guys and nothing of what he did, that he was in an elite unit. Maybe he knew something was going on. Payne asked, "What were these guys doing? Did they know it was illegal?"

Burns smiled pleasantly. "An unauthorized unit isn't illegal in itself; there are many such outfits in the 5th pulling secret missions, perfectly legitimate. This is just a case of one commander going bad and abusing his rank and position for personal gain. We doubt the men in the squad knew what was going on."

"Then why would you transfer Willingham to PIO? And I don't understand what you want from me, either."

"Just consider it," Burns said patiently. "We thought it better to transfer him here, where there's no connection to his previous commander. Think of it as protective custody. As for PIO, it's the logical choice, since we can arrange to send him into the field easily and without drawing undue suspicion. You will be going together on missions I assign you. On the surface you'll simply be doing journalistic assignments for civil affairs. It works out."

Burns poured himself a glass of water from a frosted-over metal pitcher sitting on the desk. After drinking it down he filled the glass again and put it in front of Payne. Payne took it and drank thirstily.

"You're an honest upright soldier; you want to do what's right, don't you? Maybe—most likely—draw an early out after this is settled? A promotion could be in it for you as well. That means quite a bit more money for the six months you have remaining. There's your wife to think about."

Payne sat stoically, unresponsive, feeling as if he was being bought rather than doing the right thing.

"Couldn't you just talk to Willingham yourself?"

"Of course we considered approaching him directly, but we can't take the chance," said Burns. "You must understand a combat soldier's mentality. There's a certain privilege getting picked for an elite outfit. It's a thin line we're treading here, Specialist. I'm afraid if we were to level with Willingham he would balk out of a sense of devotion, which would kill the investigation. We cannot chance that; it's too important. That's why we've selected you to help us. We need someone we can rely on, someone with a proven record and a patriotic sense of duty. You also have some field experience, which will make things easier."

"I've only gone to a few villages and places, and always with an escort," Payne said. His hands fidgeted awkwardly and he slipped them under his thighs. "Just what are we supposed to do on these assignments?"

The CID officer did not hesitate in answering. "We need tangible proof of the whereabouts of missing hardware that we believe Shellhammer's selling to ARVN commanders or local provincial officials. You and Willingham will be sent to photograph the equipment as we locate where it is, probably interallied forts or refugee camps. We're hoping Willingham might recognize the ARVN people at these places and it's up to you to find that out and report it to me."

Burns reclined in the chair with deliberate slowness, elbows gliding along the armrests and his demeanor very relaxed, as if to coax Payne into the same attitude.

"I know it may appear somewhat underhanded, what I'm asking of you," Burns said in an empathetic tone of voice. "And I have no assurance you won't tell Willingham about this meeting. There I'm taking a chance; I'm relying on your record as a soldier who obeys his orders. If you can get Willingham to tell you the locations of missions his squad went on for Shellhammer, it would be extremely helpful."

The officer leaned forward and tapped the pipe against the desk to emphasize his words: "The missing armaments are going to the enemy. Your cooperation can help save Americans from being killed."

"I understand that, sir. But I don't particularly like the idea of spying on a guy I'll be working with."

"Let me assure you that Willingham is in no way under suspicion for his role. He was only following orders. If anything, he's to be commended as a soldier who performed his duty in an outstanding manner, pretty much the same as you under different circumstances. That will be recognized for both of you after your job is done and we have the evidence we need. You shouldn't think of it as spying, Specialist. Think of it as your duty."

Listening to this, Payne could not stop his imagination from conjuring up the weight and feel of jungle gear, the flak jacket laden with heavy grenades, a Bowie swinging on his hip, the shotgun tucked menacingly under his sweaty armpit, striding confidently and powerfully with a grunt buddy into some vil ready for action. His heart pounded in his throat; but it was not from eagerness at the thought of wiping out some VC village, but rather from the fear of it, that it might actually happen. He knew Willingham was trouble the moment he walked into the office.

"The other guys in his squad," Payne said, searching for an out. "What about them? Seems like you could get them to tell you what you need. Without having to go through all this elaboration."

"Afraid that's impossible," Burns said, for the first time showing impatience. "It goes back to the reason Willingham wouldn't necessarily want to talk to you about his past duties. The men in his platoon are all dead. Died in an ambush a few days ago. Our Corporal Willingham was the only one to survive. That makes him our only source. So you can see how important his knowledge is to us."

Burns watched Payne carefully, reading the shock, and he went back to his empathetic tone. "It can affect you that way afterward, clamming up and just wanting to avoid people, feeling guilty that it was you who came out alive, wondering why you made it and nobody else did. Your mind can do strange things after going through something like that. You can understand why this investigation has to be handled this way, why it's imperative we have your cooperation."

A sudden wave of shame seized Payne as he recalled how tactless and insensitive he had been in his persistence to hear Willingham tell him about his experiences in the boonies, eager to hear a bedtime story. Willingham's taciturn, sullen reaction to his thoughtless curiosity made sense now. Of course Burns was right; he wouldn't want to talk about losing his buddies, not when he was the only one left to talk about it.

"Why?" he said. "How did it happen?"

"We're not sure of the circumstances. We know what happened, but the ambush itself is too sketchy to draw any conclusions, other than the fact that four American soldiers died. Willingham had been separated at that moment from the rest of the squad, according to his report. But, for obvious reasons, you can't rely on an only survivor's report. The ambush may or may not be connected with this investigation. God help us if it was, anyone who would set up his own people. If it is connected we are dealing here with the worst kind of human being. We don't want to think that, but it is feasible, a possibility. Can we count on you?"

Payne could not say anything. He stammered, blinked his eyes, trying to buy a little time to think what he should say.

Captain Burns waited a moment for an answer, and when he didn't get one he lowered his voice. "You can look at it another way," he said. "There are a lot of places in Vietnam that aren't as comfortable as you have it here at Long Binh, places that aren't as safe. And I believe that Ann, your wife, has taken up activity contrary to the Constitution of the United States. It could get nasty for her, too.

Think about it, Specialist. You have your orders; it's your choice."

Burns got out of the chair, put his pipe away, and came around the desk to stand next to the door. "It may be a while before you hear from me," he said to Payne's back, as though it was all settled. "It could take time before we get a solid lead locating the contraband. I will notify your lieutenant when the time comes for an assignment. Until then, get friendly with Willingham, get to know him. He may open up after a while and make our job easier."

Payne took the cue and walked to the door. He didn't know what else to say, so he said, "I'll do what I can, sir."

Chapter

5

Payne stepped out of the XO's air-conditioning and into a bright blast of midmorning heat. The heat at once took his breath away, but he didn't notice; he walked with his hands in his pockets down to the company area and back, taking his time to figure out how he would approach Willingham. The guy wasn't stupid and Payne was going to have to be careful in his new role as an undercover snoop for the fucking CID. With time he might loosen up and want to talk, Burns had said. But he meant break down, and then Payne could move in on the sucker when he started spilling his heart out with grief.

Payne did not know if he could do it, if he had the cunning to pull it off. Or even if he would. Maybe he wouldn't. Maybe he would just lay it on the line: Listen, Willie, the CID wants to know just what the fuck you were doing out there while your buddies were getting wasted. Yeah, that's right, they're too bashful to ask themselves.

He kicked a can around, thinking about it, feeling pressured by an urgency to decide whether to sell Willingham out or not, for that was how he saw it. He wanted to confide in Willingham; his first inclination told him to. Willingham was suffering inside and if he knew about his ex-commander's activities, it might help him get over it quicker. Payne considered the terrible ambivalence Willingham must be going through right now, reliving the deaths of his comrades while pulling easy time at Long Binh, as if that were his reward for not dying himself. It would have to be a horrible thing to endure.

Payne could not imagine how it would affect him, if he would be out for revenge or fall apart with grief or just take it for what it was and be thankful to be alive; he was sure he couldn't hold himself together as well as Willingham was doing. You had to admire the guy for that.

But this business went against Payne's sense of propriety. He was supposed to become a fucking stoolie, just like that, as if it were a routine human thing to befriend someone, to gain his confidence for the sole, calculated purpose of extracting information from him. The whole thing sucked.

He got back to the office still unsure of himself. He felt weak in the legs and his eyes shifted about furtively, like a weasel looking for a place to hide. He was relieved to see that Willingham was not there. He didn't have much confidence in his composure at the moment; he was not certain he wouldn't just say fuck it and tell him what was going on.

He went about his work in a self-conscious, snappy mood, growling with impatience at Lai Sin for pecking at her typewriter instead of using it. Fortunately, the lieutenant had taken off and he didn't have to make up a lie to give him. He was glad when word came down that Top had called a noontime formation. It got him out of his brooding.

A little before twelve he walked down to the company area to find the entire company gathered outside the orderly room, milling about nervously; something was up.

The first sergeant ambled out of his office spitting tobacco juice and talking to the company clerk. When the noise quieted down, he informed the men that a sapper had been captured in the wire early in the A.M. and higher had panicked over it, putting the post on alert. The first sergeant stood in front of the ranks looking bored, as if to suggest there was nothing worth getting excited about. If anything, he appeared vexed at the effort he had gone through getting two hundred men together in one assembly at lunchtime. His attitude relaxed the column even before he began his speech.

This was Top's second tour of duty and he himself was not ready to panic. It was only rumor, he said, that the NVA was building up for an offensive in the province, nothing to get worried about. Higher had blown it all out of proportion.

"Thing is, men, we don't give a flying fuck if the man was Charlie, do we?" he growled. "Because we all know that half the mamasans doing our laundry is VC, don't we? But that don't keep your laundry from coming back clean, do it? The thing is, men," he said, "is that there's rumors. Rumors is the only thing we've got to worry about around here. Now, what this rumor means is, is me and every first sergeant on post has now got to work overtime on our duty rosters. We don't like it and you don't like it. Some of you will find yourself pulling guard ahead of schedule. But that's the extent of this problem. That's it, go get your chow."

The new roster had already been posted, and Payne's was one of the names advanced. Tonight. It made for a short afternoon till the four o'clock muster. Payne stuck around for lunch, still brooding.

After chow he checked in the office long enough to grab a camera and notepad, writing on the sign-out board under his name, "USO on story/guard duty P.M."

He picked out one of the girls with the Miss America entourage to interview and photograph. The show had started its tour at Long Binh; Bob Hope was not with the group. The girl he selected was Miss Arkansas; he thought that fitting, since she represented his home state and he could ask her questions she could respond to easily: Did she love the Razorbacks or what? Was she planning to hitch up with a wheat farmer or check out the city dudes from Little Rock? Questions that had nothing to do with her title, her attitude about the war, even her inevitable plans to find stardom in Hollywood. They all aspired to be starlets, you could see it in the hard-edged determination written on their faces; it had given them all a similar look of self-righteousness and cunning, an ironic acridness.

It was a tame, folksy interview, and the girl, whose name was Jennifer Ann changed to Jeannette by her agent, stayed on her toes, never giggling or acting like a girl. She was eighteen; maybe she had not been a girl since she was ten.

At four o'clock he and nine other GIs stood for inspection with their weapons and gear, then jumped on the truck for the guardhouse, a large hot bunker where you and thirty or forty other guys were supposed to get some shut-eye before your watch. Payne smeared insect repellent on his exposed skin and sat outside, watching the stars.

When Payne's turn came at midnight they put him on tower guard instead of bunker; in a bunker he would have been alone. He climbed thirty feet up the rungs of a ladder. He stayed straight, no smoke, no booze. His watch partner was a sergeant E5, a lifer recently busted down a grade. Something to do with rigging slot machines at NCO clubs. He whined about it the first couple hours; Payne offered to take first watch so the E5 could crash and shut up.

Guards referred to time on the perimeter as showtime, for what happened out there in the dead of night got you seeing things that did not exist. Minutes belly-crawled through the lonely, sultry night so that sometime before the long wait ended in the holy light of dawn you began to look upon sights that the combination of drugs and sleeplessness created, alien sights. If your imagination was fluent, it could be a hellish nightmare, mosquitoes dive-bombing through the bunker slit like B-40 rockets, rats with the yellow glowing eyes of vampire bats stalking you from the black recesses, waiting till your eyes closed to tear out your throat. Later still, mongooses and cobras materialized and danced in the wire, playing you for the fool.

Payne stood behind the mounted M-60 feeling the weight of it, the cold gray metal under his fingertips, and let his imagination travel beyond the concertina wire and into the jungle. He and Willingham uncovering huge caches of heavy warfare machinery deep in triple canopy, barely escaping under great barrages of firepower. Decorated for bravery. Ann standing proudly at his side for the ceremony at the Washington Monument. And decorated posthumously, Ann accepting the great medal at the commemoration, that too at the monument. She would have shaved her legs and armpits and worn a bra for the event. He imagined Willingham turning on him; in one script Willingham ripped off a mask and became the enemy, a dark, flat-faced dink, laughing his ass off at Payne before he cut him down. Once or twice Payne shot him.

It got him thinking of another, darker possibility—maybe Willingham escaped because he knew the ambush was coming. Maybe he knew what his commander was doing and went along with it, participated in it with him.

Payne reproached himself for the thought. It seemed inconceivable that Willingham would do something like that, turn on his own people; it seemed to Payne his reluctance to talk really was out of remorse or guilt, the kind of reaction a man truly would have who had lost buddies he was tight with.

Payne considered it again but still could not fathom how something like that would affect him; he'd never been tight with a guy in that sense, not like Willingham had, not in a combat situation. The only guy he could claim to ever have been tight with was Junior Cotton, his friend of many years who had joined the marines and died for it. He remembered what Willingham had said about watching a buddy die in combat; Payne felt the loss of his childhood friend, but he wasn't tormented by the reality of his death because he wasn't with him when it happened. He had not been there to witness his father's violent death either, and the secondhand knowledge had severely blunted the impact of it; Payne would not have used the same word, but he was tight with his father too.

He knew the advice his father would give him in this predicament: Use the judgment God gave you, not God's judgment. He'd taught Payne at a very early age to follow his own sense of right and wrong, not what he might think someone else would do even if it went against the crowd. Payne believed he had pretty much lived by that principle and now decided he had done the right thing in telling Captain Burns he would do what he could. Now, in the wee hours before dawn, it seemed clear to him; if he could help in a criminal investigation, he would follow his orders. It was the right thing to do.

Or, as he thought later in another lucid moment, maybe he just wanted to make fucking sure he wouldn't mess up his chance to go to Tokyo.

The E5 got up smoking dope and started pacing in a tight circle, badmouthing some sergeant major for not giving him a break, ignoring the perimeter. So Payne stayed up the rest of the night, locked keen-eyed on the wire below. Just before a dull light began to eat into the hem of western darkness he saw a platoon of phantom sappers crawling snakelike through the wire. They changed shapes advancing, merged into a huge beast of the wild, then fragmented into flying things, becoming winged lizards and twirling lassos and bouncing gingerbread cookies. Because he hadn't smoked he controlled the urge to open fire.

But nothing real entered his field and a little after daybreak he loaded his gear on the rear of the truck and came in with the other bleary-eyed troops, reported to the orderly room, then checked his weapon. He dragged his feet to the hootch, foregoing a shower, and slept undisturbed until the heat woke him four hours later.

It was a new day now and after a shower he sat at his desk in the daytime quietude of the hootch and began the ritual. The wall calendar was the first to get X'd. It hung on a nail under the screened window above the desk. The calendar was issued from the First National Bank of Cleveland, Ohio. The upflaps were of Japanese landscapes depicting serene waterfalls and humble women on their knees picking water lilies out of ponds, the colors pastel and pensive. The print hadn't been thought out with the troops in Vietnam in mind, but that meant little to Payne anyway. It was Japanese and some of the pictures were elaborate scenes of Tokyo.

He had traded his roommate, whose calendar it was, a handful of six-by-eight prints he'd shot in the delta for the right to X off the dates. He used a black Magic Marker on the high-gloss paper; the squeak it made was a pleasing sound that came with the thought of conquering another day. Good or bad, it was a day laid to rest.

Opening the pocket calendar next, he quickly scratched off yesterday in ballpoint blue. The pocket calendar was the size of a pocket Bible. Its photos were of nude women, most of them white, a few black, but none oriental. The calendar was distributed by the Armed Forces Vietnam Network radio. He had drawn the peace sign around the navel of Miss October, a vixen with a hand on her hip and a thumb thrown out alongside a lonely desert road. The idea was intended to suggest helplessness, but instead it depicted a sulky model irked by her work. The road seemed to be on a salt flat that went nowhere. The caption read, "Going my way, GI?" This was the calendar in which, by drawing a tiny cupid's heart around the date, he kept track of Ann's letters. With a baseballer's superstition, he used only a blue-colored ballpoint X-ing the days in the pocket calendar. He could count on one hand without using his thumb the number of hearts for August and September and up to now in October.

Payne smoked a cigarette and considered that. Ann's last letter was not even a letter. It was the postcard from her Washington fling, a brief, distant note written as if she were dropping a line to a casual friend—"Dear Russ, Just a note to let you know I'm in Washington D.C. this weekend. It's some scene here. . . ." And she mentioned briefly her new hippie friends, the protest march, blah, blah, blah.

He had been making excuses for her not writing; he knew it was rough going it alone in Dallas, where Ann had moved in July to take the job. It was the first time she had been on her own. Her folks were down on Payne for leaving her under a financial strain and she had had a falling out with them over it. Ann came from a good, solid family, the kind that sets and reaches goals and lives within secure limits, and they had never really accepted Payne, a man from a lower-class, broken family and now a draftee in the Nam. He hadn't even managed to get out of that.

But making excuses for her ebbing interest seemed petty now; now he was worried about keeping her out of jail or whatever might happen if he didn't come through for the CID, if Burns *thought* he wasn't cooperating. He wondered just what the CID could do to her.

The familiar slip-slide patter of sandals came to a stop outside his curtain and the laundry woman shuffled in, straightening herself seeing him there.

"I clean. You go," she demanded.

Payne crushed the butt of his cigarette on the floor and stood up. "You come back ten minutes, mamasan."

The old woman grunted and left.

Payne opened his locker. He looked at himself in the mirror, tracing a finger along his hairline. He thought it had receded, but the edges had only turned near-white from the sun. Payne had different-colored eyes, blue and a shade of green he always had trouble identifying, emerald maybe. Today the green one looked gray. He examined his teeth; they looked good, their whiteness heightened against the dark luster of his tanned skin. Ann would like that. She would have curled her lip and made a little cat purr deep in her throat and called him sexy. The thought both excited and stung him.

He slipped into swimming trunks and flipflops, grabbed a towel, cigarettes, sunglasses, a paperback novel, and walked out into the blaze of noon. At the mail room he asked the clerk if there was anything for him. The clerk grinned under a slash of freckles. He knew who Payne was but said officiously, "What's the name?"

"Payne, dipshit. Anything?"

"Hasn't been sorted yet. Come back in an hour." Clerks liked to pull that sort of thing, flaunting their dominion and making clear your accessibility to it, especially mail clerks who held great power over you.

He crossed a graded field behind the messhall where a football game was under way. Football in the heat of the day; it was crazy.

On Dulles Road he took to the culvert to avoid the pebbles thrown by passing trucks. At a dump site of dead machinery three

K-9s suddenly crashed against the fence to greet him. He threw a rock and watched them jump and tear at the wire with their fangs. You couldn't help notice the contrast between American K-9s and Viet dogs; Viet dogs turned tail at the slightest provocation, whereas these trained American hounds thrived on a good fight. You could make a theoretical comparison on a higher scale, as Smith might have done, that Viet dogs were like Viet soldiers and the same for GIs and K-9s.

As he prepared to hurl another rock a deuce-and-a-half braked alongside him. He tossed the stone aside and climbed into the cab. The number of dogs had now increased to five so that it had become a pack; the pack was disappointed to see Payne leave.

The driver was a lean black kid who sweated more than he should have been sweating. The skin around his eyes had a jaundiced tint. Even though he was sitting, there were no folds in the straight muscular line of his stomach. His shirt, on the seat between them, was patched with the insignia of the 101st Airborne, which caught Payne's eye immediately. The insignia was one not often seen on Long Binh. It amazed him how the white eagle's head could retain its brilliance when the shirt was tattered and faded. Buck sergeant stripes were sewn under the patch. Had he been a Long Binh soldier, he wouldn't have stopped for a white dude.

Payne braced himself against the jerk of the truck and took a smoke from the package the skytrooper extended with a quick, nervous hand.

"You down here on temporary?" Payne asked guardedly and peered in the outside mirror. He saw the yard dogs stumbling over each other to keep up with the truck. Finally contained by the end of the fence, the dogs went at each other, receding from view in a rage of tangled madness.

"Settlin' in for the duration." The buck sergeant slapped the wheel with both hands and grinned off the side of his face. "Got it knocked now, no shit."

Payne let himself go with the bounce. "You career, man?"

"Not likely. Twelve more days and I'm outa here." The grin took on a sudden new shape, one that lowered the edges of his thick lips, as if the thought was one of disappointment or remorse. "Goin' home," he added in a low voice almost inaudible under the engine drone.

"Where you from?"

"Eye Corps. Places around."

Payne flipped the cigarette out the window. "In the world, I mean. Where you from?"

"Shit, man. Philly. But I don' know if they ready for me back there yet. Know what I mean?" The skytrooper palmed the gear shift as if it were the breast of his woman. "Say man, I be here goin' on three days now. Hard to get to know folks round here, you dig?" The cigarette bobbled in his lips as he talked. He studied Payne with watery yellow eyes. "You a juicer or what?"

Payne scratched open a mosquito bite on the inside of his thigh. He watched the skytrooper's sweaty hands grip the wheel with a tautness around the joints that lightened his black skin. The knee of his free leg jumped rapidly. The man was hooked and Payne didn't want anything to do with that.

"Any gook hanging around the gate can get you whatever you want, man. You can drop me up ahead," Payne said, pointing out a truck wash.

The skytrooper raked an arm across his brow. His yellow eyes traveled the length of Payne's white body, from head to sandals, assuming the checked hatred that had become a part of his soul. "Man, you don' know shit 'bout this fuckin war, do you? Bet you been right here your whole fuckin tour."

The heat rose in Payne's cheeks. He kept his eyes downcast.

"I could tell you shit, man, that'd blow your fuckin mind—" The black kid stopped abruptly and made a hissing sound. "But you wouldn't want to know 'bout that shit. No, you better off just where you is, man. Here you go," he said, pulling off the road.

He looked at Payne again, his need to get high contained by pride. "It's the world that worries me, man. No shit 'bout that. You a lucky dude, man. Take her easy."

Payne jumped down from the running board. "Hey, wait! I could turn you on," he said too late. The truck roared and spit gravel, the door slamming shut with the forward thrust. "Shit," he muttered, watching the truck disappear. He stubbed a toe kicking a rock after it.

He was breathing hard when he reached the Red Cross recreational complex. The commons was surrounded by a well-manicured ornamental hedge with a high wrought-iron gate for an entrance. A wreathwork of purple and red bougainvillaea climbed along the gate's arch. The bougainvillaea seemed to have been growing there a long time.

The pool was laid out after the Howard Johnson's in Houston. Succulents in bloom bordered an elevated patio with tables crowded under tin umbrellas of red, white, and blue. The tables were occupied to capacity. A few women sat among the men, drinking from glasses with tiny Japanese parasols whose colors matched the table shades.

He spread the towel in a sunny spot away from the patio and arranged his thongs neatly at the edge of the towel and lay on his back. The low-volumed brass orchestra of Herb Alpert carried from the bar and a mixed aroma of steak and chicken or duck drifted across the pool. A breeze had come up.

The intense heat drove Payne into the water quickly. He swam under water, welcoming the silence and weightlessness as though the blue water could purge his mind of place and time. And it could. In high school he lettered in swimming, the butterfly. Upper body was his strength. Ann had been a swimmer too, and they worked out underwater stunts that were more sensual than graceful, touching each other with gliding hands and legs in a kind of fluid prelude that always seemed to arouse Ann more than him, and usually ended in a footrace back to his apartment.

Thirty laps exhausted him and he lay wet under the sun. The smell of the barbecue reminded him he hadn't eaten since the afternoon before. Having no money, he resigned himself to a smoke and settled down with the paperback, falling asleep after five pages.

A voice roused him; it seemed to be calling his name through a tunnel. He blinked and rubbed the salty sweat from his eyes and focused on his cubemate bouncing on his haunches next to him. Payne sat up.

The disapproving expression on Kink's face meant nothing to Payne. His roommate was an actor of sorts, assigned to Special Services, and he was always using Payne to try out a different persona.

"You're getting bar-be-cued," he said in a lispy singsong, his arms folded across his chest. Peter Lorre, maybe. "Better apply some lotion before it's too late. I won't be responsible when you scream in the night."

The character evolved into that of a matron, a nurse. The imitation sucked and Payne said so. "All right, mother," he growled.

Kink recoiled with a hand at his throat, assuming the martyr role. "Some day you'll wish you had listened to me. Honestly, the kids they let in the army these days—"

"You looking for me or what?" Payne said, using the towel to wipe the sweat off his neck. "You didn't happen to bring along any cash, did you?"

Kink became Kink, or who Payne thought might be the real Kink. "They're showing a doubleheader Bogie at the rec later. *Casablanca* and *Key Largo,* which happens to be my favorite Edward G. flick too. It may be his best, it's debatable," he said thoughtfully. "He was fucking sensational in that one. Remember how he crept up out of the boat hatch, saying 'We can split the dough, you and me, whadda you say, soldier?' looking like fucking Renfield in *Dracula.* You just know the guy would double-cross his own fucking mother. Ever see more convincing acting? I mean Johnny Rocco was disgusting as he was pathetic but you actually liked him at the same time. Shit, it *was* his best flick."

Kink had an angelic face when it was for real. He began undressing. "Anyway, thought I'd catch some rays out here first. How much you need?"

"Five."

Kink dug the money out of his wallet, then stripped off his pants. Underneath he wore a pair of maroon-and-blue polka-dotted boxer swimming trunks. In them his basketball legs were strings. Payne laughed.

"Jesus, Kink. Where'd you get those?"

Kink hiked to his full six-three frame. "Nice, huh? Turns on the women. Speaking of which, I think I recognize one of those dames on the patio. Maybe she's got a friend. Want me to find out?"

"Hold hands at the movies?"

"Say, where were you last night anyway?" said Kink. "You OD in the bunker?"

Payne squinted, looking up in the sunlight. "You're going to have to start making formations, Kink. Top's going to crawl all over your ass when he catches you missing. Better check, you might have guard tonight."

Kink broke suddenly and dove into the water. He swam a few laps and came back and rested his head at the pool's edge. "Oh yeah," he said. "You got a letter. I put it on your bunk."

Payne was following his nose toward the grill and condiment counter adjacent to the bar. He turned back. "From Ann?" he asked hopefully.

Kink blew snot in the overflow pocket. "Nah. From some guy in-country."

"A letter?"

"Yeah. From Cam Ranh. A marine, according to the return. How the hell do you know a fucking jarhead, anyhow?"

Payne squatted with a frown.

"Guy named Cotton," Kink added.

"What!" Mixed emotions seized Payne; he first thought it was a cruel joke. "The fuck you say. What's the first name?" he said, his voice high and irascible.

"Don't remember."

"Is it Charles . . . Junior?"

Kink said, "Sounds right. A pal of yours?"

Payne felt like kicking him in the face. "You playing one of your little games on me, Kink? If you are, you're not going to be laughing this time."

Kink pushed off. "Fuck you, Payne. Remind me not to pick up your mail in the future."

Payne jumped in the water and caught up with him. "If this is some kind of fucking joke, tell me. How do you know about Cotton?"

"Shit, man, what's your problem? I told you, you got a letter. That's all there is to it."

Payne grabbed him by the wrist. "Don't fucking bullshit me, Kink."

Kink's height gave him a footing. He twisted Payne around and pulled him under the water by the hair, then let him up. "I'm giving it to you straight, Fido. Who's the guy, anyway?"

Water got into Payne's windpipe and he went into a coughing fit. After a moment and he had calmed down, he said, "He got killed a year ago in Dak To."

"Really," Kink said in his wise-guy voice. "Well, there it is, man. The fucking Nam."

Payne tried thumbing a ride back to the company area, but no one stopped. He paced himself at double time, watching the ground race under his sandals and holding back the hope that it might be for real, that it was not the kind of sadistic joke often played on a soldier's folks, who would get a fake official-looking letter declaring their son KIA, the remains on the way home. He couldn't remember mentioning Cotton to anyone except Willingham. Could he have done this, was it mixed in with this fucking investigation?

A sudden wind blew dust off the parched ground, getting in his eyes. It was a cool wind that smelled of rain.

He had tried to forget about Cotton in basic training. He was at Polk then, in the fourth week, when his mother wrote him that Junior was killed. The joke back then had been on him. The Nam was every trainee's nightmare. Drill sergeants instilled the fear: "This is the facts. One out of every four of you shitheads is gonna die in Nam." It wasn't until a week or so after her letter that Cotton's death got to him and he couldn't keep his face straight. It would happen on the rifle range or over mess, places where he couldn't escape the other guys. They thought it was the fear, that he was counting himself as the one-in-four statistic. And they were not entirely wrong; losing someone you had been close to brought the fear closer to home.

His grief was magnified by the way his mother had broken the news, as if it had occurred to her as an afterthought: "Do you remember that boy Junior Cotton? Well, he's dead, too. . . ."

For his mother, it was as though Junior's death had been just another hometown casualty. But there were things impossible for her to have forgotten. He and Cotton had run around together since the third grade, through Cub Scouts and Boy Scouts. They'd graduated high school in the same class. When they were thirteen she had caught them masturbating in the yard tent and had eased their embarrassment by laughing her cryptic laugh and telling them to get to sleep, they were keeping the neighbors up. Mrs. Payne was the only person Payne knew who could reassure Junior there was nothing in the dark for him to be afraid of; in the middle of the night she would come into the room, tying her housecoat, and read to them or make up some funny story, sleepy-eyed but always animated. She became a fill-in mother to Junior, whose own mother and father stayed drunk on corn liquor, or vanilla extract when money was low. Payne couldn't imagine his mother would have forgotten teasing Junior for stuffing himself at the dinner table. "Three helpings of potatoes, Junior?" she would say. "My, my. Your mamma let you eat like that at home?" How could she have said, *Do you remember that boy?*

But later he understood how she must have felt. She watched the nightly news; she had a son going through infantry training and another already in the service, in God knows what part of the world. She had detached herself from the fear, prepared for the day the news came of her own son's fate. He grew to understand that his mother was just another unwitting parent obsessed with the myth that Vietnam meant her boy would die, even though he wrote her that he was safe at Long Binh. As safe as the folks in Texarkana.

The sky suddenly turned dramatically dark, breaking up the distant horizon and advancing an oncoming rain with a cooler sweeping wind. It was a low sky that rolled and rumbled angrily and moved faster than seemed possible. Payne dropped off the main road and headed through the 199th's area. This was not advisable, for the infantry unit was composed predominantly of blacks who didn't like Whitey trespassing on their turf. But Payne stayed clear of the barracks and quonsets and kept in the open, passing the orderly room and OBQs where he would be in less danger of ambush.

By the time he made it to familiar territory, the fine reddish dirt was surging on gusts of wind that became twisters in the fields and made wind-flapped sails of the clothes strung outside barracks. Mamasans ran about frantically removing their laundry. Before he reached his barracks the sky was the shade of night. He made it inside the hootch before the first wave hit.

The letter was addressed simply to "Russell H. Payne/Long Binh, Vietnam," no unit included. As he opened it his heart began to thump as if small bombs were going off inside his chest.

It had been dated four days ago; it never took four days for a letter to travel in-country. The fucking mail clerk, Payne grumbled inwardly; but it was a fleeting irritation, for he knew he was lucky that it had got to him at all. He toweled down before reading it, then turned on the desk lamp and sat for a minute holding the letter; receiving a letter was a special moment and it required this preliminary indulgence, like grace before Sunday supper.

The rain splattered intermittently through the screen window in a fine mist. Chill bumps raised the hair on his arms, and his hands trembled slightly holding the letter. He allowed himself a smile. It was from Cotton all right, for he was the only person who ever called Payne "Henry." The letter was written poorly, as though by a palsied hand, and he had to read slowly.

Dear Henry,

I couldn't believe it when I heard you were in the nam. I thought since you was in college you would have been on the other side and got out of it. But when I got down here at Cam Ranh this old boy Hilburn that was transferred out of your outfit happened to mention your name one day when we were talking. He's an orderly here. I guess if you really are down there at Long Binh and get this letter you will be surprised to hear from me too after three years. Has it been that long?

I'm in this hospital recooping. In i.c.u. where I have this great view out my window of a guard tower. Real class. I got myself the million dollar wound this time, but I don't know if it was worth it.

It's a funny thing how I found out about you, Henry. Hilburn was talking about how yall frag monkeys down there for entertainment. He said yall rig up boobies in the rubber outside the wire. I pulled some stitches when he told me that. Fraggings happen sometimes where I was but fragging monkeys, that cracks me up.

Hilburn started talking about this guy called Payne that had got more monkeys than anyone in the outfit. That sounded like something you would excel at. You always was a crazy fucker. And Hilburn confirmed it when he said this guy had different colored eyes and was skinny. It had to be you, said you talked like a rebel. Fucking A, that's Henry alright. Boy was I happy to hear that. I guess I shouldn't be since that meant you're in the nam. But from what I hear though, sounds like you got it pretty good down there.

I didn't know what happened to you since you took off for college. I still feel bad that I didn't keep in touch. But you know how it goes. Knowing what I know now I think I was just jealous of you. You did the right thing. It's just too bad you didn't get to excape the army even though Hilburn says you guys got no sweat down there at Long Binh. Is it true? I sure hope so. You wouldn't want to be where I was.

I got it on my birthday. Some party. This is my second PH, plus a Bronze and maybe a Silver. But big deal. I took some shrapnel in the neck the first tour, from our own arty. Fuck me. Just goes to show you how fucked this stinking war is. I thought I was going to get bagged at the time, but it just bled a lot and they had to remove part of my vocal cords. I'm all washed up with the church choir. Remember when we were in that play together and we had to sing that Over the Rainbow song? I was scared shitless. I thought I knew what scared was. Anyways, the Corps don't care if you can't sing.

I had to stop writing and now it's the next day. They did some more cutting on my chest last night to get out some more metal. Nobody knows for sure what kind of round I took but whatever it was shattered in my lung. I figure it was a dumb dumb. Dinks can play dirty.

You ought to see all the tubes they got in me. I feel like some kind of giny pig. But I'm high as a kite right now and don't feel a thing. I think they want to take out some of the lung, even though they have not come right out and told me that to my face. But that's what I think. After a while you learn how to read these hospital types.

I wished I hadn't come back for another tour. It's the Corps, it can do that to you. The first tour really was not that bad. I was down south in the highlands that time getting paid to squirrel around with them mountain Yards. But this time I got assigned to an outfit up around Phu Loc and all we did was night patrols. Shit did I hate that. I took the round at night. I wasn't the only one to get it that night. I was lucky really. I lost some good buddies, Henry, and I tell you I won't ever be the same so long as I live.

Anyways, I'm not writing to tell you that. I sure hope you get this letter. If you do I hope you will write me. The address is on the envelop. I'll tell you, it's good just knowing someone I know is still hanging in there and especially someone from home. And God dam, my best buddy most of my life.

Please write. I would rather hear from you than have a piece of ass. Which reminds me, I finally married Judy, if you didn't know it. We have a boy too and another one on the way. But I won't be smoking any cigars, ha ha. Mamma writes sometimes and I get a letter nearabouts every day from Judy, but you know how it is. It is not the same as knowing somebody over here even if they are down at Saigon, ha ha.

Your old buddy,
Junior

P.S. I don't weigh 190 anymore. I'm down to about 140. Your mom would be proud of me.

Sergeant Ortega hesitated in the doorway looking at Payne, who stood under the falling sky digging his feet in the mud. He was stripped down and holding his hands out as if to grab at the hailing rain.

"It's lightnin' out, man. You gonna get struck," Ortega said. The hootch leader was tucked inside a poncho.

Payne held his face skyward, his eyes closed. Sergeant Ortega talked from under the protection of the outside stairs.

"Better get your ass inside," he said and, getting no reply from Payne, added, "Say, man. You okay?"

The rain felt good slapping his skin, pulling out the goose bumps. He felt alive.

Chapter

6

It was a new season now; the rains would cause changes in the routine, make things harder. Mosquitoes would multiply; the swimming pool would close down earlier; movies might not be shown; your boots would have to be cleaned every single day. The first day of the new season had opened with drama, bringing hard swift showers that beat the tin like a platoon of drummers. The first day the sporadic downpours went late into the night, bottoming out with such pell-mell fury that it wasn't unreasonable to imagine the beginning of the end had come, as though the thunderous turbulence had been hurled on the sleeping land in a paroxysm by a petulant and fickle god whose anger would just as quickly retreat into the gentle dripping of rain.

Payne lay in the position you lie in when you think in bed, hands behind the head, unmindful of the wavering buzz of insects around his ears. He felt peaceful and at ease in the dark tranquility of the hootch. He had had a dream, and in it he and Cotton ran through the woods, a dream as real as at one time it had been.

He drifted into a sound sleep. When he again woke it was to the contrastingly bright, bustling familiarity of twenty-five grumbling men getting ready for the new day. He got up feeling refreshed; Kink was still sleeping and he didn't bother him.

Before leaving for work he tried again to write Cotton. He'd started four or five letters and ended up crumbling the paper, giving it up, too embarrassed. This time he was determined to finish. He made his setup at Long Binh sound more perilous than it actually was. He even thought about saying that he was working for the CID in a high-level investigation that could get him decorated; how about that for your old pal? But the thought only brought out his underlying shame. In writing to a man who had been wounded in combat he was painfully aware of the extent of their differences, and he felt small, as though his tour all of a sudden had meant no more than the mere passage of time, as if the experience of his few travels and articles was child's play up against what Cotton had been through.

He wrote that he was a journalist and could go anywhere he wanted in the republic and promised he would come to Cam Ranh. He included the office phone number in case they planned to move Cotton before he could arrange the trip. It took him an hour to write three-quarters of a page.

It would make him late to work, but fuck it, Payne decided, and also took the time to write his mother. He was concerned with her health. She had sounded depressed in her last letter, complaining of recurring side effects from the hysterectomy she'd had eight months ago, believing with nothing to base it on that she had cancer. She usually looked at things like that in the worst possible light, but it still worried Payne. He asked if she had heard from Rick, if his ship was in the Pacific, in the Tonkin again. Payne had not gotten a single letter from his brother and he was concerned about him too.

The sun was already up when he got to the office. The lieutenant, appearing anxious and distraught, called him in first thing.

"I don't like it," Finn said, frowning at Payne from behind his thick glasses.

Payne prepared himself for a speech on punctuality; it was seven-thirty and he was an hour late. But that wasn't what the lieutenant did not like.

"I've a good mind to call this Captain Burns back up and tell him so, too," Finn went on. "He could use MACV's staff for his damned projects. I don't even know what he wants you to do out there."

"You mean today? Already?" Payne said on a rush of adrenaline.

Finn nodded glumly. "No notice at all, just calls me first thing this A.M. and orders me to pack you off. 'A priority assignment,' the man says. Damn, we've got priorities too. . . . Well, I guess there's nothing I can do about it," Finn said finally, not wanting to push his defiance too far. "At least I can be thankful you're not getting reassigned."

"Am I going alone?"

"That's another thing," the lieutenant fumed. "He specifically said our new man's to go with you. Ordered it. Hell, why not send the whole damn section?"

Finn sighed and added, "But I suppose that's all right. I told Captain Burns we function on the buddy system around here too, and Willingham, I guess, is used to field work. It's better he go along."

"Where is he?" Payne said.

The question gave Finn the chance to get in his reprimand. *"He* was on time this A.M. But I don't know about him. The guy doesn't seem to want to get with the program, hasn't even gotten a haircut yet."

"I don't think you ought to push him too hard just yet, sir," Payne found himself saying. "He's not exactly used to this kind of duty. I'd think he needs a little time to readjust."

"Nonsense," Finn said impatiently. "Who needs readjusting to desk duty? But thank God he didn't give me any lip about this assignment; in fact, he even brightened up when I told him about it. Couldn't wait to get over to the armory for his weapon."

Payne got back to the subject. "Does Burns want me to call him or what? Where are we going?"

"He's an officer, Payne. Refer to him by his title."

"Roger that, sir. What's the fucking deal?"

Finn eyed him sharply, puffing his cheeks, but let it go. "No need to call him," he said. "You're suppose to go to a refugee camp at a place called Xuan Loc. I guess that's about sixty kilometers northeast. Take a map. He wants you to get photos showing army assistance out there, the construction and materials we're providing. He said to see the ARVN in command. He emphasized getting the photographs to him as soon as you return, this afternoon."

"Right."

"I can't figure why you'd be getting the info from ARVNs if the article is on pacification. What did Captain Burns tell you the other day?"

Payne shrugged. "Guess they're after the ARVN side of it since they're the ones we're trying to pacify. It's a civil affairs project.

That's about all Burns—the captain—told me."

Finn lifted what chin he had and gave Payne a concerned look. "Well, be careful," he said. His expression turned wistful, a look Payne hadn't seen in the lieutenant before.

He handed Payne a form authorizing him to check out his .45. "Won't be as cumbersome with your camera equipment. If I weren't so busy I would—" he added, cutting himself off, then finishing his thought. "I wouldn't mind going too." It was a comment oddly out of character, but he seemed sincere.

Payne shrugged. "Aw hell, Lieutenant, you wouldn't want to go. Nothing in those camps but a bunch of scrawny people, not worth wasting your time over."

Finn's expression stayed fixed. "Yeah, but it's part of the war, Payne."

When he returned from the armory, Willingham was carrying a sixteen and wearing a heavily loaded clip belt around his waist, his Die High rumpled bush hat flopped over his ears. Still wearing the worn-out fatigues and scuffed boots. He had taken a bath in the past two days, but that was all; he still smelled like the jungle. Seeing him the armed grunt lightened Payne's nervousness, giving him a boost of confidence, and he approached Willingham with a friendly smile.

Lai Sin looked at him sourly and sat mute and frozen. She stayed that way until they left.

"You ready to move out?" Willingham said with a rush. He was chewing gum, an anxiousness in his movement. Payne felt it too and stood tall. "You bet," he said.

Sterr put his newspaper aside and handed Payne the travel orders. He glanced from Willingham to Payne. "Wear your flak jackets and helmets on the road," he said, "just as a precaution."

Payne grabbed six cartons of film from the refrigerator, zipped them inside the camera case along with notepads and a pile of Tootsie Rolls, and said to everyone around for no particular reason, "We'll be back."

The road leading off Highway 1 was slab concrete, old and apparently hardly used; grass grew high in the cracks and cavities. There were cattail weeds growing tall in the gullies alongside the road. Narrow and unmarked, the road guided them through rubber country, snaking across uncluttered flatland that accessed plantations built during the French era. Many of the plantations were still in operation and were identified by outlying faded signs; every one they passed was a subsidiary of Michelin.

It was still cool after the night of rain, but the road had already dried.

Willingham drove. There hadn't been any argument about it. He said simply, "Better let me drive," and Payne climbed into the passenger side. Willingham had the sixteen across his lap, pointing to his left, close in. He wasn't wearing a shirt under the heavy flak and it gave him a look of power and raw toughness, the motherfucker look.

"You like being out here, don't you?" Payne said. "Carrying a gun again."

Willingham glanced at him and grinned. "You're looking real spiffy. Those polished boots are liable to get a little muddy today. Tell me," he said after a moment, "just exactly how much shit have you been into? Out in the countryside, I mean."

"I've been around," Payne blurted, feeling for the second time today the sting of his uneventful tour. "I ain't no fucking cherry."

Willingham tossed both hands in the air. "Just asking." His jaws worked the gum as he looked at Payne, eyeing him judiciously as if trying to make up his mind about him. "You feel it, the freedom?"

"Yeah." Payne did feel it and it frightened him.

He concentrated on the trees, searching high where a sniper might position himself. Where clusters of dense branches overhung the road he reflexively scrunched into the flak jacket and scanned from under the edge of his helmet. His imagination went to work as they passed through the unsecured terrain, even though Willingham was hauling ass and making the jeep a difficult target by driving all over the road.

"What's this assignment all about, anyway?" asked Willingham. "The LT was sketchy. Fucker looked like he was going to cry. A real Class A candyass."

"I guess you had some meanass lieutenant before. What was he, airborne, Green Beret, all that gung-ho stuff?" He had given Payne an opportunity and Payne jumped at it.

"Yeah, as a matter of fact. But he's a lieutenant colonel, not some buttercup."

"No shit. Your platoon commander was a lightbird?" said Payne, finding it easy to act astonished. "How'd you rate that, you with some kind of special outfit?"

"That's right," Willingham said. He drove with his chin thrust forward, jerking the steering wheel to avoid the pot holes, driving fast as though racing an obstacle course.

"Tell me about him," Payne said, holding on to his seat, "this fearless leader. He really Green Beret?"

Willingham nodded in the affirmative. He wasn't wearing a helmet and his floppy hat hung loose on his shoulders so that his long hair blew in his eyes in the open jeep. "Shell's okay," he said. "Not a bad man to be under. Knows what the war's about and does his job, a guy that looked out for his men. Not exactly your Mr. Finn. So what's this business we're doing today?"

Payne watched Willingham carefully as he talked. His face didn't reveal much, but Payne chose to take that to mean Willingham was not aware of Shellhammer's activities, that Burns was right when he said Willingham and his squad had been unwittingly used.

Payne said finally, "You should take it easy on him, Finn's still the lieutenant."

Willingham sneered. "Some LT. What about this assignment?"

"Pacification. We're just taking pictures of stuff at a refugee camp," he said and, probing further, added, "You ever been to Xuan Loc?"

Willingham gave him a passing glance. "Don't think so. Why?"

"No reason, just curious."

They'd been on the road an hour and were now passing through more paddy country. Clumps of woods separated some of the fields and others were divided by straight rows of tall bamboo. Up ahead, where the paddy fields came to an end, was a denser woods. Payne heard a ping and said, "What's that?"

Suddenly his side of the windshield shattered into a spiderweb and a hammer hit him high on the chest. "Oh shit!" he said and dropped in a ball to the floorboard.

The jeep accelerated and swerved hard to the left, then back, the tires protesting in bursts of staccato squeals. The .45 on Payne's belt dug into his stomach. His mind went blank and he didn't think to pull it; one hand clutched the top of his helmet, the other squeezed Willingham's leg. It went like that for a while, Payne welded to the floorboard, harboring the single absurd thought of running water, the whine of the transmission in his ear.

The whine diminished slowly, like the whistle of a faraway shell, then fizzled out completely. He heard Willingham say, "Clear . . . you can remove your fingernails now, sweetheart." The jeep had come to a dead stop, idling in a drone.

Payne lifted his head and saw paddy fields flanking the road.

"You hit, man?" Willingham said, looking down on him with big eyes.

Payne climbed back to the seat. He released the flak jacket straps and unbuttoned and pulled back his shirt. There was a bluish splotch on the collarbone. He moved his shoulder around; the bone was tender but it and the skin hadn't been broken.

Willingham brushed back his hair, relaxing. "A born survivor. Consider yourself a lucky dude."

"Christ, I didn't know what to do, man. What the hell should I have done?"

"Nothing else you could do." Willingham spoke in a calm voice, but sweat ran out of his hairline. He slapped the wheel affectionately. "Runs okay for a fucking army jeep. Someone's pulled the governor. Cowboy probably."

"Did you see him?"

"Made out the angle of fire." He picked up the sixteen and propped it on his thigh, barrel skyward. "Solo. Probably some kid out cutting his teeth, wanting to make a name for himself. Want to make a play for him?"

Payne thought he meant it and said, "Fuck no, man. We got a job to do. Let's get out of here."

Willingham displayed his horse grin and shrugged. "You're in charge."

They were closer than Payne estimated and reached their destination in about ten minutes. The encampment was a city of tin and tents, spread out in a winding valley. Huts of tin sidings shimmered under the sun, randomly dotting the valley floor, and strings of joining lean-tos extended up into the scrub-covered hills. Smoke rose in tiny pillars throughout the valley.

A descending muddy access led off the road and took them in; a prison-style fence topped with rolled barbed wire surrounded the compound. It struck both of them as odd, a refugee camp that had been fenced in. The gate was guarded by two sloppily dressed ARVNs who halted the jeep. The Viets split and walked to either side, jabbering and working their hands impatiently. Payne showed his press card and travel orders. The ARVN stuck a finger in the bullet hole through the windshield, wiggled it, and grinned. Then he said something in a harsh tone that sounded like a question. He repeated himself in a louder voice.

"What's he saying?"

"Something about our papers," Willingham said. "They want you to take your headgear off."

The guard obtusely studied the press card, looking between it and Payne as though trying to decide if the photo was really Payne, then flipped the card over several times in an officious manner, showing his importance. Then they were waved through.

Willingham pulled into the center of things. There weren't any GIs in sight. The place swarmed with black-clad refugees. In the camp's center, an open arena surrounded by three circus-like tents, people stood and squatted in long lines around the tents and shelters. Several trucks sat idle in the open area. They were ARVN vehicles, not U.S. Payne saw nothing bearing U.S. stenciling.

Willingham stopped the jeep next to one of the large open-sided canopies, under which more refugees lay and squatted on mats around small cooking fires smelling of camphorwood. Women suckled their babies quietly. Other than the children's there was very little activity, and a kind of muted chanting filled the strangely silent compound.

The subdued, almost zombielike atmosphere struck Payne as unnatural. It was unlike other refugee camps he had seen, where families awaited relocation with outward ease, even ebullience, the promise of safety written in their activity and faces. But here they seemed collectively fearful, as if they had not escaped danger but were waiting for it. There seemed to be very few men who weren't bent with old age, and everywhere he looked there were armed uniformed Viets. That too seemed peculiar.

Payne unconsciously rubbed his shoulder. "There's no Americans here. I don't like it," he said, stripping the flak jacket.

"Leave it on," Willingham said. "You're right. I don't like it either. Keep your eyes open."

A swarm of kids converged on the jeep before they could step out. Willingham pushed aside the tiny hands that clung to his pants and forged through the mob of slight bodies. Payne caused a scuffle dispensing Tootsie Rolls. He clicked off a few pictures of the naked children, trying to pick out the dirtiest, and failing to distinguish, searched the crowd for close-ups of the most wasted. The smell of raw sewage permeated the air.

A Viet officer in regimental dress blues and a yellow neckpiece stepped out of a trailer set back from the tents. The trailer was a silver-bullet-like Airstream with black curtains drawn behind closed louvered widows. Two Viets carrying M-16s followed behind him.

"Get a load of that," Payne said. "He's got a fucking living quarters out here."

Willingham tensed visibly at the sight of the ARVN officer. Payne could see the shock of surprise that caught him, the sudden flare of his nostrils and tightness in his jaw and neck strings. Willingham recognized the man. Burns had hoped for that.

"Know him?" asked Payne.

Willingham looked at Payne with unrestrained hatred in his eyes. "Yeah, I know the motherfucker. Quite a nice little coincidence," he said, containing his rage.

The ARVN had a pudgy face and a well-fed belly. He was smiling congenially. As he approached the Americans, his smile broadened, revealing side teeth of gold. If he knew Willingham, he was not showing it. He flicked a hand at the crowd of children and they scattered.

He stopped and the guards stopped behind him. "You are the men sent to make verification?" he said, his accent marred only by a soft *r*.

It was a strange question, unless, Payne thought, he knew what Burns had sent them for. In which case, why would he welcome them openly? Payne said cautiously, "We're here to take some pictures. You're in command here?"

The officer nodded. "Major Su," he said by way of introduction. "You gentlemen must be hungry and thirsty after your drive. Come in and have a drink and we will talk."

Willingham had been watching the man with a flat expression, revealing nothing of the emotion he had shown moments ago.

Su entered the trailer first. The two guards hastened across the grounds and joined a group of other troops. Willingham lagged back a few steps and grabbed the back of Payne's flak.

"I'll tell you why later, but you have to let me handle this," he whispered with a look of such intensity Payne agreed without question. Payne felt light-headed and a little numb.

The trailer was air-conditioned; the sputter of a gasoline generator droned outside. It was dark inside.

Major Su turned on a light and pointed to a built-in couch. "Have a seat, gentlemen. What will you drink? Rum and Coke is good this time of day."

"After we finish our business," Willingham said, taking a few deep breaths as though he were winded from the walk. Payne could see it was to calm himself. He took a seat and placed the sixteen across his lap.

"Yes, yes, of course, business first," the ARVN said in an ingratiating tone. "You Americans must always take care of business first. You are operating on the colonel's instructions, I believe?"

"Yes," Willingham said quickly. "The colonel."

Payne thought he saw Willingham wince; it was very sudden and he couldn't be sure, for Willingham at the same moment quickly jerked a handkerchief from his pocket and wiped his neck.

"Your timing is perfect," Su said. He seemed pleased. "Yesterday would have been too early, tomorrow too late."

"Good. Let's do it," Willingham said, rising. "We will be taking pictures of the refugees too. For our article."

Su frowned. "What article? This is necessary?"

"Of course it's necessary," said Willingham. "We're army journalists; it's part of the job." He eyed the ARVN suspiciously, as if testing his awareness of the mysterious collusion between them. Then he looked at Payne. "Isn't it?" he asked.

Payne stared blankly at him. Willingham was taunting the Viet, playing some kind of daring game.

The major shut the refrigerator and dropped ice cubes in a glass. "I know of no other business you have here. Are these orders?"

Willingham nodded tiredly. He stepped closer to the Viet and looked down on him, measuring him. "I have to spell it out? There'll be questions asked otherwise."

"Of course," Su said. "I was not informed of this. That is all."

Payne heard something in the distance that sounded like a burst of automatic fire. He peered through the blinds but saw nothing out of the ordinary. He looked again in a moment, and then spotted the group of troops coming out of the treeline of the forest. They were heading toward the trailer, walking with their weapons slung across shoulders or dragging them along the ground by the strap. Payne got up and stood by the door.

"Some troops are heading this way," he told Willingham in a tense voice.

Willingham looked hard at Major Su, his hand on the trigger cover of the sixteen.

"Relax, gentlemen," the Viet said calmly. "They are only my soldiers coming to report." He finished off a second drink on a long swallow and tossed the ice in the sink. "If you are ready?" he said and opened the door to a flood of sunlight.

The three stepped down as the soldiers reached the trailer. Su talked to one of the men, who nodded lazily and pointed his rifle at the brush where the men had come from. Su waved his hand as he had done to send away the children, and the men dispersed in different directions. They were an undisciplined bunch, following no particular military etiquette in manner or dress, a renegade outfit.

"I will show you what you have come to confirm," Su said. His small eyes were dark and beady, like the eyes of laboratory mice.

"Why don't you hang around here and take some shots," Willingham said openly to Payne.

"Like hell. We're sticking together."

Su showed his gold cuspids again; he was amused. "Shall we proceed?"

Willingham said, "Hold on a minute," and walked Payne out of the ARVN's earshot. His face was tense with excitement. "Listen, Payne. You don't want to get mixed up in this. You've got to go along with me like everything's cool. It's got to look right. Take some pictures of the camp."

"No way, man. Who is he to you?" Payne said, his throat parched. "What's going on here?"

"I don't know. I'm not sure exactly. Something. Just trust me on this."

Payne had his hand on Willingham's arm. He shook his head adamantly. "I'm sticking with you, man."

Willingham leveled his eyes on him, then sighed on a long breath. "All right. Just try to act normal."

The Viet walked ahead in quick, short steps, leading them past rows of corrugated huts and lean-tos. As if frightened by his presence, peasants cleared out of Su's way, withdrawing inside shelters or shifting direction, avoiding looking at him. Off to the side a young boy was slapping a rubber sandal up and down in a puddle of sewage water, shrieking with delight. He stopped abruptly when he saw the blue uniform and crawled inside a shack.

There was a commotion of some sort in one of the shelters. A man in black shorts and an orange turban sat lotus style outside, swaying back and forth and chanting, a skeletal figure in a trance. There was moaning and short muffled wails coming from inside. A woman emerged from the hut in a flurry carrying a battered pot that was apparently hot from the way she shifted it from hand to hand. Noticing Payne, she threw him a quick glaring look, one that Payne took as pleading, asking him for something.

Payne fell back from the other two and poked his head inside the hut. It was dark and thick with aromatic smoke; defined shards of sunlight filtered through the cracks between slats. On a blanket lay a naked woman whose outstretched hands were in the grasp of two other women, midwives. Her legs were spread and bent at the knees, her feet suspended off the ground. Her huge stomach convulsed in the throes of labor. Payne glimpsed the pate of the bloody head stretching the lips of her vagina. Flies buzzed in delirious circles, trying to alight on the protruding head. Payne set his camera.

The woman with the pot reentered the hut and began jabbering to Payne in a low voice. Suddenly she withdrew, staring behind him at the doorway.

"You must leave," Su's voice called at his back, and Payne stepped out of the hut, rapidly snapping off three or four hip-level shots as he retreated.

Outside he heard the infant's first cry. He smiled expectantly at the man in the turban whose eyes remained closed, his incantation continuing in the same monotonous drone.

Catching up to Willingham, Payne said, "I never actually saw a childbirth before. Looks pretty painful."

"You shouldn't've gone in that hootch," Willingham reproved. "It was sacrilegious, disrespectful."

It seemed an incongruous thing for Willingham to say, and it left Payne a little bewildered, at a loss for a response.

Willingham walked on, sticking close to Su. His eyes searched everything as he walked, in the cautious way of a grunt. Payne followed his lead and searched the treetops and thicker brush. As they passed the last of the shelters the path narrowed, taking them along a ravine and then into high grass. Here Payne watched his surroundings more intently. They walked downhill to an unmanned gate which Su unlocked and relocked once they had passed through. Willingham stayed very close to him. The trail ended at the gate, but a squeeze had been cut in the vegetation. Here the growth was denser, part flower and part jungle. Beyond a thicket of elephant grass and some vine-covered banyan trees, there was a hacked-out clearing the size of a landing zone. Near it stood a large shed sided by tiger-stripe canvas with camouflage netting strung over it, presumably to prevent aircraft detection. Yet there were crisscrossing marks of chopper skids embedded in the crusted mud.

"Inside," Su said, indicating the shed. He hiked up his pants by the belt loops and assumed a self-congratulatory stance. "I will wait outside while you make verification."

"No," Willingham said and, indicating Payne, said, "He will wait outside. You will go inside with me."

He made a display of handing Payne the sixteen, as though for Su's benefit. "You know how to use this bitch?"

"Shit," Payne mumbled, seized by the conviction that something terrible was about to happen. He nodded, trying not to let his nervousness show, and tightened his fingers around the trigger guard. The safety was already switched off.

Glancing sideways at Payne, Major Su stretched his thin lips into a half smile that was as flat and unreadable as his small eyes. "He is not a soldier," he said. "Very well, I will show you."

Willingham took the camera from Payne and walked behind the ARVN across the clearing. He followed the Viet inside the shed.

Payne fine-tuned his ears. Rustling noises he had not heard a moment ago set his eyes in motion scanning the trees and knife grass. He backed into the shoulder-high grass at the sound of a twig cracking, still keeping the shed in view, but furtively searching the forest around the edge of the clearing which was too thick to see into. He crouched on his haunches. Nothing moved except his hands rubbing the pollen off his arms and face. There was no wind. His mind stayed clear, but he couldn't keep his heartbeat down and it pounded in his dried-out throat.

The seconds crawled by like hours as he listened and waited with the stillness of a cat, resisting with great restraint the urge to scratch or rub away the grass itch. Then he heard something else, a muffled grunt, like that of a pig's squeal. It came from across the clearing, where he trained his eyes and rifle on the closed canvas door of the shed.

Another long minute passed and then Willingham appeared, moving quickly into the clearing, searching. Payne stepped out of the grass.

"Let's go," Willingham said, taking back his sixteen without slowing his pace.

"What about him?"

Not until reaching the locked gate did Willingham say anything. He unlocked the chain and pitched the key back through the wire once they were on the other side. "He thought something might be missing and wanted to check it out," he explained, slowing the pace.

"Something like what?" Payne said, almost shouting.

"Nothing," Willingham said. "Keep it down."

The hut where the woman had given birth was silent now, the man in the turban gone.

Willingham walked casually through the congested area of the camp, snapping off shots without stopping or talking, heading straight for the jeep. He climbed under the wheel.

The soldier who had talked with Su earlier approached the jeep. He came quickly, looking around the compound, apparently puzzled at not seeing his commander with the Americans. Willingham started the jeep. "Get ready," he said, looking excited. His face was animated and flushed.

The guard broke suddenly, running toward the jeep and waving his rifle. He shouted, *"Bai tu. Bai tu!"*

Willingham let him get to the jeep, then caught him across the nose with the butt of his rifle and hit the accelerator. "Shoot if they take aim," he said in a rush, tossing over the sixteen, the tires spinning and throwing mud.

Payne leveled the rifle behind him and watched the confusion. A din rose instantly; guards converged around the downed man and people scattered for shelter, scrambling around in a fast-spreading panic. The first shot did not come until the jeep was well beyond the gate. On the road, Payne saw a truck wheel through the gate. Ten or fifteen of the cowboy troops were standing in the truck bed, brandishing weapons.

"They're coming after us," Payne said. He was excited but unafraid.

The tires screeched hitting the pavement. "They won't catch us," said Willingham.

Payne kept the rifle trained behind him. Down the road a few clicks, once he was sure they had lost the pursuing truck, he said, "What was in that shed?"

Willingham was still pushing the jeep for all it was worth. "Perishables," he said. "Nothing but fucking perishables."

Chapter 7

The sky broke shortly before they reached the main gate, and Payne had to lean forward to keep out of the downpour. He had his hand under the flak jacket and was caressing the lump on his shoulder. Until now he hadn't noticed it; now it throbbed.

Payne had to point out the fact that it was raining on them. "You want to pull the fuck over so we can snap down the canvas?"

Willingham did not even look at him.

At the guardhouse an MP stuck his head out to tell them one of the windshield wipers was not working, better get that fixed. Willingham went on through without a word, driving with his head craned outside, letting the rain slap his face. He had stripped the flak jacket earlier, and in the rain-dimmed light his skin had a ghostly tint.

Payne noticed the handle of a sheathed hunting knife stuck in the back waistband of his pants. "I didn't know you carried a knife," he said in the rain.

Willingham drew back in, his hair soaked, face slick. "Trusty tool. Never go out without it." He grinned crazily. "I love the fucking monsoon, man. It does something to you, you know? It like renews everything, purges your soul, washes all the shit away and makes everything right again. Know what I mean?"

He'd been in that kind of mood all the way back, in a manic state, talking about odd things, philosophizing. The jungle, what a magnificent example of nature's cycle; how virtuous the people were who lived in it, mountain people. Carrying on and on about the Montagnards, whose land this really was, how he dug their ways. Things like that.

On the way back Payne had tried to get some answers, why had he broken that guard's face, questions about the ARVN commandant. But Willingham eluded his questions and went on talking about the monsoon, how great earthworms smelled, non sequiturs. Crazy talk.

When he was sure they had lost the truck of renegade Viet troops, Payne had said, "Fuck, man. You had to of broke that guard's nose. You didn't have to pop him that bad."

"The fuck I didn't. What do you know, you don't know what they're capable of."

"What'd you do to that major, Willie? How did you know him?" Payne had asked for the third or fourth time.

"Doesn't matter now."

"Shit, man, I did like you said, I let you run the show. Now talk to me, damn it."

Willingham had looked at him as if he was about to backhand him. "We got out of there, didn't we? Just shut the fuck up and get off my case about it," he said, and Payne finally dropped it.

Willingham wasn't going to tell Payne anything he could take to Burns. The ARVN major had meant something important to him, something to do with his past. He had controlled his hatred, become calculating. But Payne couldn't figure it; Willingham knew Su, but the Viet didn't know him, or at least he did not show it. The Viet had to fit in with the investigation, of that Payne felt sure. But there wasn't any kind of armament at the camp that Payne saw. It left him blank for explanations, thinking he was involved in something more complex than he had been led to believe.

Payne had come close to telling Willingham what was going on, about the CID, his previous commander, all of it. It did not matter that Willingham wouldn't talk; he understood that. It seemed to Payne that Willingham was dealing with more than losing his squad, something worse, and Payne needed to know what was going on with him before he told him about the investigation. Yet holding off now made him feel he was betraying a friend, like a Judas. More than anything else not confiding in Willingham made him feel cheap, knowing he wasn't coming clean with a guy who today had probably saved his life, a guy who was turning into a friend.

Willingham punched Payne and pointed to a concrete wall they were now passing. The structure loomed twenty feet high, without windows, and extended for four blocks alongside the road. "What the hell is that? I keep seeing it."

"The stockade," Payne said, relieved to hear Willingham making a sane comment. "They had a big riot there last month. It made *Newsweek.*"

"No shit."

"Yeah. The article coined it LBJ—Long Binh Jail. Some soul bros burned down a cell block, no doubt your bloods from the bush. Some dude was killed and the warden got beat to a pulp. You didn't read about it?"

"LBJ," Willingham mused. "Fuck me."

"What do you say we get a drink. I could use one about now."

"No time," said Willingham.

What do you mean, no time, Payne thought, but let it go.

In a moment Payne said, "Hey, you remember me telling you about the friend of mine I said got killed over here?"

Willingham was again leaning out in the rain, fingering his wet hair as if washing it out. He drew himself back in and squirted a mouthful of rainwater at Payne and laughed. "Sure I remember. Said you was blood brothers; you think I'd forget something like that?"

"I didn't know," Payne said. "Anyway, he's fucking alive. I got a letter from him. Couldn't believe it, man. It sounds like he's all fucked up, but he's alive. They've got him in a hospital in Cam Ranh, getting operated on."

By his open expression Willingham seemed sincerely happy to hear it. "I'm glad the dude's okay, man. God love him."

"I'm going to try and visit him."

"Sounds like the thing to do. But, hey," Willingham said, "don't go expecting the guy to be anything like you remember him. I don't mean what he looks like either. I mean who he is now. He was a grunt marine, you said."

"I don't. He was in some bad shit, from his letter. He was wounded before and that's when they thought he was dead. Came back for a second tour. I don't know what to expect."

"Nothing. Don't expect nothing," said Willingham. "Just take him for who he is now. And go see him. Don't just think about it. Do it."

"All right, I'll do it. Shit," said Payne. "I'm getting hungry," he thought aloud. The rest of the drive was in silence.

At the Information Office the lights were off but the windows were raised. Night had fallen with the rain. They went inside and found Sterr sitting by himself in the dark. He sat in a lump at his desk drinking whiskey from a coffee cup and looking at the rain pound and splatter in the windows. Payne turned on the lights.

Taking all his gear and the camera, Willingham went directly into the darkroom across the hall. "I'm going to soup the film," he said. "Don't disturb."

Payne looked at him in surprise. "You learn how to do that already?"

"Had a darkroom at home," Willingham said and shut the door.

"Where's everybody?" Payne asked, making a rush of motion that slung water across Sterr's desk top.

"Split," Sterr said. He was having a hard time steadying his eyes on Payne. "Pull her up and have a drink with me."

Payne stripped the flak and gun belt and, toweling his hair, took the cup of whiskey Sterr offered. "Guess what happened, Sarge?"

"They're not going to let me extend," Sterr said, looking gloomily at Payne. "I'm leaving right after New Year's, that soon."

"Ain't that a shame."

Sterr sighed tiredly and turned back to the windows. "What happened?"

"I got shot." Payne pulled his shirt aside and showed him. The bruise now had spread across the shoulder and down into his chest and there was a lemon-size lump on the collarbone. "Sniper," he said coolly.

"God Aw-mighty. What the hell happened?"

Payne rebuttoned the shirt, making a show of being careful. "On the road. The windshield'll need replacing. Willie said the dink was in a tree."

Sterr perked up. He proceeded to barrage Payne with questions, wanting to know how many shots were fired and from what angle and what was Payne thinking, did Willingham react. Payne answered tersely, avoiding telling him he curled up in the floorboard and didn't really know what happened.

"Willie knows how to drive those roads," he said. "Probably what saved me, and him too."

"Get your ass over to medical," said Sterr, "and get the paper-work in. You've got to document it, then I'll get you the forms for the Purple Heart."

Embarrassed, Payne changed his tune, feeling as if he'd been caught lying to the scoutmaster or something. "Well, it's not like I really got wounded, Sarge. It's not even bleeding."

"The hell you didn't get wounded."

His surge of excitement died as suddenly as it had started and Sterr became thoughtful again, staring beyond Payne, the melancholy returning. His lumpy jaw hung heavily, giving him a hound-dog look.

"I've been over here, altogether I'd say about thirty months total, and I never have even seen Charlie," he said miserably, pouring whiskey into his cup and then Payne's.

When the phone rang, Sterr answered it quickly, his voice clear and sober. "PIO. Sergeant Sterr speaking, sir."

It never ceased to amaze Payne how he could throw all those consonants together so easily, even when he was sober.

Sterr cupped the receiver and whispered to Payne, "Captain Burns. You want to take it?"

Payne mouthed no.

Replacing the phone in its cradle, Sterr said, "What's he got you doing that you have to go into an unsecured area without an escort?"

"I wish the hell I knew."

"It stinks," Sterr said. He struggled out of his chair like an old man. "That shoulder must be killing you, Payne. Come on, I'll get you numb at the lifers' club. You can get over to medical in the morning."

On the way out Payne tapped on the darkroom door and shouted through it, "Hey, Willie. Want to hit the NCO club with us?"

No answer and he rapped louder.

"Get the fuck off," Willingham said angrily.

"What's eating him?" said Sterr.

"It was a long day. Let's go."

They left Willingham to close up shop and walked down the hill in the rain, Payne with his off-post gear under his arm, Sterr with one of Lai Sin's umbrellas held uselessly over the two of them.

"I'd like to like that guy, but he sure makes it hard, don't he?" Sterr said.

"I guess he's got his problems."

"Yeah, I'm sure he had it rough before. But sooner or later he's got to get rid of that chip he's carrying around. He can't go on bucking the system. Bad for everybody concerned," Sterr said. "I'll talk to him sometime."

Payne threw down Chivas Regals on ice and smoked cigarettes and listened to the sergeant and two of his lifer buddies explain why a lifer needs war-zone duty; war promotes, and the more tours the quicker those promotions came; plus there was the hazardous-duty pay and sometimes the combat-duty and TDY pay. It added up when you had a family to take care of, which the lifers all agreed this young fella ought to think about. Wasn't he planning on having a family? The military was an orderly, secure way of life. It had a lot to offer a man, especially when he was just starting out. Their reasons made sense to them and Payne nodded understandingly. He didn't feel like getting into a debate over it, as Ann undoubtedly would have done.

By the second hour, Payne's status had elevated to that of a hero; Sterr insisted he show his wound and Payne obliged, slipping back his shirt as though the pain were unbearable, when he hardly felt it. He told the lifers their return fire might have picked off the dink, he couldn't be sure, but they weren't about to go in the jungle and look for the body or the trail of blood. "Coulda been a little ambush party waitin'," Payne said, his tongue thick as a cow's. When he left the crew of hard-core juicers, he could hardly focus his eyes.

Later, watching *Bonnie and Clyde* at the clubhouse, he went to sleep and fell out of his seat before the girlish C. W. Moss delivered his infamous line, "Just blowed it away," which Kink would mimic for weeks to come and Payne wouldn't get; in Kink's estimation the line would become immortal, equivalent to "Frankly, my dear, I don't give a damn." Sometime in the night a mouse did sprints across his chest, but too deep in fatigue and drink to notice, Payne smacked his lips and rolled over. Sometime later the pain in his shoulder woke him and he chewed four aspirin.

In the morning he walked into the office late again, at nine, unshaven and dehydrated. Sterr smiled pathetically at him. His bulbous veined drinker's nose was a shiny pink-blue. "Told the lieutenant what happened, that you had to go to medical and would be late. Did you go?"

"Guess I'll have to now," Payne said in an occluded, raspy voice. "Anything to drink in the refer?"

"Nothing but tomato juice," Sterr answered pleasantly. "Want a Bloody Mary, little hair of the dog?" How could he feel like joking, Payne wondered.

Payne found only cranberry juice in the refrigerator and screwed his mouth up in disgust at the thought of drinking it but popped holes in a quart can and drank it halfway down. "Shit," he said, "the stuff ain't half bad."

The office was practically deserted with Langley TDY somewhere and Cowboy and the lieutenant covering a ceremony at Sealy Field, Willingham not around either. Lai Sin was pecking on her typewriter. She looked good today, wearing a tight sweater and knee-length skirt of different shades of blue and blue mascara, all of which gave her puffy half-Chinese eyes a blue tint. She looked good because Payne was hung over and when he was hung over he was horny.

"You see Willie this morning, Sarge?"

"Hide nor hair."

Lai Sin picked up the ringing phone. "For you, Lussell."

It was Captain Burns. He was angry and came straight to the point. "Immediately, Specialist. That meant yesterday when you returned."

"We got back late, sir. There was nothing there, some trucks, a trailer. I didn't think it—"

"You don't think. That's not your job."

He could hear Burns's labored breathing on the phone.

"Was there anything unusual at the camp, anything at all?" Burns said in a less strident tone.

"Well, the people there. I don't know, they seemed afraid. That seemed unusual."

"Yes? Go on, how so?"

"They didn't seem like refugees waiting to resettle; they acted more like prisoners, like they were being held there or something. And there were a lot of ARVNs around, guarding the camp. It had a fenced perimeter. Why would it be fenced?"

"Not unusual in that area. How about Willingham. Did he recognize anyone there?"

Payne hesitated, unsure of himself.

"You there, Specialist?"

"Yes, sir. Not that I could tell. He didn't say so. We took some shots of the place and left. I didn't see any U.S. equipment." He talked in a low voice, with his back to Sterr and Lai Sin.

The popping sound over the line might have been Burns lighting his pipe. "I'll want to see the prints."

"Yes, sir. I can bring them down today, right away."

"Just send them by courier, with the negatives. Have you gotten any information out of Willingham yet?"

"Nothing, sir."

"All right. But keep at it. I'll get back to you." He told Payne where to send the stuff, care of civil affairs, MACV, and hung up.

Payne guzzled the rest of the cranberry juice and had some coffee and more aspirin. After a while, when his head had settled down to a languid ache, he went to the armory and turned in his field gear, checked for mail, went to the PX for food supplies for the hootch, and got back to the office around eleven. Cowboy was back, but Willingham still hadn't shown up. He thought about going down to his hootch but had a better idea.

He searched Willingham's desk. Cowboy watched him curiously, and Lai Sin frowned disapprovingly, as if he were violating something sacred. He ignored them both. In the bottom drawer, stuck under an unopened box of Russell Stover candies, he found something, an address book. The entries weren't the ordinary things you put in an address book, such as addresses of family and relatives and friends in the world. He didn't see any Stateside addresses or phone numbers. Instead, it had alphabetized listings of American and Vietnamese names followed by some kind of military code—"Box Trap/Ban Don" and "Fat Cat/C. O. Muong Drak." He didn't find Shellhammer's name under the S listings, nor Su's. There were other notes appearing to indicate the sizes and topography of villages, their populations, with the number of males in parenthesis. The information could have been references to patrols Willingham had been on for Shellhammer, just the stuff Burns was looking for. He turned pages and found more of the same kind of entries. Why would he keep a coded record of his unit's activities, if that was what they were?

"Why you do that, Lussell," Lai Sin finally said, as though mortified. "You no can do. Bad you steal oth-ah people."

Payne smiled benignly. "Even him, the bush man? I thought you didn't like Willie."

She gave him a haughty look. "He still oth-ah people. I only 'fraid him. I no no like him, only 'fraid."

"Well, it's okay, Lai Sin. I'm not stealing from him. Just looking for his part of a project we're working on."

She narrowed her eyes suspiciously, unsatisfied. Cowboy turned up his radio and told her to mind her own business and get back to work or he would keep the volume up. He always threatened her with that when she spurned his advances. Payne wasn't the only one who found her especially sexy today. She had disdain for the psychedelic music Cowboy played—"bad noise," she called it.

"Yi-ie. You have no lee-spec Viet Nam," she said to Cowboy now, as if Hendrix or the Grateful Dead also violated something sacred to her, and turned contemptuously back to her typewriter. Nobody understood such comments.

Payne put the book back in its place and went into the darkroom. He found Sterr lying on the floor, his head inside a supply cabinet and a clipboard resting on his bent knee. He was snoring. Payne nudged him with a boot and Sterr roused, bumping his head and moaning himself awake.

"I've got some stuff to do, Sarge. I can finish the inventory."

With great effort Sterr lifted himself and brushed his hands. He handed Payne the clipboard without comment and left.

Payne turned on the safe light and got busy developing and printing from the only roll he had shot at the camp. He used the chemicals Willingham had left from last night. The last shots on the roll were of the woman giving birth. The negatives were underexposed but salvageable, and he had gotten the framing right. He made prints from two of them, hung them to dry and then finished the checklist for Sterr. Some of the items on the form were obsolete or meaningless, such as color chemicals which the darkroom was not set up for, but he searched anyway. Maybe Langley was trying to set up for color. On a dusty shelf under the sink, he ran across a sheath of fresh-looking negatives.

He took a strip of film out and placed it in the enlarger, focused, and hissed, "Shit," then quickly locked the darkroom door and studied the lighted image. Some of the bodies had been laid out neatly on the ground and others were hanging upside down, each suspended above one on the ground so that the heads almost touched in a uniformed row. He counted ten bodies laid out on the ground and ten suspended. All the bodies appeared to be male, all shirtless and dressed in pajama pants.

He rapidly checked the rest of the negatives. They were all of the bodies from different angles, except for the last three negatives on the roll, which included an additional body that was easy to detect because it lay haphazardly across two sets of legs, as if it had been left where it fell. Payne made a print. As the print wavered to life, he recognized the face belonging to the body lying haphazard. These were the pictures Willingham had taken in the shed.

Under the ultraviolet light the suspended bodies appeared three-dimensional. Payne blinked and the image of the bodies shifted in relief, like living black ghosts jumping off the paper.

A few of the bodies had been decapitated but the grotesqueness strangely did not bother him, perhaps because it was shot in black and white with little evidence of blood.

He turned on the fluorescent light for a better look. Su's face was clearly visible even though the head had been drawn back sharply, showing a gaping slash in the neck; but the face was turned toward the camera as if positioned that way on purpose. There was a lot of blood around his body. Payne studied the figure closely and thought maybe Su's hand was made into a fist, but it looked more as if the fingers were missing.

Payne slumped on the stool, tearing at a package of cigarettes. He filled his lungs with smoke. Willingham had cut the man's throat. It did not really surprise or disturb Payne, but why had he done it? What was it that had made Willingham go so far as to kill him? Payne's mind reeled recounting the events at the camp. The gunfire he'd heard from the trailer—could that have been the renegade soldiers murdering those people? The people they were supposed to verify? Verify for whom? Su had said the colonel, and Willingham said, yes the colonel. Would that be Colonel Shellhammer? Maybe the victims were VC, but it seemed more likely that they were refugees from the camp, which would explain the common fear that permeated the place. The fear of becoming fucking perishables.

Payne paced the floor, going through some raw emotions; this discovery made it much more serious and deadly than he suspected or could have imagined. And he was in it up to his neck; he'd already lied to Burns. He paced the darkroom thinking, searching for answers, deciding what he would do now. But he'd gone this far for

Willingham, so why not stick his neck out a little farther, at least until he could get some answers, until he had the chance to find out from Willingham what was going on.

Replacing the sheath under the sink, he torched the print with his lighter. It was too wet to burn, so he folded it in his pocket and went back across the hallway into the office, taking the clipboard and prints of the woman giving birth. He took some deep breaths to regain his composure before stepping into the lieutenant's office.

"That's it?" Finn said, not looking at the glossy Payne tossed on his desk. "Only one?"

"They're not even supposed to be for us. What do you want."

Finn rocked back in his chair, folding his hands behind his head. "Don't you have something else to report to me?"

"Like what, sir?" He wondered if Finn was in on it too.

The lieutenant pushed himself forward. "Like what? Like getting shot at, that's what. You'd think that's something you'd remember. Sergeant Sterr wants me to put you in for a Purple Heart. Certainly can't hurt the section, a Purple Heart," he said beaming. "How bad is it? Let me see."

There was a knock and both men glanced simultaneously at the closed door. An insistent scrape, like cat claws, was barely audible. It was Lai Sin's fingernails. Her scratch-knock had always irritated Finn. He barked, "Yeah. What is it?"

Lai Sin cracked open the door and pushed only her head in with customary tentativeness. "Telephone Loo-tenyant Finn."

"It's only a bruise," Payne said, leaving. "There's not much of a story with the picture, but I'll get some copy out of it."

"All right. But don't go playing up the mushy side like you're inclined to do. Angle the piece appropriately."

"Right."

A few moments later Finn stormed out of his office, shouting obscenities.

"The shithead's done it," he yelled. "What the hell am I going to do with him. He's going to take the IO down the drink. Shit."

"What's that, sir?" Sterr said calmly. "There a problem?"

"A problem? A problem? Yeah, you might say there's a problem. It's Willingham. He's in the stockade. I'd say that's a problem, wouldn't you? They want me to come down; they want to question me about him. I'm going to have that shithead transferred out of here. He's a lunatic." The lieutenant looked like the lunatic.

"What'd he do?" asked Payne.

Finn looked at him, restraining his fury. "Nothing much. Just went on a shooting rampage. Seems he shot up the retrograde depot. But he only destroyed a few pieces of machinery, about thirty thousand dollars' worth, they said." He grinned crazily saying this. "He was dressed up like some maniac in a loincloth, painted himself up like a damn barbarian or something. They told me he had a string of fingers around his neck. *Human fingers,* for Christ's sake. He held the MPs off till midnight, and then he tried to run them down in an APC, tried to kill them all. The guy is insane."

"I didn't know he could drive a tank," Payne said, trying to assuage the lieutenant. "Don't you have to have training?" Oddly, Payne was not surprised at this news; it didn't sound like the action of someone insane. It sounded like the act of a man trying to get something terrible off his chest.

The lieutenant barked like a dog. "He's done it."

"I'll go with you, sir," Payne said. "There's something you should know before you go over there."

Finn cooled down a little on the way. Payne insisted on driving; in the lieutenant's state of mind he would have probably gotten them killed in an accident. Killed in action in the rear. Finn wasn't much of a driver even under normal conditions.

Payne made a case for Willingham's behavior, telling Finn that his platoon was wiped out on patrol, that Willingham had lost some close buddies and was going through that nightmare every day. "That's why he's so moody. It finally got to him, I guess, putting up with all the bullshit he has to go through here. You've got to try to understand that, sir," he added. "What are you going to tell them?"

"I didn't know that," Finn said reasonably. "Why wasn't I informed of that?"

"I just found out yesterday, when we were in the field. It must have gotten to him, being shot at again. You have to understand."

Finn grew thoughtful and stayed that way until they arrived at the stockade. Payne followed him through the main gate, over which was inscribed, "We Welcome Command Failure." Payne was not allowed to go inside the compound.

"I wouldn't bring up this stuff I've told you, sir. It might—"

"I'll take care of it from here, Payne," the lieutenant snapped.

Payne left him the jeep and hitched a ride back to the Stretch. He went to the infirmary and got his shoulder looked at. No bones fractured, severe contusion, light duty recommended, forms signed. He then changed clothes and went to the brigade swimming pool and did laps, sidestrokes to favor his good shoulder, and slept on a chaise lounge until the sky darkened. While it rained he drank beer and shot pool at the clubhouse. Later that night he won twenty-eight dollars at poker, enough to order the Seiko watch he wanted for Ann's Christmas present. Immediately after the game broke up, he filled out the mail-order form to mail off first thing in the morning before he had the chance to blow the cash. Anything to keep his mind occupied.

Kink stumbled in stoned on acid and Payne took him out back and held his head while he puked. After getting Kink to bed, he began a letter to Ann without once stopping.

He wrote, *How can I convince you how important it is to me to hear from you?*, and went on to work himself into a state of reckless disregard to reason, accusing her of abandonment and selfish irresponsibility and even infidelity. "Why else would you be so indifferent as to not even write me a goddamn simple letter every now and then?" he wrote. "Just what the fuck do you think I'm supposed to think? I'll tell you what I think, Ann. I think you're so wrapped up in your hate causes and your job and probably in some other guy that you just don't give a flying fuck what happens to me."

On that he stopped abruptly, his writing hand cramped and trembling. He knew it wasn't Ann causing him to lose control. He was hurt she hadn't written, but he was not angry at her. It wasn't even anger; it was fear. And he knew it.

He tore the letter into little pieces so Kink couldn't read it, then took the photograph out and sat at the desk staring at the dead bodies, as if for the first time it was really death he was seeing, really war. The war was out there and he felt himself drawing closer to it.

Payne had run around all day keeping himself busy, avoiding the thing about Willingham. But he couldn't run now, and he lay wide awake in the droning rain that came down like hail on the sleeping barracks, unable to put his mind to rest. He didn't think of his wife. He thought about Junior Cotton, imagining running through the shady woods with him, and then imagining the forest being the jungles of the Nam. He thought about it in a real sense. The fear of knowing your body could be torn apart at any moment. Willingham lived with that fear too.

It wasn't fascination anymore. He knew it was real.

Chapter
8

Cowboy located Payne in the messhall, sitting at a table with Sergeant Labouisse. They were smoking cigarettes and playing blackjack.

"The lieutenant wants you," he said to Payne, and stretched to see the under card Payne briefly flipped up. Payne was dealing. He had a queen in the hole and a six showing, a losing combination.

"Hit me," Labouisse said.

Payne grinned. "You sure, Buzz? I got a six showing."

The mess sergeant was lousy at blackjack, and Payne had agreed to a few hands to prove just how bad he was. Buzz Labouisse was one of Sterr's lifer buddies, proficient at his job but a loser at cards.

"Yeah, yeah. Hit me."

"The lieutenant is anxious, Payne." Cowboy moved over next to Labouisse and looked at his down cards and grinned when a three was cut him. When Labouisse nodded for another card his cigarette ash fell on the green T-shirt that covered his slim belly. He let the ashes rest there.

"What's he want? I'm at lunch," Payne said, flipping a seven card across the table. "Another?" he said to Labouisse, who fingered the loose skin under his chin, frowning with indecision. He had ten points showing, meaning he could bust. The mess sergeant didn't fully understand odds or how to finesse a bluff. Nor did he pay much attention to the other players' cards He was always too busy telling stories about the messhalls of his past, speaking of them as if they were old lovers. His sentimentality was without shame or guise and that was why Payne liked him.

Payne took the opportunity to give him a lesson in finesse. "It's like my old pappy used to say, Sarge. If you got to think about it, stick. If you don't have to think about it, stick anyway. I've got a six up. But then again," he added, "who knows? You might make it."

Labouisse was trying for five-and-under, which by hootch rules would pay double on his bet regardless of what Payne had. The mess sergeant had doubled the bet and five dollars was on the hand.

"Don't ask me," Cowboy said to Payne. "I'm just delivering the message. But he sure sounded anxious. Go for it," he said to the mess sergeant.

As if already resigned to defeat, Labouisse raked his card tentatively for another and was delivered an eight. He used all his fingers to add the total. It was too much and he looked menacingly at Cowboy, who shrugged.

"Greed'll kill you in this game, Buzz," Payne said. He handed Labouisse the deck. "That's how much, twenty-three, you owe me?"

The mess sergeant dutifully removed his wallet and dug into it.

"Nah. Forget it," Payne said. "I took enough of your money the other night."

"I pay my debts."

"Tell you what, hold it in reserve. I might be short in a future game."

That satisfied the mess sergeant; he pursed his lips, which were thick and bright red against his pale skin, and offered Payne a sackful of his private stash of doughnuts.

"Take her easy, Buzz," Payne said, and walked with Cowboy up the hill to the IO.

"Why so urgent?" Payne asked, squinting against the sun. He'd left his sunglasses somewhere, in the hootch maybe.

Through a mouthful of doughnut, Cowboy mumbled, "Told you."

As they passed Finn's window in the quadrangle, the lieutenant glanced up from his desk with the phone at his ear and waved his arm excitedly. He was there to meet Payne as he stepped inside the office.

"Come on in here, Russell." He rarely called Payne by his first name, which probably meant it was good news; he'd gotten Payne approved for the Tokyo assignment.

The lieutenant smiled proudly, shutting the door behind Payne. Payne's heart fluttered waiting.

"*Life* has to have you sign this release before they can credit your pix," Finn said and waved a paper.

"What picture?" Payne said, disappointed. "You want a doughnut?"

"What picture?" Finn's eyes bulged with incredulity. He picked out a chocolate-coated doughnut. "Don't be coy, man. The refugee woman delivering that kid. That pix. We've hit the big time. *Life* wants to run it. How's that grab you?"

Payne became thoughtful. "How'd they get it?"

Finn shrugged. "Sergeant Sterr. I'll be the first to admit I made a mistake. But Sterr knows his business. Anyway, it's the kind of thing that'll go all the way up to division. Probably net us another citation."

The lieutenant took a glossy of the picture out of his middle drawer and admired it. He had reluctantly approved using the photo in the newspaper when Payne turned in the accompanying article, short as it was; five inches of copy. He had to convince the lieutenant of its relevancy to pacification.

Payne said, "Won't hurt your chances of making first looie either, will it?"

Finn's excitement was electric. "Looks that way. It's a stroke of luck. The timing couldn't have been better, considering this other mess I've got on my hands. I'm going to give you a few days' R&R, Payne, because you deserve it. Didn't you mention wanting to go somewhere?"

"Already put in for it, if you remember. I'd like to go over to Cam Ranh to see a friend; he's in the hospital there."

"Well, you got it. When do you want to go?"

"You really are getting promoted, aren't you?"

"I can't cut you loose right away though, be a few days yet. That okay?"

Payne said, "Yeah," and signed the release form for *Life* magazine.

"You see this?" the lieutenant said, still very excited, his finger jabbing the photograph. "It couldn't've been better if you'd set it up. Damn good work. Outstanding."

Payne leaned over the desk and took a look where Finn was pointing his finger. The blanket the woman lay on was stenciled

"U.S. Army" in full view where the newborn's oblong head had come to rest.

The picture had caught the woman craning forward, straining to view the tiny wrinkle-faced creature whose arms, instead of reaching out, were folded across its stomach as if it were in no particular hurry to come into this life. A ray of sunlight illuminated the mother's face; strands of black hair were matted to her glistening forehead and cheeks; her open mouth, frozen in painful relief, exposed blackened teeth. A plateau of thick smoke hung ominously over the scene. The flies on the baby's face gave the impression the child was dead, with the mother and midwives just on the verge of discovering it.

"What I want you to do now is write a longer feature," Finn said. "A heart-wrencher, and we'll use it in the magazine, with the pix on the cover, of course. Something that illustrates the humane side of our efforts with these people."

His about-face dismayed Payne; he hadn't cared at all for the picture until *Life* became interested. Now he was talking about building the magazine around it.

"Use your imagination. But think of life going on, how there can be hope even in war."

Payne laughed. "Sure. But I doubt *Life*'s going to treat it that way. The kid looks dead."

"What?" Finn said, assuming the bemuddled open-mouth look that reverted his boyish face to pubescence and made him look like an idiot. "Sometimes you really blow my mind, Payne. . . . Anyway, get the secretary to type up the R&R request and I'll sign it and clear it with your CO. We'll get you there Asap."

"Thanks, Lieutenant. I appreciate it."

"No problem. An outstanding job."

Payne opened the door to leave.

"Just one more thing," Finn said.

Payne rolled his eyes and said, "Uh huh." There usually was just one more thing.

"Shut the door," Finn said. He removed his glasses and squeezed his eyes as if he was suddenly very tired. Payne shut the door and leaned against it.

"They're releasing him this afternoon. They've decided to drop the charges, aren't even going to make out a report. I don't get it. But I'm not knocking it."

Payne got it instantly; the CID had done it. He shrugged: "The army works in mysterious ways, sir."

"Well, anyway, it's a relief," Finn said.

He slipped the glasses back on and studied Payne. Payne had his hands inside his pockets, an act the lieutenant considered flagrant insubordination, a particular pet peeve of his.

"I know you two are friendly, sort of like buddies," Finn said, groping for his lead-in, overlooking the pocketed hands.

"I wouldn't classify us as buddies."

"Well, I got that impression. The point is, I want you to try to keep him out of trouble. I understand he had a rough time before; I appreciate you telling me about it. But he's got to get squared away. This sort of thing can't happen again."

Payne smirked at him. "What is it, I'm supposed to be his mother now?"

"Just keep an eye on him. All right?"

"Anything else?"

"Yeah," Finn said easily. "Don't walk out of here with your hands in your pockets."

Certain privileges came with being the momentary darling of IO and Payne decided to use one of those privileges by taking the rest of the day off. He made a customary stop at the post to check for mail, and the freckle-faced clerk grudgingly searched around and found a letter for him from Ann. He immediately got the hiccups.

He tore open the envelope and read it on the way to the hootch. Later, using the pocket calendar, he would count to thirty-eight the number of days since he'd last received a bona-fide letter from his wife, but he would dispatch the aggravation and disappointment of that long period as easily as if his contrary thoughts were someone else's troubles, for Ann had written from the heart and he fell in love with her all over again. It was turning out to be one of those rare days when everything went his way.

Waves of goose bumps stood his hair on end as he read and reread the letter, and the hiccups wouldn't subside. Not once did Ann complain about her job; neither did she have anything derogatory to say about Long Binh. He could almost hear the sound of her voice floating off the pages.

She said she was losing weight without him around to see that she ate. Dinner, she wrote, was the loneliest meal. She missed looking at his crazy two-tone eyes in the morning light. His absence made the sun porch of her small apartment a gloomy place; he didn't even know there was a porch at her apartment. She wrote: "Even the house plants are wilting without you here to cheer things up. We need that funny laugh of yours around, you know?"

She said she would think about him at the most unlikely times lately and wanted to know if Long Binh really was as safe as he'd made out in all those prior letters, or had he just been saying that to keep her from worrying? She seemed especially worried about his getting malaria.

She was concerned he did not have enough spending money and hoped his chances had improved for a promotion before coming home. He dismissed the sudden thought that the CID had gotten to her, used persuasion. He decided it didn't fit; Ann was too stubborn and it would have shown. He could have read it between the lines.

She wanted to go dancing the first night he was back. "I'm dying to see you and hug you, and you can bet I'll be there when you get off that plane!" She even wrote, "Oh, Russ, I want you inside me so bad."

It was a great letter. His eyes welled up. Tears broke as he circled the date in his pocket calendar with a tiny blue cupid's heart. He allowed himself a measure of hope that before it was over the calendar would have a whole lot more of those little blue hearts. He went to the showers and masturbated thinking of Ann in the gossamer negligee she said she would wear his first night home. The despair he had lapsed into over the past few months was softened by a tenuous reassurance. A simple letter had that much power.

Payne was shooting pool in the clubhouse when he caught sight of a tall man wearing a Hawaiian print shirt and beige golfer's slacks. He didn't recognize the man as Willingham. He had never seen him in anything but fatigues. He didn't know it was Willingham until he pulled off a three rail bank on the eight ball and the tall man croaked, "Fuck me."

He had not seen Willingham since the night after the refugee camp, him in that manic-crazy way; and now, even seeing him dressed like a tourist and all smiles, Payne felt a sudden pull of nerves, a tightness in his chest. He'd had time to work it out while Willingham was locked up and had his mind set on telling him about the investigation, hoping he would be able to read the truth of Willingham's involvement or innocence by his reaction. But now, laying eyes on him again, his resolve faltered and he found himself again uncertain. He wished the whole fucking thing would just fade away.

He had enjoyed the uneventfulness of the past week. It had been easy time, like his tour before the wild man showed up to complicate his life.

Payne chalked his stick and said indignantly to his opponent, "Tough luck, dude," and while the next challenger racked the balls, he reticently joined Willingham where he sat at the bar watching.

"Some shooting," Willingham said with admiration. He was formulating a scheme in his brain. It was easy to tell when he was plotting something, for his jaw swelled up and his eyebrows moved around like caterpillars over quick, searching eyes. It was the same narrowed look he had had their first night together at China Village, playing the arrogant captain for a fool. Payne was glad to see the shifty look; it meant he'd regained some of his colorful side.

"Whatever it is, I'm not interested," Payne said with strained joviality. "I'm just lucky today. . . . How you been?"

"Eating good." Willingham hollered for a beer. He looked rested, as though he had been on R&R. Maybe he had.

"What's this getup?" Payne flipped the lapel of his palm-and-sun shirt.

"Dig it. My old lady thought I could use some street duds. She always comes up with something far out on my birthday."

"Your birthday?" The thought struck Payne as strange. Somehow he hadn't thought of Willingham having a birthday; he seemed ageless.

"This very day. Good timing, don't you think, just when I've become a free man? Gone is the teenager; now I've got to start acting my age." His grin was self-mocking.

"How'd it go in there? You look better."

Willingham drained his beer and set both them up with another. "Wasn't so bad," he said, wiping the bottle's cap rust on the tail of his new shirt. The scratches on his arms had healed. "Talked to a shrink that thought a Section Eight was in order. Fuck you very much."

It was still early in the afternoon and the club was subdued, their voices carrying. Conscious of this, Payne stirred uneasily and spoke in a soft voice.

"There some reason you wouldn't take a discharge if you could get it?" he asked half-jokingly.

"What, and leave Long Binh? You cracked? Besides, I got my brilliant future to think about. How am I going to get into law school with a Section Eight?"

"They'd sure as fuck take you at Berkeley," Payne said. "There a law school at Berkeley?"

Willingham dismissed the subject with a movement of his eyes.

"Any guy that'd do what you did has got to qualify for a medical," Payne said, pursuing. "It could have got you shot, or a fucking dishonorable."

Willingham eyed him disinterestedly. "Look, Payne. Everyone's entitled to slip a little every now and then."

His disinterest had settled into resignation, and a faint sign of contentment or self-satisfaction, the inner glow that comes with having put to rest something troubling; it was the look of sweet revenge Payne saw in his countenance. He had worked out part of the dark side killing the ARVN.

Willingham was growing restless; he'd already finished his second beer and wasn't doing anything about ordering another.

"Piss on all that," he said, shifting his weight on the stool. "I been cooped up a whole fucking week and I felt like partying. Thought I'd head over to a club they told me about inside that sounds pretty cool and use up some of this." He flashed a crisp fifty-dollar bill.

"My old man," he added sarcastically. "That's how he communicates."

On impulse Payne quipped, "Don't knock it, man. At least you got an old man." It was a rare display of father-envy and it surprised him.

"Sure," said Willingham. "You interested in going along and help me spend it? The LT let me have the jeep. Said, 'Go ahead and take the afternoon off, take the jeep.' Like nothing had happened. The guy can throw you."

"What club? You're not talking about the fucking Paradise, I hope."

"That's the one."

"Shit," grumbled Payne, "I thought it might be."

On the road Willingham produced a Parker Lane and Payne cupped his hands against the wind to light it. He sucked it deep and sat back, letting his brain go on auto-cruise. He could never be sure how hard the stuff would hit and consequently what he could expect from himself. Weed was as far as he would go with drugs; he'd seen the harder stuff make too many zombies in the hootch. Fucking heads. Payne liked to think he had it over them in the maturity department, but Kink and the other heads thought differently; they considered him uncool. They thought Payne was just plain chickenshit.

The weed was potent, a Thai strain loaded with opium, and after two tokes the road smoothed out as though the jeep had Cadillac suspension. The oncoming sky seemed to change too; instead of the rolling black rain clouds that flashed inner bursts of light, the horizon took on subtler shades of amber and purple, like soft shifting lights on a stage. Because he was partially color blind Payne normally wouldn't have noticed. But he did now and took a moment to marvel at nature's awesome beauty at work.

"Good smoke. You get it in jail?"

"Know what we ought do?" said Willingham. "We ought to do a story on LBJ. There's guys in there you wouldn't believe, just the situations that got them there."

"Yeah, you for one. Pulling that stunt at the depot," Payne said, trying again to broach the subject, before he got too loaded to handle it right. But Willingham was on his own frequency and wasn't going to be sidetracked.

"There was this one dude in the Conex next door who's going to do thirty years for fragging his LT. Doesn't sound unusual on the surface, but listen to this." Willingham wrinkled his face up, as if he were about to laugh or cry.

"The whole platoon agreed the guy had to go and they drew straws," he started. "And this dude got the job. They were on patrol and he was still deciding if he wanted to do it in the field or back at base camp. They had stopped at some vil to chow down and the dude got the sign from a good-time Coke girl and walked down to the water for a quicky. While he was getting it on the LT came up. The dude decided, *All right, fuck it. Now's as good a time and place as any to do him.* But the LT says to get his ass back with the outfit, he'd take care of the gook. The dude thought he was either going to ball her too or waste her, which I guess really surprised him, so he hid in the bush to see what the LT was going to do. He said he was about to toss a frag and take both of them out when the chick stopped blowing him and made a dash for the stream. The LT's pants were around his ankles and he was left looking stupid, trying to pull his pistol when he was blown to bits. The gook had pinched one of the dude's grenades while he was fucking her. And when the LT broke in she waited and stuffed it in his trousers instead. The LT had actually saved the dude's life by coming down there. Ain't that a bitch?"

Willingham went through a stop sign without slowing. A horn honked and he turned sharply to eye the driver. Payne thought he was going to pull over and jerk the guy out. But he kept going.

"So he's in for a murder he didn't commit," he went on, shaking his head. "It's just crazy enough to be true; I believed the dude. . . . Fuck a story, we could do a book on the place, call it something like *Badass Grunts*. Collaborate. What do you think?"

Payne thought he was serious. "Nah. Nobody'd ever read it. They don't want to know. Nobody gives a shit about baby killers."

"Sure they do. People love that kind of shit. It's us housecats nobody would read about, too fucking boring."

Payne cackled sardonically. "Not with you in the rear. Nothing boring about that."

Willingham threw the jeep violently into second, gearing down for a traffic jam approaching the crowded PX. "Look at this. Looks like fucking L.A."

"The lieutenant says they're not going to charge you." Payne took the smoke deep in a long, desperate draw, hotboxing it.

Willingham flashed a horse grin. "How about that shit."

"You know why?" Payne wheezed.

The question caught Willingham. "Do you?"

Payne held off exhaling until he had to, then coughed it out. "Got a pretty good idea."

Willingham fixed his stare. "Well?"

The blast of smoke put Payne's head in a spin; he laughed. "War paint; out there in his underwear shooting tanks and shit, holding 'em off like fucking Custer. And get this for a kicker, wearing a string of fingers around his neck." It was a ludicrous laugh, the kind that shields something hard to face. "All that's true, ain't it, pal?" he said. "Tell me, where'd you get the fingers?" He added incredulously, "Fucking fingers!"

They came to a dead stop behind a tractor trailer revving its engine and shrouding the jeep in diesel exhaust. There was a lot of noise going on, horns, a C-130 roaring down the nearby runway, Viets yapping as they bicycled past the jeep.

Willingham's look was searching, as though he were again trying to size Payne up. "I went a little crazy there, but I'm all right now. Had some time to think it over."

"Is that right," Payne said. "Think *what* over, goddamn it?" He had stopped laughing; the color on his face was high now.

You could see by his grimace Willingham didn't want to take it any further; he might have wanted to just forget about it too.

The traffic thinned out and he popped the clutch, getting rubber.

Payne sat up in the seat. "I found the negatives," he yelled. "I know whose fingers they were. Now I want to know why you killed him, why you cut his fucking throat."

He braced himself saying this, half expecting a violent reaction, and it surprised him that Willingham only sighed, letting his chest sink as though, oddly, a burden had been lifted off his mind. He lowered his sunglasses and gave Payne a hard stare. "You going to turn me in?"

Payne rolled his eyes. "What the fuck you think, man? But I sure as hell want to know why you did it. Talk to me, tell me something."

Willingham took a final toke off the joint and sent it sailing. "I guess you got a right to know," he said, his eyes back on the road now and both hands on the wheel. He spoke easily. "We were on a recon mission. The orders were to leave the vil alone, no firing. It was a friendly vil. But just after we pulled out, about half a click out, we ran into an ambush. The motherfucker that did it was him, Su."

"How'd you know that?"

"I knew," he said bitterly. "Lassiter knew. We both saw him in the vil. There weren't supposed to be any ARVNs there. The CO told us in the briefing, no ARVNs, just civilians. But still there wouldn't be any reason an ARVN wouldn't want us to spot him. He disappeared in some hootch soon as we walked into the vil. He was nervous, you could tell. Lassiter and I talked about it when we left; it was a strange thing for an ARVN officer to do. That was just before we took the hit. He did it; there's no other explanation."

"The CO the Green Beret you were talking about?"

"Shell? Yeah."

"Why'd he send you there?"

Willingham gave him a baffled, irritable look. "What the fuck difference does that make? Shit. A recon. That was part of the job, pulling recons." He didn't want to answer; he seemed defensive, as though there were something about his job that bothered him enough to want to put that too out of his mind.

"You killed him for revenge then," Payne said as a statement.

"You've got to do something." He was still looking at Payne. "It wasn't much; it won't bring my buddies back. But it helps a little."

Payne opened his mouth, about to ask him how come he was here to talk about it, but it didn't seem right to ask that now. He opened his mouth again to tell him about the CID. But again he stopped himself, needing to absorb what Willingham had just told him, try to figure it out on his own if he could. It boiled down to the fact he still wasn't sure where Willingham stood in all this confusion.

And then Willingham made it harder. "You said you knew why they let me out," he said. "Let's hear it. Why?"

"I said I had a good idea," Payne said. "How do you think something like that looks for Public Information? Fucks up the image," he said flippantly. "We're important stock, man. Can even get away with fucking murder."

Willingham laughed now. "Shit. Who you trying to kid. That's not why they let me go."

"Well, that's what I figure." Payne made himself sound sincere.

"Then you're a dumbshit. Fuck it. I'll find out myself."

They hit the four-lane and Willingham gunned it. Abruptly he said, "You should fucking be ashamed of yourself, Payne."

It was an offhanded comment that left Payne speechless. He rearranged his cramped nuts, wondering just what in hell Willingham was talking about now.

"I mean it, man. You violated that woman taking pictures of her. All they got left is their beliefs, their honor."

Payne laughed sharply. "It's all right to kill 'em, but leave their honor alone? That what you're telling me?"

Willingham lowered his sunglasses again and glared at Payne with cobalt-blue eyes. He looked ridiculous in his floppy bush hat and surfer's shirt. He turned quickly back to the road and swept past a flatbed.

"It's like taking something personal off a dead person," he said.

"Some things you just don't do. Some things you've got to respect. They have to have something to hang on to."

Payne looked at him as if he really were crazy, and maybe he was. Weren't your fingers something personal?

Traffic picked back up rounding a corner that took them along the high wall of LBJ. Across the road was the Paradise Club.

"You better watch it, man, or you'll end up back behind that wall," Payne said seriously.

"Not me. Once is enough."

Payne glanced up in time to see a bicycling Viet lose his balance and fall under the wheels of a Sealand tractor-trailer. A mangle of bicycle and body flapped like a loose recap against the asphalt as the eighteen-wheeler rolled by.

"Did you see that," he said, following with his eyes, his mouth twisted out of shape. "Jesus fucking Christ!"

"Poor dumbshit gook," Willingham said and grinned his horse grin. "Let's party."

Chapter

9

The Paradise was a squat quonset sitting in the middle of a great mud field halfway between the airfield and the jail. The airport served as a connecting point for personnel traveling between the highlands and the delta, and flight delays often brought transients to the Paradise to kill time. Many of these men were returning from in-country R&Rs, miserable troops who guzzled drinks without respite, wanting to drown the thought of having to return to a jungle base camp after three days on the serene surf-lapped beaches of Vung Tau. Sometimes a generous MP on handcuff detail would allow his prisoner a last drink at the Paradise before he got swallowed up in the iron jaws of LBJ. Stretch soldiers rarely patronized the place, for there was not much happiness at the Paradise.

But it was just the kind of joint Willingham would like.

Swinging the jeep off the road, Willingham shouted, "Hang on," and opened it up across the tarmac behind an ascending airplane. He cut a figure eight in the mud before pulling up to the whitewashed rocks leading to the entrance of the club. He had produced another Parker Lane, and Payne, getting his head right for the place, hyperventilated it, then ate the roach. He had learned that from Willingham.

In jail Willingham had heard they carried a good selection of Beach Boys songs on the box, and entering, he went straight to the Wurlitzer. He'd said "Little Deuce Coupe" was his favorite, that it was the anthem of car-loving Southern Californians like himself who actually did cruise the boulevards searching for elusive rich girls in T-birds.

Payne stood off to the side, out of the way of traffic, while his heady brain adjusted to the transformation. The pulsating strobe lights played tricks on his eyes, making nickelodeon caricatures of men in motion. He blinked several times to get in focus and then moved into the lounge area.

The Paradise was the most bizarre bar he had ever been in, any-time in his life. Along the curved quonset walls and ceiling were mural-like paintings of some of the Disney characters, Peter Pan in fatigues and steel pot, a grown-up naked Snow White, Dumbo with rotor blades for ears. Each of the figures was trapped in some sort of dead-end situation in dark, canopied terrain, the intent being that an elusive enemy stalked them out there and something ominous was about to happen.

The irony appealed to Payne's present sensibility, which he summed up with a doleful shake of the head, mumbling to no one but himself, "There it is." The paintings were bold and uncontrolled, not the work of an artist. But studying them through the intense profundity of good smoke, it occurred to Payne that the connection to Milton was ingenious, for whoever had thought up these images had associated more from *Paradise Lost* than the name. The guy had taken Milton's predominate concern, that of man's fall from his initial state of innocent virtue and so forth, and applied it to the Nam.

Shuffling along the sawdust floor with eyes still riveted to the ceiling he said it again, as if suddenly he had hit on a revelation of immense significance, "There the fuck it is, man."

He found an empty table and sat there for some time trying to comprehend the full importance of his discovery. But the noise was too distracting and he gave it up and lit a cigarette.

The place was three-quarters filled with soldiers, some in utilities and others in street clothes, huddling in small groups around the slot and pinball machines or sitting at tables laden with beer bottles and plates of steak bones; the Paradise was known for its T-bones. The strobes emanated from the dance arena where a few troops made the pretense of dancing while feeling up oriental women in micromini-skirts.

He caught sight of Willingham spreadeagled over the jukebox, owning it, reading and punching buttons, the neons lighting up his face like a Rembrandt.

"Sounds of Silence" was playing now, the delicate pristine voices barely audible amid the dissonant clamor, as if the general effort was to drown out the prissy song. GIs wouldn't have picked that song; it was a number Viets liked. You could find it on every jukebox on Tu Do Street, and nightclub bands included an instrumental arrangement in their repertoire. They didn't sing the lyrics because Viets couldn't memorize that many English words or even pronounce most of them, much less understand them. The song's popularity with the Vietnamese had to be its melody, which was nothing like off-key Vietnamese music, so that, finally, its popularity was inexplicable.

Payne gawked at a girl in spike heels standing on the boots of a soldier, her uplifted arms pulling the skirt above the contour line of white panties.

Willingham stepped in front of his view. "In-fucking-credible. Some of these tunes you can't even get in Huntington. They've got a new one I haven't even heard about, 'Heroes and Villains.' Great title, huh?"

He pulled out a chair and sat. "Maybe we could use it as the title of our book. *Heroes and Villains*. Yeah, I like the sound of it. What do you think?"

Payne supported his heavy head in the palms of both hands. He rolled his eyes at Willingham. "You know," he said dreamily, "I never really listened to the words before."

"What, the Beach Boys' new one? Me either. That's what I just got through saying."

Willingham had unbuttoned his surfer shirt down to the navel so his hairy chest could dazzle the women.

"No. The one on now."

"Simon and Garfunkel? That piece of shit?"

"Yeah. But now I can see why they have it here," said Payne. "It fits. I was thinking it's too slow and poetic for the type of derelicts that come in here—no offense, man. But it's fucking brilliant. I just couldn't see the writing on the wall. . . ."

Payne grinned like a clever moron, waiting for Willingham to ask him what he meant. But Willingham's attention was elsewhere, his leg pumping and eyes wandering around the floor.

"I mean, just think about all the metaphoric bullshit in the song,

like graffiti being prophecy and praying to neon gods. It's not supposed to be figured out. You don't know what the fuck they're talking
about; you just nod your head and think, 'Yeah, man. There it is.'
Hey, you listening to me?"

Willingham sighed languorously. "Sure. You're full of shit. . . .
Do the tunes play in the order they're picked or according to the
numbers?"

"The numbers. Anyway, that's why it's on the jukebox in this
place," Payne said, getting desperate. He was losing track of his
thoughts and starting to think things about the girl in the white panties. She was trying to keep the soldier's hands out of them.

Willingham seemed perplexed. His hands were poised on the
table, ready to jump up at any moment. "What song, the Beach Boys'
new one?"

But Payne had gotten himself in a philosophic hole and was
determined to dig his way out. He screwed up his face stubbornly.
"Stop fucking with my head. . . . Don't you see? These turkeys can't
figure it out just like they can't figure out why the fuck they're over
here fighting, or whatever they're doing, cleaning shit burners or
loading ammo. Whatever. The point is there's no sense to that song
and whoever operates this place knows the guys coming in here don't
understand it. See how it connects? Shit, it's the same reason they
named this joint Paradise. Because that doesn't make any sense either. Look at that, you think there's any sanity in giving Mickey
Mouse a satchel charge?"

Payne blew a smoke ring and sat back, pleased with himself.
"The Paradise," he added, pumped up. "What a great fucking twist to
give this dump a name like that."

"Heavy," Willingham said, still with the nervous leg. "Get me a
beer. I'm going to circulate."

Then the Stones' "Ruby Tuesday" reported from the jukebox and
Willingham went into a scoot across the floor, snapping fingers and
twirling in a quick pirouette around a table, his shoulders low, his
head bobbing like a rooster's.

A waitress sat her tray in front of Payne and began clearing the
empties. She was dressed in a short red-and-white checkerboard affair
laced with fluffy brocade and accented in front by a tiny black apron.
She was supposed to be a French maid.

"My name Lin. I take care of you. What you have, GI?"

"I'll have Chivas Regal Scotch with ice, no water, and a bottle of beer. Make it two."

"Chinee or Amelican?"

"French. But cold. It has to be cold."

She drew close to Payne as she wiped the table. "You want T-bone? Plenty good today."

There was a fresh aromatic fragrance about her, the perfume of a flower he recognized and liked but couldn't name, maybe gardenia, though not as pungent.

"Hold the steaks," he said, breathing her scent. "Maybe later. Hurry back with those drinks now."

He watched after her. She moved quickly and with feline agility around tables where huge men grabbed at her and said things which she smiled or nodded at in passing.

"Hey, buddy. Mind if we sit down here?"

Two men stood over him, a shrimp and a fullback, both dressed in slick polyester pants and print shirts that might have come from the PX in Vung Tau. They had the awkward look of soldiers out of their element.

Payne shrugged and they sat. "You guys going or coming?"

"Coming," the fullback said at the same time the shrimp said, "Going." They eyed one another and chuckled.

The shrimp showed gapped teeth and deep dimples when he laughed. "We're going back to our outfit," he clarified.

"Yeah, that's what I said," the fullback agreed. "Coming back from luxuriating on the beach."

"Say, man," said the shrimp. "Don't think we're trying to crowd you or anything."

"Nah," Payne said.

"That guy who was here with you a minute ago, you know him?" The little man grinned broadly, saying this.

"Willingham, ain't it?" the fullback answered.

They were a team.

Payne sat up. "You know him?"

"Got-dam, I told you it was Mountain Man," the fullback said. "Fucking Willie—'Don't call me Willie Boy,'" he added in a deep, mimicking voice. "Yeah, we know him."

"Shit, he was our squad leader for four months," the shrimp added.

"Five months," his buddy corrected, and then corrected himself. "'Cept when he wasn't on special detail."

The shrimp elbowed the fullback. "You always was jealous of that."

"No I wasn't, man. I ain't no fool."

"Fuck you say," the little man said.

"Anyways, he was the best squad leader we had," the shrimp said to Payne. "First of the Fifth, Bravo company, number one platoon. Known in the 5th as the Deadly Dozen, see, because of our devastating ability on the field of battle, highest accredited body count in the battalion and that—"

"You do talk," interrupted the fullback. "We didn't never have no highest body count, man. You know that." He turned to Payne. "Jesus here tends to exaggerate things. We didn't know shit what happened to Willie; knowed he got transferred, but that was all. Swear to God I didn't never think we'd see him again. What's he do down here?"

"IO. I heard his squad got wiped out." Payne pushed himself forward.

"What the fuck's IO? Interrogation?"

"Information," Payne said. "Public Information Office. Every command's got one. Nothing outstanding. Didn't you say you were in his outfit?"

"We was. It was the lurp squad got dinked." The fullback had a bull neck and a healthy set of teeth, bucked in the front, which gave him his bumpkin look. "We was mostly pulling shit runs in the highlands, when Willie was the team's ace. Wasn't connected to the colonel's lurps. Those guys were the privileged; the few and far between." He sounded a little sarcastic.

"Is that Colonel Shellhammer you're talking about?"

"Yeah," said the shrimp. "But he got moved too, right after the incident. I think. Ain't that right, Bruiser?"

Bruiser wagged his head.

The little guy sat back in his chair and lit a Camel. He had the thin, fragile fingers of a musician, the first two yellowed with nicotine. "But Willie, man. He made it. The fucker wiped out that nest of slopes single-handed. Broke the rules doing it. We figured that's why they shipped him out."

"Yeah," the fullback laughed. "So every man's been trying to break the rules ever since Mountain Man done it and got his transfer."

"Should've gotten the Silver, with a fuckin handful of clusters," said Jesus. "Or even the medal for valor. Yeah. Nobody got informed what really happened since it happened on one of those secret missions. But it's a fact he greased those dinks, that we know for sure, and him the only guy to tell about it. Mountain Man was gone before the fucking ghoolies even got to the site, never to return."

He talked with a slower Southern drawl than Payne's, but spit his words, something like a lobotomized James Cagney.

The shrimp was thoughtful. "It must of been pretty bad, though. Those guys were tight. Willie must get to feeling awful rotten at times. I guess, huh, Bruiser?" He said this frowning at his buddy.

"One evening we're all sitting around blowing dew, Mountain Man, Lassiter, Snake, and the others, before those dudes go off for their ritual, and we never see them again," Bruiser said, his eyebrows narrowed and touching over his thick nose. "All of a sudden. We always thought there was something fishy about the team buyin' it like that."

"Yeah," said Jesus. "It was the way the CO made it sound like they were on routine patrol when everybody *knew* it was a secret action. It smelled, all right. Those guys, see," he said to Payne, "were the meanest mothers in the battalion, the fucking division. All of 'em specially selected for the duty. They never talked about it; they were sworn to secrecy." There was a trace of sarcasm in his voice, too, which sounded to Payne like envy.

"What do you call him Mountain Man for?" said Payne.

"Didn't tell you that, huh?" said Bruiser. "Had to do with their ritual. He'd get up like an Indian. You know, smear himself with grease and put on his loincloth and they'd get together privately the night before they was to go on a mission. Hell, sometimes he got up like a Monty just for regular patrols with us, wearing his diaper with his eggs and bandolier and hunting knife. Sometimes sandals, sometimes wear his boots. A real sight to behold, the Mountain Man. Said you never knew when they was gonna strike, or we was gonna run into a ambush. He figured that it'd take the dinks a split second to decide if he wasn't just a Monty, and that split second was all Willie would need for his edge. That's probably what saved him, whereas the other guys bought it. You reckon, Jesus?"

"Could be, man. Sounds possible."

"Where the hell is he, anyway?" said Bruiser.

They all looked around but didn't spot Willingham. Payne said to the shrimp, "You the guy that tells that monkey and fish story?"

Bruiser laughed from his belly. "Don't go gettin' him started on *that* business." He stuck out his hand to shake Payne's. "Anybody Willie'd tell that shit to's got to be okay."

It was one of those bush hand dances and Payne couldn't get it. Finally they just shook the regular way.

A slot-machine bell went off and a crowd instantly gathered to help the guy collect the spilling quarters, which instantly turned into a shouting match between two insignias. It took three or four seconds before the first shove. Then the fight began. Payne was familiar with both patches, the lightning bolt of the 25th and the horse head of the 1st Cav. Everyone at Long Binh knew the insignias. They both had reputations.

Bruiser jumped up and excitedly pointed out Willingham. "Wouldn't you know it," he said. "To the rescue."

The shrimp sighed and rose less enthusiastically. "Aw, fuck. I hate these scenes. C'mon, man," he said to Payne, who hadn't moved from his chair. Payne stood but didn't leave the table. It wasn't his fight.

Not all the dozen or so men swinging fists and elbows were in uniform. Three of them wearing flowered shirts, all barrel-chested older men, the bartenders, were in the thick of it, popping heads with batons. One of the bartenders, while dragging a horse head along the sawdust floor, used a headlock to flip another man riding his back. Willingham was another in civilian clothes. He was on his back on the floor with two undesirables on top of him who were trying to hold his arms under their knees so they could hit his face. These two wore the lightning-bolt patch. They appeared too drunk to coordinate themselves and perform the job with any effect, and Willingham, getting a knee under one of them, lifted him in a swoop over his head. A chair, smashing, broke the guy's fall.

Payne watched Willingham's old-unit buddies push their way through the thick of bodies to give assistance, the shrimp following in the wake of the fullback. The soldier struggling in Willingham's scissor lock, gasping for breath, clutched at the air with outstretched claws. Willingham leaned on an elbow as if bored. He didn't need help. When he recognized the two men standing over him, he unlocked his ankles from the breathless lightning bolt and sprang instantly to his feet, bear-hugging the two of them at once. He pulled on Jesus' ear.

The girls left stranded on the dance floor were huddled together curling long hair around their fingers, giggling, it appeared to Payne, and the Beach Boys sang Willingham's anthem.

The fighting was mostly wrestling and ended as it started, in a rancous shouting exchange, with a few bloody noses and every face glistening with sweat. About half the brawlers were black. It was over after the bartenders tossed a couple of men out the door; then the insignias separated and went about their business as though nothing had happened, the horse heads strutting back to the girls on the dance floor. They seemed to have exclusive rights to them.

". . . not lookin' so hot right now, buddy," Bruiser was saying to Willingham, his thick arm slung over Willingham's shoulder, giving little tugs of affection.

Willingham had blood on his mouth. He glanced passingly at Payne. "You guys met my pal Payne here? The one with all the balls?" he said nastily.

"Yeah, an okay guy," said Bruiser.

"Took a sniper round and he's getting himself a PH," Willingham added.

"Wait a minute. Here, at Long Binh?" said the shrimp. He seemed both bemused and baffled, but then Willingham's buddies flashed Payne the approving look. Payne flushed.

They huddled around the table. The sweet-smelling waitress appeared and dispensed bottles of Budweiser beer in front of all four, no Scotch. She stood back with hands at her hips, scrutinizing Willingham with a maternal frown as he attended his bloody mouth.

He gingerly patted the lip, which had already begun to swell, then looked at the napkin as if expecting to find part of his lip on it.

"You get sock, huh?" the girl said. "Bad place here, many crazy GI. Lin bring you band-age with T-bone. You want T-bone now?"

"Just same same again, sweetheart," Willingham said, undressing her with his eyes and bobbing his brows lustfully. She had nice rounded legs, not too much light between the thighs.

Jesus playfully flipped a fingernail at Willingham's arm, like a towel pop, but missed. "Better lay off," he teased and said to the fullback, "Hey, Bruiser. Remember that babysan that souved him up at Fobey's Lake? Shit, wouldn't nobody in his right mind of gone after that beast—nobody but the fucking Mountain Man, the unit's forward cunt tester."

"Yeah," Bruiser said, his buck teeth twinkling. "That's what we should've dubbed him. Forward cunt tester, man. Our FCT." He spoke to Payne. "A real sucker for the Viet'nese cunt, always gettin' souved by some bush beast. He still do it?"

"Not many bush beasts to get around here," Payne deadpanned, void even of ironic humor. He felt awkward now, ashamed of his display of cowardice and a little piqued with envy from the sally he didn't fit into with this regrouping.

"What's new in the outfit?" Willingham said to the fullback. "You get your stripe?"

Bruiser snorted. "Got shafted. Nobody's gettin' promoted. They moved us from Nha Trang permanently. We're located over around the border now, working with the Viet'nese. It ain't so nice over there."

"Mostly fuckin night patrols," Jesus added. "We're still pulling S and D's, but it ain't with the Monties anymore. These ARVN people ain't so aggressive, caint train 'em. They're lazy."

"What are fucking Monties?" Payne quipped impatiently.

All three looked at him as if they hadn't seen him before, as if he had just then sat down to join them, a new guy in the group.

"Montagnards," Willingham said in a desultory tone of voice, indulging the new guy. "Forest dwellers. Used to pull details with them. Good people, never turn on you. People that are worthy of our respect," he added as if to reproach Payne again for the photograph that went to *Life* magazine.

Bruiser smiled at him. "Don't miss it, huh," he said. "But, shit, you got it easy now, don't you, man?"

Willingham dropped his eyes as if the question stung him.

"Best fucking counterguerrilla forces in-country," Jesus said to Payne. "I'll tell you what. These ARVNs don't hold a candlelight to them. We got three men in division up for the Medal of Honor, but they ain't earned shit. It's the Monties that ought to be getting them medals. Hell, there wasn't much we could teach them; all we did was give 'em the firepower. They could of taught us. They'd hump all fucking day and night. They saved our asses more than once just sensing an ambush. Saved my fucking ass."

Jesus lowered his face and stared for a moment at Willingham. "Damnation, Willie. How'd it happen, man?"

The reunion had been waiting for this, but the question hit like an unexpected blow to the chest, knocking the wind out of their intimate high spirits.

Willingham sucked beer from the good side of his mouth. He looked solemnly at his ex–bush buddies with a long face and said simply, "We got turned on, set up."

"I knowed it, got-damn it!" Bruiser said furiously. "It was them got-damn Yards, wasn't it, man? They set you up, didn't they?"

"It wasn't the Monties," said Jesus. "It couldn't of been them, man. Could it?"

"Fuck if it weren't," Bruiser argued. "You can't trust 'em worth shit. None of 'em."

Payne listened to their squabbling quietly, watching Willingham. He was sinking into the dark side, but it was different around his old buddies. They understood and shared his grief. It increased Payne's sense of shame and made him suddenly realize how stupid and petty he was behaving, how his banal adolescent jealousy could not fit in here.

A minute of intense silence followed. They all nervously guzzled beer. Then Willingham said, "We didn't use Indians on that mission, Bruiser. You can't blame them."

Jesus slapped the table. "Told you, man."

More beer guzzling and cigarettes getting lit. The music shifted to something less jazzed, one of those wailing country pieces that stilled the dance floor and made you want to throw yourself on a railroad track with your mother.

Finally Jesus blurted, "Yeah, but you wiped those motherfuckers out. You did that much, man."

"I hid," Willingham said, averting his eyes. They had become watery and you could see he was trying hard to hold it back.

Jesus appeared stunned. So did Bruiser.

Willingham went on in a soft voice that cracked despite his effort to keep steady. "I was off taking a piss when it came down. I hid and waited in the hedge. And when they started cutting for souvs, I sprayed 'em."

"Fuck, man, that's fuckin got-dam horrible," Bruiser said and shook his big head in a gesture of helplessness. In a moment he added, "But what the hell else could you do? You guys wouldn't of ever got in a situation like that if it wasn't set up. You ain't got nothing to blame yourself for, man."

"It ain't like you didn't do nothing, Willie," Jesus added. "You got some payback."

His eyes still downcast and distant, Willingham rose from the chair and walked off. His legs were lead now; he was not the lithe figure strutting across the floor a few moments ago. The men at the table silently watched him lose himself in the crowd.

"Damnation," Jesus said. "That ain't like him. He always bounced back, always. We lost guys before."

"Yeah, but how would you fucking feel, man, if you had to watch me and Satchel, the guys, man, getting our fucking ears and balls cut off. Huh?" Bruiser said. His tone was angry. "That's a fucking situation I hope I never have to be in. I don't know how I'd fucking react either. Just what in hell could you do?"

"I guess just what he did," said Payne, picturing the scene as best he could. "And it'd make you feel just as bad too, as helpless. I guess he's got to have some time to work it out."

"I think we ought to drop the subject," Jesus said. "I think you're right. Go get him, Bruiser."

Bruiser nodded and left the table.

When Bruiser reappeared a few minutes later, Willingham was with him, carrying a bottle of beer by its neck, swinging it as he walked. They were discussing something Willingham seemed to have an interest in.

Willingham didn't sit; he hiked a leg in the chair and said simply to Jesus, "Yeah. I got some payback."

He grinned faintly, the fat lip throwing his face off balance. "I got the motherfucker that set us up."

"I'm sure glad you're here, man," said Jesus. "I'm sure glad to see you. You made it, you fucking made it."

"That I did," Willingham said in a way that lifted the shroud of depressing air. Just the way he said it and let an uplifting glint come to his eyes. There was something in Willingham's ability to shift a mood that was frightening.

"I made it to the rear with the fucking gear, man," he added, stiffening, pumping himself up. "And let me tell you guys, you won't believe all the shit there is to do down here."

He squared his chin looking around the bar.

Payne knew the look; it meant he was thinking something that was bound to get them in trouble, and Payne, eager to belong but against any better judgment, said, "We've got a jeep, don't we?"

Lin floated back across the floor with the tray balanced on her fingertips. She put it down and clasped her hands, cocking her head with childlike perplexity. "You want T-bone now? The cook he ask many time, 'GI ready for steak yet?' Lin don't know what say."

When nobody responded, she dropped her shoulders in a show of disgruntlement and walked away, calling after herself, "Crazy GI here all time."

"Can you guys swing it for another night?" Willingham said in an overly exuberant voice. "Lafferty still the XO?"

Bruiser nodded yes.

"Call him up. Tell him your flight's down and you'll have to hitch a lift with a convoy or something tomorrow," Willingham suggested; he had the shifty look again, his jaw jutting and eyebrows squirming. "If I know Lafferty, he'll buy it."

The fat lip distorted his horse grin, as if he'd been to the dentist. He pulled out his crisp birthday bill. "This'll get us a room without cockroaches. Imagine air-conditioning. And this," he said, spreading his wallet and fanning more bills, "will take care of the entertainment. The women of Saigon, man, are the best you'll ever get in the Nam."

"You'd know, wouldn't you?" Payne said teasingly. Willingham had never been to Saigon.

"Damn straight he'd know," said Jesus. "Mountain Man's our fucking FCT."

Bruiser looked at Jesus and Jesus looked at Bruiser, and they both looked at Willingham.

"How do we call?" Jesus said.

Chapter
10

The stretch of highway between Long Binh and the city was good unscarred road, running arrow-straight across flat open paddyland. The rain clouds had shifted farther eastward, opening up the sky, and the foothills along the northwestern horizon were blue and wavered ghostlike in the sweltering haze; the sawback ridge reminded Payne of the low hills of east Texas in August. He had grown up there, in Texarkana, a divided town of dual allegiance. He came from the Arkansas side, which denied him the privilege of saying Texas when asked, "Where you from back in the world, man?" He said Texas anyway. It wasn't like being from Cincinnati or Philadelphia. When you were from Texas you didn't say Lubbock or El Paso or even Dallas, you said Texas with a tough coolness, like you would say Danang in the Nam.

The grunts on leave from the highland jungles didn't ask Payne where he was from.

Though straight, the road was narrow and crowded with all manner of traveling conveyances. It brought out the race driver in Willingham; he pushed the jeep with maniacal delight, skirting around lambrettas and smoking buses and oxcarts as if he had forgotten it wasn't rush hour on a L.A. freeway. Hot wind whistled over the windshield, slapping Payne's face and drawing water from his eyes. The polyestered grunts in the back seat yahooed and threw empty beer bottles at road signs and waved at the packed grenade-screened buses as they sped by. Wanting to show that Willingham's total disregard of life didn't bother him either, Payne shifted his wide-eyed stare from the road to the backseat and hollered over the rush of wind, "How come they call you Jesus?"

Willingham answered on a boisterous laugh pitched to the wind. "We named him that after the Bible character, cause every time he'd go to take his souv, he'd cross himself first. Crazy, huh? And Bruiser here," he said, turning full around to grin at Bruiser, "is an animal of the meanest breed, from the cat family. He liked to play around with the dinks we took in before we'd send them to interrogation for their work. Really enjoyed it."

"Persuasion," Bruiser corrected. "Interrogators like to call it persuasion."

Heedless of his driving, Willingham had let the jeep sway into the oncoming lane, and it was now heading straight into a huge truck. Willingham whipped back just in time.

Payne kept his foot mashed on an imaginary brake pedal most of the trip, a nervous eye peeled for MPs along the way, saying, "Cool it," when he spotted one lurking in the shadow of a fruit stand or behind a pagoda, places where they hung out waiting for foolhardy GIs like these. But Willingham smirked at Payne's caution and continued on as if he was doing the Baja 1000; he seemed to think the highway was a lawless free-for-all. And because the MPs Payne spotted were asleep, it *was* lawless.

Willingham attempted a pass no one could have made, and Payne hollered, "Ohh shit." Willingham skillfully corrected his course and gave Payne a contorted fat-lip grin, as though the maneuver had been for his benefit, a test. Then the race driver started cursing the jeep, saying he wished they had his old man's CJ-7 and gave a rundown of its mechanical data. "Cop-car power," he boasted to his pals.

"Yeah, I know," Bruiser said. "You done told us maybe five hun'ert times about that particular vehicle."

"Never seen anybody so damn crazy over a damn car," added Jesus.

"Off-road vehicle," Willingham corrected. "Baja machine. Ain't no car."

Payne could not help but say it: "Hey, Willie. Show us the snapshot of it, man."

It was a good forty-five minutes to Tan Son Nhut. Willingham made it in thirty, a record time that seemed to Payne a miracle. He swerved onto a narrow street backed up with traffic, and came to a dead halt. The exhaust from diesel and two-cycle engines mixed with the smoke of cooking fires along the street and choked off the air, casting a pall so dense the sun was blocked out. Willingham, all of them except Payne, seemed entranced with the bustling marketplace. It was a maze of joined plywood stalls under sheets of pressed beer-can tins. People swarmed around the grass mats that spilled out into the street, displaying their wares of olive drab clothing, cigarettes and liquor, fake leather jackets with gilt dragons stitched on the back, C-rations and canned vegetables, radios. Kids ran around playing with Hula Hoops and New Year's favors, dated stuff American kids would snub. The market smelled gamy and of fish kept too long in the sun. There was a constant roar of blatting horns and turbine engines revved behind the close concrete wall of Tan Son Nhut airport.

"This is it. Saigon," Willingham said excitedly, and pulled over at a run-down hotel with a sidewalk bar. On the balcony above the bar laundered GI skivvies were strung to dry.

"No shit, just lookit," Bruiser chimed in.

"This is just the fringe, the ghetto," Payne said, complaining. "You don't want to stop here."

But Willingham cut the engine and got out, followed by his buddies. Payne climbed out too and they took a table outside.

Bruiser wanted "33" beer so they all had that and small cups of spicy shrimp, both cold and good. The pug-nosed girl waiting on them stood over the table holding back a burdensome blanket of slick ebony hair. She surveyed the group woodenly and suggested going upstairs for a rest under the fan. She was a hog, but that didn't seem to matter to Willingham. The others guffawed and made jokes about his past bush beasts.

Payne said they ought to wait till they got downtown to get a whore. He informed them that out here, by the airport, confederate draft-dodgers thrived by ripping off impatient GIs, didn't matter who they were, cherries or R&Ring boonierats, guys like Willingham who couldn't wait for a piece of the city ass they'd heard so much about.

"You have to play it cool, especially out here, man," said Payne. "They'll rip you off while you're getting it on, right under your eyes.

And what're you going to do, beat the girl up, waste the cowboy? This ain't the bush, it's the city."

The girl's huge breasts swayed as she shifted her weight from foot to foot. Practiced at intimidation, she started popping her nails and heaving sighs of impatience.

"Wouldn't happen with me," Willingham said hardheadedly, though he seemed ready to acquiesce. Jesus and Bruiser chuckled in harmony and Willingham waved the girl off with a scowl. She yapped shrilly, turning away.

"*Didi nau,* bitch," Willingham snapped after her and grumbled, "Fucking slope cunt."

"Swear to God, Mountain Man," said Jesus, "you can change your tune like nobody I ever saw."

"Yeah," added Bruiser, speaking to Payne, "he's like that guy Jekyll and Hyde about his beasts. Downright confusing."

"What's confusing?" retorted Willingham. "A cunt's a cunt. My dick ain't got no eyes."

He said this for the benefit of his old buddies, Payne figured, trying to make light of a complex paradox, when it went a lot deeper than what he was letting on. They were right, though, it was hard to figure where he stood with these people, either sex.

Willingham drove more reasonably along the tree-lined streets downtown, letting the little three-wheel cars and Hondas pass with their families of five and six people impossibly fitted on the bikes. It was odd because there were no speed limits in Saigon, just the white mice to keep in check. All three of the men with Payne carried on as if they'd never been to a big city before, taking in the sites like kids at the zoo. Payne obliged their curiosity, pointing out some of the landmarks, the pre-French and French influences, the huge ornate cathedral, largest in Asia, the elaborately carved graystone opera house, now empty, where operas were no longer performed.

When they got to the park square facing the National Assembly building, Payne had Willingham pull over under the shade of a blossoming tamarind tree and pointed out the huge statue of the weary-looking steel soldier in the center of the park, a sculpture not unlike the one of American marines raising the flag on Iwo Jima. "He's charging the front doors of the parliament," Payne said, incredulity in his voice. He noticed the blank expressions of his companions.

"Don't you get it? It's the nation's monument to the GVN. And they've got the soldier attacking the government's headquarters. Something fucking ironic about that."

"Bet it's a fucking ARVN draftee," said Jesus.

Willingham shrugged carelessly and gunned the jeep. "Which way to Tu Do?"

"Take a left at the next corner, I'll show you a place you'll fit right in," Payne said with a good-natured smirk, making fun of the three jungle grunts masqueraded in burlesque. Payne was the only one in fatigues.

"Here you have it, the Pearl of the Orient," he said. "That's what it used to be, anyhow. Imagine coming here back then, when the French ran things. It had to be some kind of classy city then. Now it's the biggest refugee camp in the world and the most corrupt. But, hey, you want to see something really bizarre, go over to the Vien Hoa Dao pagoda and stand there when the sun streaks across the marble floor in the late afternoon," he said, his voice high. "It's mystic, man, like Buddha's descending on you or something."

"Jesus Christ," Willingham grunted.

"Naw, man. Buddha," said Jesus, showing dimples. "The guy said Buddha."

"Saigon," Payne said, letting the word roll off his tongue, relishing the sound of it. He had been to Saigon ten, twelve times, and it always got him excited.

"Park it here," he said. "We're going to this place. Best drinks in town. I'd say y'all look like the banana daiquiri types."

"Shit, they ain't gonna let us in there," said Bruiser.

The street-level veranda of the Continental Hotel was lush and cool and dim. Rows of potted acacia trees shaded the tables from the sun. The floor was a handsome tile of symmetric design upon which clothed tables were spaced comfortably apart, each under an overhead fan hanging low from the high ceiling. There was a fragrance of jasmine in the air. Given its close proximity to Tu Do Street, the terrace was astonishingly serene.

Most of the tables were unoccupied and they took one close to the street; never mind that they were exposed to danger, that was where Willingham wanted to sit. Bruiser was reluctant to sit; he was waiting to get thrown out.

"Sit your butt down," said Willingham, who had fitted his sunglasses in the pocket of his surfer blouse and had dragged a chair from another table where he propped his boots, getting comfortable. Payne thought for a moment he was going to pull out the snapshot of his old man's machine. The birthmark on his temple was the color of rust in the refracted sunlight.

A white-jacketed Viet waiter pranced up to them, smiling. "Gent-amen. What will it be today?"

"My buddy here will have a banana daiquiri," Jesus said, indicating Bruiser. "For me, make it strawberry."

The waiter returned quickly with a tray of large frosted tumblers and longneck bottles of beer.

Willingham paid in greenback, which was illegal for soldiers to use, and the waiter beamed. Willingham grinned sardonically. "To the Saigon Warrior," he said to Payne and gave a little self-ridiculing salute with his bottle. "I wish like hell you guys didn't have to go back," he said with a sudden thoughtful frown on his brow. "I want you to know I never asked for this housecat duty, and if it were possible I'd trade places with you in a minute."

"Let's just make the best of it right now, okay?" Jesus said, firing a cigarette with his delicate hands. He might have resented Willingham for saying that, the way he looked up sharply at him and then off to the street. He didn't want to think about going back to the war.

"Where y'all from in the world?" asked Payne, looking for a way to tell them where he was from.

Bruiser and Jesus both told him, but made their responses a terse single word—"Kansas" and "Alabama" respectively—that closed the subject. Neither did they want to think about the world. Their tours were not close enough to DEROS to think about a future.

Payne let the subject lie; he realized he should not have brought them here. Maybe not even to the city, for the taste of it could only worsen the reality of what they had to go back to.

"I know a place we can go where the women keep their health cards up to date and won't treat you like shit," he offered, not really knowing of such a place. "Chinese types. Soon as we finish up these drinks. All right?"

"I guess," Bruiser said weakly, not sure of Payne anymore.

"I know about his idea of Chinese," Willingham said. "Forget it. There's another joint I heard about." He looked at Jesus. "You'll go for it, supposed to be all makes and models of women, some real queens with meat to them, hair on the cunt."

"You mean they got Monties, too?" Jesus said expectantly.

"That's what I mean, sweet little Indians."

"Sounds good to me," said Payne, relieved that it was out of his hands. He didn't care if Willingham knew what he was talking about or not.

The waiter came around with unordered seconds, and nobody moved to reject them. The attention had shifted to a table in the back of the bar where three civilians sat leisurely in their chairs. You couldn't help but overhear them; they talked in the loud, ostentatious voices tourists use in foreign countries, as if by virtue of being Anglo and American they were a superior class. The conversation announced them as journalists. One sounded Australian or English, the other two American. They had purposely taken a table in the recesses; most foreigners who knew about such things stayed away from the street as a precaution against anarchists lobbing grenades. The journalists were all under thirty and wore khaki shirts with more pockets than they needed; they kept their hair long and ungroomed as a sign of their loose attitude about the war.

The journalists were swapping war stories in the unchecked tongue of too many drinks. One of the Americans was recounting his latest escapade on a navy patroller on some remote finger of water in the delta. He said the boat had been immobilized and the crew had to sit on the water overnight and at one point came under attack. The green tracers, he was telling his companions, were beautiful the way they squirreled through the air like luminous penlights. "This jive seaman," he said, slurring his *s*'s, "was standing on the bow taking a piss when a flash came twirling across the water and caught him in the leg, exploding like a flashbulb. Weird goddamn thing. Anyway, the guy went in the water and the firing stopped. It was freaky the way the VC stopped firing soon as he hit the water. We pulled the guy out and the firing started back up. Nobody could explain it."

Willingham craned his neck in their direction, exaggerating his posture to let the man know he was looking at him. "That wasn't VC, pal," he said across tables. "That was locals pissed you were pissing in their waters. Guy should've had better sense. It was the same as pissing on them."

The reporters stared blankly at Willingham without comment and in a few minutes they left. The one relating the incident glanced back embarrassedly as he reached the sidewalk and got in a rickshaw.

Willingham guzzled beer, raking a forearm across his chin.

"Sure cut their water off," Payne said. "Is that true, what you said?"

"What do you think, some asshole comes up and pisses in your garden, polluting the source of your food? Of course it's true."

Willingham looked around the terrace in disgust. "These fucking journalists don't know any more than the military what this little country is all about. They don't want to understand. And neither do those pompous figureheads just elected. That GVN monument proves just how little all these short-lived regimes know about their own country; the country belongs to the peasants and Indians. They been here forever and they'll be around long after all these bullshit figurehead governments are gone, just like it's been for the last two thousand years."

"You know it, Mountain Man," said Bruiser.

The soiled sky, finally making its move, dropped a gray-black curtain on the amber glow of late afternoon, and lights began to flicker on up and down Tu Do. They had been here too long already and now the terrace began to fill with the twilight cocktail crowd, composed mostly of civilian contractor types and a few token Vietnamese; the Viets stood out like foreigners in their white dinner jackets and fine-linen *ao dai* dresses.

"What the fuck we waiting for, let's do it," Jesus said.

As they left, a legless Viet appeared from nowhere and crawled down the hotel's tiled steps behind them. He moved sideways like a crab and clawed first at Bruiser, then grabbed Willingham's pants, the big men. The crippled man's livelihood was begging; he counted on handouts just to spare you his unsightly presence. Willingham obliged by wadding up a greenback five and tossing it on the sidewalk. A gang of kids, also appearing like magic, scrambled madly for the bill, but the wasted Viet outmaneuvered them and slithered back up the steps, where he disappeared in some hole in the bougainvillaea and jasmine, a cavity where even the street kids couldn't find him.

"Felt charitable," Willingham volunteered. "Poor fucker reminded me of an old papasan I once knew."

"I never have rode in one of them things," said Bruiser, pointing out a passing lambretta. "You think we could?"

"Sure," Payne said.

Willingham alone objected, concerned about the safety of the jeep.

"Don't worry about the damn jeep," Payne said and waved down a smaller pedicab, one with facing double seats. The flimsy vehicle was designed for Viet passengers, not the bulkier Westerners, but they all piled in despite the driver's protest. He livened up a little when Willingham showed him a ten-dollar bill. The weight put tremendous stress on the single axle as well as the ninety-pound Viet's legs; Bruiser pushed off to help him get going then slipped gently back in.

Inside the cramped cab their arms rubbed and knees protruded to shoulder level, making them all seem very large and awkward.

Willingham took a joint out of his shirt pocket and lit it between his knees, inhaled deeply, and passed it to Jesus.

The driver pedaled slow-motion off Tu Do and onto the broader Nguyen Hue Boulevard where, with his enormous load, he could better measure the traffic.

Along the parkway dividing the broad thoroughfare to the boulevard, artists had spread their lookalike Modiglianiesque canvases to face the traffic, and black marketeers paraded a cornucopia of Vespas and oscillating fans, T-shirts, liquor, and refrigerators, hawking at passersby. At intervals, MPs and white mice cops stood by as if to protect the bootleggers from being robbed.

The three tourists watched the commotion along the buzzing street. Payne, uninterested in the scenery, his thoughts back at the Continental, said to Willingham, "Yeah, but those reporters are just doing their job. It's not that easy straightening out all the bullshit they're fed over here."

Willingham laughed. "That's not what the assholes do," he said. "What they do is twist things out of proportion to suit their egos. Make it sound like they're out there on the front line when they are actually hanging around base camps all decked out in their Hang Ten shirts and Sears and Roebuck boots buying quotes and snapshots off grunts. And those are just the ones that get that close to the action."

"That's right," said Jesus. "You can tell they don't do shit by the pictures they take of Monties. You've seen 'em; makes 'em all look like aborigines from fuckin Africa somewheres. They got this image, see, that they want you to think is what they're like, so they take pictures of the ugliest ones, toothless old fuckers with big wide noses and lumpy foreheads and these dumb eyes like a cow's. Same thing they want us to think of American Indians. So that's the image everybody has of 'em. Shit, man, they are beautiful people, some of them."

"Yeah, that's the impression I had of them," Payne confessed openly. "And I'm a fucking journalist."

Willingham looked at Payne like the new guy again and went on. "I bet you half your civilian reporters don't ever get any further north than we are right now, doing nothing more in the day than listening to the brass preach how they can see the light at the end of the fucking tunnel. That's your bullshit. They ain't helping the war effort, they're fucking it up."

"Yeah," said Bruiser.

"So what have you got against them?" Payne said, poker-faced.

Willingham, caught off guard, hesitated a moment. Then he slapped Payne's knee good-naturedly. "Touché."

The driver seemed to know the place Willingham had described and did not look back at his passengers. He was sweating profusely through his halter shirt, the drops of sweat flying inside the cab. Payne wiped his face, but it didn't bother the others.

A squat Renault roared by with a load of American sailors hanging out the windows shouting and flapping arms. They were hollering obscenities at some peasants squatting on the curb.

"Talk about your assholes," said Payne. "There they are."

"Aww, they're just having a good time, letting go," said Bruiser. "Same as us."

A group of whores in slit dresses lounging nearby in the doorway of a neon soul bar mistook the sailors' shouts for catcalls and coaxed them on, and as the taxi sped on by the women turned their attention to the slower pedicab. "Hey, you. GI Whitey," one yelled. "You come here yo good-time mama."

Willingham pushed off Jesus' shoulder to gawk. He tried to stand inside the cab and nearly flipped it. Payne reached over and pulled him down by the back of his pants. "Be cool," Payne said, assuming his role as official tourist guide. "You're in the concrete jungle now, my terrain. This here's soul-brother territory we're passing through."

"So what?" Willingham said but didn't pursue it.

The bicyclist, coming into the marketplace on the river, finally gave out. His legs, like strips of sinewy leather, tried to push the pedals but they worked in quivering uselessness, his exhausted skeletal arms glistening in the street lights. The guy would pedal himself to death by the time he was twenty-six.

The pedicab came to a dead stop in the center of the market street, and the GIs climbed out, grunting from the stiffness and making faces at the overpowering stench of rotten fish swirling around in the rain's front wind. The driver collapsed on the handlebars. Payne said he'd pay and argued with the Viet and gave him four MPC dollar bills, the proper fare. The pint-sized man complained bitterly, calling after Payne, "Numbah ten GI, fuck you." Willingham didn't offer to up the fare.

The place they sought was on the edge of the market. The sign said "Port 'A Call," with a smaller sign underneath that read, "Sailor —GI Welcome." The two-story building extended over the bank of the brown-sludge Saigon River; apparently it had once been a restaurant with a magnificent view of the serene river; it would have been converted a couple of years back when U.S. sailors began shore leave in abundance in the city. The overlooking windows were now sealed up.

The entrance was a low-topped door strung with beads through which Americans had to lower their heads as they fanned the beads aside. It was crowded and smoky inside, the air hot and thick from lack of ventilation. Large support beams stood six or seven feet apart against which sailors in uniform leaned with women between their spread legs, the cool stance of negotiation. A busy craps table occupied the very rear and there was dancing on a sunken floor. The buzz-saw roar of voices came from having to shout over the cacophony of two electric guitars and electric drums; it was a Viet band playing something indecipherable.

There were, as Willingham had promised, women of all descriptions, including a few blacks and even a Caucasian whore, who was at the moment occupied. They pushed and wormed their way to an opening at the bar; it took almost a minute for a trio of free women to work through to the troupe of fresh meat. The quickest of the three slid in between Willingham and Payne, apparently establishing dominion over the both of them. Directly behind her the other two women fell on the arms of Jesus and Bruiser, who immediately got into an argument over one of them. Since Willingham was preoccupied ordering beer, the first whore shifted to Payne, hooking both her little claw hands on him. He didn't like her looks or her pushy manner and told Willingham to take her.

"Sure?"

Payne nodded he was sure."You hear about this joint in the can too?" he asked, and Willingham bobbed his head in the affirmative. "Figures," Payne said.

Willingham surprised Payne by dismissing the girl, saying he wasn't interested in women right now. "Let them have their fun," he said of his buddies, having to shout. "We can do this anytime."

He was scanning the place for something; in a moment he brought his search to rest on a small alcove partially veiled from the mass by beads, like a private dining area. "Think I'll try to negotiate a little business," he said to Payne.

"What kind of business?"

"Who knows?" he said, shrugging. "Who cares? Maybe get me a Nikon or a fucking motorbike to putter around on."

Payne looked blankly at him for a moment. "Why don't you just buy whatever you want? You can afford it."

"And take the fun out of it?"

Inside the alcove that captured Willingham's interest was a diminutive black-faced man in pimp's clothes. He was engaged in conversation with two women but glanced at Willingham with equal interest, as though inviting him to come over. His ebony-black hair had a smooth sheen and was parted square in the middle like a hairtonic ad out of the silent-screen era. The women too had dark skin; they seemed to be his personal property. Willingham said, "Ten to one that's the guy I want to see," and, sucking his distended lip, walked off toward the man in the zoot suit.

"You better be careful, man," Payne said after him.

Bruiser was making dissuasive gestures at the whore, who had now snuggled into the big man's armpit, contentedly sipping her tea. But he wanted the other girl and was still trying to talk Jesus into swapping. During this squabble the girl they were arguing over smiled suggestively at Payne. She had a nice smile.

"I'm telling you, man, you don't want this one," Jesus shouted irritably, unable to pay attention to the whore because of his troublesome friend. "You ought to be able to tell the difference by now. You don't like 'em, remember?"

He was telling Bruiser that the girl was a Montagnard, but Bruiser said he was full of shit, where were the beads and big lips, the nose bone? "Maybe she's a half-breed, but it's half Chinese," he said, flinching as the unwanted whore playfully goosed his ribs.

Jesus threw up his hands. "All right. If you're gonna have a shitfit about it, take her."

The girl in question had the features of a South Seas islander, high cheeks and wide, liquid dark eyes, a skin of lustrous night-shaded complexion; Payne understood why they were fighting over her. As her eyes caught his she smiled again and held him a moment under the power of her stare.

It seemed a rare quality for a Viet whore to take the arguing as she did, demurely, without showing offense. The whores Payne had thus far encountered all possessed an impossible sultry pride, seizing any excuse to become offended, even when being fought over; it was their way. But this whore was different. Payne wanted her too, he suddenly realized, and said, "Well, if you guys can't work this out, maybe I ought to take over."

The band mercifully stopped for a break; everyone in the place seemed relieved, even the three band members themselves. They wore shiny, skin-tight suits that were supposed to give them the Beatles look and had their porcupine hair preposterously pulled forward in bangs so that each of them, rather than resembling Paul, John, George, or Ringo, looked more like Alfalfa.

"I don't want no damn regular gook, or one of them fucking African niggers, either," Jesus was saying, searching for another woman who was Indian.

"What the hell's the difference?" said Bruiser.

"Plenty. Most these beasts ain't going to show you a good time. Look at 'em," Jesus said in a voice, that without the bandstand racket, carried beyond his group to bring some looks. He was worked up and didn't notice. "Damned if I'll screw a nigger," he said again. "I want me a Monty, a bitch I can deal with."

"Damn, we gonna get into this again," Bruiser said, sinking on the bar stool. Both whores eased back too.

"Your fault, Bruiser."

"Why don't y'all just flip a coin and settle it," suggested Payne, catching the mockery in the comments of some nearby sailors; it was the kind of drink-inspired service-rivalry talk that invariably led to a brawl.

"How about one of those over where Willie is?" Payne added. "They're Indian, aren't they?"

Jesus followed Payne's pointing finger. "Looks to me like he's got dibs on 'em."

"What's he gonna to do, screw 'em both at once?" said Bruiser. "Go on, go for it."

The sailors, moving closer as a group, thought it was a good suggestion. One of the five swabbies said, "Yeah, hotshot, go for it." And to his buddies, he added, "I kinda like this one for myself."

He was referring to the girl with the South Seas face. Of course, Payne thought. She seemed to be a natural source of trouble, but he could see that she hadn't been soliciting it. Oddly, it seemed to Payne, she was interested in him, the way she continued making those suggestive passing glances, her eyes downcast and inviting.

Bruiser came off the stool and stood tall with his barrel chest pushed out, ready for the fists to fly. He didn't say anything; he just smiled wickedly, sizing up the group, as though, half amused, he was deciding which of their heads he wanted to bang together first. You could see the boozy glaze clear from the forward sailor, who involuntarily shrank back as if from an inner, sober voice advising him not to tangle with the big man.

Bruiser was undaunted by the threat of simple dangers like this, and maybe, after his long weekend, he was even homesick for a little fight.

The others seemed to sense it too, but there was the U.S. Navy's reputation to save now, and the swabbies hiked up too. Before it got started, Payne stepped between the sailors and the Indian girl, not touching her or looking into her face, but slightly bowing in her direction as he had read somewhere was customarily proper with these people, and said to the boisterous swabby, "What do you say we arm-wrestle for her?"

Bruiser had given him courage he didn't know he had until he said this. Perhaps the girl also contributed. It turned out to be the right thing to say, for everyone except Bruiser assumed a looser posture. The sailor said, "You're on, troop."

"Both hands," added Payne, figuring he'd take the guy easily lefthanded and maybe pull a draw with the right. The sailor was about Payne's weight. "Winner gets the girl, the loser a free drink, his choice."

Collectively the soldiers and sailors cleared a table and they got at it, left hand first. Jesus made a couple of side bets on Payne, which encouraged Payne even more; it made him feel stronger. The band, now back on the tiny elevated stage, was tuning up for more noise.

Making his preparation a show, the sailor removed his blouse to reveal the upper body of a weight lifter, and his buddies cheered him on with skin slaps; on Payne's side, in addition to Bruiser and Jesus, the two whores became his cheerleaders, the liquid-eyed girl stepping up next to Payne, as if she had already decided she was his girl.

The sailor's grip was strong; he had devoted a lot of ocean time doing hand rolls and working with barbells, maybe pushups in counts of fifty; he flaunted those workouts now, getting set. The blood vessels along his hairless arm protruded like welts. Payne started to sweat before the acting referee lifted his hand from the wrestlers'. But it was not a contest lefthanded; Payne, with a lifetime of upper-body strength from swimming, put him down in less than ten seconds; the weight lifter, he decided, was fluff.

Bruiser and Jesus slapped Payne on the back. "Okay, buddy," said Jesus, "you just got to do it with your right now. Tear 'im a new asshole."

Payne wagged his head vigorously, feigning supreme confidence when in fact he felt very little confidence in his right-side strength. Once the contest was under way the ligaments in his neck grew taut as piano wires and his arm began to quake after but a few seconds. The ground rules, Jesus pointed out, were if neither man's arm went down within a minute and a half it would be considered a draw; seeing the sweat dripping from Payne's hairline and down the wires of his neck, the swabbies readily agreed and made more bets.

It was a long minute in Payne's life; he drew wind like a deep-diving snorkler and grunted and strained. The sailor's eyes, which he kept steadily in focus, remained unfaltering and determined, for now the navy was at stake. But he could not pull Payne's hand any closer to the table, and after Jesus called time, the righthanded duel was determined to be a draw.

"GI beat sail-ah!" the unwanted whore declared, making a small clap with her hands.

Payne left his wasted hand jerking in spasms where it lay, and asked the defeated sailor what he wanted to drink.

"Forget it, man," the sailor said, not unpleasantly. "You done it fair and square."

The sailors bounded off with supportive arms hugging their downcast companion, who was shaking a fist at himself. The band clamored into the next set.

The whore Payne presumably had won approached him timidly; she lifted Payne's limp hand and pressed it against the side of her face. It seemed a strange gesture.

"You very handsome man," she said close to him. "Most handsome all GI, all American," she added, gesturing around her.

Payne looked upon her with hungry eyes. "You want some tea?"

"No, no, no," she said. "You no buy me tea. You no buy nothing me."

The girl moved in closer, backing Payne up against the bar. He studied her; she had good teeth and small erect breasts, maybe seventeen years old. Her char-black hair was pulled tight in the back, giving definition to the delicate lines of her high cheeks and dented temples.

"Why I no see you before?" she asked, faking annoyance with him. "You no bad soldier who all time fight. No?"

Payne nodded and looked off, a little shamefacedly. "I'm a Saigon Warrior, honey. I work up the road at Long Binh. You know it?"

"Surah. Everybody know Long Binh. I have *beaucoup* friend Long Binh. What you job, GI?"

Her movements were quick but somehow not obtrusive. She was personable and seemed a bright girl.

"I write stories about the people of your country, good stories," he said, now a little boastful. "In *Stars & Stripes*. I'm a journalist."

The girl pressed fully against him, the softness of her body causing an excitement in Payne that weakened him. "You like Vietnamese people, I know this," she said in his ear. "I like you very much, too. This no place for you."

"This is no place for you, either," Payne said.

"Sometime you come my home."

Payne said he would like that very much.

"In delta, land much watah, no tree."

"I've been there. I like it down there."

The girl frowned at some inner thought. "I no can be you girl-friend here. Long Xuyen where I live. You come see me. I make you very happy, you see."

"Well, that's nice of you, but what's the problem—"

Before he could finish, the girl abruptly excused herself, saying, "I sorry now," and performed something of a curtsy and left. He followed her with his eyes as she quick-stepped through the crowd to the small alcove where the man in pimp's clothes and Willingham were talking.

"Why'd she leave?" he asked Jesus. "Damn."

Jesus grinned. "A real honey, ain't she? I told you there were some beautiful Monties."

"You're fucking A right about that," Payne said, watching after the girl, unable to keep his eyes off her.

"But there weren't no choice," said Jesus. "She couldn't make it with you now."

"How come?"

In the next moment the pimp and all three girls, and Willingham as well, turned their attention on Payne and gave him in unison a kind of salute.

"What's that for?" he asked Jesus. Jesus was now an expert on Montagnard Indians; Smith the medic had suddenly been ousted from that position in Payne's estimation.

"A sign of their appreciation for what you done," Jesus said with authority.

"What? I didn't do anything."

"The fuck you didn't," Jesus said. "You defended the girl's honor."

"You mean that bullshit with the sailor? No kidding?"

"It's a subtle thing with Monties. Half the time you don't know if you're defiling them or honoring 'em, they got so many crazyass beliefs. I couldn't ever figure 'em out completely. But I know she'd be shamed in front of her friends if she were to take you upstairs. That's what I was talking about."

"Then what the fuck's she doing here?"

"Seems a little ironic, don't it. But there it is, man, your crazy Monties. Bruiser could never understand that about 'em."

Payne couldn't understand it either. He scratched his head, looking across the room at the girl. He hadn't given a thought to his own so-called honor, that secret little oath to stay faithful to his wife, and he knew he would break it just like that for this whore. Now he realized his fall from faithfulness didn't bother him at all.

"She lives in the delta," he said to Jesus. "Asked me to come down and see her. Guess that's what I'll have to do."

"The delta? Shit, man, ain't no Monties live in the delta."

Payne didn't want to believe the girl had lied to him and he dropped it; maybe Jesus didn't know every goddamn thing. "What the fuck's Willie doing, anyway?"

"Yeah," said Bruiser. "Personally, I'm 'bout ready to try that bar, what is it, the Freegate? Heard lots of good shit about that one. I'll go get the fucker."

He shook off the unwanted whore, who seemed finally to get the message and pouted with a vengeance, walking off in the opposite direction from Bruiser.

Bruiser seemed desperate to stop time; it was getting late and curfew would be on them soon. The two soldiers on extended leave had talked wildly of things to do, hit an opium den, find a cockfight, try to get themselves a whore, in a hotel maybe. Anything to keep their minds off tomorrow. It imposed upon them a palpable gloom that seemed impossible to alleviate.

In a minute Bruiser and Willingham were back at the bar, Willingham commenting that since he didn't have the jeep he'd have to wait to pull off the deal with the gook in the zoot suit.

The bartender, a stout Oriental with a goat's tuff of wispy hair on his chin, placed a large colorful drink in front of Payne. "For you, my friend," he said, pointing to the alcove where the group of Indians again made their saluting gestures.

Payne grinned broadly at Jesus and said, "This is a fine fucking bar."

Willingham squeezed Payne's biceps. "You got to be stronger than you look. Sure impressed those Indians."

"So what's the deal with the little man?" asked Payne.

"No wheels, no thrills," Willingham said with no trace of scorn. "It'll wait till *mañana*."

"Speaking of which," added Payne, "I'm the early man tomorrow. If I stay the night, I'll never make it back in time. Why don't you guys hit the Freegate; there's enough time I can still catch a shuttle. You don't mind, do you, if I cop out?"

No one objected. It seemed to Payne that the suggestion, in fact, was a welcomed one; Willingham even gave him the keys to the jeep—"Get there faster and we won't need it anyway."

The reminder that he was still an outsider stung him. In truth, though, he wanted them to leave so he could try to make it with the Indian girl; but before he had finished saying goodbye to Bruiser and Jesus, trying again to get the jive handshake down and wishing them good luck, the girl and her dark-skinned companions had disappeared. And then the three bush buddies had also gone, leaving Payne to finish his colorful drink alone.

It struck him then, in a moment of reverie, that in just a few hours he had grown to like the two grunts almost like brothers. He recalled what Willingham had said about making friends in the bush, how quickly you became tight; it was the way of the bush, the tightness grunt soldiers had, a tightness a REMF soldier would never know. But Payne felt it, and now he felt that telling them goodbye was a final act of departure; and in his reverie, the dead face of his father flashed across his mind, regarding Payne with an empty half smile from inside his casket. That too had been a final act of departure and neither had it immediately affected Payne.

Chapter

II

Kink was making his peculiar sleep noise, not a snore but a soft nasal gurgle that often woke Payne and caused him to have to clear his own throat; it was a woman's irritating snore. Finally fed up, Payne jumped out of bed and banged his cubemate's bunk against the floor. Kink smacked his lips and the noise briefly stopped.

In the residual quietness Payne dozed, drifting on the intimate repose of a luminous sexual fantasy with the girl of last night, until his solitude was again broken, now by the abrupt scream of a siren sounding over the company loudspeakers. It was five-fifteen. Immediate hysteria erupted in the sleeping hootch and the hallway quickly filled with wide-eyed men shouting to know what was happening. Sergeant Ortega had to use a bullhorn to overcome the circus. "Get dressed and fall in at the orderly room. Double-time it!" the disembodied voice blared down the hallway. The day was beginning to look like a bummer.

Five minutes later Payne stood at parade rest, second row, third man in the first platoon, waiting for the CO to talk. Top took his place at the CO's side and straightaway appeared to fall asleep where he stood. Payne spread himself out to take up the space of two men, his and Kink's. Though the sky was still pitch dark, floodlights from the barracks and orderly room lit up the field like a prison yard.

Most of the men had rushed to the formation partially dressed and stood barefoot, shivering and nervous. The CO was not one to push dress code and himself had left his shirttail hanging out on one side, the shirt half unbuttoned, as if to set an example. He was considered cool.

Following Top's cursory head count, the CO took over. Kink wasn't missed. Payne looked over at the platoon where Willingham should have been, on the quirky notion he might be there; of course he was not.

"Okay, men. Today is conversion day," the CO said, pausing to let that sink in. "Unless you're on your second tour of duty, you probably don't know what that means. Well, I've made a special effort to get up this early just to tell you."

The CO was short, barrel-chested, and bald except for a half-tire of brown hair above his ears, just enough hair to make plausible an appearance at the barber shop. From that distance he reminded Payne uncomfortably of Captain Burns.

"Today and tomorrow you will all be required to turn in your MPC for new script. This little surprise maneuver is pulled about every two years to put the hurt on the black market. You all know about the black market. You will find that your maids won't be in to sweep your rooms for the next two days. No Vietnamese will be allowed on post. Why?" He grinned at Top, then continued without the grin. "Very simple, men. If your maid were to come in to make your bed, she would want to sell you all the MPC she had managed to stuff in her laundry bag. She would want to sell it to you before you convert your old money to new money. She would want either greenback or piaster. She would give you a good rate of exchange. And then she would give the new MPC to her papasan downtown and our little surprise would fail. You will have until eighteen hundred hours tomorrow to complete your banking transactions. Top, fill the men in on the details and take their questions. And remind them that holding greenback is not legal either."

The CO walked into the orderly room, letting the screen door bang behind him. You could see him standing over the coffee urn and then sipping from a steaming cup before disappearing into his inner office. It appeared to Payne the entire company of men had their eyes on him, watching him sip his hot coffee.

Payne got to the office earlier than was required of the early man and put some coffee together, then went around opening windows. Dawn would arrive in a few minutes, for the crickets and birds could be heard growing impatient. When the coffee quit rumbling, he poured a cup, lit a cigarette, and took out the notebook he sometimes used as a diary. He got the notebook at the PX in Cam Ranh on his first day in-country with the idea of keeping a daily record of his tour. But that had been a discipline he hadn't kept up after his tour became routine, and there were gaps in the diary often stretching three weeks apart. The later entries were limited to things out of the ordinary, accounts of his field trips, of the impressions he'd had of villages and villagers, the few Viets he met and had spent some time with. Ten pages covered a weekend he'd spent with a back-alley family in the delta, in Can Tho, who had taken to him the way some poor people take to a missionary. He never understood why they treated him with such favor; it seemed gratuitous, having no advantage for them.

He also had written at length of the resurrection of Junior Cotton, how upon learning he was not dead it had changed his perceptions of the war, as if that had been the biggest thing that made him recognize the ironic nature of the war and how little he actually knew about it. And that was the last entry; not a word was recorded concerning Willingham killing the ARVN or the CID investigation, nor the butchered bodies at the Xuan Loc refugee camp. It would have been dangerous, even stupid, to put down his feelings on that, offering in black and white information that could incriminate a friend for murder. It seemed unnecessary to include anyway, for he was not likely to forget it.

He thought now he would write something about the Indian girl, but that seemed superfluous since there was nothing in a real sense to say, only a strangely mystifying attraction he had felt for her, an attraction he knew went beyond sexual desire but not how much beyond. And if he couldn't write something of a concrete nature, without embellishing the entry with fantasy, he thought, why write anything at all?

He thumbed through the notebook, fanning pages, thinking about drawing stick caricatures on the blank sheets to make a motion picture, X-rated maybe, a boy stick chasing a girl stick. Finally he wrote a short entry; but it was vague and avoided what he wanted to explore: "What gets me is how everybody seems to have all these different opinions and attitudes about the Vietnamese, even the ones that are the enemy. Are they so different from any other people?" It was another copout.

He was on his second cup of coffee and third cigarette when the lieutenant came in quietly, dragging himself.

"What brings you in so early?"

"Couldn't sleep any longer," Finn moaned, lifting a foot on Payne's desk to retie a shoestring. "Slept with my contacts in and dreamed they fell in the toilet. I had a hard time unfreezing them."

He was impeccably dressed in khakis, the butter bars and other brass ornaments highly polished, his shoes glossy. He had made a sore of a pimple under his eye that looked like it would hurt if so much as the wind touched it.

"Want some aspirin?"

Finn took the aspirin and closed the door to his office behind him.

Payne lit another smoke and put away the foolish notebook for something more pertinent, business, and started putting together an advance article on the command's upcoming events for Thanksgiving.

In a moment the lieutenant reopened his door and invited Payne in.

Finn reclaimed his seat and gazed in silence at Payne. The whites of his eyes were networks of tiny red lines serrated like the edge of a hacksaw.

"You look like hell, sir. Sure you didn't throw a drunk last night?"

The lieutenant was preoccupied. He put his magnifying glasses on one ear at a time, grimacing as the glasses came to rest above the butchered pimple.

He spoke solemnly, in a philosophical vein. "I don't know, Payne. It seems to me we're just beating our heads against the wall," he said; it was an odd twist, confiding in Payne, an EM. "What do you think? I mean, do you think this pacification thing will actually make a difference?"

Payne assumed he was serious; Finn usually was. "I guess there could be worse things we could do," Payne offered. "Bomb hell out of Hanoi, for instance. I guess what it comes down to is we don't really understand these people and so we don't know how to help them."

"That's the point. There's nothing clear cut about it."

"You want some coffee, Lieutenant?"

"Just between us I think we started something we shouldn't

have," Finn said. "This new election is a mockery, a damned insult to democracy; the people are split and fighting against each other and us, too, when what they really want is to just grow their crops and harvest their land; they *are* farmers, after all. Frankly, I don't think we have any business staying here any longer."

Payne shot him a quick grin. "You know that kind of thinking's not going to help get you promoted."

The lieutenant grimaced painfully again. "I'll get promoted. Then it will be just a matter of time before I'm made captain, if I choose to make the army a career. That's how it works; they suck you in."

Payne rolled his eyes and let them wander around the small office where they settled on the bowling trophy prominently displayed on the shelf under the air conditioner. It was a small trophy, a plastic figurine of a bowler in action, which the lieutenant's team had won on Finn's 270-something. Since he had won it, the team allowed him to hold the trophy.

"Is that what's bothering you?"

"It bothers the hell out of me. The way things are going Stateside, I don't know if I want to stay in the military. But I do like it." He looked at Payne a moment. "What would you do in my case?"

Payne smirked and then snapped at him: "I'd go downtown, get drunk, and find me a whore, and learn something about this goddamn country."

Finn's myopic eyes were easy to read; he didn't know how to take that. "You serious?"

Payne realized he was venting his own clouded frustrations and spoke easier. "It'd be a start, wouldn't it?"

The lieutenant sat erect. "I'm an officer, Payne. I can't do that sort of thing."

Payne couldn't figure this joker; Finn acted it, but he was not military stuff. He was too soft and too childlike. Yet you couldn't really say he was a dufus OIC, or that he did not treat his men fairly, that he was not thoughtful. And that, Payne concluded, was the baffling thing about him.

He went back to the T-day article.

The morning passed, and Willingham had not shown up for work, which gave Finn a reason to bark, and he barked at everyone about it. He threatened with seeming intent to report him AWOL. He stopped short of taking such a drastic measure only after Sterr assured him Willingham was doing a story, that he'd simply forgotten to write it down on the sign-out board.

The barking had gotten Lai Sin nervous and she was having a hard time pecking at her typewriter; constantly using the white-out on the mistakes she made, she got nowhere all morning. Twice Payne sat on the edge of her desk and talked softly, trying his best to help her regain her composure, and he thought his efforts helped a little.

At noon he broke for chow. He was going on assignment afterward and had the jeep. He spotted Willingham at the rear of the messhall, pacing impatiently.

"How much cash you got?" Willingham said anxiously, climbing into the jeep as Payne was getting out. Mirrored glasses hid his eyes, but he looked sallow, like someone who'd been on an all-nighter.

"How'd it go last night? Did they get off okay?"

"Yeah, yeah. Had a blast," he said, dismissing that subject with a wave of his hand. "I'm going to make a killing. Couldn't've asked for better timing with this conversion thing. You want in on it?"

Payne grinned. "A killing, huh? How's that?"

"The gook, man. The dude I was talking to last night. Supposed to meet me here. The fucker was supposed to be here half an hour ago."

"The post is off limits to them today," Payne said.

Willingham displayed one of his finest horse grins. "When will you learn, these little restrictions only encourage them. He'll be here. If you got greenback, you'll turn a better return. You interested?"

"Hell yeah, I'm interested," Payne said. "My money's at the office."

"Better hurry."

"I guess you know the lieutenant's on a rampage. Threatening to report you AWOL."

Willingham shrugged. "I'll cry to the LT later. Go get your dough."

Payne wheeled up the hill to the office, considering the numerous ways he stood to get ripped off but deciding to go for it anyway. He broke his own rule by robbing his contingency fund, which had grown to thirty-two dollars. Returning, he found Willingham still pacing. He pulled the jeep near a shit burner and Willingham again got in. He raked a sleeve across his sweaty forehead.

"Fucking dinks," he snarled. "You never know."

"I only got thirty-two bucks. Don't fuck me."

A chopper banked low over the messhall on its approach to the hospital annex. The shadow eclipsed the sun momentarily and a swirl of dust rose in its wake. At the helipad the chopper hovered, careened, then touched down heavily. Willingham removed his sunglasses and kept his eyes trained on the machine until the blades had stopped thrashing and were strapped down. The chopper was making a body delivery.

"Bringing in marines," Willingham said.

"How the hell you know it's marines?"

"The bags, they're brown. Must be some bad shit going on somewhere if they have to ask the army for space. . . . There he is."

Payne didn't see the truck until it had become a sudden burst of fireworks sputtering around the corner of the messhall. It was a vintage deuce-and-a-half, bumperless, with frog-eye sockets for headlamps. A head no bigger than a monkey's pogoed in and out of view over the arc of the steering wheel.

A small man got down from the driver's seat. The truck percolated as if it were going to die, but it didn't and the driver went directly to the hood, raised it, climbed inside, yapped at it, jerked something, and the truck hissed at him then settled down to a languid silence. The Viet slithered out of the engine cavity and soundlessly hit the ground.

"C'mon, let's see what we can do the dude for," Willingham said.

Payne had not seen him up close last night, but the Indian was a completely different character today. Dressed in a fatigue shirt that hung loosely to his knees over baggy black pajama pants and U.S. Army boots, he was any other Vietnamese peasant. He might have weighed ninety pounds, no more than a skeleton contained inside a dark ruddy skin. On his oversized head was an army softball cap, partially covering a wild growth of skunklike hair. His was a drawn and battered face that had seen a lot of hard times.

"You're late, buster," Willingham quipped, then said to Payne, "They're like that. Don't understand when you say be here at a certain time you by God mean it."

He was trying to intimidate the Viet, Payne thought, in order to get the advantage.

"Crawl unnah wire, take *beaucoup* time get truck," the Viet said, blank-faced. "You no want make deal, okay. No make deal. I go."

Payne looked at Willingham from his distance and let go a dog-like chortle; his bluff had backfired. The Indian grinned at Payne.

Willingham grunted and walked to the rear of the truck and threw back the canvas. Inside was a general store on wheels. There were six or seven refrigerators the size of duffel bags and stacks of cardboard and crate boxes stamped with the symbols of manufacturers from Japan, Australia, Hong Kong, the U.S.S.R., and the U.S.A. Ducks hung upside down in bunches along the framework, and in the forward corner was a disheveled stack of automatic weapons, BARs, AK-47s, and ancient bolt-action rifles.

"Look at all this shit," exclaimed Payne.

Willingham pointed out an avocado-colored refrigerator. "I'll take this one. Back the truck up to that platform over there."

Payne helped unload the refrigerator and put it in the jeep while the Viet moved the truck. "It's got the wrong kind of fucking plug," Willingham complained.

He leaned against the truck and cleaned his glasses on his shirt-tail. "This next part's going to be a little tricky now, Payne. He was supposed to come before the chow rush. If you want to help, we can load his stuff faster. But you'll be in it if something goes wrong."

"What do we do?" Payne said.

"Somebody'll be pulling KP since the gooks aren't here today. I've got to get inside the messhall and get out some potatoes."

"Potatoes? Shit."

"We have to get the KPs distracted. Got any ideas?"

"Hell," Payne said, "just go in there like we own the fucking place. They won't know the difference."

"The mess sergeant would."

"Labouisse? Don't worry about him, I know him. I can keep him occupied if he's a problem, but you'll have to get the stuff out by yourself."

"All right," Willingham said. "Give me your dough. I'll see what kind of funny-money exchange I can get."

Two acting KPs were in the kitchen trying to figure out how to operate a dishwasher. The mess sergeant, on the other side of the kitchen, sat on a stool with his back to the wall and a cigarette held idly between his fingers. His slumped head made a sudden bob. He was asleep despite the chowtime clatter. The cigarette had a long ash attached to it that was curved impossibly like a meat hook.

One of the KPs looked up as Willingham opened the cooler door. "Loading some stuff," he explained. "The mess sergeant around?"

The troop pointed out Labouisse and went back to his business with the dishwasher, scratching his head in confusion. There would be a couple minutes before the cigarette in Buzz's fingers burned down, and Payne helped Willingham move ten sacks of potatoes to the loading dock. The Viet dragged the sacks into the truck. After the last one was loaded, Payne left them at Willingham's signal and went back inside, checked Labouisse, and then strolled over to the KPs, who still hadn't figured out the machine.

Payne turned a large knob halfway, then another a complete revolution, pushed the start button, and the machine went to work. "You'll have to figure out how to use the potato peeler by yourself," he said and winked.

He glanced again at Labouisse in time to see him jump off the stool and shake his hand fiercely, as if he'd been bitten by a snake, then stick two fingers in his mouth and suck on them.

He quickly got out of the messhall and was standing next to the Indian in the truck bed, helping the little man arrange the heavy sacks, when from nowhere, as before, a copter banked low over the messhall. It was a Chinook this time, coming in too low, and the swirl sucked off the deuce-and-a-half's canvas. Duck feathers soared skyward. Payne's cap vanished in the twister; he managed to snatch the Viet's cap out of the air and return it to him; the Viet pursed his lips and slightly dipped his head, a gesture Payne thought was an expression of gratitude.

He worked with the Viet, retying the ragged canopy while Willingham impatiently stood by. Then Willingham pulled the jeep forward, waving his hand at Payne. "Let's hit it, man. *Vamos!*"

Payne had his eye on the stack of weapons, on a long-barreled bolt-action French gun. He asked the Indian if they were for sale. Seemingly eager to please, the little man rummaged through the pile and picked out an AK-47. He presented it to Payne with a show of formality.

"No problem you, you numbah one. I no forget you very honorable man. I give you for this, for nothing. Okay," he said. In so many words he added that he could not guarantee the rifle would fire.

"That's all right," Payne said. "I don't think I'll be using it. Thanks."

The Viet seemed to be in no hurry to leave; even as Payne was walking toward the jeep, the Indian persisted in holding his attention.

"You like girl last night, huh? She like you plenty much," he said, becoming more animated. "You know Long Xuyen? In Mekong? You come Sing Song bar, GI bar, I show you numbah one time. You bring carton cigarette, GI cap. We make deal. I introduce you girl. Okay."

"You live there, too, at Long Xuyen?"

"Big family live Long Xuyen, in village. You come for surah?"

He was talking so only Payne could hear, drawing him closer with a near whisper as if he wanted to make a point of excluding Willingham. Payne reasoned it was because the Viet didn't particularly care for Willingham's derogatory manner; he was a Viet and had his pride or honor, or whatever it was that made them function the way they did.

Payne had heard of the particular bar mentioned, had heard it burned down in the summer when the town came under attack. "The Sing Song wasn't destroyed? I thought it burned down."

"No. For surah Sing Song no gone. You come, ask for Sar-junt Mike. I fix you up with girl. She numbah one virgin girl. Sar-junt Mike my name. Okay."

"Yeah, she's number one all right. Mike, huh? Sergeant Mike," Payne said, grinning. "I'll just bet we could make a deal. Maybe I will look you up," he said and told the Viet to get lost before the mess sergeant came out and threw him in the automatic potato peeler.

"When you come?"

Payne said he didn't know right now, he'd have to work on it.

"You come soon." And then he added a word Payne had never heard a Viet use before: "Please."

The wheeler dealer Sergeant Mike showed a gold tooth in a mouthful of space and rot and climbed into the cab of his truck.

"You come. For surah Sar-junt Mike fix you up good." He gave Payne a V sign bouncing against the shake of the machine.

Willingham was flicking his gold-plated pen, which seemed to curb his anxiety. He had his head tilted back against the seat, staring silently at the weapon in Payne's hand.

Payne stood next to the jeep for a moment admiring the rifle. It was well used and dented, the stock oily. He had owned only one gun in his life, the single-shot .22 rifle his father had given him for Christmas when Payne was nine. His father's instructions had been, "Use it only for target practice and squirrels. Nothing else." Payne remembered the very words because he had asked why not rabbits or crows and his father's angry response surprised him. He had said sternly, "Because I'm telling you." When Payne was able to hit a can at fifty feet, his father took him squirrel hunting. On his second shot Payne popped a gray squirrel high in a pine. The squirrel fell from the tree, clipping branches, and hit the ground heavily. His father gave him another bullet and said he had to finish off the animal. It was different seeing the squirrel up close, flopping in the leaves, bleeding from the mouth, its nose and eyes moist, and Payne recoiled, begging not to have to shoot it again.

"You have to put it out of its misery, son. Hit the head," his father said, and that night, when Payne was in his bed still crying over it, his father had stood tall and dark in the doorway and voiced in a harsh, deep tone his disappointment with his son. "Let this be a lesson to you, Rusty," he'd said. "You will always be faced with things you don't want to do, things a lot harder to handle than shooting a squirrel. I hope to God you will learn to face them better than you did today. Now stop that crying."

Payne had hated his father for years after that, after his death, and when he had occasion to remember him, as now, it was the looming dark figure in the doorway he saw, and the disgrace he felt never changed.

Willingham's reaction to the rifle was one of incredulity. It surprised Payne, who hadn't thought it was all that big a deal. It wasn't like getting a real souvenir. But Willingham couldn't get over it. He said the Indian giving away an AK was incomprehensible, mysterious even, that he must be after something in return. "He definitely has something up his conniving little sleeve. Bet he tried to make you a deal, didn't he? Told you the girl you were salivating over last night was a virgin and you are going to be the lucky dude that gets to pop her cherry. That about right?"

"You heard him."

"I know his kind. Fucking VC. You better watch out if you ever decide to take him up on it."

"You seemed to get along fine with the guy last night," said

Payne. "How come you gave him so much shit today?"

"He wasn't the same dude today. Today was strictly business. Let's get this thing over to the hootch and grab some chow."

"You ought to check in, cool the lieutenant down."

"Later."

After dropping the refrigerator off at Willingham's room and the AK at Payne's, they headed over to the Paradise for lunch, which Payne did not object to. Willingham offered to buy the steaks.

"Nah. Treat's on me this time," Payne said, waving the roll of money Willingham had gotten for him in the exchange.

On the road Willingham looked sideways at Payne, shook his head again in dismay, and said, "I've seen dudes who'd fucking kill each other for that souv. It's been known to happen. I can't figure it out, why he fucking *gave* it to you."

"I didn't treat him bad; I caught his cap," Payne drawled. "Must of meant something to him that it didn't get dirty. Fuck if I know. But the guy was all right, number one. They aren't all slimebag VC. You got me three hundred bucks from him, didn't you?"

"Just my luck to get another gook lover to hang around with," Willingham said. He made it sound facetious, as if he weren't taking himself seriously.

"Hell," said Payne, "I was a nigger lover growing up. No reason to be any different over here. Pull over, I got to take a leak."

Standing at the edge of the road, Payne took out the thick roll of MPC Willingham had traded for his thirty-two greenback dollars. He had delayed opening the roll of cash, considering the moment something to build up to, like reading a letter, wanting to relish it. He'd already thought of the things he might use three hundred dollars for and had started dreaming of future enterprises. This could be the start of something lucrative; he could see himself and Willingham pulling off deals in Saigon, selling cigarettes and stereos, fucking potatoes. Hell, who knows how far they could take it, with Willingham's savoir-faire and verve. He figured to send a wad of it to Ann for her Christmas shopping—"Here you go, Annie baby. Live it up, there's more where this came from. Ain't war beautiful?"

He removed the rubber band from the roll and spread the bills. His eyes suddenly grew large. Under the outer ten-dollar MPC bill was nothing but piaster.

"Goddamn it!" he shouted, turning toward Willingham. "Didn't you count the money?"

"What?" Willingham said from the jeep.

"The fucking stuff is all pi, fuckhead. There's not more than thirteen, fourteen bucks here. I've been gypped. God*damn it!*"

Willingham sat up in the seat, his chin hanging loose in confusion as he unrolled his wad. "But I watched the bastard count it," he said, looking at his own handful of worthless piaster. "I watched him roll it up and hand it to me. I watched him."

Payne jumped in the jeep. His jowls were tightened in knots. "You stupid bastard," he hissed. "I thought you knew what you were doing. . . . The fucking gook." He didn't know what he wanted to say.

"Stop bitching, you did all right," Willingham said. "You got your money's worth with that AK. Think of it like that."

Payne didn't think of it like that; he crossed his arms in a silent, unmitigated pout.

Willingham sighed consolingly. That he too had been ripped off didn't seem to affect him adversely; it was only money to him. At first he tried to hold it back, but by the time they were a click down the road, laugh tears were running down his cheeks. He looked at Payne and the guffaw started over again.

"'But they aren't all slimebags,'" Willingham mimicked with mock sympathy, which was the most he could get out before bursting into a higher pitch of laughter.

"Shut the fuck up," Payne said.

Chapter
12

Payne tossed the covers in a panic, fiercely blinking his eyes. "Fucking goddamn rat," he muttered and shivered. Total darkness encompassed him. This time the mouse had tried to root in his armpit. It was the same every time it happened, tickled into semiconsciousness by the slight touch of tiny claws and whiskers, then the scurry across some part of his anatomy and gone, disappeared, leaving Payne fully awake and fuming. That the rodent only sought a warm place to nest and had never nibbled or even scratched him didn't soften his overblown rancor, and he lay in bed plotting how to catch the rat and the slow, torturous death he would put it through.

The mouse caused the loss of precious sleep and he had had it the same as he'd had it with Kink's insufferable snoring; and doing something about those things was on his mind when he got to work. He had momentarily suppressed more important concerns so that when he picked up the ringing phone he was caught unaware.

He answered as usual, as policy dictated: "PIO, Specialist Payne speaking, sir."

His delivery was not as clean and quick as Sergeant Sterr's, but he got the string of words out, this time without tying his tongue in a knot.

He knew before the voice spoke that it was Captain Burns; he could almost smell the phosphorus of a match being sucked into a

168

pipe. The voice was a brief and firm and immediate summon to MACV.

Payne explained he would have to take the bus and would be there Asap. His alarm did not escape Sterr, who said he could get him a lift to Saigon, no problem, but Payne said he would rather take the shuttle.

He had a few extra minutes before the eight o'clock departure and, in a decisive moment of fear and panic, he went to the hootch where he removed the photograph of the slaughtered Viets from its hiding place in his locker and burned it over the wastebasket. His better judgment told him it was a mistake to destroy the picture, that it was evidence which might be important to him. But now if things got sticky he wouldn't have it to use against Willingham, and when the picture was ashes he felt better, as though in a small way he had done something right, shown some strength of character.

But it didn't help his apprehension when, an hour and a half later, he stepped into Captain Burns's drab office and found two other men with him. One was a lightbird colonel, a thin man with a fierce, anxious look. The other was in civilian clothes, a light blue seer-sucker suit and a narrow necktie. Under a flattop cut of hair was a stolid face with close gray eyes that Payne sensed had the potential to show compassion.

All three of them, however, appeared restless and agitated, as though they'd been waiting since the phone call and their patience was now exhausted. All three appraised Payne with the kind of sup-pressed contempt you would imagine of men preparing to interrogate a suspected enemy; a grim atmosphere imbued the small smoke-filled office.

Captain Burns returned Payne's salute and switched on a reel-to-reel tape recorder. "Sit down," he said, devoid of cordiality. "These gentlemen are Colonel Sayers from 6th Psychological Operations and Mr. Fouts from the Central Intelligence Agency. You will be asked some questions concerning your photographic assignment at Xuan Loc. Be advised this is for the purpose of an investigation and that what you say is being recorded."

He adjusted the microphone on his desk and noted his own pres-ence, the date, and Payne's full name and rank, which he asked Payne to confirm aloud.

The civilian started. His hands flitted about carelessly, a gesture seemingly incongruous with his stamped, mannequinlike appearance. He might have been thirty years old. "There's no reason to be nervous, Specialist," he said in a monotone. "This is only a routine interview. You'd be surprised the number of people we talk to about the most trivial matters."

He raised the corners of his mouth slightly to convey reassurance. "Now, let's get the groundwork out of the way," he said and asked several questions to establish that Payne had received prior orders from Captain Burns and that he and Willingham had in fact been to the Xuan Loc refugee camp as ordered. Payne confirmed the questions by answering the agent as he would an officer. "Yes, sir," he said repeatedly.

The lightbird colonel lit a fresh cigarette off the one he'd smoked halfway down. He continually crossed his legs. Reclining behind the desk, Burns puffed his pipe. Payne desperately wanted a cigarette.

"Now," Mr. Fouts continued, "did you have contact with a Major Vinh Loc Su, the ARVN commandant of the camp?"

"Yes, sir."

"Suppose you tell us what transpired."

"Transpired?"

The intelligence agent patiently rearranged himself on the edge of the desk. "What I mean is did he show you around the grounds, put any restriction on you? Did Willingham know the man?"

Payne's toes started to itch. He curled them inside his boots, which only made the itch worse.

"No, sir. He invited us inside his trailer for drinks—rum and Cokes I think it was, or lunch if we wanted it. We didn't have anything."

Colonel Sayers leaned forward and pointed at Payne, shaking his finger like a swagger. "We have a problem here, Specialist. Su has disappeared. As far as we can determine you and Corporal Willingham were the last of our people to see him."

Sweat began to trickle down Payne's sides under his shirt. He pulled his arms in. "Disappeared, sir?"

"That's what I said," the PsyOps officer retorted. "We have reason to presume he's dead or he's deserted, which seems unlikely. But let's get things straight here; it doesn't really matter what happened to him. Nobody much gives a damn about these ARVN advisory people anyway. Except where our people are involved. The problem is that the reports we have indicate he disappeared about the time you were at the camp. We further understand that you assaulted an ARVN guard before you left and fire was exchanged. You seem to have been in quite a hurry to get out of there. Why?"

Mr. Fouts offered Payne a cigarette, which he accepted along with a light. The familiarity of the act made Payne self-conscious of his moves.

"All we did was go in there, take some pictures of the camp, and leave. We didn't see any army equipment there."

"Then you deny that you struck the ARVN? That fire wasn't exchanged?"

Payne drew slowly on the cigarette so that he wouldn't lie too quickly; he had expected at some point to be questioned about the assignment and had already decided what he would come straight on and what he wouldn't. "No, sir. There were some guards pushing around some of the refugees at this one tent when we were leaving. I guess they were soldiers. We heard some firing. But we didn't know what the problem was, and we weren't about to stick around to find out."

The CIA man said, "You have some reason to think the men weren't ARVN personnel?"

"I guess they were. But they were sloppy and undisciplined. There didn't seem to be any formality or authority outside of the commandant."

Sayers laughed sharply. "Nothing exceptional about that."

"Let's get back to Major Su," said Mr. Fouts. "Are you certain Willingham didn't know him? Maybe he did and just didn't say. Is that possible?"

"If he knew him, he didn't tell me," Payne said convincingly. "There was no reason for me to think he did."

"All right. As close as we can ascertain, Major Su vanished at the time of your meeting with him. Do you know what became of him?"

Payne exhaled smoke through his nostrils and screwed up his face in the pretense of remembering. They might be stringing him along, but he was almost certain they did not know what had happened in the shed. If they had evidence of the body, they would have known the fingers Willingham insanely had made a necklace of were

Su's. But it seemed to Payne that even if these men did know, they didn't seem to care, and he tried to relax.

"No, sir. He showed us around the place. He didn't stay with us the whole time. I guess he had other things to do."

Burns had been sitting quietly behind his pipe. He pushed himself forward. "You gentlemen should know that some of the pictures Specialist Payne took there will appear in *Life* magazine. He also was wounded by sniper fire as a result of the assignment."

The information didn't impress Sayers. "That wouldn't have been from your hasty retreat from the camp, would it, Specialist?"

"No, sir. It wouldn't. It happened on the way there. It wasn't any big deal."

Mr. Fouts began to pace. "Suppose we move along. Are you familiar with an allied government program called Open Arms, known to the Vietnamese as Chieu Hoi?"

Payne shook his head.

"Voice your answers, Specialist," Sayers said, indicating the tape recorder.

"No, sir. I don't believe so."

"It's pretty well known," Mr. Fouts said and hesitated, as though waiting for Payne to change his mind. Payne sat quietly.

"Then I'll explain it to you. Under the program the enemy is given the chance to surrender with clemency," the agent said. "The guerrillas are paid incentive money to stop fighting and return to GVN authority, which theoretically should curtail the VC's strong hold in the countryside. So far there's been an enormous number of ralliers and both our government and the GVN claim the program is working. But the truth of the matter is it hasn't put a dent in the VC's ability to control the hamlets. Money's involved, and that creates corruption."

"Particularly with the GVN," Colonel Sayers snapped, as if to set the record straight. "These hamlet chiefs and advisers are taking large sums of money by falsifying the number of VC supposedly defecting. We can only speculate as to the magnitude of the corruption, but it's widespread and it's insidious. For some time now we've been tracing the activities of this particular ARVN commander— who, as you know, has now conveniently disappeared on us."

Mr. Fouts said, "We've linked Major Su to an excessive number of enemy defectors in Long Khanh and other provinces. The trouble is most of these people weren't defectors but refugees. Are you beginning to get the picture?"

"I'm not sure. I thought this was about missing armament."

"What's this about armament?" The agent seemed perplexed.

Captain Burns intervened. "Specialist Payne was under the impression he would be looking for stolen army ordnance. At that point I did not see any reason to involve him in the full scope of the operation."

"All right," said the agent. "You can forget about stolen armament, Specialist. We're not concerned with that. I believe Captain Burns has filled you in on Colonel Shellhammer. Is that correct?" he said. He kept his voice steady, a practiced interviewer.

Payne watched the reels turn. "Yes, sir. He mentioned him," he said, directing his voice toward the microphone. There was an edge to his voice now; he had been lied to and used, tricked, presumably as a test of his collusive reliability.

"Then you are aware that before he was assigned to Saigon Support, Willingham had been with the 5th Special Forces Group? And that he was a demolitions specialist detailed to a clandestine long-range reconnaissance outfit which Shellhammer commanded?"

Payne wagged his head sideways, grinning wolfishly. "I know what Captain Burns told me before. I didn't know Willingham had anything to do with demolitions. He hasn't talked about his previous duty. You'd think he would . . ." he said and caught himself, realizing he was making a mistake letting the anger of his emotions come out.

"Yes? Why's that?"

"Well, because," Payne stammered. "I mean, guys getting transferred to the rear from a unit like that usually like to brag. You know."

"But not Willingham."

"No, sir. He doesn't talk about it. But he's like that anyway, reserved."

They all looked at each other with long faces, sighing.

Mr. Fouts wiped his moist forehead with a handkerchief. He reached over and cut off the tape recorder. Colonel Sayers, lighting another cigarette, came to the edge of the couch.

Payne noticed there were no pictures or plaques in the room; the walls were naked, like a newly occupied room or one used only occasionally.

"So far, Specialist, you have a record you can be proud of," Mr.

Fouts said pleasantly. "Captain Burns recommends you, says you're an exemplary soldier. Your dossier supports Captain Burns. You have a wife, I believe?"

He was making it a question.

"Yes, sir."

"She seems to be politically active, what the agency terms a malcontent."

Payne frowned. "Who isn't? So what if she is?"

Raising a hand, Mr. Fouts said, "No problem. Just showing you that we have checked you out so you'll appreciate our confidence in you. You may have reservations about the war, but like you yourself just said, so what? Just about every noncareer soldier does."

He loosened his tie and patted around his collar line. He looked at Colonel Sayers, who had placed a manila folder on his lap and was looking inside it.

"You've spent some off-duty time with Corporal Willingham since his transfer," the PsyOps officer said, flipping a page. "Clubs, bars, restaurants at Long Binh and here in Saigon. Some women maybe? Having yourselves a regular R&R," he said, looking up with a sneer. "Tell me. Who's been footing the bill for all this extravagance? Willingham?"

Payne reached inside his pants for his own cigarettes, tearing the package to get at one. "I wouldn't call those things extravagant, sir. Willingham's father is a lawyer, I think. He sends him money. But I pay my own way."

"If you're that tight you must know what happened before he was transferred."

"If you mean about his squad getting wiped out, yes. But *he* didn't tell me," Payne said defensively, angrily. "Captain Burns did. I don't think I'd want to talk about that either, sir. Would you?"

Surprisingly the PsyOps officer nodded, as though agreeing with him. "He might have been decorated if it weren't for the circumstances. And it's completely within reason that a man could go a little crazy as a result, pull some stunt and get himself locked up."

Sayers had an expression on his face that might have indicated a sympathetic attitude toward Willingham; he again addressed the folder on his lap. "There aren't many incidences where our people sustain that high a percentage of casualties, and something like that can't be swept under the rug. We don't allow our personnel to just disappear like these people do."

Mr. Fouts glanced at the PsyOps officer with the slightest sign of impatience and undid the top two buttons on his shirt. He turned his attention back to Payne. He was in charge here.

"It was a stunt, a stupid one," he said in a voice meant to advise Payne. "Back to the point. Shellhammer used his lurp team to scout out potential villages and, we suspect, to intimidate civilians into defecting. Major Su was the colonel's Vietnamese contact in Long Khanh Province. Now he's missing. We think Su was terminated because he had somehow become a liability to Shellhammer. For the same reason it's not unlikely that Shellhammer was responsible for the ambush that destroyed the lurp team," the agent said, leaning close to Payne. "Think about it, Specialist. His own men. We're dealing with a dangerous individual."

Mr. Fouts finally removed his coat and draped it over the back of a chair and leaned against the desk, folding an arm across his chest; half-moons of sweat darkened the armpits of his white shirt. "You can see how important Willingham is to us in this investigation."

"Is that why you got him out of jail?" Payne said, asking only to hear them say it outright.

"He's of no value to us locked up," said Mr. Fouts. "We need to find out how the colonel works his deals, names of his other ARVN counterparts, locations of the places the defectors came from, that sort of information. Understand we're not interested in implicating Willingham, only finding out what he knows. It's going to be your job to act as our eyes and ears."

"I can't get anything out of him, Captain Burns knows that," Payne said, augmenting his objection with a sour look.

He realized immediately the stupidity of the comment and the PsyOps officer reinforced it.

"Your job, Specialist, is what we make it," Colonel Sayers said. "If we decide to let you go to Tokyo or send you to the DMZ, we'll do it. You're a soldier and you'll do what you're told."

Mr. Fouts pushed himself off the desk and walked behind Payne and caressed the back of the chair.

"You will have to admit," he said softly over Payne's shoulder, "that Willingham being at the refugee camp at the same time Su vanished is quite a coincidence. I'll assume you've been square with us here. You can see if Willingham's mixed up in it he's not going to play along with us. But you, Specialist, are in the position to find out what he knows."

Colonel Sayers rode the edge of his seat while the civilian talked. It was now his turn again, and he spelled out Payne's options more clearly. "When you're called on the next time, we're going to expect results. If you don't do as you are instructed I can personally assure you that you *and* Corporal Willingham will face serious consequences. I hope you read me."

Payne crushed the stub of his cigarette in the ashtray on Burns's desk and sat back with his eyes lowered and fixed on the floor. "Yes, sir."

With that, Captain Burns came out of his chair smiling. His smile had a crook in it from the flawed upper lip and it gave him a sinister look when Payne thought the smile was sincere. "If you've found out anything at all so far, tell us. Don't hold back," Burns said. His voice was pleading.

He waited a moment and when Payne said nothing he added, "I'll notify your lieutenant when we have another assignment for you to carry out. I don't think you have to be told what it would mean if you talked about this meeting."

This time nothing was said about rewarding him with a promotion or an early out. No deals to coax him into betrayal. This time he had been threatened.

He went straight to the bus stop and caught the next bus back to Long Binh. He went over the things they had said, how he had been lied to, the innuendo against Ann, the treachery against Willingham. Yet despite his apprehension of what was to come, he was left feeling only anger. What right did they have to put him in this position? The possibility had been suggested that Willingham was involved, and maybe he really was mixed up in the corruption, receiving money, as loosely as he had been spending it. Maybe he had assassinated Su for Shellhammer. Christ! Payne thought, maybe he had been forewarned to get out of the way when his unit was ambushed; was it possible he was in it that deep? What the hell was Payne supposed to do now?

He went straight to the office, storming through the place like a boxer at the sound of the bell. He rapped on the lieutenant's closed door and opened it and entered before Finn could say, "Enter."

"I want a transfer," Payne demanded.

Folding shut an issue of *Free Press,* Finn gave him a stare that was void of the usual boyish glaze he got when confronted by the unexpected. He pursed his lips playfully, as if restraining a burst of laughter.

Then he said, "Hmm. Why?" as if now trying to calm Payne down.

"To a different command. I don't want to be sent to another unit in ours; that won't help."

"Help what?"

"Never mind. Just get me transferred. I've had it here."

Finn grinned. He found Payne's unlikely temperament amusing. "In a hurry, huh?"

"Look, sir, I'm not going to be of any use to you anyway if I have to jump whenever those assholes from civil affairs say jump," Payne said. "You can fill my slot easily. Guys are dying to get to the rear," he added with as much sarcasm as he could command.

"So that's it. I'm the one who's supposed to get pissed off about that. What does Captain Burns want, to put you on TDY status?"

"No. But why the hell am I working for PIO if I've got to fucking answer to him whenever he wants? Yes, sir, sir. Yes, sir, your fucking highness."

Finn rocked back in his chair, still amused but acting thoughtful. "Well now, where am I going to find someone to replace my best man? Somebody to take pictures the nationals want to use? Not Langley; I see him so seldom I've forgotten what he looks like. Sergeant Sterr's rotating, can't be him. How about Willingham?" he said in a facetious tone of voice, apparently trying to humor Payne.

"I don't give a fuck. I just want moved. Get me transferred to the delta."

"Yeah. Can you imagine trooper Willingham running the paper? I'd have to make the Tokyo trip myself; wouldn't that be a shame."

Payne sighed thickly. "Sir, nobody owes anybody anything around here."

"Profound, Payne. Simply profound." The lieutenant came up in his chair. "I think it's time you took a little rest and relaxation. Didn't I promise you a three-dayer to go somewhere?"

"Yeah, to Cam Ranh," Payne said, his vehemence softening.

"To see a friend, I believe. Do it; take off tomorrow. Get yourself back together."

"All right, I will."

That helped a little, but Payne left the office the way he'd come in, in a rush. Outside he stopped at the window closest to Sterr's desk and said through it, "Sarge, can I talk to you out here a minute?"

Sterr came out. "You and the lieutenant have a little difference?"

"Can you put in the paperwork to get me a transfer? I wouldn't ask you if it weren't important."

"Want to tell me about it?"

"I can't. All I can tell you is I'm in some deep shit."

"That civil affairs officer, what's his name?"

"Yeah, and I've got to get reassigned."

"What's he got on you, Payne?"

Payne shook his head stubbornly. "Just can't say, Sarge. You want to help me out or not?"

"You know it takes a constitutional amendment to get a transfer," Sterr said gently. "It's not the thing to do right now anyway, not when the lieutenant's putting you up for Spec 5. You'd lose that if you were transferred."

"I don't give a flying fuck about promotion. I just want out of here. You can do it, Sarge. Get me to the delta."

Sterr cocked his head. "Now listen to me, Payne. You can't just run away. That never solved anything."

Payne threw up his arms in a gesture of hopelessness and left.

He was relieved Willingham wasn't there to confront; considering the state he'd worked himself into, he could easily say something he might regret.

He spent the remainder of the afternoon drinking beer and failing to make straight-in shots at pool, and after the evening rain he went to China Village and stayed until curfew. The Filipino called Rosebud wanted to know why Willingham had not been back to see her. "He good man, numbah one," she said, and Payne retorted, "Oh yeah? Bullshit." She left him to drink alone. None of the other girls bothered him either.

He kept asking himself why he hadn't just told them what he knew, that the Xuan Loc compound was a prison where people had been murdered. That there were photographs to prove it. That there was a record in Willingham's desk filled with coded names and places which had to be what they were looking for. It would have been over; he would have been out of it.

But he knew why he hadn't told them; for the same reason he had burned the incriminating photograph. It was what he didn't know that kept him from talking; he wasn't sure what Willingham's role was in this dangerous affair, but he was sure he himself had been wronged; he wanted to believe Willingham had nothing to do with it, that he had been unwittingly exploited by his ex-commander and really was tormented and haunted by the loss of his buddies. And Payne couldn't turn on him without knowing because he was sure if it were the other way around, Willingham would not turn on him.

Chapter

13

Sterr had stumbled down the corridor of Payne's hootch late in the night, drunk and worried, to inquire if he seriously wanted a transfer. Payne rubbed the sleep out of his eyes and said, "Fucking A straight," and the sergeant again tried to dissuade him. He said it was foolish, that he didn't appreciate the luck of his present assignment and the delta was no place to be; Payne poured him a shot of Scotch and listened mutely while he talked over Kink's snoring. "What is it these young hotshots say, you owe it to your body? But I could probably help you if you really want to be that dumb," Sterr said and, rising with great effort to leave, mentioned there had been reports of sporadic activity up around Cam Ranh and advised him to take along a sidearm. "Pick it up in the morning. I also took the liberty of manifesting you on a flight—Jeeze, how do you put up with that guy's noise? . . . Think it over, Payne."

At the terminal Payne found his name had not been logged in for the passenger flight, but the NCO in charge checked through the departure-arrival schedule and found a supply ship heading out shortly for Cam Ranh. Maybe they would make room for an extra body. He walked Payne outside and pointed out a Chinook. "That one. Better run."

"Thanks," Payne said and crossed the blinding concrete.

Under the huge idling rotors, Payne squinted and held down his cap against the fierce wind. He shouted at a crewman who motioned him aboard, and Payne stepped up the loading ramp. He worked his way around the load of unmarked containers and sat in the webbing by a window. He was the only passenger.

He hadn't thought to bring earplugs and had to palm his ears against the thunder of liftoff. Once airborne it was quieter and he viewed the countryside through the porthole. As Long Binh grew smaller and finally vanished from sight, he let the problems that concerned him there also fade and set his thoughts anxiously on the purpose of the trip. But there was dread mixed with his anticipation, as though he was going to a dark place where he would encounter not the man Junior Cotton but the specter of his boyhood companion. He had an inexplicable, uneasy feeling about it, like the aftereffect of a bad dream.

Explosions of white clouds dotted the sky. The paddy fields below made an elaborate chessboard of the landscape, catching the sun like cubes of shiny brown mirrors. The terrain changed quickly, reminding Payne how small this country really was. In ten minutes they were out of the first paddyland and into foothills, gliding over the lush canopied folds and ravines of a mountain range that could have been the Smoky Mountains. Farther north the land became florid and tropical, a panoramic canvas of green glittering jewelry, and Payne looked down on it reflectively as the jungles he and Cotton had dreamed of someday conquering.

He indulged himself with that thought rather than the other, remembering back to the summer of 1957, when he and Cotton had built the raft that would take them to Africa. It was the summer his father died, and Payne remembered it as being the worst and finest summer of his youth. It was an impossible, fantastic plan that he and Cotton took with great seriousness, for both had the intense, headstrong vision that accompanies the sagaciousness of ten-year-olds. To the adults they were building the raft as a joint Eagle badge project, although neither was yet a Boy Scout. The real purpose, to explore the Dark Continent and bring back riches, was kept a secret, sealed in blood by an oath, which made them blood brothers. They designed the craft after the image of Huck Finn's. The idea, Payne had believed, was his because Cotton wasn't the smart one. Cotton had the muscle, which wasn't muscle really; it was fat. But he was strong as a hoist and it was his grandmother who had the barn that was big enough to house the construction of the raft. So they became partners.

In a boy's logic the plan was simple and perfect; they would haul the giant raft down the meadow to the creek and then, when the creek rose, bottom-push it to the Arkansas River, which would get them to the Mississippi. From there it was a cinch. Payne had the trip mapped out before the first log was cut: they'd snake down the Mississippi to the calm, blue waters of the Gulf and sail along the arc of Mexico, stopping for a fiesta here and there for some good times, then on to the mouth of the Amazon where they would catch the trade winds, kick back with jugs of Kool-Aid and Hardy Boys adventure books until the great winds delivered them to the continent of Africa.

That was the way Payne planned it, economizing on supplies; but Cotton had his own ideas. He wanted to take his pillow and said they would need guns when they got there to shoot the cannibals. He wanted to ransack the diamond mines, whereas Payne suggested going after the big prize—ivory from the lost elephant burial grounds. Payne was convinced they would end up two horror-stricken skulls on sticks if they went into diamond country. But Cotton thought the burial grounds were more sacred than diamond country and there was no question that their heads would get shrunk if they invaded burial land. Consequently they had fights in the planning stages, which Cotton won by putting Payne in bear hugs and scissor locks. He got his pillow included in the list of priority items, but the booty they would steal remained an open subject.

It was June of that year that Payne's father was found dead in the office of his furniture store. His gun, a Luger, lay on the floor next to the body. The coroner determined the shot had been self-inflicted. Payne was not allowed to set foot in the small office, even after it had been scrubbed clean and the store put up for sale. He had hated his father then, after the squirrel incident, and refused to shed tears at the funeral; but he would soon regret with terrible shame his open announcement that his father's death meant nothing to him. It was a regret he never got over.

Unable to cope with the tragedy, Payne's mother had to send her two sons off for the summer and Payne was allowed to stay until school started on Cotton's grandmother's farm outside Moscow, Arkansas. Payne and Cotton had already planned out the raft and trip. But after his father died, Payne took it upon himself to modify the plans; he decided that when they departed on the voyage they would never return. Another fight ensued over that idea.

He remembered Cotton's grandmother as a generous and pleasant woman. She loved her only grandson with an intensity that extended to Payne and earned him lavish helpings of cobbler pie. She was a petite, bent woman whose teeth clacked when she smiled and whose eyes, as Payne recalled, were filmy and blue, like india ink spilled in milk.

The first few days were spent cleaning the ground floor of the neglected barn. Payne loved the smell of that barn, its earthen musk and the dead hay pollen floating in the still air, the odors of the dairy cow and mule lingering there like a part of the construction. He thought of it as a museum.

The partners quibbled over whose blisters were worse, but the fighting decreased; the first week at hard labor, they didn't fight at all.

Then the unexpected happened. Melissa showed up to throw a monkey wrench in their plans by announcing she was going on the expedition with them.

"Ha!" Payne said and stuffed a handful of creek mud down her shirt.

Melissa lived down the road. She was older by two years and taller than either boy, but too skinny to demand their respect. But she got respect after Payne went further and called her "Birdlegs," and she hit his jaw. Instead of hitting her back, Payne pouted up in the loft, wasting half a day's work.

She was back early the next day, and Cotton, grinning crazily, said, "Here comes that girl back, Henry. You better run."

"I got fifteen model ships I built myself sitting on the shelf in my room," she said proudly. "You want me to show you dummies how to saw that tree up?"

The partners understood then the trouble they were in for.

But Melissa pulled her weight, and after a week, Payne whispered to Cotton, "She's smarter'n any girl I ever saw."

"You just like her cause she's a girl," was Cotton's reply. "What are we gonna do with her in *Africa?*"

After the thunderstorms started in July, they didn't have to do as many chores because Grandy, as Cotton called his grandmother, didn't want mud in the house. They had complete afternoons to work on the raft.

If Grandy wanted to talk with the boys she did it at lunch. Melissa ate with them every day now except Wednesdays when she had to take her "got-dam pee-aner lessons," and on Sundays.

In no time Grandy became like Payne's own grandmother. Sometimes he slipped and called her by his grandmother's name, but she didn't seem to mind. She gave him a crooked, clacking smile that made him at once forget the embarrassing slip.

Grandy didn't talk much, so what she said stuck on Payne's mind. One day when Melissa wasn't there for lunch, she said, "That little Melissa ain't so tough as she carries on. She's still a girl and you boys have got to look after her."

Payne didn't understand what she meant until Cotton told him that his daddy almost drowned once when the creek rose, which it was doing now. "Grandy's a worrywart," he said. "My pa could take care of himself."

The comment struck Payne the wrong way and he ran up to the loft. All afternoon, while it rained and the thunder echoed through the darkened barn, he hid in the hay and cried. He wouldn't come down until Grandy came out to the barn with an overcoat over her head and called him down for supper. She sat beside him on the bed that night and put her frail arm around him, saying nothing, just holding him and rocking as if they were in a rocking chair. He felt even sadder and cried even harder feeling her bony chest and thin-skinned hand against his face.

After the hull was finished, the partners had a discussion and felt it would be all right to get the mule and haul it down to the creek for a test float. When they told Melissa she got carried away and started jumping up and down; her enthusiasm rubbed off on Cotton and excited him so much he couldn't eat his lunch. After some blackberry pie, they did it. The hull of the raft was ten feet by ten feet and weighed a ton. But the creek was high enough to support its size, and it floated.

Cotton told Payne to go back up to the house and get the rifle. Payne took his .22 out of the closet and, not knowing if he would ever return, sidled over to the sink and put his arms around the old woman.

"My, my. What on earth?" she said, and hugged him with wet hands.

Then she said a strange thing. She held him at arm's length and took her time wiping something off the corner of his mouth. By the look in her milky eyes she seemed to know the partners were on the threshold of becoming heroes in the jungles of Africa.

"Listen to me, son," she said. "When things look the darkest, there's nothing more important to a body than having a friend at your side. You remember that always, you hear me?"

Payne didn't know what she was talking about, but he nodded anyway.

She took a long breath and put her hands together as if about to applaud something in her thoughts. "I was thinking of letting you boys drive the car out on the road come Sunday. Think you can reach the pedals?"

"Yeah!" Payne said and hiccuped. He tried to think up some more words to say but he couldn't get anything different to come out, so he said, "Yeah!" again and banged the screen door. He ran through the wildflowers, getting slapped in the face by giant sunflowers. By the time he reached Cotton, his hiccups were coming like heartbeats.

"Guess what," he shouted at Cotton, who was standing on the tied up hull like George Washington.

"Where's the gun?" Cotton said.

"Grandy's gonna let us *drive*."

"I already know how. Besides, we don't have time now."

"Not now, idiot. Sunday."

Melissa wanted to learn too. "All right," Payne said, "but you're after me."

Grandy was good for her word, and Payne learned a little about driving an automobile on Sunday. He learned a lot that summer; after panicking in reverse gear and denting the bumper on the front-yard tree, he learned it took a great deal of practice to drive an automobile, just as it would take to navigate a raft; the partners hadn't taken into consideration the narrow culvert the raft would have to clear just a hundred feet downstream.

He learned that Grandy was right about the meaning of friendship, too, for the loss in his family was softened and partially replenished by the comfort from another family that he would go back to in his mind for many years to come. The dream of someday conquering jungles had not slipped away either, only the fulfillment of it had.

The sea came into view at an angle. There was a haze over the green water that turned the destroyers anchored offshore into ghost ships. Along the horizon a formation of silhouetted gunships migrated northward, gradually pulling into the shape of an arrowhead. The zigzagging coastline as far as Payne could see was Florida white, and as the chopper leaned into its steep combat descent, a city of shiny corrugated rooftops flashed in the sun.

As a showpiece of American ingenuity, Cam Ranh Bay outdid Long Binh. It took the Army Corps of Engineers and Seabees only a year of wielding their great mechanical arms to erect out of a mosquito-infested sandpit one of the greatest harbors in the Orient. As many as twelve freighters at a time could dock in the harbor and the dual ten-thousand-foot runways accommodated the military's largest transport aircraft, the C-5A, which delivered and retrograded the Army's great burden of warfare machinery.

Cam Ranh was also the major terminal point for incoming and outgoing U.S. personnel, mixing hardened veterans and bewildered replacements, both of whom spent their first and final days suspended in a numb limbo at the turnstile of an uncertain future.

It was here that Payne had stepped off a wide-bodied jet eight months before and choked on the blast of oven heat, his knees weak with a case of the nerves.

As the helicopter touched down heavily, toppling smaller boxes and rearranging Payne's insides, a sense of *déjà vu* seized him, the vacuous, gut-heavy feeling of again being alone on the brink of the unknown. Only now the reason was different. Cotton would not be the same person he had known, and what was he going to say to him? Would he gawk at him after seeing how much weight he had lost? How would his boyhood partner react to him, a fucking REMF? He did not even know if he would still be in the hospital.

He shook the thoughts, thanked the crewman, and made a dash under the waning whirlwind. It was ten degrees hotter here than at Long Binh and more humid. Mosquitoes attacked him immediately.

Through the roar and hiss of airport noise he thought he heard a faint pop, like that of a distant grenade or mortar, and he scanned the rising mountains that lay just inland. He guessed it was his imagination, for the sloping hillsides appeared tranquil with nothing to indicate any kind of ordnance.

The chopper had landed near the main processing station, Vietnam's Grand Central Station. As he entered the huge hangar Payne's guts began to rumble as if from a sudden viral attack. A thousand uniformed men loitered on the vast floor, waiting nervously. A simple red stripe across the floor divided the men heading to Oakland and home from those heading inland to points unknown. Considering the number of men, the place was extraordinarily hushed. Pink-faced cherries whispered among themselves while gawking across the red line at the dark figures waiting solemnly to depart.

A processing clerk told Payne there were two hospitals; the one he wanted was across post adjacent to the perimeter. The churning in his stomach turned to quick, sharp pains and he found a bathroom on the veterans' side of the terminal and closed the door of a booth. The voices in the bathroom suddenly stopped and someone rapped on the toilet door.

"Yo, cherry. Don't let it get to you, man," a voice called. "This only your intro."

"Sound like he done already got the pucker factor," said another.

"Welcome to Nam, babycakes."

There was some forced laughter.

Payne waited until the shuffling of boots faded and the outer door shut and then he left.

He walked quickly under the rising heat, taking a plywood cat-walk next to the mud road. The inland side of the road was flanked by a wall of sandbags and concertina wire, and beyond that by bright ore-red sandbars where stagnating saltwater pools swarmed with armies of mosquitoes.

He walked past boys with clean white faces and quick, searching eyes that took in every moving thing as if it were a sniper. Their nerves overwrought, some of them stepped off into the mud to allow a man wearing a holstered gun the right of way. A few disconcerted troops saluted and Payne returned the salutes nonchalantly, trying to both acknowledge and discourage the formality. He felt empathy for the new soldier, a man on the eve of his tour whose disoriented nervousness had reduced him to cowering behavior out of his awed sense of expectation.

The *déjà vu* hit him the strongest observing the new guy; the recollection was as lucid as if he himself had just arrived in-country. The newness didn't bother Payne now, but he remembered how you would jump like a cat at the whump of helicopters and hold your breath in the shitters. The new guy would assimilate and adjust quickly, but those first days he would suffer an unrelenting dizziness from realizing this was it, that he was actually in Vietnam. He was already familiar with the names of places—Hue, Pleiku, Danang, the DMZ—and the names drew mental images he tried to suppress but could not. He listened in a state of horrific expectancy as weary combat vets spoke of firefights, napalm, body bags, children with grenades, of taking body parts for souvenirs, of raping village gooks and fragging officers. He wondered if it were all really true; he wondered if he would become like that, if he would be sent to one of those places that made the news or somewhere unknown that would become a place in the news when he got there. He wondered if he would become one of the numbers in the weekly death count, ten thousand dollars to his folks.

When he reached the hospital Payne was sweating heavily. The hot air had him panting for breath as though he'd run all the way.

The wings of the octopuslike hospital stretched from the main body like huge gray arms, its closest wing almost touching the perimeter. Beyond a narrow clearing outside the fence rose foothills of virgin terrain, a natural cover where the enemy could easily hide. High guard towers interrupted the fence at hundred-meter intervals; one of them would be the view through his window Cotton had written about. Payne entered under an elongated awning. An MP stood aloofly at parade rest at the door, his glazed stare appearing to register nothing of this world.

The water, from a fountain, was ice cold. After taking a long drink he held his wrists under the fountain to cool down his blood. The heavyset nurse at the front desk could have been a female wrestler, but when she inquired, "Can I help you, Specialist?" the unexpected soft feminine lilt of her voice drew a blush from Payne.

As he talked the nurse traced a red fingernail down a roster of names and said the person Payne wanted was in ICU, second wing down the corridor. That Cotton was still here struck Payne ironically, with conflicting emotions; he didn't know whether it was good or bad.

"Can you tell me his condition?"

She dropped her eyes and nodded. "He's in ICU," she said in answer. "The duty nurse can tell you more. If you want to get him a book or something, there's a PX next door."

Payne smiled, showing her the worn copy of *Huckleberry Finn* he'd brought. "This one ought to do the trick."

A sudden concussion shook the lobby, breaking a window and sending a tremor along the floor. The nurse gasped and put a hand to her throat.

"What is it?" Payne said, searching the lobby.

He followed the nurse's eyes to the MP who had planted himself in a wide crouching stance directly in front of the door, as though he could single-handedly defend the hospital.

"I'll show you to the shelter," the nurse said calmly.

"Is this common?"

"It happens, nothing to worry about."

He followed her through a pair of swinging doors. There was a commotion in the hallway where patients were leaving rooms. Someone inadvertently kicked the crutch from underneath a man who was watching the activity from a doorway and he took a fall in front of Payne. His leg had been amputated above the knee and the stub protruded through a rolled-up pajama leg. Crisscrossing lines of black sutures, like columns of marching ants, held his discolored face together. Payne took hold of him under the arms, trying to get him to stand, but the man wouldn't help. He gathered himself in a sitting position in the door frame and tucked his good leg under the stub. "Get lost," he said, pushing at Payne with the crutch.

Payne moved on, turning back once to look at the slumping figure. The man covered his face with both hands.

He'd lost the nurse but followed the flow along the hall. Another explosion hit somewhere, its shock rattling the corridor, and the traffic quickened. A siren began to wail. He checked the faces of the few white men in bedclothes and looked closely at those on gurneys. Even if he saw Cotton he didn't know if he would recognize him, except possibly for his red hair.

A man in a body cast bumped Payne rushing through a door marked "Intensive Care Unit." The man coughed painfully from the gray smoke spilling through the door after him.

"Is a guy named Cotton in there, do you know?" Payne shouted above the siren.

"Yeah. Maybe, I don't know," the man said, ambling on under the awkward cage of his cast.

Payne went through the door; it was dim and tunnel-like. Out of the smoke a charging gurney materialized, grazing Payne's side. It carried a black man whose eyes were shut, his face loose and placid.

Coughing, the attendant barked, "Get Ten C. We've still got one in there."

Payne read room numbers—"6-C," "8-C"—glancing inside and finding empty beds with IVs left dangling. Something loud and hard like sudden decompression bolted him against the wall and pinlights danced in the dark.

When his eyes opened he saw the blur of cream-colored linoleum, an acrid odor blistering the membranes in his nostrils. There was a lump on his forehead where the floor had taken his fall.

He rose, wobbly. The siren had changed to the short bursts of a ship's battle-station alarm, and between blares he heard sputtering clips of machine-gun fire. The door to 10-C was shut; he pushed it open and stepped into a furnace.

Small flames and smoke curled through a gaping hole in the outer wall. Fingers of yellow fire licked at two beds, one of them made tight as a basic training bunk. The occupant of the other bed lay in a cataleptic curl on the floor. Blood had formed in a small pool under him. Tubes running from the man's nose and both arms were drawn taut from their overturned sources. Payne knew it was Cotton without seeing the man's face; it was a white man with dark red hair. The color of his hair had not changed.

"Junior! Fuck, man."

Payne tore a piece of curtain not yet on fire and covered the body, then jerked the IVs from the broken bottles. He thought at first Cotton was dead, but his arms moved, and Payne lifted him quickly and carried him through the hole in the wall like a man carrying his bride. He seemed light, but that was the adrenaline.

Laying him on the grassy sand and pulling the cloth off his face, Payne traced a finger along Cotton's cheek to the scar on his upper lip. He couldn't feel the scar under the whiskers, but he knew it was there.

Once in junior high Payne had gotten so angry at Cotton he threw a punch at him. It only skimmed his neck, but the intent infuriated Cotton and he chased Payne across backyards in the semidarkness of dusk. Payne could run like an animal and he led Cotton, teasing him with come-ons, then running off again. The angrier Cotton became the louder Payne laughed. Knowing it was a vicious thing to do, he led Cotton through a yard with a low clothesline and turned beguilingly to watch Cotton's feet fly out from under him.

One of Cotton's eyes opened partially in a flutter as if he were winking at Payne, as though to tell him, "That was kid stuff, Henry, don't sweat it."

Payne put a hand at the nape of Cotton's neck. The blood covering his chest glistened in the sunlight. There was nothing now of the dark and unknown he had dreaded confronting.

"Junior? Damn it, can you hear me?" he said, watching Cotton's eye close again. "Look at you, man. I've got to do something for you. Junior!"

Cotton lifted a hand to the back of Payne's neck, pulling him close. It was a powerful grip.

He whispered with a painful grimace, "Buddy. Oh shit." Then the grip eased and the hand went limp again.

Payne got up and looked around expectantly, as though looking for someone to tell him what to do. He saw movement in the roll of ground wire and ran that way. A boy was tangled in the wire, half naked and bleeding from barb snags. His porcupine hair stood on end like magnetized metal filings. The boy saw Payne pull out his gun and tried to scramble, cutting himself more on the barbs. Payne chambered the .45 and flipped the safety, taking aim at the sapper's head. The gun shook in his hand, and as easily as it would have been he could not squeeze the trigger.

Footsteps pounded close by and someone shouted, "Do him. Shoot the motherfucker!"

For a moment there was no sound at all, then a babble of fire hammered Payne's ear. The voice next to him followed: "That's one motherfuck ain't no more. You better get on out of here."

Payne turned away without looking in the wire.

An orderly was extinguishing the fire in the room. Payne asked if Cotton was going to make it. The orderly didn't know; he had been taken to an OR.

Payne opened a drawer next to the smoldering bed. The letter he had written was there along with other letters, from Cotton's wife, another marine. He studied the snapshot of his wife and the kid. Judy was a plain-faced and kind-looking woman with an eager smile; the boy on her lap smiled too, at something to the side of the camera. The boy might have been two. He had amber-red hair like his father.

In the corridor patients talked about the attack. Just a diversion, they'll hit the airport next. Nah, the supply depot. Fuck you say, they'll hit us again. Fucking dinks love blowing hospitals. They all agreed they'd seen worse.

No bunker call had been announced, even though the sirens wailed into the late afternoon. Payne waited at the bar close to the hospital. Every thirty minutes he walked over to inquire about Cotton. At dusk the sky turned into a flaming blood-colored vista. The nursing staff had changed. The new desk attendant could say only that Cotton was still in the operating room. At least he hadn't died.

When next he asked the nurse and she told him Cotton had expired, that she was sorry, Payne took the first ride he could get and left Cam Ranh. The supply convoy was heading thirty clicks north to Nha Trang. He rode in a jeep. The major at the wheel wanted to know what business Payne had in Nha Trang and Payne answered him sarcastically, "Army business."

At one point the major tried to console Payne. "People die in war, soldier. You get used to it."

It was late when the convoy arrived. Payne got out short of the compound and went into the town. He wandered around dimly lit streets that smelled of stale bars and rotten fish. It was the same everywhere in Vietnam—stacked sandbags and rolled wire, litter strewn in mud streets, the odor of rot. It was a poor, filthy country of pint-size people who had bad teeth and wore bedclothes, who shouted at you in excited, grating voices. Incomprehensible people. He was sick of it.

He had no business here, only time to kill. A sudden flash of yellow lit up the far end of the alley he'd strayed into and the aftershock jarred him, putting a tic in his eye. It was happening here too.

He listened for the whistle announcing the next hit, but it was too far away and he felt only the concussion. The clamor on the street turned into a panic, people in black pajamas scurrying aimlessly like a rush of startled cockroaches.

An MP grabbed a piece of his shirt. "Get off the street, soldier. Get back to your unit on the double. We're under attack."

Extended beads of automatic fire erupted a few blocks away and the MP dashed off in that direction. Payne backed into the metal netting of a closed shop and searched the abandoned street with quick, nervous eyes, drawing a blank and wondering what to do.

Across the street was a dilapidated hotel. He spotted a girl in the shadowed doorway, hiding like a cat as if she were unused to the buckle of in-coming. Seeing him she turned to display her breasts, her assets, and he cautiously crossed the street.

A mamasan seized his arm and pointed excitedly at the watch on his wrist. "Curfew!" she hollered, as if to assure him that was all he had to worry about. She took hold of his hand and placed it on the girl's breast.

"You come in. You safe here." The mamasan's grin exposed black teeth from a lifetime of betel.

She took the modest wad of money from his hand, searched his face, then pushed two of the bills back into his shirt pocket. "You numbah one GI, you."

She bolted the door behind them and turned out the foyer light.

He followed the girl three flights up. In the room Payne stood by the window where the air was hot, staring vacantly into a spotted orange horizon that shifted colors on his face. Fires rose on inlets from the sea.

The girl yakked with a dried-up man in the hallway and shut the door soundlessly. She became businesslike now. Payne expected that. She chattered as though he understood her talk.

She might have been thirteen or ten, a child who should have been snuggling a teddy bear and dreaming quixotic things. He both envied and hated her youth, and took a kind of sadistic, spiteful pleasure in knowing this whore had never had a childhood.

He sat her on his lap facing him and studied her face as though it were a painting. She glared fearfully at the blood on his shirt. When he took it off she made a smile appear. Her teeth were not yet ruined.

Payne touched her cheeks and let his hands slip along her slender shoulders and down the slight arms to her hands. Her tiny hands disappeared in his. As he unbuttoned her blouse and pulled it aside, the girl lowered her eyes. He thought her utterance was a giggle.

Thunder bolted through the room, causing her to shiver and tilt her head quizzically, as if she did not comprehend Payne's indifference. She began talking again in a hyper voice. Payne put a finger to her lips, then covered her mouth with his and ran hungry fingers through the black silk of her hair. Her breath was hot, a little sour.

She was a whore because of her woman's breasts; Americans liked tits. The points of them had already turned leathery. He bit down on a nipple and squeezed under her armpits lifting her. She gave a screech and twitched, offering a make-believe moan of pleasure.

His teeth were set on edge as he laid her down on the slab of wood and stripped off her blacks. Her eyes, following his hands as he undressed himself, pretended to know desire, flaring slightly at his erection. He pressed a hand between her legs and watched her writhe as though in pain or ecstasy, throwing her arms out.

He stood over her a moment, letting her fake magic work, then rolled her over on her stomach and pinched the small buttocks in one hand and let saliva drip there. Holding her under his knees, he forced his way. She thrashed angrily and violently trying to resist, but she was powerless against him. Her screams were smothered in his large hand.

When he let her up she dressed silently, trembling, and left the room. He gave her what was left of his money and his watch, but it didn't change the ambivalent sense of shame and satisfaction he felt.

Thick, soiled air hung in plateaus, and bits of plaster crumbled from the ceiling. He crouched in a corner and watched a cockroach race up the far wall, as if rushing from the incomprehensible, evil thing that Payne had become.

The old man burst in shouting at the top of his tiny lungs. Payne understood his rage. Payne waved his gun. *"Du ma,* motherfucker," he said. "Get the fuck out of here."

After dressing he stood by the window again and watched the sampans burn on the water. Fire was spreading from shacks to buildings, and the street below was choked with buglike people and pedicabs and canvased trucks. He saw an MP collar and push a running man to the ground and shoot him through the head. Payne dropped to his knees and vomited on the floor.

He lay on the slab bed listening to the sirens wail and the diminishing bursts of fire. There was a single picture hanging askew on the wall across from the bed. The picture was an etched print of peasants in a paddy field, all of them bent in the labor of work, their hands and feet lost in the water, their pajamas rolled up to the knee. He sighted the .45 at a peasant in the picture and fired.

Chapter
14

"We get this kinda shit on occasion, don't mean nothing," the driver said. He was a talker. "Less you get casualties, 'course. Like the man say, let 'em blow theirse'ves back to the Stone Age, if that ain't 'bout where they is now. You know? Fuck 'em. I mean, man, they don't need us helping 'em; they been doin a pretty good job wiping theirse'ves out long before we got here. Who gives a fuck these dinks destroy their own temples and shit anyways?"

"Yeah," said Payne, "who gives a fuck."

The driver said to call him Fleet, the nickname that stuck from all the raving he did about the Fleetwood convertible he left in the care of a buddy back in Jersey. "Sho' do miss that vinyl wide body. And that sweet Rosie spreadeagled in the backseat. Know what I mean?" Yeah, Payne knew—knew his buddy was taking care of Rosie in the backseat.

Fleet said he had big plans of making it as an independent in the interstate trucking business back in the world. He was on a short-timer's high. "I be ready, man," he said. *This* experience behind me, I would haul fuckin nitro, no questions asked. The mafioso got the industry tied up in knots back there, but I don't have no 'tentions of lettin' that bother me none. I aim to correct it. You know?"

Payne listened to his prattle part of the time and occasionally nodded.

He was not ready to face things back at Long Binh and had

hitched on with the convoy out of Nha Trang. The convoy was going to Bien Hoa, a few miles from Long Binh. Fleet's fourteen-wheel flatbed was the fourth vehicle in the ten-truck caravan, each hauling three sections of huge concrete conduits. The haul was two hundred miles and took three days. They spent the first two nights on the side of the road and bivouacked the last night inside an ARVN compound near Ham Tan. Payne slept with the mosquitoes in the cab of Fleet's truck all three nights.

From an operations officer at Nha Trang he had learned that an NVA sapper outfit staged the attack to coincide with the harassment at Cam Ranh. The enemy body count totaled only five from both the town and base, no VC and no American casualties reported. He wondered why the man he'd seen the MP shoot wasn't counted as VC. He wondered why Cotton had not been added to the casualty stats of Cam Ranh.

Payne left the convoy at the north gate of Long Binh. He thanked the driver for the ride and wished him success back home.

"Ever get on the turnpike, look for the red Peterbilt that say Ramblin' Rose on the door. That be me, man. Maybe you find me cruisin' them Texas highways some day, never know. Maybe then I call her the Yeller Rose. Be cool, Tex."

Payne walked the three clicks to the Stretch. Long Binh seemed strange and distant, like a place out of the past. He hadn't bathed or shaved in four days, and when he checked in at the IO everyone but Willingham gawked as if he were in fact a stranger. Willingham slapped his dusty back with lofty regard.

The lieutenant was incredulous.

After the initial shock he said, "You've been AWOL since O-seven-hundred yesterday. What do you have to say for yourself."

Payne shrugged. "Guess this means movie privileges." He sat down and lit a cigarette and released a plume of smoke over the desk.

"Look at you. You *smell*, for Christ's sake. Where have you been?"

Payne dumped an ash in his hand, then blew it on the lieutenant's floor. "Had to bum a lift with a convoy. Ever been up Highway One, sir? Runs along the sea much of the time, beautiful scenery."

"Damn it, Payne. What's the matter with you? You could have at least called; you've always called before when you got delayed."

Payne's sigh turned visible with smoke. He lifted himself out of the chair, suddenly disgusted having to look at Finn. "Is that about it, Lieutenant?"

Finn squeezed his eyes. "I haven't reported you yet; I'm going to let it go this time. Would you mind putting that cigarette out, it's burning my eyes."

Payne crushed the cigarette under his boot. Finn watched him with a look suggesting he too was disgusted. "You're scheduled to get your medal in Colonel Whitson's office in an hour. Get yourself cleaned up first," he said. "Dismissed."

Before leaving the office Payne asked Sterr, "Where'd Willie get away to?"

"Said he was going to lunch and then to the morgue to do a story," Sterr said and read the question on Payne's face. "Don't ask me. With him you never know what's going on."

Payne nodded agreeably.

"But you've got to give him credit," Sterr added. "He sure knows how to push the lieutenant's button. The lad seems to be getting his shit together."

"Glad to hear it," Payne commented indifferently, not trusting himself to pursue the subject with Sterr.

"Did you think it over?" Sterr said. He could see Payne did not know what he meant. "This notion of getting transferred."

"I haven't thought about it."

"Well, when you make up your mind, young Payne, let me know," he said, exaggerating his tone with benign sarcasm.

Clean-shaven in crisp fatigues, Payne stood at attention as Colonel Whitson presented him with the blue leather box containing a plastic bust of George Washington. Cowboy took pictures of the handshake. Payne stared grimly at the floor while Colonel Whitson read from the citation how in the line of duty Specialist 4 Russell H. Payne, after sustaining a wound by sniper fire, distinguished himself conspicuously by protecting his comrade and defending U.S. government property without regard to his own personal safety and so forth. The citation read like a medal for bravery; it was a false, glorified account of what had actually happened. Payne wondered about the guy who wrote the citation up; what kind of job would that be?

During the short, informal ceremony he tried to imagine Ann's reaction seeing his picture in the newspaper, reading the paragraph or two attesting to his heroics and injury. But he couldn't bring forth a picture of Ann; the image that came to him was Cotton's wife at the graveside, listening to another string of meaningless words. But those words would count.

Outside he tossed the medal up and down in his palm. It felt heavier than it was. He walked with Cowboy across the quadrangle back to the office.

"Is it true what he said about you shielding Willie and that other stuff?" Cowboy asked gullibly.

"You write up the release, then it'll be true."

Payne laid the medal on Sterr's desk. "I don't know what to do with this, Sarge. Why don't you take it for a souvenir."

Sterr pushed it away. You could tell he had stayed sober last night, perhaps even for a couple of nights. "Keep it."

"I didn't earn it."

"Yes, you did. Someday, when people change their minds, and they will, it'll be something to show your children, something you'll be proud of."

Payne laughed at the idea. "I doubt it, Sarge," he said. Sterr, he decided, was out in left field, but he nevertheless dropped the PH in the depleted contingency-fund tin; it might buy him a little respect from Ann, if he decided to tell her.

He looked for Willingham in the messhall, which was cleared out and being cleaned up. The smell of roast beef in the ovens aroused his somnolent appetite. It was amazing, thinking about it, how often lately he had found himself hungry. Missed meals. Sometimes going without eating all day and not remembering it. That was the kicker, not remembering he was hungry. He hustled a gook KP for an apple and orange and ate them on his way to the morgue.

A dustoff sat on the heliport outside the hospital annex; heat waves rose off the turbines. Payne stole a look inside it. It hadn't yet been hosed down. Blood was slung across the fuselage and firewall and a syrup-thick puddle on the deck was still wet. The puddle of blood didn't put off the odor he thought it would. A piece of flesh the size of a hamburger patty was stuck to the floor grating as if seared to a grill. Neither did it have a smell.

There were other guys he knew from back home who were somewhere in the Nam, and now it seemed important that he know where they were and what had happened to them. Maybe one or two of his other high school pals had bought it; maybe their remains were inside this morgue right now waiting to be sent home.

No one was around; the ghoolies, the guys whose job it was unloading the medevacs, had taken the wounded troops into the hospital or inside the refrigerated coolers in the annex, those men who hadn't made it.

Admissions & Dispositions and Graves Registration were housed together in a rectangle of joined boxcars. Whitewashed rocks marked the walkway to the entrance. A youthful Spec 4 with wavy blond hair stopped Payne abruptly as he stepped inside, informing him officiously that the morgue was restricted.

Payne pulled out his press credentials and said he was looking for a tall guy, another journalist, doing a feature story on the place. "He probably has a camera. Name's Willingham, you seen him?"

The Spec 4 changed faces. "Oh, you mean the guy from the *Stars & Stripes*. You with him?"

"That's right, he here?"

"He's with Sergeant Zielinski. C'mon. I'll show you."

Payne followed him along a narrow hallway where gurneys stained with various shades of red and brown were shoved against the walls between cooler doors.

"You guys doing an article for the *Stripes*, huh?" the blond kid said, looking back as he walked and shaking his head. "Crazy, man. I could tell you plenty stuff you wouldn't want to write about. The shit goes on in here, comes in some of these bags—it ain't all bodies, I can tell you that. Check this out," he said, stopping in front of a cooler.

He depressed a lever and the heavy refrigerator door swung open on a narrow compartment fashioned after bunking quarters in a submarine, dimly lit by an overhead mesh-wire light with about twenty-five watts of glow. There were eight bags, four on each side, laid out on aluminum-slab tiers. Payne stood off to the side, respectful of where he was.

The Specialist wiped his hands meticulously on the backside of his fatigues, then unzipped a bag on the third tier down. He opened the bag to the point where knees would be and spread the flaps.

"Fucking marines," he said approvingly. "You gotta hand it to them, they got imagination. Neanderthals all of them, but they sure can come up with some clever shit. Check it out."

With delicate fingers he lifted for Payne's inspection a pink, hairless scrotum containing a pair of huge testes. The scrotum was the size of a football.

"Mountain oysters!" the youth cried and laughed as if he still couldn't believe it himself. "Dig it. The fucker got his groin blown away—here, take a closer look," he said, jerking the body bag roughly against the unyielding chunk of body. Most of both legs were gone too. "So his buddies threw in these pig balls, just to drive us up the wall."

Looking at what was left of the man, Payne flinched, his stomach rising. He pictured some farm boy from the Ozarks running through a burned-out village after a squealing pig and then cutting it. His squad would have gotten a big kick out of stuffing the balls in the body bag of a dead comrade. He could picture their sweaty faces, aglow and wild-eyed with the kind of perverse madness they needed to keep from going insane.

"How come they're bringing marines here?" Payne wanted to know. He had backed up to the door unable to stomach the sight any longer.

"There's been some pretty heavy shit up around Cambodia lately, along Uncle Ho's trail. A lot of Neanderthals are working the bush around there, part of the First Division. Least that's what this latest shipment was," he said. "Third Field's too crowded to take them. And we have the facilities to handle the overload. We've got the lowest consistent cooler temp anywhere in the Nam, right here on Long Binh." The ghoolie wanted to be quoted.

Willingham appeared and stepped around Payne, poised his camera, and said, "Here, let's get a shot of that. Just grip them nuts and grin."

The blond kid quickly replaced the scrotum in the body bag and zipped it closed; the sound of the zipper traveling over the hunk of meat had a finality about it that sickened Payne.

The kid turned out the light, crowding them to shut the compartment. "Afraid that's unauthorized," he said, trying to make his voice authoritative.

In the hallway Willingham turned to Payne. "Must've been one helluva trip, judging from your looks."

Payne sloughed it off with a shrug.

"So, you looking for me or what?"

"No. I come here after lunch every chance I get," Payne replied.

Outside he said, "What'd you tell them you were with the *Stripes* for?"

"To get in, why else."

"I could figure that. But what'd you want at the fucking morgue?"

"To see where all these jarheads have been coming from. And I was right."

"You've got a perverse sense of curiosity."

"Just learning how to be a journalist," Willingham said through his horse grin. He looked healthy, in good spirits. He wasn't wearing his Die High boonie hat. His hair was cut above the ears and his skin was tanned evenly. He had the look of a rear soldier, even studious, as if he really was coming around, conforming. It made it harder for Payne to broach the subject.

"What do you make of that, those pig balls in the bag?" Payne said.

"The guy wasn't liked very much," Willingham said. "Some of your primitive Indians'll do that with their dead. It's a ceremonial rite. They bury animal parts with the dead or string the entrails in trees. The rites can go either way, be honorable or dishonorable, sacrilegious, depending on what kind of animal and what part of its body goes in the grave. Burying the person with pig balls ain't exactly complimentary to him in the everafter. If that marine dude had been an Indian, his soul would be damned with shame and his family disgraced forever. His squad knew that. He must of made some enemies. . . . So what'd you want to see me about?"

Payne put him off with another shrug; he was going to confront him; he'd set his mind to it. But it was harder than he thought to get it out.

As they walked toward the office, he said evasively, "I hear you and the lieutenant are getting to be regular bosom buddies. You trying to brownnose him into something? Going to Tokyo in my place, maybe?"

Willingham dropped the pleasantness in his expression. "What the fuck's that supposed to mean?"

"I don't know," Payne said. "Just trying to figure you out. Where's your boonie hat?"

Willingham stopped him. "Listen, Payne. I'm not going behind your back. You can get off that shit right now."

They reached the lawn at command headquarters and walked across the quadrangle. Payne hesitated, said, "Wait a minute." He felt suddenly weak, wanting to be swimming underwater or in bed with the covers pulled tight.

"You know what I did," he said. He was looking at the ground. "I turned in some guys for shooting a buffalo. I did that; turned in my own people."

"No shit," Willingham said satirically. "Well, hell, that wasn't very nice of you."

"Those guys were just letting out their frustrations. Like Bruiser said, they were only letting go."

It didn't interest Willingham; he started to walk inside. Payne stopped him.

"That happened six months ago, when I didn't know anything. I shouldn't have done it. It was none of my business."

A couple of officers passed along the sidewalk and Payne gave a halfhearted salute. Willingham, leaning against the jeep, didn't seem to notice them.

"Something went down in Cam Ranh. What was it?"

"It's not that."

"Who you trying to kid? I can look at you and know something happened. What was it?"

Payne felt a deep sense of shame telling him about the attack and Cotton and the sapper in the wire. "I was close as I am to you to the dink that killed him. Somebody else had to shoot him; I couldn't. You would've."

"I wasn't there. You probably did the right thing in your mind. You got nothing to be ashamed of."

"How many men have you killed?" Payne said, breathing hard, working into it.

Willingham slid into the jeep, his look flat and unrevealing. "That's history. Doesn't matter now."

"It matters to me. I want to know about the lurp team. I want to know why you were ambushed."

Willingham stared at him a moment. "You already know about it. Let it go."

Payne took a couple of steps fumbling with a smoke, trying to collect himself. "You told me that gook major did it. And you wasted him for payback. Yeah, I know that. What I want to know is why the squad was ambushed. Was Shellhammer behind it?"

"What?"

"I have to know, Willie. Was it planned for you to be the only guy to make it out?"

That got the delayed reaction Payne was expecting; a swift hand seized his throat, powerful steel fingers, like Cotton's.

"What are you fucking insinuating?" Willingham hissed.

Payne couldn't break the grip with both his hands. He had to kick off the jeep to free himself. "Fuck you, man. I could have already turned you in. But I haven't."

Willingham settled back in the driver's seat. He slumped in it and started playing with his gold-plated pen.

Payne rubbed his neck. "I'm not fucking around with you. Tell me if you're mixed up in it."

Willingham eyed him thoughtfully, with derision. "Mixed up in what?"

"Did Shellhammer go on the missions with you, the illegal ones? The team was illegal, wasn't it?"

"No," said Willingham. "The squad was unauthorized, not illegal. There's lots of outfits like ours working for the CIA in counterintelligence and shit. You just never hear about them."

"Your team worked for the CIA?"

"Could have been, I don't know," Willingham said. "We wouldn't have known if we were. Special Forces has *beaucoup* units that pull jobs for them. We got our orders from Shell; we didn't know what the missions were for. We were never told and we never asked."

"Could he have been using the squad for something illegal without you knowing it? Like getting civilian head counts so he could claim them as enemy defectors?"

"Where the fuck you come up with these ideas, Payne? Shell's tough and he may be a little too gung ho, but he's as straight as they come."

"As fucking crooked as they come."

"You better tell me what in hell you're driving at, Payne."

"He's been documenting civilians as Chieu Hoi ralliers. Your squad collected the data and he falsified the records and took the money they're supposed to get for defecting. Did you know that?"

"The fuck you say."

Willingham came out of the jeep again. Payne thought he was

going to take a swing at him and he backed up. "Think about it, Willie. Why were you ambushed? You think it was just a coincidence you were on one of Shellhammer's missions? That gook Su worked the other side; he split the money with Shellhammer. They were in business together. If your outfit was set up, it had to be Shellhammer who was behind it. Can't you see that, man?"

Willingham ran his hand along the fender, innocuously scraping off particles of dried mud. The edges of his face were set hard.

"I don't see how."

"They said you wouldn't believe it," Payne said. "They were right."

"They who?"

"The fucking CIA. I'm working for them. I'm the goddamn stool pigeon that's got to get you to talk."

And Payne told him about the investigation, how he was supposed to get on Willingham's good side so he could extract information out of him, that the assignment to the refugee camp was set up to see if he recognized anyone there.

Willingham was perplexed but listened with interest. Outwardly he refused to accept what Payne was telling him, but you could see in his eyes that he was backtracking, piecing things together to see if it could be true. He didn't want to believe his former commander could have done the things Payne was saying. But Payne could see he was thinking it was possible.

"Do these people know I did the motherfucker?" Willingham asked.

"They only know he's missing. As far as I know they haven't connected him to what happened to your outfit. I don't think they know; if they did, it wouldn't take much to figure out where your finger necklace came from. I didn't tell them and I'm not going to."

Willingham nodded, his way of showing gratitude. "Then that's why they dropped the charges on me."

"You're catching on."

Willingham looked squarely at him. "You can believe me or not, but I didn't know about this. I thought there might be something on those missions, small stuff, but that's to be expected. We all just let it pass. I didn't know, Payne."

Payne nodded. He believed him. "That's why I stalled them. But it's not over yet. The thing I can't figure," said Payne, "is why he would have his own outfit wasted."

Willingham absently picked mud out of his fingernails with the ballpoint pen, his eyes darkly transfixed beyond the present into a time before. "If Shell did it, no, it's not over," he said. "Not yet."

Chapter
15

Payne sat on his ankles on the rack, the AK-47 across his knees. He traced a finger along the length of the rusted side plating. He wondered if it was louder than a sixteen and if it jammed as easily in quagmire terrain, if its impact really did tear out more flesh. He tried to picture the man on the other side whose weapon this had been, how many of the imperialist enemy he'd snuffed and how much pain those Americans might have gone through, what thoughts occupied them in their dying moments. He wondered, too, why the Montagnard calling himself Sergeant Mike so freely had given him the weapon, if it were as valuable a trophy as Willingham made out. The Indian had all kinds of rifles and this one didn't work; it probably meant nothing to him. The AK wasn't as streamlined as the sixteen but it was about the same weight and handled similarly. He could fit only the very tip of his little finger into the muzzle.

Lolita was showing in the clubhouse next door. It was the closing scene with Quilty sadistically riding Humbert, playing him for the fool with yet another sinister deadly game. Their maniacal voices exploded through Payne's window like staccato gunfire. They were fighting over the girl. No longer the nymphet, the young woman was now a wife and mother, struggling to have a normal life after the bizarre and abused merry-go-round of a life she'd been through with these two men. Both men would die because of the girl, because of their lust for her.

206

Payne had seen the movie twice in the world. He had liked it even though it didn't stand up to the book. It was not a popular movie at Headquarters and Headquarters Company; it wasn't James Bond or a spaghetti western; only a handful of troops were watching it and they were quiet.

He wasn't in the mood to see the movie again, for he felt a debasing sense of empathy for Humbert, whose perverse abuse of the child was all too freshly familiar to Payne. Presently the gunshots sounded and the movie ended and chairs shuffled in the clubhouse.

He put the weapon away and settled back with a new paperback. It had a prologue and prologues irritated and bored Payne, usually because they were preponderantly stuffy and unnecessary to the actual story. The first paragraph of this one confirmed it and he snapped pages to Chapter One. It was one of those recondite novels that shuffled time and tense and points of view like a deck of cards, for no better reason than to prove to the pissed-off reader that The Novel, sure enough, was in its death throes. Fuck this shit. He sent the paperback flapping to the waste pile under Kink's empty bunk, where it belonged, and dug out his battered copy of *Huckleberry Finn*.

But neither did he feel like reading of boyhood adventures.

The hootch was noisy; he could make out at least four different tunes going—"Peggy Sue," something from the Grateful Dead, Jefferson Airplane, a song from "Sergeant Pepper's Lonely Hearts Club Band." There was more music playing in other cubicles, but those muted tunes surrendered to the higher wattage. Some shouting and laughing and vibrating thuds rounded out the cacophony. A scent of sweet-smelling Cambodian weed seeped into his room, breaking the rules. A typical hootch night.

Payne stepped over to Smith's old cube to see if he could strum the new guy's twelve-string. He didn't know the dude's name. The new guy wasn't in and Payne took the guitar back to his room. He had a Scotch up and played "Jingle Bells" in the C cord, followed by "Silent Night" in the C cord. It was just as well he couldn't hear himself sing.

He wondered if Ann would be spending Christmas with her folks or with his mother. She hadn't mentioned. It didn't matter.

Time was moving on; day after tomorrow was Christmas. The IO had yet to receive its tree from the Red Cross, or the care packages. The weather was 110 these days with high humidity and monsoon rains. The *Stripes* said snow hit New Orleans in a freak winter cold spell. It sure didn't seem like Christmas.

But that didn't matter either. He stopped strumming when a dominating blast of Chuck Berry issued through the hootch, the up-beat cadence throwing Payne into a foot-stomping jig dance. Like all Chuck Berry songs it didn't last long, and Payne went on to something else; he rechecked the wall calendar—fifty-three and a wakeup. Under fifty was another magic number; he considered himself close enough to celebrate and had a couple more Scotches up while he worked out a recondite X-mas-in-the-Nam number in the C cord. The lyrics were meaningless, not worth repeating.

It was a dull, lonely, typical hootch night, but pretty soon it was over and the enveloping dark arms of sleep swept the hootch to places faraway.

After chow the next day he came up on Lai Sin having her lunch outside the office. She had a towel spread on the grassy edge of the quadrangle and was squatting under an umbrella eating rice with her fingers.

"You always eat alone, Lai Sin," he said. "How come?"

She threw her large round head outside the rim of the umbrella. "I like eat alone. Have big family," she said and arched her arms to form a huge circle. "Make much noise, always talk. Yak, yak. It nice be alone."

Lai Sin patted a spot on the grass for him to sit. She continued with the rice and tiny pieces of shrimp. Payne sat on his haunches and gazed at her; all her features were round, like an arrangement of soft moons in various stages of emergence. He watched the dainty way she fingered her food and chewed with her lips closed. She had to constantly push back her hair to keep it out of the bowl.

Payne plucked a weed and chewed on it and looked off into the distance, enjoying the serenity of the moment. He sleeved the sweat trickling from his hairline.

Lai Sin placed the empty bowl against her ankle and touched the end of the towel to the corners of her mouth, that too a winsome motion. Her face was shiny but not sweaty.

"I going miss Sah-junt Sterr," she said. "He berry nice man."

Payne smiled at her. "Me too."

She frowned. "When you go, Lussell?"

"Pretty soon. I'm going to miss you when I do."

She lowered her face and smiled broadly, not showing her teeth. Then she frowned again.

"All GI go sometime, but I not sad," she said. "I have much joy working with Amelican, much good time to remembah. Amelican good to me, give me job. My family like Amelican too."

She gazed big-eyed at Payne, like a child. "You good for Viet Nam. And my family make special place for you at doorstep for Tet, wish much pospelity for my Amelican friend."

Payne gave a small grunt. "Well, thanks," he said. "Tet. That's next month, isn't it?"

Lai Sin shook her head sideways. "It in Feb-ah . . . Feb-ah. . . ."

"February."

"Un-huh."

"Tet's the granddaddy of your holidays, isn't it? Everything wrapped up in one giant celebration?"

"Everybody birthday. Chinee have *beaucoup* celebrate, Lussell. Ancestah, family, friend. Much to celebrate."

"What is it?" Payne said ineptly. "I mean which spirit or god is it this year?"

"It Year of Monkey," she said, batting her eyelashes. "Tet Mau Than. Cross fingah evil spirit no make day dark. I light much joss at pagoda, say pray-ah so sun shine on first day Tet."

She spoke with restraint and a faint gloom in her eyes.

"I thought you people didn't like monkeys," Payne said innocently. "Don't they ruin your crops, the sugar cane and tea and stuff? Spread diseases?"

"Monkey much part of life in Viet Nam, in China where my ancestah from. Monkey, it no like rat," she said, making a face. "But rat have year too. Same same all animal of new year, the buffalo and tigah, all animal. It is tradition. You undah-stand?"

"Let me get this right," he said, shifting off his burning haunches. "If it's cloudy when Tet begins, then the evil spirits will bring you bad luck?"

"No. No cloud. Black sky, like night, dark sky," Lai Sin tried explaining, looking frustrated.

"An eclipse?"

"Ee-kip? What that?" A wrinkle appeared across her unblemished forehead.

Payne patiently explained, watching her face lift as he talked.

"That it," she said. "Ee-kip. Pray no ee-kip. *Beaucoup* bad luck."

Payne tapped a finger against the side of his face. "Should I put something out for Charlie? Would that help?"

"Charlie? It no funny, Lussell. It berry bad luck you make fun of spirit with BC."

"No. Not that, Lai Sin," Payne said and touched her arm. He almost laughed. He withdrew his hand quickly, trying to remember which it was, their arm or knee or face, you weren't supposed to touch without insulting their dead grandmother or somebody.

"I mean the monkey we used to keep in the hootch," he said. "Our mascot. Her name is Charlie. I didn't mean the VC, Lai Sin. Maybe I could fire up some joss sticks at the bunker where she used to hang out. I don't know; maybe she's dead by now," he said. "But I'll do it anyway if you say so."

Lai Sin issued a relieved and then pleased look. He couldn't tell if she was serious or not.

"For surah. That good, Lussell. You light joss for you monkey Charlie. That good for surah." He still wasn't sure.

"Do the Indians, the Montagnards, celebrate the new year like the Chinese and Vietnamese?" He felt a sting of embarrassment asking the question, for showing his ignorance and making his lack of interest in the country seem obvious. But Lai Sin, not interested in seizing an open invitation to ridicule him, answered straightforwardly.

"Surah, Lussell. Montagnard celebrate, maybe different, but they much part Viet Nam too. Many people no think this, no think Indian citizen Viet Nam. But Viet Nam belong Montagnard same same me and all citizen."

"Yeah, they've gotten a raw deal, haven't they?" he said.

"Indian poor but good. They no want fight but maybe they fight *beaucoup*. I feel solly Montagnard."

"Yeah, me too. I met some of them. This one man gave me a very valuable present for nothing."

Lai Sin shook her head slowly. "It no for nothing, Lussell. You must do berry good thing Indian. He lee-ward you for something."

"Well, I guess I did something."

Payne stood up, his knees popping. The umbrella blanked out Lai Sin's face and he stooped to look at her.

"I'm sure you'll have sunshine for your holiday, Lai Sin, just like today," he said. "You shouldn't worry so much about the evil spirits. I'll help fight 'em off for you, okay?"

She was contemplative again and gave a tentative nod. But then she offered up her best smile, a crescent moon. It amazed him how much her face could light up when she smiled.

"I wish for you *beaucoup* joy for you holiday, you Christmas, Lussell."

He suddenly felt sorry for her, his sympathy tapped in a way that made him want to drive her to Cholon, pack up her big family, and put them on the freedom bird out of this miserable country.

Payne ambled into the office shaking his head, thinking how absurd were the kinds of superstition that put you in a state of constant worry. It reminded him, disgustedly, of his Baptist upbringing in which one feared God instead of loving Him.

The office was quiet with everyone still out to lunch. He found a note behind the dial of his desk phone, Sterr asking him to call the Red Cross and inquire if the trees had arrived. PIO had been allocated a tree with decorative articles. Payne called; the trees weren't at Long Binh yet. Something about a delay at Newport Harbor and they expected delivery tomorrow, which was Christmas Day. The army for you.

He searched the bookcase and located a four-page pamphlet entitled, "What You Should Know About Tet," put out by the Office of Information, United States Military Assistance Command, Vietnam, and skimmed through it, finding nothing that might tell him what Lai Sin had meant by making a place on her doorstep for him, a visiting American.

Under the catchy heading, "Taboos of Tet," he discovered that you could start a chain of bad luck merely with an insult. He wondered how much he'd insulted her already; he knew how much Cowboy had, and yet she didn't seem to hold a lasting grudge against him. The article didn't refer to touching a Viet or crossing your legs in their presence, which he knew to be insulting.

You were not allowed to show grief or break dishes or discuss controversial subjects during Tet. You were supposed to avoid arguments and violent emotions and pay off your debts. It was prohibited to clean your house at Tet.

Right on, he thought, recalling with a pang of guilt and bitterness those holiday mornings his mother scurried madly about the house with her sweeper, tidying up with the last bit of housecleaning before relatives arrived. Had Westerners observed such taboos he would have had a better childhood, for all the emotional outbursts and insults that had passed between him and his mother when she had him up at daybreak dusting the furniture on holidays would never have taken place.

The taboos of Tet seemed appropriate and logical.

He read that Tet was a time to correct faults, forget past mistakes, pardon others for their offenses. Was this what she had meant, offering to forgive the Americans for continuing the war in her country? The same Americans who were her benefactors?

He decided that by making a special place at her doorstep for him, Lai Sin hoped to thwart some other evil spirit for the year to come, since the MACV pamphlet also read: *What a man does during Tet forecasts his actions for the rest of the year.* Or did the pamphlet mean that to apply only to American visitors?

Payne put some of these thoughts in his notebook so that he could remember how little sense it all made to him. He was unaware that the lieutenant had returned from lunch until Finn hollered at him: "Payne! Get in here."

"Fucking Finn," he mumbled audibly and put away the notebook, just as he thought he was about to get a grasp on the complexities and strange paradoxes of this business of Tet.

Stepping inside Finn's office, he shut the door and bellowed, "Yes, sir!" and clicked his heels to attention.

"Wipe that damn smirk off your face."

Finn sounded angrier than he looked.

"Who runs this section?" he said. Payne shrugged gingerly and almost said, "Why, Sergeant Sterr, of course," but instead pointed an emphatic finger at the lieutenant.

"You're damned right. Me. It's my command and I say what goes around here."

Payne held his stance until the lieutenant ordered him to sit.

"You've been trying to go over my head with this obsession to get your butt transferred."

It didn't sound like a question and Payne said nothing.

"Well, isn't it true?"

Payne tried to downplay the accusation with a droopy-eyed, flat expression. "I just asked around. No harm in that."

Finn grimaced as if pained by a toothache. "Damn, Payne. I can't figure you. You've got it good here; you're short. And there are other things worth considering too," he said, holding something back.

Payne knew the change coming over his expression; the heat shifting to frustration.

"Look, sir, I talked to Sergeant Sterr about it," Payne said. "But he knows it would put you in a bind. And so do I. Maybe I mentioned it to Top, too, but I was just finding out what the chances were."

Payne sat back in the chair and added, "But I still want to get transferred out of here. You going to help me out?"

"We've had this talk and you know I'm not. I need you."

Finn studied him, his look now tempered to a mix of disappointment and concern. And when he spoke again, there was a sign of compassion in his tone. "You've been here three months longer than me and you haven't taken a real R&R, haven't even put in for one; why haven't you?"

"Little matter of needing two hundred and fifty bucks in cash."

"You mean to say you can't afford it?" Finn said, appearing genuinely surprised. "Doesn't your wife have a job?"

"She's just a gofer right now. Hasn't had enough time to earn anything yet. But, fuck it, I don't need R&R."

The lieutenant squeezed his mousy chin. His telescoped eyes sparkled in private thought. "Well, I'm going to forget the transfer. But I've got a little something I think you'll like."

Payne stayed silent, thinking vaguely of Tokyo.

"You've always liked going to the delta, so I've got an assignment that's taking you down there. Civil affairs story. How does that sound? Get you out of here for a couple of days."

So this is it, Payne thought, the next assignment. It had been so long he thought maybe they didn't need him anymore. Finn's deceptive tactic instantly angered him. He abruptly stood up.

"Damn you, Lieutenant. You could just come right out and say it; there's no need to butter me up first," he said and took a step and stopped. "When are we going to leave?"

Finn's jaw swung open in perplexed confusion. "Sit back down, Payne. I don't know what in hell you're talking about. It's just you I'm sending. What's your problem?"

"You said civil affairs. It's an assignment from Captain Burns, isn't it?"

"I thought I made it clear that I'm in command here. I'm making the assignment. I thought you'd be thrilled to get off post for a change. I want you to get this notion of a transfer out of your system once and for all, and I thought this might help."

Payne sighed his relief, proferring a downcast, apologetic look.

Finn relaxed his posture as well. "I do have an ulterior motive, I admit. But it's really to your benefit—that is if you still want to take the magazine to Tokyo. That's right, I got approval for you to go. But we're sorely lacking a topnotch human interest story on pacification and this assignment should fit the bill. There's a medical team working the provinces down there; it should make a good story, the kind you're famous for."

The lieutenant grinned broadly giving Payne this news. He liked things to run smoothly, and perhaps he was practicing for the time he would no longer have Sterr to help run the office.

Payne too grinned broadly, his relief soaring to exhilaration. But it was a false exhilaration, one that should be put on hold; it didn't mean Burns would not call.

"What province?" Payne asked. "When do I go?"

Finn went through some loose papers on his desk and located the one he wanted. "They left post today, be in An Gang Province the next couple days and then they're going out to our AO. You'll have to leave right away to catch them. Tomorrow."

Payne checked the *Stars & Stripes* map of the war zone taped to the lieutenant's wall. Locating the area in question caused him to issue an involuntary laugh of delight. The town of Long Xuyen was in that province where the Sing Song Bar was located, where the Indian girl lived who as much as promised him herself.

"I'll leave bright and early. Two days? That all I get?"

Finn nodded sternly. "It better not take more than two days."

"Guaranteed."

He was about to leave when Finn said, "One other thing." He should have known that.

"Do a good job," the lieutenant said, "get us an outstanding piece, and I'll have something else for you. Guaranteed."

"What would that be, sir?"

He grinned and Payne grinned back.

"Your promotion," the lieutenant said and sat back, looking self-satisfied from all his good news. "Which means you'd better bone up on your General Orders when you get a chance. Better make it soon, though."

It was strange in this humidity that his sweaty face hadn't spawned a single pimple ready yet to butcher. A pair of big eyes shifted playfully behind his magnifying glasses.

"The magazine goes to press three weeks from tomorrow. Try not to screw up in the meantime."

Payne had let the illusion of Tokyo fade from his mind; somehow it had lost its hold on him, the allure seeming now to be a childish thing. "Could I ask you one other thing, sir?"

Finn nodded.

"Would you not mention where I am if anyone asks?"

"Why's that? Who's going to ask?"

"Especially Captain Burns. It's just nobody's business but yours, the IO's."

"Like I said to begin with, Payne, I run the show around here. And if I don't want to give out information about my section, well then by God, I don't have to."

"I appreciate it, Lieutenant."

For a brief moment Finn seemed to actually focus on Payne. He said, "I was sorry to hear about your buddy. Willie had to tell me."

He was calling him Willie now.

"Why didn't you come to me about it?" Finn said with a hurt look. "You can confide in me, Payne; that's part of the LT's job."

Chapter
16

The standby peasants filed up the rear of the fat-bellied aircraft with grim reluctance, cowering in mute hysteria behind the wind-blown rip and roar of spinning props. They squatted on the floor of the vibrating cargo vault in tight groups and remained frozen in place as if awaiting certain death. The children picked up the fear of their elders and cried in their clutches through the twenty-minute flight. Payne tried to distract the kids closest to him by making clown faces and passing out gum, but his heart wasn't into it and he couldn't break the spell. When the Caribou rumbled to a stop, the death sentence commuted, the Viets snapped up their meager possessions and fled yakking down the tailgate in joyous relief.

Payne stepped out among them into a blaze of sunlight and sweltering humidity, himself glad to be on land and free of the whining peasants; it was hard not to be affected by the extremity of Vietnamese emotion, but he had his own to contend with after the painful talk he'd had with Ann. He did not need the gloom of their ignorant little fears to make things worse.

Payne didn't stop on his way through the terminal to arrange for a return flight. He might, he thought in his present state of mind, stay as long as he fucking well pleased; he had gotten the disparaging letter, her yuletide *gift*, late yesterday and the helplessness to act on it had only increased the want to avenge his hurt and anger.

It would help being in the delta, away from Long Binh, for down

216

here he was a free agent, responsible to no one; the press credentials gave him carte blanche to go where he wanted, do whatever he chose. And he chose to find himself a whore, a particular whore for whom, in the aftershock of Ann's confession, he now felt an urgent, desperate need.

He took a taxi and ordered the driver to the army compound where he figured to square himself away before hitting town. The road was flanked by squat palms whose crowns of long sweeping fronds swayed in the breeze like huge manservant fans. Lazy puffs of cotton-white clouds roamed the sky in cross-moving plateaus, adding depth to the atmosphere. The earth flattened out in the delta, and where there weren't slabs of concrete, a deep lush green dressed the land.

On either side of the road two rows of concertina aproned the tall wire fences. On the way he bitterly reread the letter.

The letter was inside her CARE package, in which she had thoughtfully included a corkscrew and a jar of Woeber's horseradish mustard, a treat that could only be gotten in Springfield, Ohio; she said it was the last of their stock. He wondered why she sent the corkscrew. The CARE package clincher was the T-shirt. She said it was the same T-shirt she had worn at the Washington rally; it had the peace symbol emblazoned on the front and in multicolored lettering on its backside, the words, "War Is Good Business/Invest Your Son." He felt humiliated by the gesture and could not figure her reason for sending the shirt.

The letter, though only alluding to the confession—"Rand has been so good for me"—had struck him with such purposeful cruelty, he put in a call as soon as he read it and paced the office floor, chain-smoking until he was patched through to her four hours later. Her voice had been like a voice in a dream, calm and logical-sounding, and Payne tried as hard as he had ever tried to understand the cool flow of her words, how Rand was being a good friend, not Jody. A pal taking care of more than Payne's car for him. "Yes, Russ," she relented, very soberly. "But I never claimed to be perfect, I have weaknesses. He's been a good friend, that's all. You have to understand that."

She had also said, "I love you, Russ. But I don't understand you."

What had he done that she couldn't understand, that was what he wanted to know. Gone to the fucking Nam? And why couldn't she have just kept it to herself? Surely she knew that telling him she was fucking his friend would hurt. But then, of course, Ann was one of those *honest* persons.

"Fuck it," he said to his kneading hands and the driver turned, arching thin black eyebrows.

"You want Chinee girl, Joe?" He profiled a mirthless grin.

Payne sneered at him.

"Maybe no like girl. Like boy."

"Just fucking drive," Payne said.

After a moment he said, "You know where the Sing Song Bar is? Take me there instead."

The driver's prune face shifted to gleeful condescension. "You the boss, Joe."

Payne was traveling light on this trip, having hastily thrown together his stuff and just making the flight; he had left behind his steel pot, flak jacket, and weapon. Neither had he thought to bring along any merchandise such as cartons of cigarettes to deal with the Indian Sergeant Mike; the man probably had just fed him a line of crock about living in Long Xuyen anyway, he thought now. All his luggage was in the camera case—a couple of handkerchiefs and a change of socks and underwear; he'd packed with gray disinterest.

Long Xuyen resembled the part of Saigon around Cholon, but without the French influence. It was dirty and crowded like the city but lacked the rabid energy; here in the southland life was low-keyed, not unlike the humid and humble southland of Payne's origin. There wasn't much concrete and hardly any shade trees. Most of the streets were mud.

The Sing Song was on the north side of town, at the edge of the slums. The stench of rotten fish hit him as he stood out of the tiny car and argued over the fare. He threw two dollars in MPC through the window and the sullen-faced Viet left him in a pall of oil-blue smoke.

Payne squeezed through a curtained door past two young girls in women-of-the-night clothing, whose prowling hands he brushed off. Inside the bar was dark and he had to adjust. It suddenly struck him that coming here was a mistake, that his reckless abandon was going to get him into trouble. He wished he'd brought a weapon.

He sat the camera case on the stool next to him at the hook in the bar and took a head count around the long, narrow saloon. The Sing

Song catered to GIs, but there was nothing in the way of ornaments, reindeer or Santa Claus stencils, to indicate the Western holiday. A few American servicemen, maybe eight in all, were leaning against the bar or seated at open tables, no more than three to a group. The tone was contained to hushed voices. A few women in fake leather microminis sat cross-legged on the laps of soldiers; two couples were slow dancing to melancholic Vietnamese music filtering down from a source in the dark recesses. With its off-key, funereal strings, Vietnamese could be the saddest music in the world.

He didn't recognize any of the women as the Indian girl and there were no Viet men save the bartender, who leisurely worked his way toward Payne. A raised platform behind the bar put the diminutive bartender eye level with him. Speaking to the man, he realized he didn't know the girl's name: "Two beers if they're cold, one if not. I'm looking for Sergeant Mike, he around?"

"You friend Sah-junt Mike?"

"Yeah, pals and business associates," Payne said in a flat tone of voice, though he felt a touch of excitement that the bartender knew who he was talking about. "Just got here from up north. Where can I find him?"

The Viet manufactured a slight grin. "You no find Sah-junt Mike; he find you."

Payne shrugged indifference, like a businessman not needing the business. "Sure. Tell him I'm—"

He cut himself off when he spotted the girl. She had strolled in from the rear of the saloon. She was dressed differently but he would have recognized the face anywhere. The girl stood in the open space and made a survey, passing over him without recognition. Or so it seemed, for then she put her hands to her cheeks as if jubilantly surprised and came his way in a flourish. Her rush gave Payne a start, like the height of elation one feels at his welcome-home party.

The girl touched his arms for a quick look, then embraced him in a hug. "I no think you come," she said. "I look for you all time Sing Song."

"Here I am," Payne said brightly, though disbelieving her. He was conscious of the way he held her in his arms, not wanting to hurt her. She seemed to him very fragile.

"This my good friend," she announced to the blasé bartender. "Most handsome GI in all Viet Nam."

The bartender nodded amusedly and placed two bottled beers on the counter, then retreated to attend a soldier calling for drinks.

The girl snuggled up to Payne. Her exuberance seemed overdone and it occurred to him despite the magnetism he felt for her that he was going to get taken for a ride; but he put that thought away and indulged himself with the impetuous impulse at hand, the call for a bed.

He guzzled a beer in one tilt, offering her the other. She wet her lips with a tiny sip. "You rather have tea?" he asked.

"You no buy me tea. Maybe I have tea but you no buy."

The bartender, Johnny-on-the-spot, produced the small glass of amber liquid. He didn't stay to collect Payne's offered money.

The girl was dressed for business, in high heels and a short, tight-fitting skirt and sleeveless blouse, but it wasn't the common whore's wear, wasn't gaudy; if not for the tinkling wristful of brace-lets, Payne thought of her dress as something Lai Sin might wear, titillating but tasteful. She was more beautiful than he remembered from the bar in Saigon; majestically sculpted by Polynesian genes, with huge dark candlelight eyes, a smooth almond skin, and lips very red and not too thin. Her hair was worn in a chignon held in place by an ornate yellow pin and strung with a diadem of beads; she was a princess.

To take the edge off his impatience Payne lit a smoke. He had to squirm on the stool to ease the pressure in his lap where the girl had pressed her small pliable body with obvious intent. She slipped a hand inside his shirt and played with the hair on his chest.

"I like you very much, you want dance?"

He declined with a nod. The girl showed bright teeth behind that same smile that had melted him before and took his hand, pulling him off the stool. "I tell you I make you happy you come see me," she said. "Okay, you come my place now."

He shouldered the camera case and picked up two more beers the bartender had just placed on the bar and let her lead him out. She walked quickly the way she had entered, through the rear, taking him across a narrow alley of exhausted tin-fronted buildings. Her place was intact, but the adjoining structure was a shell of twisted iron rods and rubble.

Inside, in a small, tiny-windowed, bare room with a slab of

teakwood for a bed, she turned to him and grabbed his genitals. "Melly Christmas!" she said sprightly.

The abruptness of the gesture seized his heart, and despite the effort to resist, his suppressed emotions suddenly broke.

"What wrong you?" she asked, releasing. "You no like me? I know you like me."

Payne turned his back to her and after a moment his choked breathing was again under control. He squeezed his eyes clear and looked inside the only other room, a closet with a cooking stove and cans of Sterno stacked neatly on the floor in a corner.

Coming back to the girl, he smiled easily and ran his eyes the length of her body, his urgency now unleashed.

"I no know you name," she said.

"Joe," Payne said off the top of his head, his mouth thick with saliva. His hands became huge and clumsy in his effort to help her out of her clothes. She did not remove the beaded necklace and bracelets of fake smoked platinum. In both earlobes were small discs of white wood. Without the shoes her height shrank considerably.

The lovemaking, at first awkward, presently became passionate, ruled by a whetted voraciousness she as well seemed desperate for, as if she too had been jilted and desired the fragile reassurance of being needed. He thought her rapture strange for a whore, but it didn't seem phony and he turned himself loose with her.

Later, he finished off the warm beer with a cigarette, sitting like a buddha while the girl rubbed his shoulders. She really did like him.

"Why you wait so long see me, Joe?" she asked petulantly, pretending to be injured.

Payne lifted his shoulders in a shrug.

"You very good me in Saigon, you remembah? I no forget."

"Yeah. I remember you left."

"No right I see you then. Must understand."

"Yeah. That's all right. I'm with you now," he said lazily, inclined to go to sleep after his pleasure at her knowledgeable hands.

"I no good girl," she said.

Payne turned and grinned at her, pushing smoke through his nostrils. Hiked up statuesquely on her knees she was still only eye level with him. The glistening dark shape of her body aroused him again. He patted the flesh of her thigh.

"Must work hard for money go university at Saigon," she added when he said nothing.

"You've taken your exams already?" he asked, knowing something of the educational process. High school students had to take a comprehensive examination, the *baccalauréat,* and pass before they could go to the university. He knew also that it was rare for peasants to take the exam, particularly the unrecognized class of Montagnards.

She nodded. "In Can Tho next month before Tet. I scared death no pass. But I very smart."

"What will you study?"

"Antho-polology," she announced proudly, lifting her chin. "I study Indian of the world. It very good thing know. Know where you come from. For example. Where you come from?"

"Long Binh."

She punched his back with a tiny fist. "Long Binh. You say. You no come Long Binh, Joe. Where you come from?"

"I come from Texas."

"They no have Indian there? Surah. Plenty Indian there." She laughed as though she knew all about Texas. "Maybe you Indian. Maybe ancestah Indian. You know your ancestah, then you know what life about, who you are. I come from mountain, my family all Indian. France soldier call Montagnard. You know. But I very smart. Maybe I go home when I educated and teach family bettah way," she said seriously, and then grinned broadly. "Maybe I go Paris instead, huh? I so smart."

He thought fondly again of Smith the medic, the only man from his hootch ever to be killed in a combat situation, and of Smith's notion that an anthropological study would support his theory linking the rhesus monkey to Montagnard tribesmen. He stared affectionately at the girl, deciding for certain that Smith had done too many drugs, that Jesus, with his song of praise for Montagnards, was much closer to the fact. This Indian girl spoke even better English than Lai Sin; she was bright and ambitious, and with the exotic beauty of her wide, high-boned face and demure graciousness, you could easily imagine her on a glossy postcard, the pride of Samoa.

She was unabashed and without shame at being a whore, too, which put Payne at ease and made his attraction to her guiltless. He was in no hurry to leave.

The girl seemed in no rush to pack him off either. Maybe business was slow at Christmas, the extra GI money having gone home in the way of tax-free gifts from the Orient. As for himself, Payne had taken an all-or-nothing chance on a big hand of Guts last week, a bluff from which he came out fifty bucks ahead, and he wasn't hurting for cash. He could pay.

The girl had not yet asked for money or even intimated it was part of the deal, but he wasn't so predisposed or presumptuous as to think she had brought him to her room just because she promised him a good time, without wanting something in return, and even though he was ready to pay for his pleasure, he decided to let it ride and see what happened.

As if exhausted the girl fell against his back and dropped her arms across his shoulders and sighed. She pinched the hair on his thighs and bit his earlobe. "How long you stay me, Joe?"

"Fifty-one days," Payne said automatically, the time he had left in the Nam.

She began counting on her fingers. "That long time. Maybe you get tired me and go. Maybe you nevah come back me." It was said in a sulk meant to make Payne tell her the lies one tells a whore.

"Maybe I won't even go," he obliged.

She pulled a hair out of his leg and raked teasing fingers by his swelling cock, and then abruptly pushed off him. "You want come with me? I take you see you friend."

Payne turned to see her begin dressing and made the grumbling noise associated with rejection. "You mean Sergeant Mike?" he said.

"That what I mean. I know you want see him. He want see you."

Payne was curious how she knew he knew the black marketeer and asked her, "He tell you about the potato deal, giving me a rifle?"

"He tell me everything, he my friend too. You want go?"

"Sure. Where is he?"

She took the butt of the cigarette from his fingers and disposed of it in a beer bottle. "In my village. We go now."

Payne dressed quickly, tying his laces carefully so as not to dirty the room with the mud on his boots. He watched her reclothe herself in different wear and primp herself without the aid of a mirror. She put on black and white and turned into a peasant.

Again she led him by the hand in a rush, avoiding the bar and taking him out of the alley, where she hissed for a lambretta. They were the only passengers and she played with his knee pocket, unbuttoning it and grinning as if she were searching for goodies inside a Christmas stocking. He removed her hand gently. He said there was nothing in the pocket for her and she indulged herself with a pout.

Payne gazed at the people in the streets and at the buildings, which now did reflect the French touch. The buildings bumped each other and had thin, overhanging balconies with filigreed iron railings where potted plants were hung to bask in the sun. The few trees on the major street had massive trunks and spread widely to great heights, the leaves deep shiny green and leathery. The air was cool against his wet skin. He was already thirsty again.

The motorcab took them outside of town in the opposite direction of the army compound. The girl rested her head on Payne's shoulder, her man for the day. Dwellings soon gave way to paddies. Beyond some road stands and shrines, they came to a small village visible from the road. A gateway stood at the entrance of the square. Unlike most villages there was no name-bearing or political banner spanning the archway. It was a flimsy gate resembling the goalpost of Payne's high school football field. The gate leaned sharply, as though it were about to fall.

"This Paang Dong," the girl said proudly, lifting her head from the pillow of Payne's shoulder. She spoke to the driver and he dropped them at the goalpost and headed back toward town without taking payment. Payne walked silently behind the girl. It was a village of thatch-roofed hovels.

"Very nice place. You like," she said.

Piglets slopped about in the mud and families of chickens and ducks roosted in the cool muck under huts, about half of which were raised on stilts. There was no electricity. It looked like a very nice place all right.

The larger dwellings appeared to be all roof, the corners rounded off and close to the ground; pigsties and wicker coops were attached to these villas near the doorways. Half-naked kids played in the mud under trees, and women in groups of two and three sat in their yards around mortars, hulling rice, mindlessly working their pestles. There was no evidence of military presence, no flags or guard posts or barbed wire. A village without ARVN or American uniforms was rare and with their absence the village had an idyllic aura. It reminded Payne of a sharecropper hamlet in the flatlands of rural Arkansas

where he'd once gone with his father to deliver a cheap yellow For-
mica table and chairs. There a dozen blacks had lived in a one-room
shanty, the event memorable to Payne because of the jubilant black
faces running to greet his father's truck.

The girl broke toward a hut at the edge of the village, jabbering
in a loud voice as though to alert its occupants of their presence.
Payne stood in the open watching after her. Keeping their distance,
the mud-smeared children cautiously watched him; he wished he'd
brought along some Tootsie Rolls.

She called for him, waving an arm. "You come, Joe. Sah-junt
Mike here."

He stooped to enter the doorway and was immediately hit by the
thick smell of incense. Instead of disguising the rank odor of opium,
the joss blended with it to create a searing yet not unpleasant scent. A
fucking opium den, he thought delightedly, then warily. He squinted
to see what appeared through the haze of smoke to be half a dozen
levitating figures forming a circle. One of the figures rose and glided
toward him. Sergeant Mike, who extended his hand like an American
for Payne to shake.

"Good you come," he said cheerlessly, giving Payne the dead-
fish grip. "I think maybe I nevah see you again. Come and sit and
smoke. This numbah one stuff here. Guarantee."

He might have been angry the girl brought an American, but
Payne wasn't sure.

The men readjusted, making the circle larger to accommodate
Payne and the girl. The men all wore loincloths and either sleeveless
tunics or blankets across their shoulders. Instead of squatting Payne
sat in a lotus position to give the impression he was comfortable in
this new setting. He thought of the money the Viet had cheated him
out of, whether he should cut the ice by making a joke about it or not
mention it at all; he wondered if Mike remembered. He decided to let
it ride.

In the center of the circle was a woven mat with bowls of food-
stuff, rice and betel and lichee nuts, and a bowl containing a small
mound of the brown stash. The expressionless head nodding could
have meant anything and Payne chose to take it as their way of greeting. None of the others offered to shake hands. He stared in awe as a
couple of the men, talking to Mike, exposed teeth that had been filed
down to points.

All the men ignored the girl. Payne began to feel uncomfortable, thinking he might have interrupted a meeting.

Passed a long bamboo pipe, he drew from it tentatively, not knowing if he would choke. "Thanks," he stammered, choking. It was pure stuff all right, going immediately to his head and easing the knot that his shoulders had drawn into.

The hard, sinewy faces around him seemed suddenly to turn gentle. He had a sudden urgent desire to touch the girl, to brag to these men what a great fuck she was. The idea flashed across his mind of mounting her right there, in the middle of the circle, raking the bowls aside and giving it to her on the mat while they watched.

"Christ!" he said rather loudly, now feeling as though he too were levitating. "You're absolutely right about this stuff, Mike."

He passed the pipe to the girl, who gave Payne a seductive look; she took a tiny puff, which somehow embarrassed him.

He was then offered a bamboo stem and looked to Mike questioningly.

"To honor you, a foreigner," Mike said. A large clay jar was rolled to the center of the group, its small opening uncovered and water poured into it. The men took turns inserting their straws, each chanting before drawing the liquid and sucking a little longer than the previous man.

It was rice beer, the taste at first bitter but later becoming smooth and weak. Payne drank thirstily, spilling some and wiping his mouth on his sleeve; he grinned sheepishly. He was undecided how his overall behavior so far was being construed, whether it was acceptable or rude. The faces surrounding him did not offer an answer. It crossed his mind what Jesus had told him about these people, that he could never figure out whether he was defiling them or being respectful. Even stoned Payne hoped his demeanor reflected the latter. He thought it had with the girl, at least.

Mike looked at the girl, giving her some kind of sign with his eyes, his okay perhaps for bringing the GI. He then came back to Payne with his unreadable eyes.

"Smoke from pipe and drink from jar," he said. "Only for the man worthy our respect. You such a man. I not forget you in Saigon bar. You show great courage and much honor to my people, respect Vietnamese people. I give you gun for this Long Binh and honor you

now Paang Dong. You say you name to us now. And I make introduction you."

"Joe!" the girl quickly exclaimed and giggled. "He name GI
Joe."

"Henry," Payne heard himself saying, lifting his eyes from his
lap. He knew he had relaxed in that moment, for there was a flourish
of movement from the others, as if they all knew exactly what was
going on in his mind and just then welcomed him into their private
lives.

The pipe reached him again. He swallowed the bitter smoke.

"Okay. Henry. No problem. My name not Mike, you know,"
Mike said. "My name Tieng-of-the-Two-Face. This Saang, my sistah." He pointed at the girl without looking at her. "Saang-the-Smart-
One. She work hard many year. Someday be great woman, cause
much problem. Is reason she smoke with the men. You like my sistah?"

Payne felt a heat blush on his face. He smiled at the girl and tried
to make a joke: "I guess maybe you do know Mike—Tieng." The
words died in his mouth.

"I not sistah like you have sistah, Joe," she said helpfully.
"Many ancestah back. Long long time back."

"Many generations removed?" Payne suggested brightly, trying
to hide the blush. She nodded. "How many?"

"Many," she said, counting on the fingers of both hands. "Ten."

"Eleven," Tieng-of-the-Two-Face said. "American nevah count
so far back, huh? But my people live by the law go way back, law of
ancestah we honor." He stretched his hands wide and a few of the
men barked laughter at the gesture.

He introduced the others, four of them by epithets and the other
two by a single name. Payne wasn't going to be able to remember the
names—he was having enough trouble trying to act polite—much
less assimilate through the powerhouse haze of opium and rice beer
what he was hearing. But he understood that being with these people
was a rare privilege and he made a special effort trying.

The man Tieng seemed to favor the most, who sat next to him,
was called Kroong-the-Warrior. His teeth were mutilated, the upper
row filed completely down and the lowers shaved to pinpoints and
painted, it looked like, with black lacquer. He bared the lower row of

them menacingly like a fighting dog. At his side was a bush-hook machete.

Payne sensed disdain or irritation from the man called Kroong-the-Warrior and averted his eyes.

"Why are you called Two-Faces? What does it mean?" he asked, taking a lichee nut from the bowl that had been pushed in front of him; the sweetness of the soft nut tightened his jaws.

Tieng palmed his kneecaps and drew himself into a small figure, making his head of wild porcupine hair wider than his shoulders. Payne noticed then the ivory plugs in the lobes of his ears, similar to the white wooden earrings the girl Saang had worn earlier.

"I have great love my country Viet Nam," he said in a low voice. "All men here same same. Many men have love Viet Nam. But must live, survive. You understand, Henry?"

Payne nodded, removing a cigarette from the package.

"Please, no smoke here. *Benh nyiim*. It taboo in house of opium. Very bad, smoke only pipe." He grinned broadly to soften the censure and his gold fang glistened in the light of the candles. *"Beaucoup* beer, *beaucoup* opium. Okay," he said and slapped the stolid-faced Kroong on the back. Maybe to lighten him up.

"Much corrupt, this Viet Nam," he went on, again addressing Payne. "A man survive only if corrupt too. Tieng-of-the-Two-Face corrupt. Sell all stuff to American, to Aussie, to Vietnamese. Maybe to VC, huh? I have great love my country Viet Nam," he said and shrugged easily, "but must make the money. So Tieng have two face. You understand, Henry?"

He was altogether a different person here, in his village, than the zoot-suited pimp or the crafty, contradictory marketeer who'd cheated Payne then rewarded him with the prized trophy, and Payne was beginning to see how you could like these Indians, why Jesus and Baby Huey, even Willingham, had been so fond of them.

"Yeah," Payne said in answer. "It's like having to pretend you're somebody you're not. But it's not right."

"No, no, Henry. No bad this name. Two face good."

Payne shook his head miserably; it had to be the opium fog. "I don't understand," he said, the words falling thick off his tongue.

"You love you country?" It was a question Payne thought he might be able to handle.

"I think so, yes."

"Then you do what you think right you country?"

"Yeah, I guess so. That's why I'm here." He cringed saying it. "I didn't mean that like it sounded."

"No, okay. Same same Tieng. I help my country Viet Nam. With money I make. Corrupt no problem. Much a part of war."

Payne squirmed uncomfortably. He was squatting now and his legs began to cramp despite the feeling that he was floating on them.

Tieng looked among the faces of his companions, as if, Payne thought, he was asking them a question by telepathy. "What you think Viet Cong, Henry? Think they have two face too? VC only citizen Viet Nam. Take money, food, all kind weapon from GI to fight GI. No different. Maybe you know plenty VC, huh?"

Again he slapped Kroong on the back; but the man was as fixed in his stoicism as a fireplug, which his solid, squat build resembled.

He was about to speak again when, outside, dogs began barking. Tieng stood up along with the others; the only knees to pop were Payne's as he struggled to lift his leaden weight.

The girl dropped behind the others. She pulled at Payne's arm. "You come this way, Joe," she said, and pushed open a straw door in the back of the hut he thought was all wall. The sun hit his eyes like a flashbulb.

The girl led him thirty meters to the water, a canal running through a palm grove, and had him lie on a bank behind the massive trunk of a palm. The dogs continued barking.

"What's going on?"

"No problem," she said, crouching on her haunches. "You stay, I come back you."

He hugged the ground and watched an ugly fat bug with red antennae methodically journey down the tree to the ground, making its way to the water. A colony of black ants the size of bees traversed close by, hauling the things ants haul. The ants marched in tandem string columns, going and coming faithfully and blindly on orders of an implacable queen hidden somewhere beyond. He tried to figure out where the nest might be, at which end of the marching lines the soldier ants the queen waited, but both lines seemed to be transporting the stock futilely to and fro. The process baffled him.

In his haste he'd left his camera case inside the hut and remembering it put him in a panic. What if it were discovered? But who would find it? He envisioned planning an escape route, treading the canal until he was far enough away he wouldn't be found. Then hide in the brush until dark. Then what? Everyone, even at Long Binh, knew the night belonged to Charlie, that the countryside was his domain at night. What if a VC troop line passed his way, or in his wandering he stumbled into their hideout or hit a booby trap? He would become like a piece of stock those black ants hauled to some unknown place, never to be found. Were there tunnels in the delta? Now his want of a weapon was genuine.

He jumped like a field mouse spotting the legs that stood over him. He'd had his face buried stupidly in the grass, as if that would make his body invisible. They were Tieng's toothpick legs, jutting below the loincloth like knotted cords of beef jerky. Any other time Payne might have laughed at the sight of the legs. He sighed breathily.

"Okay, Henry. No big deal," Tieng said the way Sergeant Mike would say. "You must go now. Not safe you stay. Too bad, much opium to smoke. Much talk yet."

His gold incisor shone like a tiny sun. Payne hoisted himself up, suddenly very tired.

"Damn, scared shit out of me, man," he said in his Southern drawl.

Tieng shook his head, holding the wry grin. "You no coward you. Brave soldier. Follow order good."

"Who was it? Were they troops or what?"

Tieng shrugged easily. "No problem. You no worry. Saang take you back town now. Maybe I see you Sing Song tomorrow. Okay."

"Yeah, okay. Maybe."

Tieng led him around the abandoned hut and pointed to the girl; she was straddling a bicycle at the gateway, clutching the sagging goal post as if to keep it from falling on her.

Saang had his camera case. She rode on the crossbar, giggling whimsically as Payne's knee bumped the underside of her leg, saying nothing of the abrupt departure from the opium hut. Segments of the road were old asphalt; he zigzagged to stay on it and out of the mud. She tried to land a kiss on his bouncing lips without succeeding and once or twice held a hand playfully in front of his eyes.

"Why you go so fast?" she said. "I like ride close with you. Make me think of little girl again. You have bike in United State

America? Maybe you little boy sometime, huh?"

She laughed.

"Sure I was," Payne said, panting. The extra weight from the mud on the wheels soon had his thighs burning. "How old are you, Saang?"

She took her hands off the handlebar to count on her fingers, pretending before she had finished to lose her balance. She screeched and tilted backward into the fold of his arm. She was not sweating at all, even in the black pants.

Saang told him she was nineteen. When they arrived at the Sing Song an hour later, she said she had miscounted and was actually eighteen. He believed her.

"I like you come in," she said, straightening her blouse, finger-brushing her hair. She hiked up her loose slacks.

He said he better not. It was now dusk and he needed to check in; he'd had enough excitement for one afternoon. "What was going on back there? Was there trouble?"

She shook her head, again dismissing the question. "Why you no stay me? I want you stay."

"It's late and I have to go," Payne said. He went for his wallet.

Watching him, she said in a harsh voice, "What you think, Joe. I no whore you." Her black eyes grew round as nickels, and furious.

"Then what!" Payne said just as harshly, finally exhausted with trying to figure these people out. They were impossible; he thought they all could use money. Wasn't that what Tieng's little talk had been about, doing what you did to get by, to survive? Wasn't she a whore?

She walked off with her head downcast and arms folded under her small breasts. After a few steps she turned and came back to him. The fury had tempered to a pout. They were good at pouting, even the princess Saang.

"You big dumb man, Joe, you no can see," she complained. "Please, you come back see Saang again. Tonight."

Payne turned soft at her shifting plea and smiled looking her over, seeing her without her clothes, about to capitulate and throw it to the wind. But he said:

"I'll come back tomorrow, Saang. Maybe later in the day. Will you be here then?"

"You give me time, I be here at Sing Song."

He told her dinnertime and said, "I'm sorry. Please take some money—for your brother's good smoking stuff. I want to help if I can."

She grinned wryly, as Tieng had grinned. "You come tomorrow, then you be plenty help. Goodbye, Joe."

On the way to the compound he racked his brain trying to figure out what it was they wanted from him.

Chapter
17

The installation was little more than a plank-and-tent outpost comprised of USARV detachment units. But these units facilitated a full range of support to combat outfits scattered from the central delta to the Cambodian border, and it was the major petroleum depot for the navy's backwater assault vessels cruising the thousands of miles of waterways over which North Vietnamese cadres infiltrated and supplied matériel to the VC in the south. The delta had the highest population of the four military tactical zones in the republic. The delta also had the highest casualty figures for civilian and ARVN personnel, and the highest concentration of Viet Cong in the Nam.

Payne found out this stuff at the office of the 2nd Civil Affairs detachment unit, from a sallow-faced Pfc who sat under a fan sweating and wheezing as though having a bout with malaria. The Pfc had been in-country less than a month and despite his sickliness still had a cherry's undaunted enthusiasm to know what was going on, a guy who hadn't yet been touched by the war. Accordingly Payne took the guy's information with cordial attentiveness without putting much stock in his estimation of VC strength in the region.

The Pfc did not know the medical team had come down from Long Binh, so Payne whiled away the time chitchatting innocuously while waiting for the CO to arrive.

The kid wanted to know if Payne had seen any action and Payne shrugged, nonchalantly mentioning the Purple Heart.

"Wow, man. What happened?"

"Ambush," Payne said and lit a smoke. The kid parroted his action with a cigarette of his own and coughed on the smoke.

The CO, a captain, came in, and Payne chitchatted with him for a while in his office, found out the team's whereabouts, and turned on the charm trying to borrow a jeep for the day.

"Afraid not. Only got one." The captain smiled. "Wish I could help you out."

Payne had spent the night in the back room of an ice cream plant that was on the grounds of a motor pool. Entering the compound he had spotted on top of the motor pool's garage the crazy vision of a giant double-scoop ice cream cone someone had painted on a sheet of plywood. He looked into the place out of curiosity, deciding the idea was worth a story. The plant was operated by Viets, and the boy who slept in the tiny back room let Payne use his cot. The old mamasan tending the huge ice-cream machines offered to wash his muddy fatigues.

His sleep had been fitful, constantly interrupted by peculiar and horrifying dreams. The one that stuck evoked the image of his father towering over him with a handgun, shouting at Payne, "I don't want to do this!" Huge tears hurled down his father's cheeks, hitting him like rocks, and when next he looked it was Ann in a black raincoat in the dark, her back to him, the figure diminishing and finally vanishing. It was the feeling the dream had left him with that stuck, as if he had fallen from grace with loved ones and could never go home, never see her again.

That he dreamed of his father was remarkable; his sentiment toward his father had long since become an objective thing, and the image of him was vague, like a figure shrouded in fog or a blurred snapshot. Yet the dream-image had sharp, accurate details—the black whiplike hairs in his nostrils and on the hand pointing the gun, the skeletal outline of his narrow face, his clear gray eyes that in the dream were albino. The dream-image could have only been his father, for the gross nose hair and sunken death-chalk hue of the face were features of the visage seared in Payne's mind from the open casket in the living room of their home.

Payne remembered his father used to wear a fedora. He kept it on the truck seat when he let Payne ride with him to Little Rock or on deliveries, and Payne would cover his eyes under the hat, pretending to be his father. On longer trips they had bet on the number of Chevrolets passing them or on pop eyes or on fatality markers along backroads, innocuous things. He could not remember his mother and father together, embracing each other or posed together in old snapshots; that too seemed remarkable.

Payne connected up with the medical team at the dispensary. The team was composed of three enlisted men and a captain. An MP gun jeep had been assigned to escort the jeep and panel truck on their rounds to three villages, the day's agenda. One of the villages turned out to be Paang Dong.

"Fall out, men. Let's move it," the group commander said to his men, whom he had stand at attention in front of the vehicles.

The two MPs, their legs slung casually around the windshield of the gun jeep, watched this business amusedly.

"You will ride with me, Specialist," the captain told Payne after the muster. "I'll fill you in on the way." Payne knew immediately what to expect from the man; he'd dealt with his kind before, the rigid lifer fortuitously pushing his weight around, pulling rank for no apparent reason. He was the kind of officer who made his work self-serving. Payne felt sorry for the EM under him; it made him appreciate Lieutenant Finn. Had Finn not told the captain to expect him, Payne would have foregone the assignment altogether.

On the road the captain, whose name was Reinhardt, informed him of the overall purpose of the army civil affairs med-help program: his team was one of hundreds throughout Vietnam providing not only medical assistance and services but coordinating educational programs on preventive medicine in thousands of villages and hamlets. These teams provided the Vietnamese with physicals, immunizations, pregnancy training, dental extractions, and oral and physical hygiene indoctrinations.

"It's all part of the pacification program and your angle, of course, is to enhance that image," Reinhardt said, instructing Payne what to write. "I'll of course require you show me your article before it's printed."

Before they reached the first village the captain demanded to look at the notes Payne had taken down. Curtly Payne refused. His notes were his business, he said, the same as examining peasants was the captain's. He could tell the man was thinking insubordination, of filing a report. He was what was known in his own parlance as a first-class prick.

This exchange took place where the small caravan had been stopped at a bridge guarded by iron-faced ARVN Rangers in tiger-striped uniforms. Everyone had to show papers. The guard who looked over Payne's reminded him of the dead man Su because of his strutting manner and the orange bib he wore as a neckpiece; it gave Payne a start and he diverted his attention to the river where kids were playing on oversized inner tubes. He turned his long lens on them.

The guards released them with a fuss of hand waving. The village was just beyond the bridge in a palm grove and the three vehicles wheeled in with the ostentatiousness of a circus, sending chickens and pigs scurrying for shelter. A rabble of children and dogs followed noisily behind the caravan.

The Americans gathered the villagers in the square and separated them into five or six platoon-sized groups which were sent to the various stations under the direction of a civilian translator using a bullhorn.

"Organizing them is the key," the captain told Payne, who had stopped taking notes. "Once we get them organized and going to their proper stations, it goes easy. We can get through maybe two hundred on a good day. But you've got to keep on top of them or they'll wander off before they get their shots and teeth jerked—strike that last remark. Use 'extraction' instead."

At the first opportunity, Payne lost the captain.

Inside a windowless concrete building a group of peasants squatted submissively before a Spec 5, who was teaching preventive dentistry with the use of a three-foot toothbrush and a set of tyrannosaurus dentures. The huge model caused the children to cry when he clacked them together. The Spec 5 enjoyed his work, hoisting his set of teeth around the room and lunging them at the children with a startling crack.

Payne ran off some film. Between groups, he asked the Spec 5 why he had to clap the contraption so loudly. "Don't you see it scares those kids?"

The Spec 5 sneered as pleasantly as he could. "That's the idea, man. You got to scare them into brushing, it's the only way you can teach these people anything." He watched Payne taking notes. "You better keep that out of your article." Payne figured he was just venting his resentment at being stuck with an asshole for a section chief.

At another station he photographed women in various stages of pregnancy; the women were apprehensive and held off entering the house as long as they could, as though a devil spirit awaited them inside. Most of them had toddlers leeched to their loose slacks. Payne took shots of an older pregnant woman whose flaccid breast a squalling infant tried to nurse. He didn't give a second thought to stealing their souls or whatever nonsense Willingham would be on him about for taking pictures of them.

He strolled around the village shooting straw huts and water buffalo and more people, smiling and dishing out the Tootsie Rolls he'd thought to buy last night at the PX. He shot two rolls of color film and two of black-and-white, a few obligatory frames of the team at work.

He devoted the bulk of his picture taking to closeups of people's faces, the subject he was most drawn to. Over the course of his tour he had collected a galaxy of portraits, and all of them could fall under a single theme. He had considered what that theme might be in a word—deprivation? poverty? war? The thing most common in the faces was what he didn't see. He didn't see self-esteem or optimism or even the promise of it. It was as though futility was second nature to these people, evident even in the bittersweet faces of kids. Or maybe this was just Payne's perception because he saw these people as an inferior order of human beings, the lusterless, hopeless faces he encountered having always been so and the interminable state of war having nothing to do with it. It crossed his mind of someday exhibiting his work, a Diane Arbus-like study of the ubiquitous low life of South Vietnam. The theme in a word would be "surviving."

He ventured to the edge of the village and leaned against a palm in the shade and wrung out the handkerchief he wore on his neck. Two boys were standing by the concertina, pissing through the wire, trying to hit the water. A chicken pecked at their feet. One boy could have been the shadow of the other. They both had strong, wide-arching streams, which dampened some geraniums on the other side of the wire but fell short of the river. Spotting Payne with his camera poised, the boys in unison snapped to attention and saluted. The shutter clicked, catching the salutes and arched streams. He lowered the camera and casually returned their salute and dished out some candy. The boys offered him their sister.

The captain had left his class in search of Payne and found him skipping stones with the boys on the river; he admonished Payne for disappearing and ordered him to stay close by. The day became long and arduous after that; he had to submit to the captain's insistence that he take this or that shot of the team commander examining a patient or instructing a group with a pointer aimed at charts on which the body's sexual organs or digestive and circulatory systems were pictured. He required Payne to take down "key parts" of his lectures on diphtheria and rat-bite fever and malaria. The civilian with the bullhorn translated.

The talk Payne enjoyed most, "Intestinal Gardening," roused him to a burst of laughter, which momentarily stifled the captain and translator. On the road to the second village Payne used his best condescending tone of voice to ask why the fuck didn't he teach them about some of the viral and venereal diseases or tuberculous and balanced diets. Even a REMF like Payne knew TB and dysentery were the most common diseases in this country, sicknesses the local sorcerers let go too long for real medicine to cure. "Vitamin B's pretty helpful for deficiency, ain't it?" he offered in advice. He knew he was stepping out of bounds bringing this up to a doctor, but he got a certain satisfaction from it. Then the captain actually did threaten to file a report for his "attitude problem."

Reinhardt kept him underfoot and too busy to break away at the last village, Paang Dong, to look for Tieng or the girl.

Payne was struck even more by the obvious contrast between the other hamlets and Paang Dong village; there wasn't a single structure made of milled lumber or tin, no wire in the bamboo pig pens; nothing ARVN or American, not even nails. He figured the villagers were all of a tribe of Montagnards, the men wearing loincloths and the women ankle skirts, and some baring their breasts. Most of them, men and women, wore their hair the same, pulled right in a knot; many bummed cigarettes from the GIs. They seemed overly responsive to the team, as though they wanted them quickly done with and gone.

Payne spotted one of the men he'd smoked opium with and asked him on the move if Tieng was around. The Indian wouldn't talk to Payne or even acknowledge he was being spoken to; he quickly darted off and out of sight.

Payne asked one of the enlisted men if he knew anything about the village.

"Just another stop," he said. "They're supposed to be forest people relocated from the highlands, according to the data sheet. But, hell, you can't go by that. They could be from Cambodia. Our info comes out of USARV headquarters. They don't know shit what's going on down here. Why?"

"No reason," Payne said. "If your asshole captain asks, tell him I split. I'll report to him tomorrow sometime."

The specialist grinned. "Shit, you're going into town, aren't you? Wish I could go with you, man."

"You ought to arrange for that guy to get a case of the dysentery or something," Payne said. "He's not exactly doing an 'outstanding' job, you know."

"Hey, man, what job? These civic action programs are just more bullshit that the army dreamed up to soothe over their conscience for the damage we're doing this country."

Payne grinned crookedly. "Can I quote you?"

The specialist looked around and said, "I put in for a transfer already. Waiting to hear."

"Good luck," Payne said. "But it's him they don't need, not you."

When the team packed up to leave, it was late in the afternoon, a dark low sky approaching. Payne wandered off behind a large hut where he wouldn't be spotted. He heard his name called and ignored it, taking shots farther along the water canal in case he was seen and needed the excuse. He wasn't, and soon saw the vehicles disappear along the road.

The rain broke before he made it to the familiar outlying hut. He poked his head through the fake rear wall and to his surprise found Tieng sitting on his heels. He was busy assembling or disassembling a rifle, an AK. A stack of banana clips lay at his side. He glanced sharply at Payne.

"Hi, Tieng," Payne said, grinning like a Cheshire cat, fully aware of the gravity of his intrusion.

"MP go, no here now?" Tieng questioned sternly, looking past Payne, searching. He didn't invite Payne inside.

"They're all gone. I was tired of being with them. I told Saang I'd meet her at the bar but thought I might as well stay here instead of going back to town since I was already here," Payne explained rapidly, though trying to sound casual, look disinterested.

Tieng studied him, at first suspiciously, then easing his stare as if making up his mind that Payne wasn't connected with the other Americans. And of course he wasn't; he was a free agent, responsible to no one. . . . His body could bloat and rot and go for ant stock before he was missed.

There was a thumping noise under the plank flooring and a trap-door lifted. Tieng frowned at Payne and then waved him inside as a stocky Viet crawled out of the floor. It was Kroong-the-Warrior; noticing Payne he bared his painted sawteeth in a snarl as if he wanted to bite him. The two Viets exchanged glances, followed by a harsh tonal lecture from Tieng. He said to Payne, "Sit and smoke. We talk."

Payne had started to bolt to the canal but decided that would do no good, that it was in fact stupid. But he felt oddly less nervous than he thought he would in the presence of the enemy.

He sat and removed his shirt and flattened it to dry on the floor while Tieng lit a pipe and passed it to him first.

"You will understand why you no see me when GI here."

Payne nodded silently. He took the opium smoke only to the top of his lungs and expelled it.

"You are not a warrior—" Tieng started and stopped to listen to something Payne didn't hear. The recollection of Major Su saying the same thing of Payne gave him a sinking sense of impotence, but it was true, he was not a warrior. He didn't even have a weapon; but that didn't matter either, for he had not been able to use it when he did have one.

"You very honorable man my people," Tieng said, to his relief. "I think you no believe fighting this war. You understand, Henry?"

Again Payne said nothing and nodded he understood, although he didn't.

"Tieng-of-the-Two-Face much like you, no believe in war. GI no understand this. GI think all Vietnamese enemy. Not so. Only love country, only take from land and live on land."

He was telling Payne something by this, preparing him; but a sudden rustle under the trapdoor stopped him. Two more men emerged from the tunnel brandishing carbines; they too were from yesterday. They were part of an outfit or were an outfit.

A conversation ensued among the men; it was evident they were talking about Payne, for they shot quick darting glances at him and made pointed gestures while speaking excitedly among themselves. But he couldn't tell how he stood with them. He became a fixture waiting. One of the men rushed out into the rain without his rifle. The pipe made two rounds before Tieng spoke again in English.

"Kroong say maybe we shoot Henry, throw body in rivah," he said, smiling. "I say Kroong, 'No can do. Henry okay, numbah one GI. No problem.' I say to men maybe Henry help us. It good have GI friend. What you think, Henry?"

"I don't think anything," Payne said, his voice on the verge of shouting.

The Viet caught his eye and held him under intense scrutiny long enough that Payne's forced coolness was about to collapse. Then Tieng said, "You no hate Vietnamese, I know this. Can see in you. I prove you I no warrior too, you no worry. Okay. Tonight I take you place make you believe what I say. You understand then, maybe then you want to help." His face grew stern.

Payne let go the air he'd been holding and sat off his haunches; like the peasants on the flight that brought him here, he felt as though a death sentence had been commuted and he would see another day. He accepted the pipe again. The other men listened intently as Tieng talked; then they smiled at Payne and touched his fatigues, though not his skin; they were playful pinches and pats and he took the gestures reassuringly. Kroong did not participate.

One of the men, acknowledging Tieng, produced from the recess a jar and a pannier of bamboo shoots.

"You drink. This join us like broth-ah," Tieng said to Payne. The pannier was passed around and each chanted softly before sucking beer. Payne understood now that the procedure was ritualistic.

There was no more talk about his busting in on them and they drank and smoked for a while in silence; someone lit joss. The rain pounded the thatch, which leaked here and there.

"Maybe you want see Saang now," Tieng said after the rain lightened to a drizzle. "We go Sing Song. You like?"

"All right."

A covered lambretta was stationed in the common as if it had been waiting on Tieng. Halfway to Long Xuyen the drizzle stopped.

Night had quickly fallen and Payne couldn't see farther than the sides of the road where he kept his eyes trained, imagining spotting others of his host's comrades hiding in wait beyond the branches and leaves that fluttered in the cast of dim lambretta light, wondering if he was being taken on his last ride to a bloody rendezvous in the black jungle.

Then the lights of Long Xuyen burst forth to commute the sentence again.

He had the chance to make his break at the Sing Song; Tieng didn't have a weapon and there were Americans there he could have easily mixed with, left with. Some of the GIs had sixteens lying on the tables or sidearms. He didn't break away because he knew Tieng was aware he could, and because he wanted to believe he was in no personal danger since they could have done away with him at the village if they'd wanted. He was flirting with a deadly kind of adventure that made him feel special, as though he had been singled out, individually selected to perform some uncertain action; and he had the option to run or face whatever unknown challenge awaited him, the option to finally see if he did have strength of character.

There was a sandy-haired American at the bar he had seen yesterday, a regular, Payne surmised, whom he started to engage in a little how-ya-doin' conversation just to demonstrate he was comfortable, that everything was cool with him. But Tieng did not want to stay in the bar. The girl had been waiting on Payne "for many hour," she said, as if both dejected and overjoyed. The three of them went to her small place in the alley and Saang cooked rice and strips of beef on the wire-framed stove. She went about the chore happily. A dome-topped Roosevelt radio was plugged into the overhead light socket, but she didn't turn it on.

"American eat very much," the girl said, serving them where they sat on the wood-slab bed. Payne's dish, a large soup bowl, held twice as much as theirs. "Eat now," she said, prodding Payne with a chopstick.

The meat had a slightly rancid taste, which he convinced himself was only the spicing, and he cleaned the bowl. The girl was pleased. She made a compliment of how well he could use the chopsticks. He refused her offer of more food.

Tieng did not leave them alone, and the girl made no advances toward Payne. She touched him with her eyes but not her hands, and he followed her lead and did the same. She was in her peasant clothes tonight and wore no jewelry. After eating they rested. Tieng talked to his sister for a while, occasionally exchanging laughs and then engaging in an argument apparently over the contents of a rucksack she produced from the closet kitchen.

The opium had worn off, leaving Payne with a headache. He was growing short on patience too, waiting and wondering what was to happen next. He could have used a double shot of whiskey.

"Curfew's at nine," he blurted, thinking it must be eight o'clock already. "If an MP sees me I'll be arrested. We'll all get in trouble."

Tieng stood and said, "It time now we go." He shouldered the heavily packed rucksack and walked outside.

As soon as he had left, the girl grabbed Payne around the waist, looking up for a quick kiss. Payne kissed her on the lips.

"You be very careful tonight, and you come back to me, Joe. I love you," she whispered. Her flat, moist eyes spoke to him of impossible dreams. "Tonight I sleep you."

"I'd like that, Saang."

The Indian was quick and moved like a shadow, leading him stealthily through alleys to the edge of town and on to the banks of the wide Mekong River. At a dark inlet Tieng pushed aside a clump of reed to expose a short, rickety pier where a small sampan bobbed gently. The sampan had a covered compartment in the middle. He instructed Payne to get inside the compartment; he pushed off noiselessly, making an imperceptible wake.

In silence Payne watched the elongated strings of lights ripple on the water's surface; then the river became dark with only an occasional light. Where there was light he could make out overhanging growth along the banks and a tree line against the sky. Tieng withdrew from the ruck a pair of U.S. boots and put them on while he had Payne paddle.

"I can't see where I'm going," he complained.

"No talk," Tieng ordered and took over.

The sampan glided along narrower and quieter water for almost an hour before sliding onto a mud flat. During this time Payne had felt a junkie's craving for a smoke; he had studied the stars to keep from thinking about it, and watched for patrol boats. He knew they were out there somewhere, but not once did he see or hear anything motorized, only the splashing of surface fish and the deep-throated cawing of savannah birds.

They left the boat under brush and walked into the jungle. The vegetation was dense and high and Payne couldn't see his hands in front of his face. The quarter-moon occasionally popped in and out of view through the higher canopy. He fingered the rope-belt holding up Tieng's trousers and followed silently, taking tentative steps in the sucking muck. The thought of hitting a booby trap crossed his mind in spite of the assurance that the man guiding him knew exactly where he was going and where to walk. Brush constantly slapped his skin and a loud swarm of mosquitoes stalked the air around his face. He lost track of time. Soon Tieng stopped and began rummaging through the ruck.

"Okay," Tieng said in a small voice. "See light?"

"No."

He took Payne's chin in his hand and directed his face at a point where a faint light twinkled through the branches and high grass.

"Yeah, I see it."

They walked a little farther, the light growing to a dim glow through which Payne could make out Tieng and the surrounding foliage in silhouette. The trees were huge here with trunk ribs high as his knees. Overhanging vines drooped like great boa constrictors from the trees.

"The fucking bugs are eating me alive," Payne whispered. "You got any repellent with you?"

"No mosquito, is grass," he said, but Payne knew what a mosquito bite was. "Make shirt long, use this."

He handed Payne something hard, a piece of coal. He sooted his white man's face and hands and gave it back. He felt stupid for not thinking to roll down his sleeves.

"Now you jungle warrior," Tieng said and punched him with an elbow. "We go close but you no can go in. Must watch."

Payne copied his squat walk through the biting lalang grass until they came upon rolled barbed wire below the grass line, the perimeter of an encampment. Payne wondered if it were electrified or rigged in any way. In the subdued light he could make out figures of men moving about hastily and could hear talking from the camp, the muted yak of an incomprehensible tongue.

From the ruck Tieng withdrew a pair of large and heavy binoculars and handed it to Payne, pointing out the focusing device. Payne looked into it. To his astonishment the entire encampment became surrealistically illuminated in a washed-out tint of red.

"Infrared," he said softly, impressed. "Where'd you get these? Shit."

Through the lens he made out three huts standing in an even line flanked by hedgerows; they were rickety structures, hastily erected as though for easy leveling. Between two of the huts were stacks of wood boxes that could have been either large munition crates or coffins. "Why are they carrying stretchers?" he said. "What is this place?"

"I go inside. Have deal make. You wait, Henry. No make noise or you die, maybe me too. Understand?"

Payne acknowledged without speaking.

"Come back soon. You look at hut there," he said, aiming the glasses for Payne. "There you see what I bring you see. Okay."

Tieng disappeared and Payne tried to follow his movements through the glasses but lost him immediately. From the hut Tieng had instructed him to view, he watched two men carrying what appeared to be a body on a litter. The litter moved lengthwise along a narrow path and out of view. He refocused on the hut. It stood between other bamboo-sided huts about thirty or forty yards from where Payne sat low on his knees. The binoculars indicated the distance at 37.48 meters. He picked out Tieng waving an arm to greet four men with rifles at the hut. The guards circled Tieng and talked for a few seconds then led him inside.

There were people shuffling about inside the oblong hut; some of them appeared to be women. As they moved away from the opening Payne saw a table upon which a body lay directly under a hanging light. It had to be an operating room, he decided, a VC field hospital. And the boxes would be coffins. In a moment Tieng stepped back through the door and again vanished into the darkness.

Waiting for him, Payne didn't hear so much as a twig snap or a rustle in the grass; then the Viet touched his shoulder. Payne jumped and gave a sigh. *"Damn,"* he muttered.

Tieng no longer had the rucksack. He stayed low and peered for a moment through the binoculars, viewing the surgery hut. There was no glare or reflection on the lens. A few minutes passed, then he said, "Okay, we go now."

"They're treating people in there, aren't they?" asked Payne.

Tieng backstepped in a crouch and Payne did the same. Stepping up his pace some distance away, Tieng talked.

"You see men who love my country Viet Nam, my broth-ah. This I want you see. Many men die in war, Henry. Some Indian, some army, all broth-ah. You say patriot of country. You patriot my country Viet Nam, huh."

"By patriots you mean Viet Cong, right? And you were delivering medical supplies, weren't you, Tieng?" Payne only wanted confirmation from him; he talked in the darkness, stumbling to keep up. He wasn't alarmed and didn't feel at all in any kind of danger; it was as though he were invincible at this man's side.

"My broth-ah very brave, die for my country Viet Nam. I help make hero."

Payne wondered how bringing them medical supplies would make heroes of the wounded; then it occurred to him that Tieng meant himself as the hero.

"But it's pretty damn risky bringing me out here," he said. "What's your rank, Tieng?"

The Viet acted as though he didn't understand the question; he grunted softly and kept going, moving through the dense growth as agile and quiet as a panther. Payne was breathing hard when they got back to the sampan.

Tieng took a different route back, traversing waterways so narrow the jungle intertwined over the close banks like braids of twisting fingers to black out the sky and stars. The dented moon tried to watch them through the engulfing growth, sneaking an occasional peek as the boat coursed the silent water. A low, still mist rose off the surface of the water, and Payne listened beyond the plinking of oar drops for other unheard sounds. It was strange and eerie gliding through the dank, confining, muted tunnels of swampland—like being lost in another time and place, like living the lost dream of a Congo adventure.

He lay quietly in the compartment, aware now of the nauseating odor of rank fowl. In time Tieng stopped paddling and bottom-pushing and the sampan bumped into land. Payne had no conception of time, how long the return trip had taken; he peered out and viewed the outline of the palms where he had hidden the day before; tiny lines from an inner light shone through the siding of the opium hut. He felt suddenly, upon seeing the familiar hut, as if he were home.

The light came from candles lining the floor mat that covered the trapdoor; no one was in the hootch. It had been left that way for him, for them perhaps, as if by prior arrangement. Tieng silently got out of the combat boots. He lifted the trapdoor and dropped the boots and the binoculars in the tunnel. A jar sat next to the mat with a long straw beside it.

"We drink now," the Indian said. "I tell you about my broth-ah."

And through his tireless but limited English and Payne's perseverance, Payne understood him to mean that the men were not being operated on back there. They were men who had been wounded, and because they were judged incapable of recovery, were being used as live booby traps; the supplies Tieng delivered had not been medical but explosive plastics which were to be placed under the clothing of the wounded soldiers. That was the activity Payne had viewed through the glasses. The drugged comrade would then be taken by boat in the night to an ambush site and left, hopefully to be conscious by morning and ready to attract the enemy with his moans. He did not mention the coffins, but Payne took it for granted they were for the ones who wouldn't get the chance to be martyred brothers. Payne didn't ask who the enemy was, whether it was the Americans—his brothers—or the ARVN, who once had been the brothers of Tieng-of-the-Two-Face.

Payne maintained an outward demeanor of attentiveness and sympathetic interest to what he was being told, but inside he was aghast at the information; his ignorance of such activities stunned him into incredulity. But a greater alarm centered on the Viet's reason for giving him this information; why had Tieng not just left it that he had delivered medical supplies? Surely his intent was not to try and persuade Payne to somehow turn traitor against his own people; what could be his motive?

With reluctance he finally asked the Indian who his enemy was, did he mean the Americans?

Tieng became animated in answer. "No, no, no, Henry," he said emphatically. "No American GI. You think Tieng crazy take you to enemy camp, show you enemy hideout, enemy secret? No, no, no. I speak of the NVA, the ARVN. Both enemy, no patriot Viet Nam."

"Well, we aren't exactly patriots to the Viet Cong, Tieng," Payne said, sounding doubtful but relieved. "They are our enemy as much as the NVA. You know a lot more than I do about the ARVNs, sure. But we're supposed to be fighting with them, not against them."

Tieng exaggerated his nod of agreement. "Yes. I know this. But you know what I tell you, Henry. I explain. How you want I explain more, huh? No can do. You understand. I no want give you idea that wrong. Okay."

Payne said yes, he could see what he meant, that he was sorry if he gave the wrong impression, but that he was just making sure. He wanted to believe it.

Presently Tieng's comrades ambled into the hootch and moved to sit in a circle on the mat. The ensuing talk seemed jubilant. They smoked the pipe and drank from the common jar, swaying their heads as if they were all drunk. Payne thought they might be.

He felt the full weight of the predicament he was now in, realizing the liability he was to them with this new knowledge. He knew about the tunnel below the floor, that the village of Paang Dong was probably a VC headquarters, at minimum harboring the enemy, that there was a field unit out there somewhere that might have been a direct link with the Ho Chi Minh Trail, where death was being manufactured, as likely as not, for his people, the imperialist enemy. Why should they trust him to keep his mouth shut about what he'd seen and knew? That was the question that made him ask Tieng:

"What do you want me to do to help you?"

Chapter
18

He did not sleep with the girl that night. After Payne and Tieng had left Saang's alley apartment, U.S. military police made a raid on the Sing Song Bar. They arrested a number of American troops on curfew violation and detained the women for questioning. Saang was among the ones detained. The women later were released and threatened with arrest if they were seen again on the street, and Saang had remained in town, looking for Payne to return to her apartment. When it got very late and Payne had not returned, she knew he had stayed in the village with Tieng; she said because they could not sleep together it had been a long, sad night for her.

He was not asleep when she entered the hut at noon but he was prostrate as though he were, sweating and feverish. Earlier he woke up thinking he was in a temple. No one was there and he felt deserted and frightened, as though he'd been abandoned. He had smoked and drunk from the jar until dawn with the Viet Cong, and when he finally lay down to sleep a spider bit him.

Saang seemed genuinely sad but said, kneeling next to him, that she could not have slept with him in the village even if the MPs had not held her, that she had prayed he would return to town. "It wrong me sleep you here," she said, patting his face with a wet cloth. "Very bad. Bring evil spirit to Paang Dong I sleep with American. Why you no come back Sing Song?"

Payne smiled through his teeth. The fever had broken and he felt better now. The wet cloth on his forehead was soothing. He rose to a sitting position and shook his thick head, which only intensified the throbbing. He moaned. The briarlike cuts on his hands and forearms were puffy and bit like ant stings.

The girl rocked back on her heels; she clasped her hands in her lap. She was a peasant again today, wearing also a conical hat that swallowed her small head. "Why you no come back Sing Song?" she repeated in a sulk, hiding her eyes under the rim of the hat.

"Got drunk and couldn't drive."

That snapped the sulking. "You funny man, Joe. What you do today? Rest of day? Not much left, huh?"

"Work," Payne said, lying. He had no intention of working. "I could see you tonight."

"I work today too. Very early. Have much rice take." She put a hand on the small of her back and grimaced. "Much work Vietnamese girl. No like work all time. I too smart, I go university someday, no take rice no more. . . . You smell numbah ten. You wash today, I see you tonight."

She stooped to retreat through the low doorway. Payne stopped her. "What did the MPs do to you?"

"No problem, happen all time," she said and left.

He wondered about that, just how often she was harassed for being a whore, or being an Indian, if it did "happen all time," if it so permeated her peasant-prostitute existence that it really was "no problem." He couldn't tell by her response, which was without color, a flat and simple catchall phrase; maybe it was just an automatic response for all Americans. She had said it to him before, but it was not an answer.

Other than a few dogs and hens passing time in the shade, the village of Paang Dong appeared deserted. Nobody around to check on him or stop him from leaving.

He didn't feel up to walking, and he waited alongside the road for a ride. The landscape was a panorama of near and distant paddy fields where small, bent bodies went mindlessly about the back-wrenching task, indifferent to an angry sun beating down on them. Humble and ignorant farmers. It was a pervasive scene in this country but the familiarity of it narrowed in Payne's thoughts to the wall picture in a crumbling hotel room in Nha Trang, a scene he had destroyed.

A boy leading an ox-drawn cart came along and he climbed in the back and tried to get some sleep. A faint leftover moon stood boldly in defiance of the eminent, unforgiving sun. Payne lit a cigarette and took one bitter draw and threw it away. He needed antiseptic for his arms.

During the night someone had produced a deck of cards, wanting to learn an American card game and Payne taught the Indians the game of blackjack. They learned quickly, when to hold, when to risk a hit, and he joked that they could make a mint playing the crew of goons in his hootch. Afterward Tieng sent a man for a chicken and Payne watched unnerved as Kroong-the-Warrior bit open the fowl's belly, disemboweling it with his pointed teeth in a bloody pursuit of the bird's heart. They each took a candle outside and stood around a tree as Kroong draped the entrails on the branches; his grinning, blood-slicked face glinted in the candlelight. He ate the heart without compunction, as if he were hungry. The ritual joined Payne in some way to them; because he had swallowed the chicken's blood, as did the others, he thought of it as a union sealed in blood, as blood brothers.

Earlier Tieng had told him a little of the history of his nomadic tribe. Payne found it difficult to believe the pitiable, ruinous past his people had endured; he thought Tieng was embellishing the extent of the tribe's disasters to gain his sympathy so that Payne would readily comply with the favor Tieng was working up to asking him.

Tieng said the seventy-eight people of Paang Dong village were all that was left of the old Sar Paang tribe, one of the most prosperous and respected colonies in all Mnong Gar country; the tribe had the fiercest warriors and the choicest land. They had been forced to abandon their homeland in the Lang Biang Mountains two years before, and the exodus ended here in the delta quagmire. Several things accounted for this, Tieng told him. After the epidemic which killed or incapacitated most of their militia, they could no longer defend themselves against the constant harassment from the Viet Cong. The various Saigon governments took no interest in impoverished forest dwellers and each new regime turned its back on them, and later their forests were being defoliated and pocked by U.S. bombs and napalm, hellfires thrown down by angered spirits.

The forest tribes for centuries defended their land with their own militia. More recently they fought the Viet Minh when the French ran

things and then the Viet Cong. Tieng himself commanded a strike
force that fought with the ARVNs and Americans as the VC insur-
gency strengthened. He said his guerrilla force gathered intelligence
in the highland mountains along the border and inside Cambodia for
the Americans and ARVNs. His force had joined with 5th Special
Forces in earlier years and he talked of the bravery and determination
of those Americans, much as Jesus had talked of the courage of the
Monties he had fought with.

"We kill many VC for American and for my country Viet Nam,"
Tieng had said. "But Saigon no like Sar Paang people, much hate."
The Montagnards, he said, were discriminated against and distrusted
by the Saigon government, which considered them subhuman and
eventually cut off the civil assistance programs they depended on after
the epidemic struck and after the great American war machinery in-
discriminately bombed their forests and villages. They could no
longer move about their territorial land planting and harvesting crops
in poisoned soil. Tieng blamed Saigon rather than the U.S. forces that
now controlled the region for robbing them of their land. It had been
Payne's people who destroyed the land, but it was Saigon that allowed it. He said, "Other army come, they go, we still have forest for
crop. No more, only hole in land. No can plant crop. Must go, leave
home of ancestah forev-ah."

Although Payne had listened with reservations as Tieng told of
the plight and fate of his people, he was certain he could not have
been stretching his story too far beyond the truth, and when the Indian
got around to his solicitation, Payne enthusiastically agreed to do
what he could. "Just tell me how I can help you," he said, "and by
God I'll do it if I can."

They had celebrated Payne's compliance with a fresh jar and a
different pipe, one with a longer draw. But his compliance was an act;
he had no intention of helping them, the enemy, but had said it anyway, for he was leery of Kroong-the-Warrior, who eyed him with
grave caution over the course of the night. Kroong was a menacing
figure, muscular and pinched-faced, and the French officer's kepi he
wore low on his head accorded him, like the boonierat's headgear
Willingham wore, the intimidating mystique of a tested warrior.

Yet the request seemed a simple enough thing, even innocuous.
He was surprised that all they wanted of him was to arrange safe
passage for ten men to the highlands for Tet, and on the way deliver

caskets to Saigon so that a few of the martyrs could be buried in the graveyard of their ancestors.

"The men of power must go land of ancestah, where tomb rest. This for Tet. Must take dead patriot Saigon first," Tieng had said seriously, as if homage to his ancestors were more important than the war. "You help see we go no problem. You have plenty authority. Get army truck for us."

High-spirited on opium and beer, Payne had then teased Tieng, pointing out that he was a first-rate con man and shouldn't have any problem getting a truck himself. "Hell, you already have a truck, don't you? That general store on wheels?" Had it not been for Kroong flashing his bush hook, he would have carried it further and mentioned the ripoff to bring home his point, even though he did not want the money back; as Willingham had said, the AK-47 was worth more than money.

"No, Henry," Tieng had said, still intensely serious. "You must go with us. Make sure no problem. You do because you no hate my country Viet Nam. You now comrade my people. Okay."

Payne didn't like that idea, the way it was put, but he kept it to himself. "Will Saang-the-Smart-One go with us?" he asked.

Saang would not go. The trip to the graves of their ancestors was only for the men who had the wealth and the power. It was settled; the beer had all been drunk, and when the birds began to chirp and twitter and the sky began to glow, Payne and his strange ensemble of blood-brother comrades had wandered off in different places to sleep.

The heavy-hoofed ox was in no hurry to get anywhere even as the boy tugged on the oxbow and then the bull's jowls while prodding him with a stick. The beast reacted as it would to a bird perched on its back, twitching its thick hide or flicking an ear. Payne tried to talk to the kid, but they could not communicate. The boy's long shorts were rolled up and he was barefoot. He dug his toes in the mud and slung gobs of muck on the ox's back then smeared it around to cool and coax the animal.

When they finally reached the outskirts of Long Xuyen, Payne jumped off the cart and gave the boy five dollars, a lot of money for a peasant kid. The boy's eyes grew large and he bowed three or four times.

Payne walked thoughtfully along a road that banked the river. There was nothing to keep him from going to the authorities. They would find a cache of weapons and a unit of VC in the village. He considered whether he could save lives by telling them about the compound in the jungle, how wounded soldiers were rigged with explosives. Maybe. But what would his people do with the information and how far would they go? Would they seize only Tieng and his comrades, or arrest the entire population of Paang Dong?

It was his people in the first place who had defoliated their forests and sent them into exodus, his people who were hell-bent on winning the hearts and minds of the Vietnamese people.

His people. The thought of it disgusted Payne. It was the Americans who wouldn't leave them to their own concerns, his people whose unctuous pride alone prolonged the war.

He wondered what Willingham would do in his place. Willingham had been there; he knew the score. He had fought the war with Montagnards and he understood their ways. But Payne couldn't imagine what he would do; there was more to Willingham's ambivalence toward the Vietnamese than he knew about. Maybe, like his buddy Jesus, Willingham felt compassion for the Indians, trusted them. Or maybe he didn't trust them at all, like Bruiser. Maybe all Vietnamese were slopes to Willingham, responsible for changing the boulevard-cruising surfer into the vindictive killer he had become. Who was to blame for that, them or us, their people or his own?

Payne skimmed a stone on the river. It was no big deal getting a truck for the Indians; he knew *he* felt a certain compassion for them. He considered them his friends. They trusted him and he saw himself being useful in a way that would not cause harm. What could be the harm in taking the dead to their resting place, to deliver his new friends to the land of their ancestors? Maybe their priorities were off track; it seemed to him they were, but who was he to pass judgment on their priorities? Maybe tradition was more important to forest people than the war. And helping them get to their homeland for the holidays wasn't exactly like aiding and abetting the enemy. Who was the enemy, anyway? That was the very heart of the matter, the way Payne saw it; just who was the goddamn enemy?

It was late afternoon now and the sky began to roll and rumble. He was gritty and exhausted and his scratched-up arms needed attention. His calves ached from all the squatting he had done over the last two days. He needed a bath and a shave and a cold beer. He found a hotel that ministered to GIs and took a room overlooking the water.

He hadn't gotten out of his boots before a girl tapped on his door, wanting to party; she cooed sweetly and batted heavily painted eyes and suggested a short time in a harder tone when Payne turned down her best-deal offer, the all-nighter, and then a half-hour round the world tour. He had to shut the door on her. Forgoing a shower, he washed his arms then stretched out on the bed. Bright particles swirled behind his eyelids and he tried to stop one, to still it, and then he fell asleep.

He was awakened by a flash of light and a noise that sounded like a gunshot. The light was a roaming searchlight coming off the river; the noise, he decided, had been a car or motorbike backfiring. It was noisy on the wet street below the second-floor window. The rain had come and gone while he slept.

After a shower he went downstairs to the bar and drank a cold "33" in two gulps, then had whiskey on ice, since they were out of Scotch. He smoked a cigarette that now tasted right and talked with a black lieutenant going on leave from the wet boonies. He was on his way to Sydney.

But the young lieutenant had not yet left the jungle. His lips continually tightened as he ranted. With vigorous pride he claimed to have personally taken out three so far; the man was beside himself with hatred. "I know goddamn well I dinged that many for sure, maybe more," he said. "Sleazy little motherfucks," he said without using much wind. "Freakin little shits."

The lieutenant was from Upper Michigan. He didn't want to know anything about Payne, which disburdened Payne of his self and led him deeper into the man's hatred. The lieutenant had a right to hate the way he did; half his platoon in less than a month had bought it from either sniper fire or boobies. Payne filled with ambivalence, wondering how many of them Tieng and his men, with their body-wired booby traps, had caused to die.

"This war ain't for shit, man. I mean you can't square off and fight the goddamn enemy, fuck no," the man said. "They trick you." His nostrils flared like huge abysmal wells in his black face. "The worst, man, was my point getting it. Right through the fuckin ass and up his body like some goddamn medieval impalement. A fuckin disgrace to die like that. They got no honor to kill a man that way, no respect for life . . . motherfuckers."

It was hard to keep from feeling the man's hate. Willingham

hated like that, when he had watched the slopes dismember his buddies, before he had learned to live with it, and Payne vicariously felt some of the pain of this man's passion.

"You shouldn't have to go back," Payne said. "You've done your part."

The lieutenant glared at him with the full extent of his hate. "You kiddin' me, man? Fuck. I *want* to go back. I got some fucking payback to settle up and I mean to take me out as many as I can before they take me out."

It was as if a territory had been set up at their corner of the bar. None of the other GIs in the lounge moved within listening distance of them. The young lieutenant's wrath had consumed him; Payne felt it too, felt it taking hold of him, and he abruptly left, leaving a full drink, telling the man that now was a good time to go to Sydney, that it wasn't raining there this time of year.

The whores in the doorway of the Sing Song issued knowing catcalls as Payne stepped by them, their crooked grins of jealousy signaling another kind of territorial possession. He searched the dimness for Saang and located her in a booth at the rear. She waved without getting up.

Walking her way, he noticed the sandy-haired GI he had seen in the place once or twice before and nodded familiarly at him; the GI had been looking at Payne but acted as if he hadn't.

"Joe, you very nice-looking man now, most handsome all GI. I let you buy me tea," Saang said and batted her Polynesian eyes. She was decked out in full regalia of necklaces, bracelets, the white ear discs, a wooden comb in her chignon along with a crown of colored beads patterning her black hair.

Payne had his cap on and the green handkerchief tied around his neck. He couldn't tell if he smelled or not. He ordered the tea and himself a mixed drink.

"*You* look nice, Saang. Most beautiful girl of all."

"You hungry suppah? I make you."

Sometime during the dead of night, in the darkness of her apartment, Saang rolled over into the contour of Payne's body and woke him curling his chest hair around her fingers. In his sleep he thought it was the mouse in his hootch.

"Oh, I scare you. Sorry . . . Joe? I talk you now. Everybody like you and Saang love you."

He touched her hair, which now draped her small breasts, fingering the down on her neck, and ran a hand along her baby-smooth back. Her breath was not sour and he tried to kiss her.

"You wait," she said, pushing easily against his chest. "You have girlfriend in United State America?" She paused very still and waited for him to answer.

He thought about that, about Ann. It was not something he wanted to think about. "No," he said.

She raised up on an elbow and looked down on him. Her face was a vague outline in the filtered residue of the streetlight. He rubbed the sleep from his eyes and waited.

"That make Saang very happy, because I want be girlfriend you. When you go Viet Nam, Joe?"

"Saang," he said, "my name is Henry, not Joe. My other name is Russell. You can call me Henry or Russell, or Payne if you like. That's my name too. But you don't have to call me Joe anymore, all right? It's not my name."

"I know. I know you name."

She breathed softly, and in the silence that followed Payne drifted to the edge of sleep.

"Joe? When you go Viet Nam?"

He put his hand in the smooth cup of her underarm. "A couple months."

"You know I go soon university Saigon. Saang almost rich now. I be very smart then."

"Saang-the-Smart-One," Payne said. "You'll do good. I'm very happy for you."

"University Saigon no good. I want go United State America, Joe. You marry Saang, take United State America."

A morning bird called through the open window; it was a lark, singing in a melancholy warble.

"I be best girlfriend you, make you happy. I give you son and we call him Joe. Saang very smart, make you family happy, very proud. Please, Joe, you take me United State America?"

Payne pulled her onto his chest and absently ran a hand along her hip and leg, deciding how to let her down.

"My country is not what you think it is, Saang," he said. "It's cold and hard and fast. You would not like living there."

"I like. I know I like," she retorted. "You think Saang make you shame. But you see, Joe. I make you very happy."

He tried again to kiss her and she kept him away. "Where are your parents, Saang? Are they helping you get into the university?"

She turned away from him. He wasn't going to pursue it, but in a moment she turned back to him. "My moth-ah and fath-ah dead. Die before I come here."

He felt instinctively that their deaths were caused by the war and not the great epidemic. "Did they die because of the Americans?" he asked against his will.

She shook her head sideways, but he had forgotten that that meant the affirmative, that she was saying yes, because of the Americans.

She remained quiet for a while and soon he released her and threw his feet over the edge of the slab bed. He smoked and watched the light slowly bring to life the dismal room.

She didn't take it well when he told her he was married. She wouldn't believe him at first because he had no ring or the imprint of a ring on his finger, even though he told her he never wore a ring. She seemed genuinely heartbroken and cried for some time, then dressed in her field uniform and went out to get him some coffee. "All GI like coffee," she said, drying her eyes.

He held Ann's letter to the morning light. It was a smear of blue ink now and indecipherable and he balled it up and threw it out the window.

When Saang returned carrying two porcelain cups she was smiling. "Sorry, no coffee. Tea. Tea much bettah. What you do today?"

Her cheerfulness brightened him.

"I'm free. What would you like to do today, Saang?"

She thought hard behind the steam of her tea. "What you do in United State America today, you no work?"

"We'd have a picnic. You want to do that?"

"What this pick-neck, Joe?"

"We'd ride our bicycles out into the countryside and sit by the water under a shade tree and eat sandwiches and drink wine. You want to do that today?"

"No can do, must take rice." Instead of pouting she grinned. "You come me today, help take rice too. Okay?"

"All right," he said, without thinking; he thought only that he wanted to be with her.

Before the sun had reached high noon he was exhausted and collapsed on the edge of a dike under a fig tree. It was the hardest work he remembered ever having done, comparable to picking cotton with his country-hick cousins in the heat of August but worse because of the extreme and constant stooping; at least picking cotton you did not have to continually stoop. Her peasant friends chuckled at him as they bounded by with heavy chogi sticks springing on their shoulders. He had refused to take off his boots and now his feet were swollen inside them and he couldn't get them off. The mosquito-infested water did not help the festered scratches on his arms.

"You no say Tieng what I say you, okay? It secret," Saang told him, squatting beside where he lay sprawled flat.

"You mean about you wanting to go to Texas?"

"He no understand. You no tell. You promise."

Idiotically Payne gave a Scout's-honor sign and made the promise to her.

"Maybe you change mind, come back some day, say 'Okay, Saang. I change mind, take you United State America now. I love you, Saang.'"

"Please," Payne said, "don't say that."

She picked a fig for each of them, and as she nibbled on hers Saang grew serious; by now he could tell something about her moods and he knew she was going to pursue the subject. But she did not; she brought up something else.

"Tieng-of-the-Two-Face my broth-ah, you know this," she said. "I love broth-ah. But I love you too, Joe. I learn love you. You be careful with my broth-ah Tieng. He good, very good person, but you be careful. You promise that Saang, Joe."

He didn't give her the Scout sign this time but nodded, displaying the show of coolness he felt he had by now earned.

"I want hear you say you promise be careful."

"All right. I'll be careful. What should I be careful about?"

She dry-kissed him on the cheek.

"Well?" he persisted. Her habit of dismissing his questions was beginning to annoy him.

"You big dumb GI, Joe," she said vaguely, not answering the question. She said nothing else about it and presently they waddled back in to the great sloppy rice field, Payne dragging his leaden feet, regretting he had agreed to this slave labor.

Late in the day he went back to post and over to the information office to take care of the lumpy seven canisters of film he'd been carrying around. He first revived himself with a few beers, nothing harder, at the tent clubhouse where a Spec 4 from IO spent his time after work. The Spec 4 afterward let him use the office lab.

The IO had the facilities to handle black-and-white but not color, and he processed the canisters of black-and-white. The grain was good; he credited the quality of the prints to the army, which had outdone itself choosing Leica equipment. He made small prints, six-by-eights, and sandwiched them between cardboards in a manila envelope which he addressed, "Public Information Office/c/o Spec 4 Russell H. Payne/USARVSUPCOM, HHC/Long Binh, RVN," and dropped in the post office depository.

He slept again in the ice-cream factory's back room, and again the boy relinquished his cot to Payne. The kid spent most of his time on post because he was an Amerasian, a social outcast. He had big feet and long legs and there was a slight wave in his amber-colored hair, something like Cotton's crop in adolescence. Payne thought he was a beautiful boy and wondered, not remorsefully, if he would be leaving a child behind.

In the morning Payne took some shots of the boy and the old mamasan, who again washed his reeking clothes; he shot them tending the large churns and outside where they loaded the five-gallon cartons into a paddy wagon that would deliver the ice cream to any number of camps in the outlying areas. The truck had bullet holes in the paneling and in the windshield.

He asked the boy if there was anything he wanted from the PX. The boy lowered his head shyly and Payne said, "C'mon, how about some boots. We can find a pair to fit those clodhoppers of yours."

The boy walked alongside him to the supply billet and waited outside while Payne looked through a bin of utilities earmarked for retrograde and found a pair that looked about the size of the kid's overgrown feet. The people down here were not plagued by the strack rigidity that permeated Long Binh. He was welcome to a pair of boots. "Heck, they just goin' to waste anyways," the supply clerk said. "Don't nobody wanna wear no dead man's boots."

The boy stuck his flipflops in the waistband of his shorts and walked off in the boots, stomping them to get the feel.

Payne went back to the IO and called Lieutenant Finn.

"It better be worth it," Finn said after he finished screaming at Payne for again being AWOL. Payne told him he had forwarded some prints and was working on two or three topnotch pacification stories, plus a yarn about ice cream cones for the field troops, that he had more pictures coming, enough to make a four-page spread for the magazine. It was all good stuff, but he needed a couple of more days if the lieutenant could spare him. He sold Finn on it.

"All right. But this better be the last time this happens," Finn said. "Two days. I'll tell Captain Burns that when he calls again today. And you can bet he will. Captain Reinhardt also called me today. He didn't have much good to say about you; seems you disappeared without him getting the chance to check over your notes."

"He's an asshole."

"Yeah, that may very well be. But he's still an officer, Payne."

"What did Burns say? Did he want to know where I am?"

"*Captain* Burns."

"Right. What did he say?"

"Well, he didn't want to know if you had any distinguishing birthmarks," Finn said in a deadpan, and the unexpected humor of it drew a laugh out of Payne. "But he wanted to know everything else. I told him I sent you to the boondocks on assignment, but I had to tell him, that knowing you, I couldn't say exactly where you were or when precisely you'd be back. Did I do all right?"

"Sir, you did just fine," Payne said, grinning into the receiver. Damned if he wasn't actually becoming fond of Lieutenant Finn.

"How's Willingham doing?"

"He's doing your job. I might have to make him the editor since you don't seem to like our company much anymore, considering this attitude problem everybody thinks you have."

Finn's tone was amicable, teasing. He added, "Who knows, we might have to make a switch in the Tokyo plan."

"Who knows," Payne said agreeably, not overly concerned if he meant it. What was Tokyo to him anyway?

He took Saang to a movie in town that night. She had never been to a theater. "No kidding?" Payne said. "Well, let's hope they show something good. You don't have to dress up."

It was a Japanese samurai film, the good sword of the East against the bad sword of the West, climaxing in a duel to the death. Both swords died, although the good sword, dying last, lived long enough to deliver the story's moral: "There is no life in the sword." It was the final line of the film which had been subtitled in four languages, Vietnamese, Chinese, French, and English. Saang pulled for the samurai from the West, even though he was evil, and cried when he was run through by the sword of the East. Payne was taken by the colorful costumes. He didn't grasp the esoteric customs, in which honor seemed to dictate the rules and take precedence over all other motivations, even their ultimate deaths, which seemed to Payne unnecessary and ironically tragic, for the warriors were brothers by blood who had been separated in their youth.

They stayed the night in the waterfront hotel where he had met the impassioned young lieutenant. This time he was charged, in addition to the room, the price of a hotel girl. He quietly paid the extra money because Saang was embarrassed and he didn't want to make a row in front of her, but it left him with little money.

Reluctantly he worked again in the rice field with Saang and the women of the village the next morning and went back to her apartment and slept the afternoon while she continued working. He took her to dinner at a restaurant on the river in the evening, and then he was completely broke. She had dressed formally in a black silk *ao dai* and flat glittering slippers, her hair left free to drape her shoulders, a single bracelet and earrings of white bone. But it was her poise and manners that impressed Payne more than her loveliness, and he thought that night she truly was a princess.

He stayed until New Year's Eve. When it came time to leave he realized the extent of his sentiment for Saang and Tieng, as though they were a part of his life now after only a week. Tieng gave him a stash of opium which he was inclined to refuse because he thought he might get addicted; but refusing the gift would have been an insult and he stuck the bag in his pocket.

Their last night together Tieng got down to specifics on the arrangements. They were to meet in Saigon at five o'clock at the Japanese pavilion of the zoo exactly a week from today to make sure Payne had things arranged on his end. Earlier if anything unexpected came up. "I be at zoo every day. Wait for Henry. We have good time, drink and smoke in Saigon. Okay."

Payne wanted to know why not the bar where he first met Saang; he thought it was Tieng's hangout in the city. But the Indian was adamant that they meet in the zoo, for reasons he didn't explain.

Grinning broadly, Tieng finally mentioned the ripoff: "Maybe I give MPC back you friend with potatoes. He friend you I no cheat. Okay."

Payne shrugged it off.

He left the cameras and lenses hidden underneath the blanket in Saang's hut in Paang Dong. He had not been inside her tiny house before; it had been forbidden for him to enter her place and he had to sneak in before dawn, when the village was sleeping. The apartment in town was better furnished; the austerity of her meager house, which was her home, touched him in a sad way. She kept all her personal things there, an old dilapidated trunk and several photographs of her family, her parents, he presumed. The room smelled of musk, like a barn, but she kept it neat. There was a stack of textbooks on the wire-spool tabletop next to the discarded door she used as a bed. One of the books, in French, appeared from its pages of pictures to be an anthropological study of highland Montagnards, another a dated U.S. history textbook in English, similar to a particular book Payne remembered from grade school.

The camera equipment would bring a fortune on the black market—enough, he hoped, to have a bearing on Saang's future. He had wanted to take pictures of them but Tieng early on prohibited that too. Payne hadn't pushed it or asked again, but he had taken some shots of Saang, which she made him swear not to mention to her brother. "It bad take picture me, make Tieng very mad. You promise."

"Will you try to come to Saigon with your brother? I'd like to see you," Payne said to her under the fig tree where they had a picnic on New Year's Eve.

She said she was smart enough to talk him into it.

Chapter

19

He beat the weather back and scrubbed himself under a hot shower.
Before shaving he evaluated himself in the locker mirror; the week-
old mustache dignified and matured him, he decided, and he left it to
grow full. After plucking out his whiplike nose hair and dressing in
fresh fatigues, he opened the mail Kink had left on his side of the
desk. One letter was from his mother and one came from an aunt who
had written him three or four times. Dorothy was his father's sister, a
thoughtful and insightful woman Payne had rarely seen when he was
growing up and barely knew. She seemed to know how much it meant
to get letters in the Nam even though she had no children of her own.
She called him Rusty, as his father had called him, and Payne had
come to regard her warmly. She lived in the Bay Area of California
and he had promised in a return letter to visit her when he got to
Oakland.

His mother had written regularly in the first half of his tour, then
slacked off to a letter every month or so. She had stopped mentioning
the television news or anything about Vietnam in her writing, but she
sent prayers and liked to gossip and down-talk Ann. He looked forward to his mother's letters with the ambivalent commingling of affection and apprehension. In this one she wanted to know what
Payne's future plans were, how many children he and Ann were planning to have. Were they going to make their home in Texarkana or
"somewhere away from home"?

Annoyance overcame his affection and he started a letter back to her: "Dear Mom, Got a surprise for you. Let me put it this way. Won't be living in Arkansas or even Texas. Got married here and am bringing home a gook wife. A little skinny but a swell fuck. Will have to live in Utah. But don't worry. They're salt of the earth folks up there, I hear, with mighty disciplined religion. BYOB when you visit." He angrily wadded it up.

The office crew welcomed him back with news of tonight's going-away party for Sergeant Sterr. "Getting two birds with the same stone," Cowboy said and showed Payne the New Year's champagne in the refrigerator.

Payne had a deep tan from the paddyland sun, which brought out the squint lines around his eyes. The crisscrossing milk-white scars along the backs of his hand and arms glowed in contrast to his darkened skin. Other than being beardless, he looked like Willingham the first day he strutted into the office.

Willingham raised an eyebrow, appraising him. "That fucking knife grass sure can be a bitch, can't it?" he said and popped Payne between his shoulder blades. "What kind of shit you get into this time, buddy?"

It was the first time he'd called Payne buddy.

"You'll like it," Payne said, cracking a grin. Taking Willingham aside he whispered, "Finn told me they called. It's got to be another assignment. He say anything to you about it?"

Nodding, Willingham said, "But it's about time; things are getting boring around here. I'm ready to boogie any time."

He was making light of his anxiety; but Payne could see it. He understood it better now, the need Willingham had to get back out there, back into his element, for he felt anxious too. It wasn't the same as before his week at Long Xuyen; he felt involved now, committed to a purpose, that was the big difference.

He stepped inside the lieutenant's office to tell him about the stolen cameras.

"For Christ's sake, Payne," Finn said, shaking his head. "They took everything?"

Payne nodded dejectedly. "Everything but the prints I sent ahead. You get them?"

"Yeah, smart thinking. You didn't get hurt or anything, did you?"

"Nah. These cowboys are real smooth. Just cut the strap and disappeared in a crowd. I chased them into an alley but I didn't figure it would be too smart to go in there."

"Right. Cameras can be replaced," Finn agreed and hesitated, staring into space. He was reflecting on something and Payne asked, "What?"

"Oh, nothing," the lieutenant said and then changed his mind. "Well, yes. It reminded me. I guess you haven't forgotten that trip you and I made back in June, have you?"

Payne grinned lopsidedly. He was going to hear a confession from the new lieutenant.

"Yeah. Well, I found my buddy all right. It shook me seeing what had happened to him; the fool had gone berserk. I mean his goddamn teeth were falling out from all the shit he was shooting up. He never even smoked before, when we were bridge partners back in school. Seems a long time ago. I stayed with him a few days; that's where I was all that time. I tried to get through to him. He was going to kill himself, and he was short then, practically on his way home. He didn't even know me."

"I've always wondered about that," Payne said. "You ever hear from him again?"

"No." You could see Finn had already dismissed the guy and he simply shrugged now at the thought. He brought himself back to the subject at hand:

"Write me up a full report describing what happened and I'll take care of it. You *were* doing a story at the time, weren't you?"

"Roger that, sir. Sidebar on dietary improvement; locals shopping in town for health foods." Payne chuckled despite himself.

Finn shot him a quick doubtful glance but let it go. "Well, glad you're all right. It could have been a dangerous situation, you know."

"Burns call again?"

Finn frowned. "You're incorrigible; it's Captain Burns. But, no, he hasn't bothered me since you called."

"You going to let us drink champagne in the office?"

"It's New Year's, isn't it?"

The man *had* changed; it must have been Willingham's influence.

Everyone from the office was there but Langley, who was on temporary duty setting up a photo lab for a new detachment unit in IV

Corps, the delta. No one could pronounce the name of the village nearest the new unit, and when the lieutenant finally missed Langley halfway through the party and asked, "Where's Langley?" Sterr had to say, "Somewhere in the delta," since he couldn't say it either. Lai Sin painstakingly slow-spoke the name of the village, trying to get it across to them, but tones cannot be transposed phonetically and the interest in Langley's whereabouts was scrubbed.

Payne had never known Lai Sin to stay after work or participate in any GI social function; he assumed she equated the high season of New Year's with her Lunar New Year and had stayed because of its importance, in deference to her American benefactors. She was cheerful and seemed to be enjoying herself.

The Red Cross tree had arrived four days after Christmas along with a string of blinking lights and some wilted mistletoe. Sterr said it didn't seem like Christmas until then. "It don't fuckin seem like Christmas now, neither," said Cowboy, getting drunk and trying his best to trick the elusive Lai Sin into standing under the clump of dead mistletoe. The men nevertheless appreciated the tree with its sparse string of colored lights. There was one gift-wrapped box under the tree.

Sterr had uncorked the first of the six bottles of champagne at five o'clock and soon was teaching the men how to circle-dance and sing beer-garden songs from the diaphragm. His was a German's charismatic enthusiasm, a stalwart old-country traditionalist's high-flying verve, which soon had the room rock-and-rolling with foot-stomping swaggers and deep bellowing voices.

After he'd put away a quantity of champagne and a heater of sake, Lieutenant Finn ceremoniously announced his promotion and allowed Lai Sin the honor of attaching the silver bars to his lapels. He attempted a speech and was booed down. Sterr tried to persuade him to at least for the love of the army *consider* re-uping but the men hissed and booed him down too.

The leftovers from CARE packages were spread across Lai Sin's desk. There was a fruit-nut cake and a tin of cookies from Cowboy's family and a loaf of Payne's mother's banana bread, which Kink had dropped off at the office while Payne was away. Lai Sin had never heard of banana bread and had two pieces. "Lookit. She's gone ba-nanas over it," Cowboy yelped, getting drunker. Lai Sin had Pepsi in the place of champagne and after much coaxing reluctantly entered the circle-dance. She seemed to like the attention and twirled shyly until Cowboy ruined it by again grabbing at her.

After Lai Sin left to catch the late bus, Willingham and Cowboy gingerly hung arms across Sterr's thick shoulders and directed him to the single present lying under the tree.

Cowboy said, "It's from all of us. Go ahead, open it."

Sterr accepted the present appreciatively, appearing touched. "You shouldn't have. Thanks," he said, gullible as Cowboy.

He went through several expressions as he unraveled a wrinkled, deflated full-size blow-up Barbie doll, before finally settling on a good-humored shake of the head. Cowboy had purchased it by mail order from an ad in the back of *Playboy* magazine.

"Just what I always wanted," Sterr said.

Willingham showed him the umbilical cord at the navel. "You have to give her a blow job to get her going."

By eight o'clock Finn was wobbling. A few minutes later he excused himself, saying he had letters to write, and the party went on with Sterr, Payne, Cowboy, and Willingham playing blackjack with Sterr dealing. Payne used the paltry remnants of his contingency-fund money, which he no longer considered sacred. Sterr produced a bottle of bourbon and poured rounds.

Sterr couldn't seem to lose; he dealt himself nineteens, twenties, and twenty-ones and nobody hit a blackjack to take the deal from him. It was his night and no one complained about losing but Cowboy, whose futile bluff in the game of blackjack wasn't working against Sterr's winning combinations. Sterr put his drinks away like water, his huge workingman's hands shuffling and dealing the cards with the deft touch of long experience, cool as a cardsharp, and eyes began to watch his hands closely. It couldn't be detected if he was cheating.

When he had won a pile of money, Sterr said he would demonstrate a feat they would not believe if they didn't object to changing the game. No one objected to changing the game.

"We've got enough time before the fireworks start that I can show you gentlemen the impossible—and take the rest of your money doing it because you're all suckers." He spoke with a confidence that was larger than himself.

"How's that?" Willingham asked, his chin on the desk and eyes narrowed to suspicious slits.

"Cockroach vapor test," Sterr announced casually. "Somebody find me a cockroach, the bigger the better."

They spread out in search of a cockroach. It took only a couple minutes. Willingham came back with a two-incher plus in the palm of his hand, and after examining each man's bug closely, Sterr chose that one.

From the well drawer of his desk Sterr produced a clear quart jar with a rubber tube in its lid and a ball squeeze on the tube. He explained that he would place the live cockroach into the jar, seal it and suck out all the air to make a vacuum and then give the bug ten minutes to die.

"Thirty," Willingham said. "Give it thirty minutes and I'll bet fifty bucks. No fucking way a cockroach can live that long without air."

Sterr reexamined the cockroach, thought it over, and said, "Why not."

"What's the catch?" Payne said.

"How do we know all the air's out?" said Willingham.

Sterr pointed out the tiny gauge sealed in the lid. "I'll get it reading below zero, but just below. We don't want the jar to implode."

Payne was out of cash and had only his Purple Heart medal left to bet. "How about it, Sarge, this ought to be worth about five ten bucks, don't you think?"

"Sure, Payne," Sterr said. "Throw it in. Let's make it worth twenty."

"No way a living creature can live in a vacuum thirty minutes and come out alive," Cowboy said. "I'll go fifteen."

When the money was on the table, Sterr went to work on the squeeze ball. They all leaned forward to watch the gauge. It dropped below the zero mark and within a few seconds smoky-gray gases began to exosmose from the cockroach's shiny black shell. Everyone but Sterr jumped back. The bug struggled to climb the glass, then started spinning dizzily around in a circle. After three or four minutes of spinning without air, the bug flipped over and kicked through the smoke with its tiny hairline legs.

"What we have here, gentlemen, is your basic dying-cockroach position," Sterr said. "You will remember it from your early training days."

The cockroach disappeared in the opaqueness of its own vapors; the gray-white smoke swirled inside the jar, filling it completely. They took turns holding up the jar, tilting it, shaking it and peering through the bottom at the motionless bug.

"It's dead as a sonofabitch," Cowboy said after ten minutes.

Sterr poured more bourbon and they waited.

"Still got fifteen minutes," Sterr said languorously and began shuffling the cards. "A round of stud while we wait, gentlemen?"

Periodically he squeezed the ball to keep the vacuum at or below zero, everyone scrutinizing the gauge like surgeons. They got through three hands of seven-card stud and then it had been thirty minutes.

Sterr theatrically cracked his knuckles and eased the turn of the lid to allow air slowly back inside the jar. It made a quick hiss releasing some smoke. He then dumped the cockroach out on a newspaper on his desk. "Now we wait till he rejuvenates."

The cockroach looked as if it had been dead a week. The three of them laughed and chattered as the minutes passed without so much as a twitch from the antennae. The cockroach was on its back, its legs as brittle as the dried veins of a fallen leaf.

Then a leg moved. Payne and Cowboy hadn't caught it. Another leg twitched and then one of the antennae. The cockroach rocked on its back and they all saw it.

"Fuck me," said Willingham.

"In-fucking-credible," said Payne.

"How'd you do it?" said Cowboy.

"Suckers," said Sterr.

The bug spread its wings as if stretching after a good night's sleep. Soon it righted itself and staggered aimlessly around a headline on the newspaper.

"Old flyer's trick, boys. Dates back to the time of Double-You Double-You One on the Philippines where they knew the secret of bringing back life," Sterr said in a blasé tone of voice, and then changed his tone: "You guys are too green and too cocky to know anything; just a little lesson to let you know you shouldn't go messing around with those that do know their shit. . . . Who wants to finish him off?"

Sterr raked in the pile of money and the PH. He dangled the medal in the air for a moment, shaping his big Slavic jowls into a grin for Payne's benefit, and pocketed it too.

It was Willingham's bug so Willingham snuffed it.

The four of them jumped in the jeep and drove to the perimeter where Sterr said the fireworks were supposed to start at eleven o'clock. Sterr had brought along a case of beer and a fresh fifth of bourbon.

Cowboy leaned outside the jeep and threw up while they were moving, and Payne gave him his handkerchief. "You okay?" he asked. Cowboy puked again.

"He's fine," Sterr said from the front seat. "It's the fruitcake. Fruitcake and champagne don't mix. Give him a beer and a shot of this."

They drove along the perimeter's mud road to the bunker numbered 68, which Sterr said would be the best place to watch from because that was the number of the new year.

"Hell. Let's go after a mongoose long as we're here," Cowboy suggested. He had stopped puking and was throwing down slugs of whiskey.

"I told you he was all right," Sterr said. "You just got to listen to me and I'll steer you right." He grinned like a lazy bear.

Willingham pulled the jeep over in the roadside ditch and they slopped through the mud to get to bunker 68. Sterr suddenly threw out his arms. "Wait here. Don't want to get blowed away."

He wore a crooked grin that was meant to show he'd seen *Bonnie and Clyde,* that he was cool. But he meant it, too, because you never knew how stoned the guy in the bunker was; sometimes a guy got so wasted he couldn't tell a friendly from a hallucination and would pump twenty rounds into his relief man, the guy strolling up to the rear of the bunker, as they were about to do now; no one else was around yet for the show.

The half-moon was high and bright and cast soft shadows.

Sterr came back and said sullenly, "I got it wrong. The fireworks ain't till midnight. Let's split over to the NCO and come back later."

"Naw, man," Cowboy said peevishly. "I want to *prove* I can catch a mongoose. This jerkoff don't believe I can do it." He pumped a thumb at Payne.

Willingham had lit a weed and had it circulating. Sterr refused when it came to him; he wouldn't touch the stuff.

"You guys are crazy," he said, looking down his nose at them. "You ought to lay off that maryjane shit. Ain't nothing but trouble."

A vehicle approached from a distance, lights off. Sterr saw it coming and said, "Put that thing out. Let's get the hell out of here."

The vehicle, a security jeep, was on them in a burst. A flashlight caught their faces and behind it a voice spoke casually. "You soldiers lose your way? This road is off limits and there's a curfew."

"Little trouble with our vehicle, sir," said Sterr, apparently assuming that the voice belonged to the officer of the day. "We were just leaving."

The beam of light passed over Willingham's face, came back, and held it.

"Don't I know you, soldier?" The voice now had an edge to it. It sounded familiar to Payne but he couldn't place it.

"Speak up. What's your name?"

Willingham shielded his eyes. "Douse the light."

When the light was lowered Payne saw the man's face and recognized him from the China Village lounge as the captain who had threatened to have Willingham busted for insubordination his first night at Long Binh. It was probably the bush hat that gave Willingham away now. But you could tell the captain still hadn't placed him.

Sterr became friendly. He manufactured his press card and showed it to the captain. "Listen, sir. The guard command was supposed to be alerted that we might be coming out here tonight to gather data for a big spread the magazine plans to do on post security. We're from PIO, Saigon Support. I told our IO it wasn't a good idea, but he said General Wheeler ordered the story personally. Didn't the general's office notify your people?"

The captain pushed back his steel pot and pinched his lip in a nervous way, as if admitting he had screwed up. "Well, Sergeant, it doesn't sound like the kind of thing that's procedural. But if that's the way you people work, okay. I guess you should carry on. You need any assistance, with your vehicle or anything?"

"You bet, sir," said Cowboy, his voice high-pitched as a woman's. "We could use a few white phosphorus flares to throw some light so we can get some really neat shots."

Sterr was sweating in the cool night air. "Aww. I think we'll just call it a night now. It's New Year's. Merry Christmas to you, sir."

He saluted faultlessly and held it. The captain took another thoughtful look at Willingham, trying to remember what it was about the dude, but said nothing, returned Sterr's salute, and climbed back in the jeep and left.

"Fucking dimwit," said Willingham. "We ought to put him out of everybody's misery. Let's tail him."

Sterr laughed at him. "You young-ass dipshits," he sputtered. "Think somewhere along the line you'd learn to roll with the punches."

They headed for the jeep. Sterr sucked on the whiskey bottle as he walked. He shuddered and pushed the whiskey on Willingham. "I'm gonna miss this stinking place," he said, prodding him with the bottle. "Go ahead, take a snort. Put hair on your chest."

Willingham took a stiff drink. He belched and grinned and returned the bottle to Sterr.

They got into the jeep.

"Fuck you guys," said Cowboy. He popped a beer and showered the open jeep with a spew.

Sterr liked that. He shook a can violently and drenched Cowboy, and then Payne and Willingham. The case of beer lasted a matter of minutes.

"You young-ass dipshits," Sterr said pleasantly, leaning into the wind. "What the hell, you'll grow up. Someday . . . maybe."

"I wouldn't bet on it," said Willingham, his face slick in the moonlight. "Not in this man's army."

"Fuck you guys," Cowboy growled again. "Let me out. I'm gonna hunt me down a fucking mongoose."

They had almost reached the company area and Willingham pulled over. "Go ahead," he said, and Cowboy got out and started walking back toward the perimeter.

He turned and shouted, "You'll see, assholes. Not you, Sarge."

"Probably going to see that good-time mamasan he sees," Sterr offered, looking after Cowboy. "Drop me at the NCO. I got some fellas to say bye to. You wanna go along, you're welcome."

He used the edge of the dashboard to stabilize himself getting out of the jeep. It was the only indication he'd given that he was drunk. Payne declined the NCO club for both of them, saying they would catch Sterr bright and early at the IO, have his coffee brewed and waiting.

"He's all right," Willingham said, burning rubber on the asphalt.

"Yeah. You want to hit the bunker? I got some special stuff."

Willingham smiled. "I'll just fucking bet you do."

Two other guys were leaving the bunker as they squatted to enter. One of them was the new guy, bunked in Smith's old cube, whose twelve-string Payne had borrowed to pluck his C-cord repertoire of Xmas tunes. Payne had never met the guy; he was a six-foot butterball; he *looked* like Baby Huey, which would explain why the superstitious barracks leader had assigned him Smith's old cube.

"Shit, you ain't a medic by any chance, are you?" Payne asked him.

The guy looked at Payne as though he didn't comprehend English; he grinned and wagged his head in a circle, which could have gone either way, yes he was or no he wasn't. He produced a cherubic smile and waddled off; Baby Huey's smile was cherubic and he walked with a penguin's waddle too. Payne thought he was seeing a ghost. "Shit," he called after the guy.

The air inside the bunker was saturated with heady smoke. Payne fanned some of it out with his shirt and then lit a Sterno and started a pipe of opium. Willingham leaned against the swollen sandbags with his legs crossed, watching him, taking the pipe.

"Oh yeah!" Willingham wheezed behind a mouthful of smoke. His eyes welled up because he'd taken too big a draw. The canned flame colored his face yellow. Payne squatted comfortably on his heels, like an indigene.

"One thing I'll say about this stinking country," Willingham said, still wheezing, "they sure got a taste for the finer things in life."

"I'm fucking turning into a head," Payne said. He was mindlessly writing letters in the dirt between his legs. The letters were Saang's name, sing spelled in the past tense.

"You think he tricked us somehow?" he said, raking through the letters. Dirt clung to his sticky hands. His fatigues were soppy and reeked of beer.

"Don't see how. We watched it come back to life. Fucking Sterr, man. I got to get me one of those vacuum jars."

The opium was smooth. It should have mellowed Payne, but he was fidgety, swaying from side to side and doodling in the dirt.

"What do you think of my 'stache?"

"Quality," said Willingham.

"Not the dope, my mustache. You think it makes me look older . . . tougher? What?"

Willingham leaned close and took his time to study him, going through a series of irreverent faces to show he didn't think anything. "Hmmm. Hard to say. Adds a touch of experience. Yeah, that's it; you look experienced."

"Yeah," Payne said agreeably, pleased with that.

"Tell me about it."

"Remember the gook that ripped me off, you got the refer from?"

"Sure. Gave you the AK. What about him?"

"I've spent the last week with him and his sister, the looker from the bar where you met him. Remember her? They're from up around Dalat. His name's not Mike, it's Tieng-of-the-Two-Faces. She's called Saang-the-Smart-One. Crazy, huh. Fullfledged Monties."

"I knew you were into some kind of shit, man," Willingham said. "Everybody thought you'd gone to the delta, including me."

"I did. They don't live in the mountains anymore. They had to relocate after we blew the fuck out of their land," Payne said. He wanted to tell him all about them but stopped short of saying they were Viet Cong. "I got to go along with Jesus; they're good people, taught me a lot."

"Gained a little experience, huh."

Willingham's eyes had a glaze over them. He seemed misty. "Yeah, they're all right for the most part. But you've got to remember who they are, that they've all got two faces when it comes to us."

"Maybe."

Willingham's misty look might have just been the opium. Payne couldn't tell. He said, "You're thinking of someone in particular, I bet. Somebody did you wrong," he said with a hangdog face. "The bush beast Bruiser was talking about, right?"

"Piss on you, man," said Willingham. He straightened up as if he was going to leave.

"Don't pull that shit on me," said Payne. "Come on, wait a minute, man."

"You don't want to know about her."

Payne really had hit a sore spot. "Why's that?"

"You'll get the wrong idea."

"What, you're ashamed to let anybody know you liked a gook?"

"That could be part of it, yeah."

"What's the rest of it? I'm interested."

Willingham lowered his eyes. He had long lashes, like a woman's. Payne hadn't noticed that before.

"She wasn't a whore," he said.

"So what if she was?" Payne said sharply. He realized his thinking of Saang being a whore made him snap his words, and he added, "Whores are only whores 'cause they're lucky enough to have looks. We turned them into whores. But at least they can feed their families."

"I used to come around and see her, see her family," Willingham said, staring at the glowing sandbags. "Fine fucking people. They had nothing to do with the war, hardly knew anything about it. They lived in a vil in the valley, nothing but hovels. There were seven kids, most of them little ones. Shit, you had to feel sorry for them. Tai was fifteen. She had this bum leg and hobbled around like Chester," he said.

There was a glow on his face remembering the girl. You could tell when he was sincere; his whole face lifted as though the gravity around it had disappeared.

Payne pushed the pipe on him, flipped a flame above the bowl, encouraging him to go on.

"She was really beautiful, man. This clawfoot came from a simple infection that never should have gone that far. She looked after all those kids; one or two of them were always sick with something. But none of it affected her disposition. She was a laugher. I guess that's what I liked most about her, all of them. Dirt poor, no chance at all in life, but she was a happy person, always finding something to laugh about. I could have taken her home with me."

"Yeah," Payne said. "I know what you mean. So how come those guys rode you about her? Didn't they ever see her?"

"She was a fucking slope, man, why do you think? Anyway, she's dead now, so it doesn't matter."

The casual, almost flippant way he put it hit Payne like a slap. "Christ. What happened?"

"What happened?" Willingham said, suddenly animated. "What happened? The rockets' red glare, the bombs bursting in air. That's what happened, man. LBJ, the fucking U.S. Air Force. The military-industrial complex happened to them. But if you mean how did Tai buy it, I personally take credit for that. It wasn't even her vil; it was the one her uncle lived in and she was there, visiting I guess. I was real good at my job."

Willingham shifted his weight, turning away. He was through talking about it.

"Were you on one of Shellhammer's missions?" Payne asked, persisting.

"Just don't matter. I blew places; that was my job. Let's drop it."

"They're just trying to survive and get by," Payne said. "I got to know the girl and Tieng pretty good and I'll tell you something, Willie. It makes you wonder just what we're trying to prove being here. It's not our war, man, that's what I decided. . . . I gave them the cameras," he added. "I told the lieutenant the stuff was stolen. The girl wants to go to college. The money can help."

Willingham sneered. "You're a fool, Payne, if you think that's what the money will go for."

"Yeah, I know. They could use it for anything, but what's the difference?"

"Probably use it for clays and frags, to blow the fuck out of us," Willingham said. "You can't trust these fucking dinks, no matter how innocent or nice they come on."

Payne stared at him incredulously. "How the hell can you say that? You just got through telling me . . . " he said, seeing the uselessness of going on. "Man, sometimes I just don't get you."

Willingham grinned coldly. "Nobody's asking you to."

In the silence that followed Payne moved in a flurry to refill the corncob pipe. That it hadn't burned down didn't matter; he had plenty of the stuff. It passed back and forth a couple of times before Payne said, "You're wrong to judge all of them like that. I don't think you mean it."

Willingham had moved to the bench and spread out on it. He was gazing into the brim of his floppy hat. His boots hanging off the end twitched as if he were getting restless instead of mellow. "When do you think we'll be going out?" he asked and turned to look at Payne.

"No idea. We might not have to if you'd just tell me the places Shellhammer sent you. That's all they want."

"Then that makes them need me, doesn't it?" he said, sitting up.

"Let's see where we're off to first. But don't get smart and try to fuck me over by going it on your own."

"Why would I do that?" Payne said.

"Just don't. You'll need me."

"I never even thought of that, man. I wouldn't go without you."

Payne, still on his haunches, leaned against the wall and stretched out his legs. He took a long pull off the pipe and passed it over.

After a while he said, "I can't see how he tricked us. Looked to me like the damned thing really did come back to life. Fucking hard to believe though, isn't it?"

"Stranger things have been known to happen," Willingham said. "But not much stranger. I got to agree."

A sudden piercing noise found its way inside the tomb of the bunker. They both looked toward the opening and then at one another. The noise was human, a loud lengthy scream. Willingham crawled out first. Payne stuffed the opium in the tin and put it in his hiding place.

Lights were ablaze inside the hootch and the scurry and chatter within resounded through the windows.

Payne noticed something moving in the moonlight at the other end of the hootch. It was low to the ground, a small dark figure like a cat. He spotted the figure again slipping between the nearby bunkers and knew it was the monkey.

"Look, there she is, man," he said, pointing excitedly. "It's Charlie. See her?"

The monkey leaped on top of a bunker and jumped to the next one and stood erect on its hind legs.

"I see it," said Willingham. "Charlie, huh? Bizarre fucking sight."

The monkey seemed to crane its neck for a look inside the illuminated interior of the hootch. Her long arms dangled. Payne heard a tiny growl followed by chirps that changed pitch, as if the monkey were laughing and threatening and challenging and condemning the men inside the hootch. This was how Baby Huey might have explained her primal sounds. Payne smiled.

Sergeant Ortega appeared outside with a flashlight. He looked frustrated but not panicky.

"On the bunker," Payne said, and the beam of light hit the monkey.

It hypnotized her. Other men had collected and were gawking at the blinded figure. Some of the men had never seen the monkey before.

"Let's get the little shit," one of them said.

"You better fuckin leave that monkey alone," Ortega threatened, as though he was at his wit's end, and said to Payne, "She belong to herself now. She come back just today, New Year's, just to blow our fuckin minds."

As soon as the light shifted off her, Charlie dipped and vanished in a flicker, as though she'd never been there. But for a moment you could still see her imprint in relief against the moonlit sky.

"What was the screaming about?" asked Payne, turning from the phantom image.

"It's that newby Smiley, the fat one I put in Smith's cube," the hootch sergeant said. "Got bit. Serve the guy right, man. I told him maybe there was a monkey come around sometimes to sleep underneath the bunk, to let it be, but he don't believe me and he don't listen. 'All right,' I say to him, 'but it's Charlie's place.' Shit, man, now I got to hassle with this shit, find the fatass dude a new place."

"Sounded like he got torn up pretty good," Willingham said.

"Nah, just scared the guy mostly. I sent him to the dispensary for a tetanus. I don't think we gonna get sued," Ortega said. "Swear by my mother's grave I thought that monkey'd done bought it out there. *El Diablo Espiritu de la noche de Ano Nuevo*—that is what that animal is, man. She back to fuck things up."

Ortega moseyed off, shaking his head, carrying the weight of an uncopable world.

"What was that he said?" Payne asked.

"Called your monkey the devil spirit of the new year. Guy's got a bad case of superstition, but that's your basic Chicano, wrecked by religion."

"Wonder where I can get some joss sticks," Payne heard himself say. He had remembered he was supposed to light joss for Lai Sin to fend off her evil spirits.

"For what?"

Payne said, "Never mind," not caring for a dose of ridicule too.

At midnight a siren started. Then the fireworks all along the perimeter, kilometers away, erupted in a kinetic display of firepower thrown high against the sky, metallic thunder thumping the land. Multicolored illumination flares turned the horizon into day. It was a spectacular and horrifying sight.

Chapter
20

The public execution square stood in full view across the street from the sidewalk café. It had been the intelligence agent's idea to meet here.

He and Captain Burns flanked Payne at the table, giving him the direct view of the square. The PsyOps officer was not with them this time. They sat under a merciless sun having drinks the CIA paid for. That was the only cordiality Mr. Fouts extended Payne this time around. Payne had been mistaken about him; the hint of compassion he'd read in the man's eyes before was not compassion. It was cunning.

"You disappeared on us," the agent said, gingerly sipping a frosty red drink. "That wasn't very cooperative."

Payne flicked sweat from his hairline. "I was working. I have a job to do and was doing it."

"You were to make yourself available on notice," Mr. Fouts reminded; his tone wasn't pleasant. "We can't have you disappearing again. What have you learned from Willingham about our Colonel Shellhammer?"

Payne looked at him when he spoke and answered straightaway. "All I know is what his squad did on their operations for him. They took head counts at villages. He told me that sometimes they were ordered to plant explosives to blow a village on a time delay, when

281

the people were in the fields—or supposed to be. He killed some innocent people, and that's why he wouldn't talk at first. It got to him," Payne said and waited a moment to let that sink in.

"But he doesn't seem to know anything about falsifying defectors. I believe he didn't know it was going on," he said, looking from one to the other. "And you can't very well expect me to ask him outright if he thinks his commanding officer was doing that, when I'm not supposed to know anything about him."

"That's reasonable," Burns said, chewing his pipe. He didn't seem to be as bothered that Payne hadn't been around when they wanted him. He casually rattled the ice in his drink. "We have another assignment for you."

Burns explained the assignment would again go through Lieutenant Finn, via him, Burns. Finn would be told only that he and Willingham were to be doing a job similar to the one they'd had before, possibly an overnight operation this time.

"I can't give you a specific day. We are working out the arrangements now. You'll be looking for refugees," Burns explained. "Confined groups of men. You will probably have to do some snooping around; but you're a reporter, you ought to know how to do that. Keep an eye on Willingham. He may recognize someone this time. We're counting on it."

Burns sat back and finished off his drink, crunching the remaining ice. He tapped the pipe on the knee of his crossed leg. Under the surgically bright sun you could see the detail of minuscule white dots along the scar line that flawed his upper lip. It wasn't a harelip after all; it was a scar, and Payne understood why he hadn't covered it with a mustache, since hair won't grow on scar tissue.

"If anyone questions you, which may happen, you simply tell them you're doing an article for civil affairs. You won't be in any danger."

Payne stroked his mustache casually, as though it were an activity he was practiced at; he didn't believe this last comment, that he would not be in any danger; there had to be some kind of risk, but his toes didn't itch this time and his sweating was due only to the one-hundred-degree temperature. He said, "I take it then it'll be another refugee camp."

"You've heard all you need to know right now," Mr. Fouts said.

"Just keep yourself at your duty station. We'll call on you soon. Most likely very soon."

The agent leaned across the table so that his breath was in Payne's face. His washed blue eyes turned friendly. "I don't think you'll disappoint us this time," he said grinning. "We have the girl."

Payne looked at Captain Burns.

"What girl?" he asked. He tried to hide his surprise behind a baffled look, but the catch in his voice exposed him. He searched his mind trying to figure out how they knew about Saang.

"You want to see her?" the agent said. He had leaned back. He waved off the waiter. Payne said nothing, and in a moment Mr. Fouts added, as though disappointed, "She wants to see you." He said she was in the barracks across the street and nodded toward the execution posts in the square. The calculated smile he manufactured was meant to show he enjoyed giving Payne this information. He stood. "I think you should pay her a visit. Now."

They crossed the street and passed by the wall of sandbags behind the two posts and went through a tall wire gate in the fence surrounding the barracks.

She was being held in a six-foot concrete compartment in the basement. The slab floor was wet and rank with the odor of vomit. Daylight filtered in from a slit along the top of a wall. Saang sat in a crouch in the corner, a lump no larger than a sack of rice. Her head lifted as the door opened; she had been beaten about the face and both her eyes were swollen, the left one closed. She cocked her head to favor the right eye and looked at Payne without moving from the crouch. She didn't show pleasure or anger at seeing him, and he took this as a cue.

"Joe," she said flatly, as if recognizing him only as another of her GI tricks.

"Yeah, 'Joe,'" Mr. Fouts laughed. "I like that."

Captain Burns had stayed upstairs. A Vietnamese policeman stood guard outside the cell.

"I know her," Payne said nonchalantly, shrugging. "Spent a couple nights with her; good fuck. What's she done?"

Again the agent looked disappointed. He sighed thickly and sucked a tooth. "For openers there's the matter of a couple of cameras and some lenses with serials traced to the information office where you work. Seems your XO ran across a stolen-equipment report turned in just yesterday for exactly two cameras and three lenses, a wide-angle, a zoom and a forty-five-millimeter. Your girl here had them. That's one thing."

"I no steal," Saang said bitterly. "I find room, tell you. Joe maybe give for present or forget, I no know. But I no steal."

He ignored the girl and kept his attention on Payne. "We don't care about the cameras, of course. I mention it to show you how useless it is for you to try to evade us."

Payne looked at Saang and thought of the posts outside where they shot people, wondering if that were going to be her fate. He felt helpless and rotten.

"She's VC," Mr. Fouts said matter-of-factly, leading Payne by the arm. "She'll talk before it's over. Let's go."

"You come see me for good time, Joe," she said to his back, the casualness of her voice seizing his heart.

They walked outside. Burns had left.

"What's going to happen to her?" Payne said. He was trying hard to display a lack of interest. He didn't know what he could do for her unless he turned in Tieng and spilled what he knew about the people of Paang Dong and the camp Tieng had taken him to, and that he was supposed to meet Tieng in two hours not far from here. He wasn't sure even if that would save her.

"Who cares? She's their meat now," Mr. Fouts said. "They know how to extract information."

"What information? What do you expect to find out from her?"

"Don't insult me. That village you liked so well was swarming with VC. We could stick you with conspiring with the enemy, put you away for being a goddamn traitor if you want to let it come down to that. But we really don't need to take that route . . . do we?"

It didn't sound as if he were bluffing, making it up to scare Payne; it sounded as if he knew Payne had conspired with the enemy.

"I could give you some information about them," Payne found himself saying. "If I do, will you get her released?"

The CIA agent waved for a cab. He looked down at Payne; he was tall, six-foot-something, and broad across the shoulders. His gaze suggested amused disinterest. "They'll just arrest her again tomorrow. But go ahead and tell me if you want."

"First I have to know if you can get her out."

Mr. Fouts shrugged with an effort. "I suppose that's possible. Depending on what you tell me."

"I can lead you to them," Payne said. "That's not all."

The agent grinned broadly. "You get around, don't you."

"How do I know she'll be let go?"

Mr. Fouts appeared wounded. It was a measure of his dry humor. "I suppose you'll just have to trust me."

"If you get her out now and give her to me, I'll tell you where to find her brother."

The man seemed genuinely astonished. "Her brother? One of them's her brother? Well knock me over with a clover. No wonder she's been so hard to break. . . . Okay, talk."

"I'm going to meet him tomorrow here in Saigon," Payne said, thinking quick and sharp. "He's going to bring me some dope in exchange for some PX stuff. We're supposed to meet in front of the Gia Long Palace at five o'clock. Maybe you'll want to have some GVN people there to take him. I'll tell them where they can find an enemy camp with an arsenal of weapons. But I want the girl first, or fuck it, I won't do it."

A cab had stopped and Mr. Fouts waved it off. He seemed impressed. "The thing I can't figure is why you people fall for these locals. . . . But what the hell. I'll see what I can do."

Payne paced the sidewalk outside the jail, feeling unsure and unconfident in what he was doing, then went back to the café terrace and took a seat. He lit a cigarette; his hands were shaking. He kept looking back and forth between the gates of the jail and the unavoidable death posts looming ominously out of the concrete.

That they had known his whereabouts in the delta impressed upon him the resourcefulness and seriousness of their intent. He never suspected they would have followed him, kept him under surveillance. How did they know where he went? How did they know about the VC at Paang Dong? They knew; that was their business. It was a strange feeling learning he had been followed, as though he had been stripped of a freedom that until now he took for granted. These people weren't fucking around, and he was getting a quick enlightened education into the workings of a system he had little understanding of, except that they were powerful and smart and insidious; and they weren't fucking around.

He didn't expect the man to believe he was meeting the girl's brother tomorrow, and he wondered why he had gone along so readily. Mr. Fouts hadn't said, for instance, something to the effect, "How do I know you're not stringing me along just to save your girlfriend?" Maybe he only wanted to impress further upon Payne the power and prowess of the CIA and the futility of evading them again; maybe he just didn't care one way or another about the girl.

He had no idea what to do with Saang if she were released, and he spent the better part of half an hour working it out. When the idea came he went inside the café and paid to use a phone. He called Lai Sin at the office. It was a long shot soliciting Lai Sin's help, for she was proud of her half-Chinese bloodline and the Chinese in Vietnam looked upon the proletariat much as those in government service did, with disdain or mere toleration at best. But her other lineage was Vietnamese. It was worth trying.

He could see the entrance of the compound where he stood with the receiver to his ear and he watched the café for anyone who might be watching him. Lai Sin answered. He ran through his story: a girl from the country he had befriended while away was in serious trouble and needed a place to stay for a day or two, could Lai Sin put her up. He kept it short and purposely vague, and it surprised him when she agreed without question. She gave him her family's address in Cholon. He wrote it on his notepad.

Lai Sin teased him. "Maybe you wife write now you have oth-ah girlfriend, huh?"

"This is a good thing you're doing, Lai Sin," he said and hung up.

He got a drink at the bar inside and waited; it seemed to be taking Mr. Fouts a long time. Any way he looked at it, he was in trouble. They knew he had been with the enemy and hadn't reported it. It was an ace in the hole they could use anytime they wanted. Now they might even suspect he had withheld information about Major Su; if Payne could conspire with the Viet Cong, he could just as easily shield a buddy who killed an ARVN. Regardless that the man was corrupt, he was still an officer in the republic's army.

The bar was crowded and noisy with chatter; outside was crowded as well. He wanted urgently to be alone. That was a thing about the Nam, you could never be alone, no matter where you were, not even in the claustrophobic smoking bunker really. Never any privacy, a place you could go and be by yourself, shut a door and be alone. He thought of something Willingham once said about his grandmother, the one with the rosebuds, that that was the thing he missed most in the world, the room in his grandmother's house. "Sure, there's things I miss in the world," he'd said. "I miss my dog and the jeep, cunts with hair. But you know what, the thing I miss most is the room in my grandmother's house; it's the most peaceful place I know." The comment had stuck endearingly in Payne's mind, for he too used to have a place like that, the small back office in his father's furniture store. It had the smell of his father; it was a secure and private room that never changed. He would have given anything to be there right now.

He moved to a vacant table on the sidewalk and sat under the unforgiving sun, holding a vigil on the jail gate. But his gaze continued to be distracted by the unsightly execution posts. Even from this distance he could make out the pockmarks and splinterings, the result of steel-jacketed bullets ripping through the flesh of the slight bodies bound to the poles. The condemned would be tied securely so he would not slip down from the weakness in his legs, a hood then placed over his head so that his last vision would be the crowd gathered in the square to watch him die; and he would know his death was sacramental, for he had only been caught up in an outside cause. But it was his countrymen who now took aim.

She seemed a fragile figure, a child almost, crossing the street under the grip of the towering CIA agent. He sat her down next to Payne and stood behind her, grinning at Payne as he patted her shoulders reassuringly.

"She's all yours," he said. "Don't renege. People are counting on you."

Saang's color looked worse in the sunlight. She quivered as if chilled but otherwise remained stoic, leveling her welted eyes on the flat surface of the table.

"Will she be followed?" Payne said suspiciously, as if to show he knew how they worked their marks.

Mr. Fouts shrugged indifferently. He produced a form. "Not by me. She's on her own now. Here, sign this."

The paper was in Vietnamese script.

"What is it?"

"A release. Sign, or back she goes."

Payne signed. Walking off, the agent hailed a cab.

Payne stopped him with a question. "Tell me something. Who was it? I mean who'd you have on me down there?"

"You should've known—you noticed him in the bar."

The sandy-haired GI, Payne suddenly remembered, pleasant-looking guy about Payne's own age. A fucking spy.

"Do I get my camera back," he said in a dead tone, suppressing with great effort a rage he knew was powerless.

Grinning over his shoulder, the man said, "Property of the GVN now. Maybe you can find it on the street tomorrow, who knows."

Mr. Fouts stooped awkwardly entering the small car.

Payne touched Saang and she flinched. The pain she was in caused him to shudder; his sense of outrage was made worse by the shame he felt knowing he had caused this to happen to her. He was unable to imagine the extent of her ordeal and the courage it had taken to endure it. It was not "no problem" this time. Payne took his eyes off the girl and watched after the agent's taxi, and for the first time in his life he had the desire to kill.

He took the girl's trembling hand and had to force himself to speak in an even tone. "They shouldn't have done this to you."

She began to cry then and hid her face in her hands.

"Let's go," said Payne.

He hailed a motorcab, got her in it, and told the driver to head toward the river, the other direction from the Chinese district of Cholon, where Lai Sin lived. After half a dozen blocks he made the driver stop and they got out. He led Saang down a crowded side street. She was weak and could not walk fast. He walked her as fast as she could move, zigzagging through the streets and alleys, then flagging down another cab. He did this again and was fairly certain no one could have kept up.

On the outskirts of Cholon he got a room and helped Saang up the stairs to the second floor. Two framed windows overlooked the street. Payne stood for a few minutes searching the people milling about below, but he did not know who to look for. Then he closed the louvered windows.

"Undress," he said. His passion had tempered in the scurry of their journey and he considered more cautiously her release; he was now trying to think as they would think.

She was sitting on the edge of the bed, absently feeling the linen. She questioned him silently.

"Take off your clothes."

She obeyed. He grimaced looking at the welts and discolored lumps on her breasts and legs. He hugged her and she hugged him back with very little strength.

He went through her discarded clothing, twisted the flipflops, and then ran his hands through her disheveled hair and examined her ears and mouth. He put a hand between her legs.

"I'm sorry," he said. He was holding her hands and looking into her swollen eyes. "I had to check you."

He didn't know what he was looking for, a bug on or in her body, a booby trap in her clothes. He didn't know who to believe; she had seemed too cool-headed in the cell. It had been more than an hour before they released her.

"I understand, I so sorry you," she whispered. "You get trouble for me."

He felt the bitter irony of her comment in his heart. None of this would have happened if he had not moved into her life, tampered with her feelings for what amounted to a few days of carnal pleasure. It had been just that to him, a reprieve from the self-pity and disillusionment he felt over his wife's petty affair; the girl had comforted him, brought him out of his despair, taken him in. She had given him her fidelity and in return he had betrayed her.

He held her shirt as she painfully slipped her arms into it; he pulled the bed sheet back and tried to get her to lie down. She stubbornly refused, instead sitting with her hands folded in her lap.

"Is Tieng all right?" he asked.

"Maybe. I loose him when they come take me. Very bad, they come. But you okay, no you problem. You very good man me, Henry, give me camera."

"A lot of fucking good it did you," Payne said, unconsciously aware she had called him by his real name. "I'm going to meet Tieng now. I'm late already. I want you to wait here."

"I come you. Maybe you no find Tieng."

"You're in no shape. Let me have your ring."

Grudgingly she slipped off the band and handed it to him. It was the only piece of jewelry she had on.

Payne started to leave and then turned back to her. "Here," he said, tearing a page from his notepad. "If I don't get back in a couple of hours for some reason, you go to this place in Cholon and tell them you are a friend of Lai Sin's. She lives at this address. But wait at least two hours. Lai Sin. You understand? Can you make it all right?"

She said she could. "Why you no let me go you?"

He gave her ten of the twenty dollars he had in greenback. "Lock the door. Stay inside," he said.

He despised himself for listening outside the door, for thinking like the CIA or the Viet Cong; he waited a few minutes, relieved that he heard no stirring inside the room.

He got to the zoo thirty minutes late, but Tieng was there, standing on the arched bridge of the Japanese pavilion. He was dressed like a farmer and feeding corn to the goldfish in the lily moat. The calico fish didn't need feeding; they were already big as river catfish.

"Tieng," he said familiarly and offered his hand. He bent low so as to make himself seem smaller to the diminutive Viet. Tieng's hand was hot and wet and fishlike.

"No call me that. Here I Sah-junt Mike. Okay."

He was trying to be cheerful, but the crack in his voice betrayed him. "You no like what happened, Henry. Many people maybe dead. Saang gone. Maybe dead, too. I think she dead."

He kept his eyes downcast and his carriage slumped, like a beaten man who didn't know how to lay down and die.

"She's not dead," Payne said. "I got her out of jail and she's in a hotel room near Cholon right now. I left her there."

The Indian looked disbelievingly at Payne, his small face pained. "You no lie me, Henry. I no like you lie."

Payne leaned on the rail of the arched bridge. The largest of the colored carp had gathered underneath in a tight circle, their mouths puckered and kissing the crest of the water, greedily waiting for more kernels. The small ones swam frantically outside the circle, trying in vain to work into the ring of larger fish.

"I can take you there now," Payne said, offering Tieng the ring he had taken from Saang. "Believe me, she's free."

Payne took a few pieces of corn and tossed them away from the circle of large fish. He saw a couple of the smaller ones take the kernels and slip quickly away before they could be overpowered.

Tieng glanced thoughtfully at him, as though about to question the circumstances of her being free. But he said nothing of that: "You brave man, save my sistah. I no forget you this, Henry."

"What happened at Paang Dong?"

"No blame you," Tieng said.

"But what happened?"

Tieng threw the rest of the kernels into the water and they both watched the fish fight over the food. Only two or three of the smaller fish were clever enough to snatch a kernel from the stuffed mouth of a larger one, too greedy to settle for its fair share.

"American drop firebomb, the napalm. Destroy the Paang Dong. Some people die, many go to camp. The Paang Dong no more."

For a moment Payne could not say anything; he turned away and took a few steps in a tight circle. He made a sound that came out like a laugh or a bark. His hands were in the way, awkward appendages, and he squeezed them into fists and pounded the railing.

Tieng touched one of the fists. "You no blame, Henry. Must be quiet."

But it was his fault. He tried to face the Indian, but he could not look at him. He said weakly that he was sorry, and the banality of his apology made it worse.

"It done now," Tieng said; he was trying to comfort Payne for his own people's misfortune, as Saang had done.

He asked Tieng, "What about your friends . . . your comrades, are they okay?" He wanted to say *his* friends, his blood brothers.

The Indian slumped again. "Maybe, I no see. No can say."

Payne looked into the flat, soiled sky, at its bleakness. "What will you do, Tieng? Where will you go now?"

"Sah-junt Mike no die, free. I will do."

First he had lost his homeland and now it had happened again, more of his people dead or displaced, Tieng never giving up the fight. It was hopeless.

But he wouldn't admit his cause was hopeless, that he was alone. Payne said, "There's ways you could get clemency, protection by the government. You know about the Open Arms program?"

Tieng's burst of laughter was bitter. "I know what you talk. Chieu Hoi. Get card, get money, fight for government. You no know, Henry. Very bad this Chieu Hoi."

"It can't be all corrupt."

"Many friend where I go," Tieng said, "many neighbor, they join this Chieu Hoi. Then my government know for surah you Viet Cong. Disappear, in prison for VC. You say, 'I VC. I quit VC, join you.' But my country Viet Nam have very bad government now, no good, no honor. You VC you join Chieu Hoi and maybe die. I no can do this."

"I suppose you can't," Payne said. He frowned. "Tieng, it was my fault it happened. If I hadn't been there—"

The Indian stopped him by reaching up and touching Payne's shoulder. He smiled and showed his gold. "You no hate my country Viet Nam. I know this all time. You see?" He displayed Saang's ring. "Henry save life my sistah. You no blame and now I know you do for me."

"Yeah," Payne said thickly. "Fucking A I'll do for you."

A loud shrieking noise erupted and spread across the zoo's grounds; a fight had started in one of the monkey cages, and before they left, it had roused the birds and tigers and other animals into a frenzy.

They took a pedicab to the hotel. On the way Tieng asked him if the truck had been lined up for the trip north and Payne told him yeah and asked Tieng when he wanted it. It was a lie; he hadn't arranged for a truck yet. But he would do it; that wasn't a lie.

"Much business take care of now," Tieng said. "Must get people from camp." He moved around uncomfortably in the seat, not used to sitting and not used to a cushioned seat. "It American camp," he said. "Not surah name. I find out, I tell you. You come with truck and you help get friend from camp. Very important right away. Okay."

"What kind of camp?"

"Must find quickly. Maybe they prison-ah. You understand? I look, I find. Maybe tomorrow, maybe three day. I no can know."

"Okay," said Payne.

At the hotel Tieng and Saang greeted each other with mutual aplomb. They didn't touch each other but Tieng's happiness at seeing Saang showed in his eyes and his gestures. Saang was sipping a Coca-Cola by the window when they came in, her hair wet from a shower. She threw her arms around Payne, for the first time showing her affection in front of her brother.

"I have a place where she can hide for a while," Payne said to Tieng. "Maybe you could stay there too, I don't know."

"No problem. Have *beaucoup* friend Saigon."

Tieng became abstracted, turning to the window and standing for a while with his back to the room, thinking something out. "Okay," he said finally, and spoke to Saang in English. "You go Henry. Maybe bett-ah for you." Then he talked to her in Vietnamese.

The three of them walked through the Cholon marketplace and down alleyways with narrow catwalks bridging the mud, searching for the area and street and finally the number of Lai Sin's home. Tieng said he knew Cholon—"like the front my hand"—but he got lost in the tight quarters.

The place they found was a concrete tenement of three floors. Lai Sin's apartment was on the bottom floor. "Good," Tieng said of that.

The front door stood open and Payne called inside it.

A stocky, broad-faced woman stepped forward into the doorway. She had on a white *ao dai* and tan wraparound sandals and appeared about to go out. She stared blankly at the three faces.

Tieng talked to her and she smiled and moved aside to allow them entrance. There were four oscillating fans in the small main room and a high Western table with eight chairs taking up most of the area. Payne looked around for the big family Lai Sin talked about, but the woman appeared to be the only one home. She didn't speak English.

"She say it honor to have Saang," Tieng said in a formal voice. "She know you, Henry, and say you very welcome for sup-ah. Saang stay, many day okay."

Payne declined the invitation as graciously as he could. He thought he might have offended the woman anyway. He told Saang he would try and see her at a place Lai Sin would tell her of. Saang, he thought, was pouting. She walked him back and spoke in private.

"Maybe you no understand problem my people," she whispered. "But I want you promise be careful my broth-ah. Tieng good man, but he fight for his country. . . . Saang want you remembah I always love Henry."

"I won't forget you. I'll see you stay safe; I'll see you again."

On her disfigured face he thought he saw a smile. "Saang so smart. Tell you I see you Saigon, huh?"

He touched her arms and then left with Tieng. She had nothing but the money he'd given her, not even a change of clothes, and nowhere else to go. But it was better than the splintered pole in the execution square, and Payne felt good about himself at least for that.

"She very nice woman, this Lai Sin mothah," Tieng said. "She Chinee but no hate Vietnamese. I think she okay. Husband Vietnamese. She say husband know what do for Saang, can hide her numbah one place if have to. No sweat."

"Where will you be?" asked Payne.

"Every day I be zoo, same same today. Wait for you. Must go now see oth-ah friend."

"Okay," Payne said as the rain broke on them.

Chapter
21

Payne waited in the general's palm garden, leaning against one of the trees with his boot propped on top of the "Keep Out" sign. He needed a shave and wore wrinkled fatigues and kept his hands in his pockets. Two officers in conversation passed and looked hard at Payne when he didn't salute.

When he spotted Lai Sin hurrying along the sidewalk promptly at seven-thirty, he came out of the tree cluster a little too quickly and the secretary jumped with a gasp and patted her chest. He asked about Saang.

Lai Sin said the girl was all right. She made her use an ice pack and said that the swelling in her closed eye had gone down some. She reassured him there was no problem about her remaining there; she could stay as long as she needed. The secretary said Saang was a nice girl, that it was terrible what had happened to her, wandering about in the wrong neighborhood where a gang of thugs had beaten her and tried to rape her. Saang had said she was in the city looking for members of her family, who had been displaced after the attack on her village. Lai Sin didn't question Payne about the story and Payne added nothing to it. He doubted she believed Saang, and her discretion eased his mind.

"You'll have to lie if you're questioned about her," Payne said as a warning. He had to say something to warn her.

"I know," she said simply, her lack of surprise assuring him she did know there was more to it, that harboring the girl was dangerous.

He sipped lukewarm coffee and tried to busy himself with the work he had been neglecting. Willingham had been doing his job for a couple of weeks now, covering for him on the paper—laying it out, sizing the photos, writing the captions and heads, the editor's job. There was a deadline to meet for both of the command's publications, and Willingham had come through when Payne needed it most. Cowboy helped some.

There was a stack of releases in his basket and the articles from his delta trip were abstractions floating around in his brain, still unwritten. He had made several starts to get even one story going but couldn't get the right lead and had given it up. He tried again now and for almost an hour stared at the blank sheet of paper in the typewriter before giving up again. His mind wasn't with it.

After lunch Cowboy returned with the mail. He tossed a letter on Payne's desk from Texas Christian University at Fort Worth, its return address printed in raised baroque script. He tore it open and read the official notice of his acceptance for the winter term beginning January 21. Along with the notice was a statement from the registrar's office waiving preregistration. He could register by proxy but would have to be there when classes started.

Ann had done it. She had briefly mentioned sending in the papers for his application in their Christmas conversation, a conversation he had tried to forget. The waiver was essential for the early out, and Ann had made sure the school included it. She was on top of things; she had come through for him. Texas Christian. Did they have a journalism school there, he wondered. Did it fucking matter?

If he hand-carried the paperwork around, he could be on his way home in two weeks, maybe even one. He could be out of the Nam in a fucking week. The thought made him giddy.

He immediately got the hiccups, which erupted more animal-sounding than human. The throaty yelps startled Lai Sin, who gave a yelp of her own and spilled white-out in the guts of her typewriter. He stuck the letter in his drawer and rushed across the hallway to the darkroom to tell Willingham the news.

There were dark problems waiting in the wings, but an acceptance to college put things in a different light. It was something he could focus on—a light, he thought still giddy with excitement, at the end of his fucking tunnel.

"Guess what, man?" he said casually, being cool.

Willingham had one of his Beach Boys tapes on, "Help Me, Rhonda." Standing over the print trays he jerked and twisted from his hips up, turned to grin at Payne then turned down the volume.

"I give, what?"

"Got accepted at a school," Payne said and hiccuped. He took a seat on the stool and hiccuped again. "I can leave this hole."

"How soon?"

"Shit, man, a week or two. In no fucking time."

"Go for it," Willingham said.

Payne felt like hugging him or something. "Shit," he said again, the thought of home beginning to sink in.

He watched a print come to life in the tray. It was a grip and grin, perfectly centered, good grain, right focus—Willingham getting with the program. Unlike Payne, he didn't even need a haircut.

"Listen," Payne said in a calmer voice. "You want to go down to Saigon with me this afternoon?"

Willingham grew interested, alert. "You heard from them? We going?"

"Not that. Just for fun, a little celebrating," Payne lied, not wanting to get into it now. "Four o'clock, all right?"

Willingham seemed disappointed but cracked a half grin. "Something tells me I'm being suckered."

Payne spent the afternoon at Stretch headquarters, filling out and shuffling forms from office to office. He had to push for assistance from every begrudging clerk. But his papers seemed to be in order and he'd know in a few days if the early release were approved. It was that simple.

The lieutenant had a staff meeting or some such thing at three-thirty and wasn't due back in the office today, since his bowling team practiced at five. With Willingham driving they got there early, twenty to five, enough time for a beer. Payne had him park across the street from Gia Long Palace and led the way to a bar adjacent to the palace. Payne took a seat by a window so he could keep an eye on the street. He didn't see Mr. Fouts or anyone who looked CIA or who he imagined would be the GVN secret police.

He didn't know if he was looking for someone in uniform or street clothes, or even if anyone would show up. For all he knew Mr. Fouts had made some other deal to get Saang out. Maybe he hadn't told them anything, just gone back inside the compound and ordered the girl released. He was the CIA.

The street bustled with more activity than usual at this hour. The reason was the group of six or seven bonzes in orange bedsheets, who were sitting on the sidewalk in front of the palace, apparently preparing to do their monk-humming thing. A small crowd of spectators, student types, milled around as though merely curious. It didn't appear to be an organized demonstration. Behind the bonzes was a shrine of candles and bronze ornaments under a couple of huge picture placards, one of a monk and the other a nun, martyrs of the cause, Payne guessed.

"You think one of them's going to burn himself?" Payne said, pointing his longneck bottle.

"Should've brought a camera," Willingham joked. He knew Langley had the only remaining camera, and Langley was off somewhere in the countryside, doing something.

Willingham leaned over the table. "You didn't want me to tag along just to look at some skinheads, Payne. Let's have it; what's going on?"

Payne sighed and lit a smoke. He wasn't sure how to tell him. "Listen. The people I told you about, the Indians, they want me to do something for them and I think I ought to do it."

"Oh?" Willingham was amused. "You never learned about volunteering?"

"It's something I have to do. I owe them. But I need your help."

"Sounds like you're losing track of your priorities," said Willingham, his amusement slipping. "Look, Payne, you've been lucky so far. Don't go pressing it. Forget this other crap with Shell too. There's going to be trouble, I'll tell you that right now. I mean it. You got a golden opportunity to go, so just get the fuck out while you can."

Payne got the attention of the white-jacketed waiter and waved for another round. It wasn't five yet. "That's not what you would do. I know it's not," he said. "It's gotten complicated. At first they just wanted me to get them transportation so they could go back to the highlands for Tet. I said sure; I didn't expect to see them again. But yesterday I got called downtown, to the jail. They had Saang, the girl. They arrested her for stealing the camera. She'd been beaten. I don't know what else they were going to do to her so I signed a release for her."

Willingham shook his head morosely. "Man, you shouldn't have done that."

"Maybe. But I doubt the army will ever find out. Anyway, Saang's out."

"Where is she?"

"In Cholon. At Lai Sin's house."

"Say what?" Willingham said, amazed. "She's Chinese. Why would she take in an Indian?"

"I don't know," Payne said, getting irritated. "Maybe she's VC too. Maybe they're all goddamn VC."

"Take it easy."

"It doesn't stop there, man. After they took her they destroyed their village. *We* destroyed it. The people that weren't killed were sent to some kind of camp somewhere. She says they're being held, maybe as VC. I don't know about that," Payne said. "But that's what Saang thinks and she wants me to help get them released. I told her I'd do what I could."

He purposely forged a half-truth of the matter, leaving Tieng out of it. To include Tieng, the black marketeer, meant more explaining. It would raise Willingham's suspicions, and sure as hell Willingham wouldn't go along with him if he knew the truth, that the lot of them really were the enemy.

Willingham sipped beer, eyeing him thoughtfully. "You're serious, aren't you?"

"I can't do it without you. I have to help them if I can."

Willingham snickered. "Another fucking hero."

"They're just trying to get by, simple people that have nothing to do with the whole fucking mess. You know that. You know what it's about. Their village was destroyed because of me. I owe it to them to do something."

"You don't owe them a fucking thing, Payne. Like you just said, they're probably all VC, which is a good bet. I can't believe you're serious."

"I don't give a damn if they are. They're good people. Being with them was like—I don't know," Payne stammered. "It was like I was part of their family. They trusted me and look where it got them. Can you understand that?"

Willingham looked away. He understood.

Payne pressed for his attention. "If I hadn't stayed with them none of this would have happened. I'm telling you I can't turn my back on them. I won't."

He had already forgotten about the letter from Texas Christian University; talking about it clarified things and he knew now that his first priority was his Indian friends.

"You're damned lucky your body's not rotting somewhere in the bush," said Willingham. "You can't make a good time into a personal thing. All this is going to be history pretty soon. Forget it, Payne," he said flatly. "You're just asking for trouble. There's nothing you can do for these people. You got to think about yourself."

"Maybe I am doing it for myself."

"Then you're really fucked," Willingham said with contempt. "This war don't make heroes, man."

Payne looked down at his hands, then up again. He didn't want to say it, but he did: "The girl you liked, wouldn't you have tried to help her if you could?"

"Lay off that shit. It don't apply."

He didn't lay off. "Oh yeah? Why the fuck not? It seems to me to be the same thing. We're both to blame for what happened to them. I don't see any difference, except yours is dead."

"Shut up, Payne."

"She was probably VC too and that makes it all right that she got wasted. What the fuck."

The blow came swiftly, like a sprung coil. It could have landed squarely on his eye or mouth but didn't and only jarred his head. Willingham following his fist across the table pushed Payne to the floor, pinning him underneath, his fist poised over Payne's face.

"Sometimes you go too far, man," he said. His eyes were watery and fierce.

Payne tried to push him off but couldn't. He had Payne by the throat, but he didn't hit him again. Willingham's weight abruptly lightened. Two GIs wrestled him to the floor. Payne got to his knees and said, "Let him go," and they did.

Payne's jaw popped as he worked it around. He tasted blood inside his mouth.

Nothing had been broken in the way of property, but Willingham gave some cash and a cold look to a hefty Asian, presumably the bouncer, who was standing there with a hand out. It was a quarter past five.

Payne silently walked out to the street, Willingham trailing him. They stopped short of crossing the street. The crowd had transformed into a mob around the Buddhists, who were now circling and shouting incantations, the huge pictures bobbing in the midst of the mob. Comprised largely of shirt-and-tie students, the mass encouraged the bonzes with upraised fists. A line of white mice cops routed through the crowd, using billy clubs to push the skinheads into the street and away from the palace gate. The scene was becoming panicky.

Two men in police-cadre uniforms approached from the sidewalk, their eyes on Payne and not the commotion. It was them. He hadn't expected uniformed types; it seemed too low on the scale for the CIA. Grinning in a friendly way, one of the policemen said, "You friend no come?"

"Maybe he was frightened away by this riot," Payne said, as if himself disappointed.

"Maybe he no come because you tell him no come," said the other officer, who wasn't grinning; his look was threatening.

"The deal was," Payne said quickly, "that if it looked bad we'd meet another time. It's just small stuff, cigarettes and booze. Small time. I wouldn't expect him to show with this going on."

"When?"

"In three days, same place, same time. That's the way we work it. I've done business with him before, for a long time, and he's always shown up—except when something like this is going on. I'm sure he'll be here then, three days from now."

"Three day, quite so. We come back three day," said the pleasant-faced man. "In three day you friend no come, you go jail. We find you. You no like jail."

The policemen walked off, ignoring the struggle their comrades faced with the angry mob that by now was overpowering them. Two quick gunshots suddenly rang out, a warning that didn't seem to affect the frenzied mob.

"We better get out of here," said Payne. "It doesn't look too healthy."

"Yeah," Willingham said. "You're right for a change."

More police cars screeched under sirens and quickly cordoned the crowd on the sidewalk opposite the palace. The jeep was somewhere in the thick of people. Payne and Willingham backed up and watched from the recess of an antique shop.

"They're going to wreck my fucking jeep," Willingham said.

"Piss on the jeep, let's go."

Willingham stood firm; he wasn't going to leave the jeep.

"Fuck," Payne said and stayed by him.

A Molotov flew through the air and splattered, spreading a white liquid fire along the curb and street outside the crowd. More warning shots went off, and then one of the bonzes broke through the line in a skittish scramble. He tripped and fell into the flame. Payne thought he might have been shot in the back as he fled. His loose flourish of robe caught fire instantly and the stunned crowd grew silent as the burning figure writhed on the asphalt in a vain, frantic effort to disrobe. The body soon stopped moving and contracted into a smoldering stump.

The riot broke up after that.

"Fucking Buddhists," Willingham said once they were in the jeep and on their way. "You believe that shit? It'll be built up as a self-immolation in the press, you watch."

Payne said nothing. He could still hear the bubbling and popping of burning flesh.

"What was all that back there with those cops?" asked Willingham, back in his element behind the wheel. The seats had splotches of red on them, blood from the bleeding heads of students, but the jeep hadn't been damaged.

The question didn't register with Payne and Willingham prodded him. "Well? What did they want?"

"That was another thing," Payne said after a moment. "I had to promise I'd lead them to Saang's brother if they let the girl go."

"You're living too dangerously, man. . . . Sorry I slugged you. Where to now, the Freegate?"

Willingham's chameleon ambivalence was bizarre. Payne didn't know if he was being facetious or serious. The Nam, he thought dismally, the goddamn Nam did that.

Chapter
22

The rain came late, after dark. Payne waited until it stopped, then walked up the hill to the office. The lights were on and the door open. The cleaners had just started on Finn's office. Payne sent them away. The mamasans bowed politely and left with their rags and buckets, shutting the door behind them.

Willingham had tried to talk Payne into staying the night in town, getting a room and a woman, blowing it out. He'd pay. He was wound up from the street riot. But he changed his mind before they got to the first bar; he told Payne, "Shit, you're right, buddy. I'm supposed to be keeping my act together," and burned up the road back to Long Binh. They had plenty of time to hit the club and the bunker for a smoke, but Willingham said he was going to turn in and went off to his hootch. *"Mañana,"* he said, just like that. He had resisted the dark side taking over, but death on the street had gotten to him.

Payne took some ice from the refrigerator and poured three inches of Scotch over it and searched Willingham's desk for the coded address book. The desk inside and out was immaculately orderly. The chocolates were still in the bottom drawer, still unopened. It occurred to Payne that he had never seen Willingham eat anything sweet or even drink coffee. He was not very observant, and that, he reproached himself, was a serious flaw for a journalist.

The book was not in the desk. He poured another long Scotch and went into the darkroom and searched for the negatives of the butchered corpses. It didn't surprise him that they too were gone. If he had found the negatives or the address book, he considered what he would do. Would he turn them over to Burns? Which was sure to get Willingham court-martialed, maybe even for murder. Payne could do that to save his own skin. Or he could use the negatives to black-mail Willingham into going along with him in this crazy notion he had to help people who were, in fact, the enemy. But without the evidence he could do neither, and he was relieved he hadn't found it, that he was freed from the temptation of having a choice.

He went to the hootch and to sleep, again without supper. Ghosts came forth in the dead of night. Cotton was there and so was his father. Ann came into the show too, her lips peeled back in a hideous glower that exposed rows of pointed metallic things, bullets. The three of them stood a long way off in rank and file, lifting rifles on command from a distant voice, taking aim. He felt incredibly weak and light, as though all the muscle in his body had been sucked out. The body set afire on the post next to him popped and gurgled like boiling soup. Three rifles steadied eye level at him; his blurry eyes magnetized to the steel shafts, the pinpoint holes exploding like can-nons, the bullets twirling as if through water. He kept thinking, *Why are they doing this, these people, the people I love? What have I done to them?*

He got out of bed and went outside to piss. He was thinking of his father, the peculiarity of dreaming of him again so soon. And why in the nightmares was he always holding a gun over Payne? Why a gun at all? Payne leaned against a bunker and lit a smoke and prac-ticed his quick-flip with the Zippo. With its age the lighter made soft, fluid clicks opening and closing, the blue-yellow flame contained within the windscreen—not the radical flame and hard metallic clink of the newer Zippos. It had been his father's lighter. His mother sent it in one of her packages; when was it, his fourth month over here? She'd written as a way of explanation for sending it, "You're a soldier at war and I guess you can smoke if you want to. Your father learned to smoke when he was in the war and never gave it up. I was always after him about it. I guess I was wrong."

Sterr was sober and looking sharp in his pressed khakis when Payne got to his quarters at O-six-thirty. Payne felt like hell. Sterr hauled two overstuffed duffel bags to the jeep and Payne carried his suitcase and AWOL bag.

"What are you doing with all this shit," Payne grumbled. The task made him sweat. He had been sweating in the night and was convinced he had malaria.

"You can collect a lot of garbage in a year's time," Sterr said. He was bright-eyed and cheerful. "Here, stand over here and let me get a shot of you."

Sterr was irritatingly fastidious about his picture taking, sidestepping and moving in, then back, as he peered down into the viewfinder of his old 2X2 camera. Payne stood in a slouch on the steps of the barracks.

"Take your cap off."

Payne removed his cap, turned his head at an angle and grinned.

Once they were settled in the jeep Sterr gave him an appraising glance. "You're looking drawn, Payne. Better start taking a little better care of yourself, eat better."

"It's my mustache," Payne said. "Gives me a leaner look, more debonair. David Niven, don't you think?" That Sterr had said nothing about his 'stache injured Payne in some small way.

Sterr grunted, chuckled. "Maybe you just need a haircut."

Payne, at the wheel, threw mud rounding the orderly room. Top was standing on the steps holding the screen door; he'd been there waiting to wave Sterr off. They went back a long way, old lifer buddies.

Sterr was leaving out of Tan Son Nhut. Although his flight didn't take off until noon, he wanted to be there in plenty of time, hurry up so he could wait. A true-blue lifer. But Payne didn't care; he wanted to talk to Sterr and now was the only time to do it, now that he was leaving.

Payne was shivering even though he had his sleeves rolled down and buttoned against the now warming air, his baseball cap pulled low above his sunglasses. Sterr asked him twice on the road if he was ill and Payne said he was all right, he just could never get used to the morning chill.

On the road Sterr didn't talk at all about going home. Payne had to ask him, "Shit, Sarge, aren't you excited or anything?" and Sterr nodded and smiled easily that nonplussing way he had of smiling when he had nothing to say, which didn't tell you if he was agreeing or disagreeing.

They had to wait in a line of vehicles to get through the airport gate. The tarmac crawled with ground and air traffic, creating a continuous thunder too loud to talk over and Sterr had to point out directions. Only after they parked and the luggage was unloaded and inside the terminal did Sterr say anything about going home, and then it was only a sentiment. "I'm going to miss it here," he said with a sigh; it was a line he liked to use, but he really meant it.

He would be flying straight to Japan and from there a thirteen-hour trip across the Pacific to Travis. His flight would not be stopping first for processing at Cam Ranh. NCOs in III and IV Corps didn't have to put up with the wait and hassle of Cam Ranh.

"Man, if my early out comes through, I'll be right behind you," Payne said. The excitement of seeing commercial jetliners, freedom birds, and the quick-paced shuffling of men starched and shined and heading home sent his mind reeling.

"Don't count on it," Sterr cautioned. "You don't want to go setting yourself up to be let down. Let me buy you some breakfast."

They walked along sidewalks between hangars and quonsets to an NCO club. Sterr had coffee and brandy shooters while Payne ate a full-course breakfast of ham and eggs and redeye gravy on biscuits with a large glass of orange juice and a sectioned grapefruit. "Sure ain't nothing wrong with your appetite this morning," Sterr said, getting tight.

The meal warmed and invigorated Payne; he finished it off with a cold beer and a cigarette. It was cool and relatively quiet, the atmosphere congenial with the low, somber voices of career men at the end of their tour. Sterr had gotten his hair cut short and was wearing all his ribbons, four rows of them. His thickset face was tan and almost distinguished-looking, the stately bust of a self-made man from the streets. He was a man who believed in himself, in what he did; he had his shit together.

He dug into his pocket and withdrew the Purple Heart medal and pitched it in front of Payne. "Here, take this thing."

Payne grinned and stuck the medal in his shirt.

"Hear anything on your promotion?" Sterr asked.

"Naw. The lieutenant'll let me know. I guess he's working on it," Payne said, adding, "He's a pretty square dude when it comes right down to it. You know?"

"Yep, he's come a long way, no denying that," Sterr said. "Just goes to show you what a man can do when he applies himself. . . . Yeah, we've had some times with him, ain't we?"

Sterr went to the bar and came back with a tumbler of brandy and another beer for Payne. His splotched drinker's nose shined even in the dim light of a lounge. It wasn't yet nine o'clock.

Payne said, "Sarge, you think we're doing the right thing over here?" The question popped out; it was not what he wanted to talk about and he didn't even care what Sterr thought; he knew what Sterr thought. Sterr was a lifer. Of course we were doing the right thing over here.

But Sterr surprised him. "No way in hell," he said in the easy tone he might use with a Filipino whore, or in front of a network news camera. "We'll win this sucker. But I'll tell you, Payne, in the long run it's us that's going to be the losers. This war ain't for shit; we should of never took it on. We're going to have to live with the repercussions of it for a long time to come, even us lifers. . . . I'm not exactly going back to the band playing."

"Yeah. Say, listen, Sarge," Payne said, drawing himself up on his forearms, his knee starting a nervous thump against the underside of the table. "You've been around and you know how things work. If a guy refuses to say something he knows could go against somebody else, say something that could get him court-martialed, how serious would that be? I mean, is it like you could be court-martialed too for withholding information?"

Sterr scratched the hair on his thick head and squinted. "Well, yeah. I guess. Who might these guys be?"

"And if this guy knew what he'd done was criminal," Payne went on, talking rapidly off his head, "but said fuck it and went ahead anyway, even though he might've been justified doing what he did, would you turn him in for it? Could you, knowing he really did the right thing, at least in his own mind?"

Sterr sneered and pushed his lumpy jaw toward Payne. "You got something to say to me, Payne, spit it out."

Payne held on to Sterr's eyes. "I'm in deep shit, Sarge," he said miserably. "I can't go into it with you. If I did then you'd be in the same boat as me, withholding information. But I'll tell you this much. I'm being used as a goddamn stoolie against Willie in some stinking investigation I'm not supposed to talk about to anyone. It's been going on ever since he came to the IO. But, fuck, man, it's gotten way out of hand and I don't know what I'm supposed to do anymore."

Sterr turned thoughtful, studying Payne as if sizing him up for a portrait. Then he stretched his burly arm across the table and gingerly tapped the pocket of Payne's shirt, where he had stuffed the Purple Heart medal.

"Remember how you got that thing?" he said. It didn't seem to be a question he wanted answered. "You wouldn't talk about it, which makes me think Willingham was the one in control of the situation, that if it hadn't been for him it might have been worse. You might of gotten it posthumous. Am I right, did he cover your ass?"

Payne remembered clearly—balled up on the floorboard, scared out of his wits, and the next thing Willingham telling him it was clear, he could stop hiding. "Yeah," Payne said, tightening his lips. "He got me out of it."

"And while you've been out gallivanting around the countryside, twice AWOL, hasn't it been him who's pulled your weight at the office?" Sterr said, not waiting for an answer. "Believe me, if it hadn't been for Willingham, you wouldn't be getting promoted, you'd of gotten busted. The lieutenant fretted over it, I promise you; he almost did it. I don't know how serious this stuff you're telling me is, Payne. But you ought to think long and hard before you go turning on a man who's covered your ass like Willingham has done. He's been a buddy to you."

Sterr finished off the brandy and shivered from its bite. "I'll tell you something else. There's two types in this war; there's us who push the paper and get by with no sweat, and there's the boys that are putting their lives on the line. The difference is nothing you can compare. Those poor kids are the ones who're going to take the pain of this war home with them, the ones that are going to be ruined even if they survive it. They're going through hell, experiencing things we don't have no conception of. It's the shit these grunts are having to do out there that distorts their perception of what's right. Hell, it ain't even that either. It's not a question of what's right, just what is.

"Maybe Willingham did something before, and maybe it was something pretty bad, I don't know and it don't matter because you've got to remember where he came from that he was one of those boys whose perceptions got turned around. And it may look like he's got himself squared away now, adapted just fine to the rear; but don't be fooled, Payne. He hasn't. You can see it. He's waiting to explode, and whatever this situation is with you, you can't go applying your judgments to what he's done—or what his experiences has done to him; it just don't apply. What you can do is reciprocate. Be *his* buddy."

Payne hadn't seen it quite like that. Sterr put definition to a side of Willingham he had been at a loss to fully comprehend or clarify. It was as if Payne had taken for granted Willingham's dark side as residue of the terrible experiences he had been through, that since he had taken some payback he really had started to get himself together. But how could he, how could he ever be the person he was before the Nam?

Sterr was right, and Payne suddenly felt for the old lifer as he would a father. He wanted to tell Sterr that, but he didn't know how. He said instead, "Sarge, I wish the hell you weren't leaving."

Sterr grinned broadly. His eyes were clear and his color healthy. "Got to," he said, failing to catch the implied meaning of Payne's comment. "Got to make room for the next man. Maybe he can get his stripe."

Sterr wanted to get another round, and no doubt another after that. Payne said he better take off, he had lots of work to catch up on, which was true, and he shook the sergeant's hand and wished him well and said he would sure as hell look him up in the world. Sterr stood and slung a heavy arm around Payne's shoulder, giving him a squeeze.

"You take good care of yourself, young trooper," he said with affection. "You'll do the right thing; you've got the makings."

As soon as he walked into the office, Lai Sin popped out of her seat, looking worried and frightened. He followed her lead and stepped back into the hallway.

"She go, Lussell."

"Where? When?' he said.

"I get up to cook, she go. No say where. Her broth-ah wait, I see him. She scared, Lussell. I worry for her."

Payne tried to reassure her with a smile. "She didn't know how long she would stay, Lai Sin. That was the plan and there's nothing for you to worry about. All right?"

Lai Sin nodded acceptingly, but her eyes told him she was as uncertain as he was.

He figured it meant Tieng wanted to see him today, that he had probably found out where the people from Paang Dong were and would be at the zoo this afternoon waiting on Payne. He would tell the lieutenant he had business at MACV and needed the jeep. He was getting experienced at lying. If Tieng was there he would lie again, tell him he had a truck lined up and was ready.

The office crew one by one drifted out for lunch. Payne wasn't hungry. He brewed a pot of strong coffee and sat down to write the delta story. This time it came and he wrote six pages in less than two hours and was pleased with what he'd done. He had hardly noticed when everyone returned after chow. The chaotic music blaring from Cowboy's radio did not bother him, even when the lieutenant twice stormed out of his office ordering him to turn it off. Willingham was busy cropping prints and had not disturbed Payne either.

He hastily edited the typos, then knocked on the lieutenant's door with the story. He still had plenty of time to meet Tieng.

When the lieutenant didn't respond, he stepped in. Finn was on the phone; he looked up and motioned Payne to sit.

". . . But, sir, we're working on a strict deadline right now," Finn was saying in a pleading voice, his reddened face a shade lighter than his crimson hair. "Yes, sir. I understand. . . . Right. Goodbye."

He slammed the phone down and glared at Payne. "There you are," he said disgustedly. "Another goddamn assignment, compliments of your Captain Burns. He expects me to drop everything."

Payne swallowed his rising heart. "When?"

"0-six-hundred tomorrow. The bastard doesn't believe in giving much advance notice."

"What did he say?"

"Get Willingham in here. He wants both of you again and I don't want to have to repeat myself."

The lieutenant turned formal with both men standing before him. He informed them that a helicopter would be waiting to lift them to a relocation camp, where they would be interviewing and taking pictures of a priority civil affairs operation just starting up. That was all he knew.

"Captain Burns said you would know what you're to do, Payne, that you are in charge," he said. "The chopper will be back to take you out at fifteen hundred hours."

Finn's formality shifted to aggravation. "He wouldn't even tell me where the goddamn place is, like it's classified. Then he says it's routine. . . . I don't know. I don't like it. Something about this whole business doesn't set right. You better get over to the armory this afternoon. I don't know if you can get weapons that early in the morning."

Willingham was resting against the door jamb, his hands in his back pockets. He listened intently as the lieutenant talked, lifting his face with obvious enthusiasm and grinning his horse grin.

"No sweat, LT," he said. "Hell, there might even be a magazine story in it. No need to worry about us if we're flying in."

A little of his self-assurance rubbed off on Finn, who said, "Well, I guess it is routine. It's just that he's taking too much liberty imposing on my staff like this. Especially right now; the guy's timing sucks."

"Sir," said Payne. "They're having some problems at MACV with the rag's composition, matching prints with the right captions or some such bullshit, and I need to get down there this afternoon to straighten it out. All right if I take the jeep?"

Finn seemed just then to notice the story Payne had put on his desk. He picked it up, appraised its length, and offered up a pleased or relieved look. The story was slugged "delta medcap."

"How good is it?" Finn asked, fanning cursorily through the pages.

"It'll make the magazine," said Payne. "With the art you can probably get a four- or five-page spread out of it. More if you let Willie the Wizard here do the layout."

"All right," Finn said, "go on down there if you have to. But get through with the editing first, and get back pronto, no dillydallying around. Understood?"

"How about I give an assist," Willingham said.

Finn had said nothing about the hands in Willingham's pockets. He shook his head. "We're running it close. I need you for some more lab work. . . . Where's that damned Langley, anyway? Why can't he ever be around when I need him."

Willingham and Payne grinned at each other.

Lai Sin caught Payne's attention by pawing at the back of his arm. She had never touched him before. "Telephone you, Lussell."

"Who is it?"

She shrugged. "No say."

"Okay, that's it," said Finn. "I want to see your face back here before I leave for the day, Payne."

Payne took the call at his desk; it was Burns.

"Is anyone else on the line?" the captain asked. Payne glanced at Lai Sin smoothing her skirt and inside Finn's office, where Willingham sat on the edge of the desk talking, and told Burns the line was private. "Has your lieutenant told you about your mission tomorrow?"

"He told us."

"Willingham as well?"

"Yes, sir."

"Good. Now listen up. We have reason to believe Colonel Shellhammer may be at the place you're going. We're not sure if he knows of Willingham's whereabouts. It may mean nothing to him or he may become suspicious seeing Willingham there, which could hinder your assignment. He might have one of his men follow you around. You're going to have to be on your toes to get the pictures. Remember, we want pictures of the locals who are concentrated or appear to be confined to huts or whatever."

Payne felt a heaviness in his chest, fearing Burns might decide against Willingham's going. He asked him directly: "Does that mean you want me to go alone?"

"No," Burns said. "By no means will you go alone. It's essential he be there with you. Understand?"

"Yes, sir," Payne answered, relieved. "I'll get your pictures. Are you sure the colonel will be there?"

"I'm telling you so you will not be caught cold if he is," the captain said. "We're expecting you to give a good account of yourself, Payne. If you do, it could very well be the last assignment you'll have to do; your early out could very well go through in a few short days."

He knew about that too; Payne wondered if there was anything these people didn't know. He said nothing and stupidly shook his head at the receiver.

"One other thing," Burns said, and Payne braced himself. "I'm

going to try and clear up the problem you have with the GVN authorities. Don't worry about the information you were supposed to give
them. Just do your job and you'll be out of here in no time. That I
will promise you."

The man was telling him they were not interested in Saang or
Tieng and weren't going to look for them—or it meant they had been
apprehended and already sent back to the dungeon in Saigon, where
they would face an assemblage of their countrymen. Payne was on the
verge of asking Burns which it was, if the Indians were free or if their
fates were more ominous, a summary dispatch at the execution posts.

He forced himself not to ask; he might find out later today when
he went to the zoo. He cupped the receiver and whispered, "What
about Willingham, sir? I would like your assurance that he's going to
get out of this all right, too."

Burns didn't hesitate to assure him. "Of course he will. As we
told you, we aren't after him. Don't worry, Payne. Just be careful.
Shellhammer's shrewd; he's a dangerous individual."

Payne hung up the phone and called Willingham out into the
darkroom. "We get through with this thing tomorrow," Payne said
excitedly, "I'm going to talk Finn into letting you go to Tokyo in my
place. 'Cause I fucking won't be here, man."

He forced the excitement, for he knew that what happened tomorrow might not satisfy the CIA and they would continue to use him
until they got what they wanted, and he still had a huge debt to pay
the Montagnards for causing the destruction of Paang Dong. And for
both these things he needed Willingham.

Willingham saw through his forced excitement; he studied
Payne. "That phone call—you know something I don't."

"Yeah." And when Payne told him his former commander might
be at the camp, Willingham visibly tightened. He stared beyond
Payne and let his eyes settle on secret inner thoughts; he laughed
harshly and balled up a fist and shook it in the air with a kind of
athlete's victory salute and popped his open hand.

"You sure?" he said, coming back, focusing on Payne.

"I'm sure that's what I was told. I'm not sure he'll be there, but
I'd bet on it. What are you thinking, man?"

Willingham went slack, as if exhausted. "That's it, then. After
this it'll be over. Let me have a smoke."

"Sure," Payne said, totally bewildered. He gave him a cigarette and a flame and watched the smoke stream out of his nostrils as if he'd been smoking all his life.

Willingham then hiked up to his full height and walked Payne out into the hall, the cigarette hanging from the corner of his mouth. "Come over to the hootch later tonight. There's something we have to do together. All right?"

"Sure." He had never asked Payne to his hootch, but Payne didn't question him for a reason why; he thought he knew why. He remembered Bruiser and Jesus telling him that the night before they would go on one of Shellhammer's secret missions, the men in his squad got together for some kind of ritual. That was what Willingham wanted now, to have a ritual with Payne.

"Sure," Payne repeated with a sense of comradeship that made him feel as tall as Willingham.

It was Finn's way to suffer attacks of insecurity as the paper's deadline hours grew closer, and he would stick to Payne, his editor, like a tick to get him through the nerve-racking ordeal, to save him. This deadline proved to be no different, and when Payne finally got away he had to gun the jeep like Willingham to get to the zoo by five.

He arrived at the pavilion a few minutes early; Tieng wasn't there. He stood on the archway and for a while watched the calico carp swimming aimlessly under the lilies. He watched the fish for thirty minutes, then sat on the grassy knoll in view of the bridge for another half hour. There was no outlandish noise; the monkeys, in their cages, seemed to have made peace. That Tieng wasn't here did not necessarily mean he had been caught; the Indian simply was not yet ready to meet Payne because he had not learned the whereabouts of his people. That was the deal; he hadn't found out anything, so there was no reason to come here; and Tieng was too smart and resourceful to get caught. Payne was jumping to conclusions. He talked himself into believing this, but his gut feeling was not as rational about it.

He waited until six o'clock, then drove downtown to the Continental, not yet ready to return to Long Binh. He had an unsettling intuitive feeling he might not see Saigon again and he wanted to get it fixed in his mind. He took a seat close to the street. The ceiling fans churned slow enough to follow a blade; the unhurried mood of the Continental was set by those ceiling fans. The Rue Catinat was very busy, a carnival of pedestrians and parading vehicles; thin blue layers of exhaust smoke hung between the acacias lining both sides of the street. The exhaust came from old dented French cars and a rabble of two-cycle motorbikes.

A group of three strutting Aussies entered Payne's stage, gabbing in their rich Queensland accents, unmindful of a passing coterie of giggling schoolgirls in white Western dresses who turned in unison to look at the tall soldiers. Payne took notice of everyone passing, picking out the Chinese full-bloods and half-breeds, the Indonesians, the peasants, and the upper-class Viets. He knew a little of all of them. His eyes followed a young peasant woman who ambled along the curb of the sidewalk as if having nowhere to go; she had a ruck on her back and in it was an infant. Its limp arms and head dangled with her steps, and he was sure the baby was dead.

The motion before him was rapid, people moving as though something urgent awaited. The urgency was the city itself struggling to keep going; like a heartbeat the city had a contained and ordered vitality, a pulse. He was going to miss this city; Saigon was a shrine to the beauty and pain of Vietnam's history, evinced in its handsome cross-cultured landmarks and vagrant war victims and refugees crowding its streets, in the whore bars and elaborate hotels and museums and crime syndicates.

He left the cool, barren repose of the Continental and walked along the street, paying attention to things that had not made sense to him before but now did—the way Viets squatted instead of sitting to eat, the beaten pride in the faces that met his, always grinning that grin Americans mistakenly took for contemptuousness. For all its power and wealth America had become a callow giant imposing and flaunting itself on this insignificant little country with a show of cavalier arrogance that the sagacious and humble people of Vietnam tolerated but could not comprehend; and as he walked along, catching eyes, he felt ashamed of who he was, of the uniform he wore.

Payne stepped lightly along the hallway of Willingham's hootch. It was after eight and dark outside. Payne had been to his room on two or three occasions, but never by invitation; he'd simply popped in unannounced; and those times Willingham had been cagey and dour, as though Payne was invading his privacy, which he was, and Payne got the message and hadn't come back again. His lightfootedness now came from a tentative expectation. He stuck his ear against the wool army blanket fastened around the doorway and listened for stirring inside; Willingham had the blanket sealed so tightly you couldn't see light around the seams.

There was a trip wire, Payne knew, between the blanket and doorway which would cause the overhanging net inside to swing down on the intruder if the blanket-door were flung aside—that and the detonator caps would do the job. Willingham had rigged the apparatus after a gang of stick-wielding blacks raced down the hallway popping heads in the cubicles.

The blanket was suddenly jerked aside from within and Willingham appeared in the door, dressed to Payne's amazement, though not altogether unexpectedly, in a loincloth and nothing else, his chest and face smeared with dark, smelly balm. He stuck his head out and looked up and down the hall and pulled Payne inside.

"Take off your boots."

Payne tried to grin, but it was more of a frown. "What's happening?"

"First thing, let's get you high."

Payne unlaced his boots where he stood and placed them by the door. Willingham sat crosslegged on a wicker floor mat, cooking a substance in a small makeshift bowl of aluminum foil over a candle.

"No way I'm going to shoot that shit, man," said Payne. "What is it? Is it heroin?"

"Neither am I. Relax," Willingham said, looking up. "It's an opiate; you'll suck it up your nose, something the Indians taught me."

Payne remained standing, viewing the room. Willingham had somehow managed to get rid of his cube mate and had kept any new guy from moving in, and he had the cubicle fixed up to reflect the closed, mysterious side of his personality. The overhead netting hung low in places so that you had to duck, moving around. Since Payne was last here, Willingham had sealed off the window with a bamboo shutter. The room was closed up like a tomb. It smelled of sweat and joss and balm, and now the addition of an acrid odor rising from his tiny stove.

He had done away with the chair and cot but had kept the mattress, which was rolled up in a corner of the room. Instead of the regulation desk lamp, there were four restaurant candles lit and placed on the corners of the bare desk. On top of the chain-locked refrigerator Willingham had traded potatoes for was a kind of shrine of framed and unframed pictures and unfired .60-caliber shells circling another lit candle. The arrangement seemed to have been given some fore-thought. Some of the photographs were of his family and girlfriend Becky, an Olin Mills portrait of his grandmother alone and one of him and his father brandishing rifles next to a six-point buck spread on the hood of the CJ-7, taken in the Baja mountains.

Payne had seen those pictures before, but there were others dis-played now that he hadn't seen. He stepped over to the refer for a closer look.

"Is this your Indian girlfriend?" he asked, pointing to a framed mosaic of three snapshots of the same girl.

The substance had cooled down and hardened now, and Wil-lingham used his hunting knife to make powder of it. "Beautiful, wasn't she?"

The girl seemed very young; there was an innocence in her posed expressions that carried through all the pictures, a kind of harmless, ignorant bliss that made her death seem especially tragic. The smile on the girl's face uncannily duplicated Saang's. Her expression was different from the ubiquitous dead-smile looks in the many pictures Payne had taken of the Vietnamese peasantry. Noticing this made him realize he could never be an Arbus, for she had the ability to photo-graph the real person, the soul of her subject. Payne had not gotten that close to any of his subjects. He had not cared about them enough to capture them as they were from the inside. The thought compelled him to say to Willingham, "You're an artist, man. You ever thought of being one?"

"Sit over here," Willingham said. The idea held no interest for him. Payne sat on his haunches and imitated Willingham, blocking off a nostril and with the other breathing in the powder off the tip of his knife. Then Payne filled a pipe with the opium he'd brought and they smoked it down.

It was a while before Willingham said anything more, and Payne sat patiently on his heels waiting, his mind and body completely at ease, almost as if he were submerged weightlessly in warm water or in space.

Presently Willingham reached over to the refrigerator, took down another picture, and laid it in front of Payne. He spoke softly and with fondness. "My squad," he said. "This here's Lassiter, the tunnel rat. Eyeball; he wore a beret. And this's Snake, mean as a viper, quick as a cobra. Snake had a baby coming. The black dude there, that's Wash, the point. He talks in this squeaky, effeminate voice; you'd think he was queer. Good with a blade. And this one with the sixty's Burke Teschke. To look at him you wouldn't think he has a one-forty IQ and quit Brown University to go airborne and tote a pig."

He used both the past and the present talking about them, as though part of him had to keep these men alive.

The men in the snapshot stood close together, arms draped across each other on a hill of sandbag bunkers, looking as mean as they could for the camera. A couple of them wore their jungle shirts, which had no rank or insignia.

"Who's this one in the boonie hat?" Payne said. He was trying to smile but he felt his face contorting for the pain Willingham was not showing.

"That's the one that's going to make it up to them," Willingham said. He stared for another moment at the picture and the only sign he gave of what he felt inside was a slow fluid blinking of his long eyelashes.

"The oldest one was twenty. Burke. What the squad would do was when Shell passed the word a mission was on, we'd come together and have a communion," he said, holding Payne with his dark eyes. "We always figured somebody was going to die, and being together beforehand made the wait easier."

Willingham unlocked the refer and punctured two cans of Pabst. He fixed another sniff of opium for each and told Payne to take his shirt off, and he began to smear balm on him haphazardly.

"Well, buddy, this is our communion."

Chapter

23

Payne woke with a start; for a terrifying moment he was unable to grasp his own identity or the dark alien surroundings his eyes beheld. A boot poked his ribs again, Willingham's boot. It brought him back. He had slept the deep dreamless sleep of a coma and both his eyes were matted together.

"It's time," Willingham said, looking down on him. The dying candlelight eclipsed him, so that half his face was consumed in darkness. In Payne's unsettled vision he appeared an apparition.

Willingham had already dressed. He nudged Payne a third time, now with the stock of the AK-47.

The night came back to him slowly. He had crashed on Willingham's floor; he had not wanted to be alone and he'd felt close to Willingham the way it used to be with Junior Cotton those times they slept in a pup tent making secret pacts. Payne had eaten one of Willingham's C-rats, ham and limas; Willingham was incredulous and couldn't get over the fact Payne had never eaten a C-rat before. "In-fucking-credible," he'd said. They pierced each other's ears with an ice pick, something Willingham said he had to do for contrition and as a belated tribute to the Indian girl Tai, whose death he'd caused. It would bond him to her memory, he had said. Payne wanted to do it too, for the same reason. The pain was no more than a pinch and Payne had suggested they do something more significant, but Willingham said that was enough. They made small wood earrings from a stalk of the bamboo shutter, both whittling and sniffing opium in a kind of ritualistic fervor. Later Payne had run over to his hootch for the AK. He remembered saying, "You ought to have it, man, not me. I want you to have it." He had made a big deal of giving his souvenir to Willingham, offering it ceremoniously like a shy schoolboy. It embarrassed him now recalling the display of sentiment.

"Fuck, what time is it?" Payne said. His earlobe throbbed.

Willingham got out two pints of orange juice, hook-shooting one to Payne. He gargled before swallowing his.

"I've been watching you sleep," Willingham said drolly. "Did you know you talk to yourself? Yeah, you were carrying on this crazy conversation with some chick, in a chick's voice. You're a weird dude, man. It's four-thirty, let's shake it."

Payne stood against the opposite wall and watched him douse the candle in his shrine and roll and tie the mattress like a sleeping bag. "Pretty weird yourself," Payne said.

Willingham stooped before the locker mirror to primp himself, parting his hair different ways and making faces at the reflection, as though he were humoring another side of himself. He tied a handkerchief cowboy style at his neck and fitted the floppy bush hat to hang just so between his shoulder blades. A web belt with canteen hugged his hip, also cowboy style. He was wearing the old utilities and cracked combat boots he wore the first time he walked into the IO and it transformed him back to his old self, a *Life* picture of the straight-leg grunt. He looked mean and ready and Payne felt easier knowing today a warrior would be at his side.

Willingham stepped out of his room behind Payne, resealing the blanket-door and setting the trip wire, and they walked over to Payne's hootch under the beam of a flashlight. Willingham brought the AK along.

He stuck the rifle inside Payne's locker.

"Thanks for the offer, but I can get my own souvs," he said. "Don't go giving this thing away to anybody, all right? It belongs to you."

He held Payne's eyes until he got a confirmation. "Sure, okay."

Payne couldn't seem to pass off any of his treasures.

He scrubbed the balm off his face and chest and dressed in fresh utilities and slipped on his dog tags, pulled Kink's big toe, and they left for the armory in the darkness.

Payne signed for the lieutenant's .45 and six clips of ammo. Willingham got a twelve-gauge Remington, trying to bribe Sergeant Ortega with a quantity of good dope for two ammo bandoliers. "What the hell you want to do, start a fuckin war?" Ortega said teasingly, laying a single twenty-shell belt on the counter. "That's all I'm authorized to dispense. Already got all the smoke I am ever gonna need."

Labouisse let them in the mess hall before it opened and they sipped coffee with him while the gook KP prepared their eggs and bacon. He wanted to know where they were off to so early, but let it go when he didn't get a straight answer.

Payne couldn't eat his breakfast. He got down a glass of tomato juice and some coffee. He made a trip to the latrine with a case of the squirts. Worried he would get heatstroke from hunger, Labouisse wrapped a sweet roll in aluminum foil and stuck it in the ruck Payne was using to carry film and the lieutenant's personal Topcon camera. Willingham finished off Payne's uneaten scrambled eggs.

"You give us a lift to the airport, Buzz?" Payne asked.

"Sure. I got nothing else to do; I'm only working," he said with worried cheerfulness. "I forget. We're squared up, ain't we, Payne?"

"Yeah. We're square."

The short trip passed in silence, and when they got to the airfield, Labouisse said, "You guys be back in time for a game tonight?"

"We'll see," Payne said. "Thanks for the lift."

"Don't mention it. Just be careful out there." Labouisse might have been a lousy card player and done nothing but cook food all over the world, but he was a long-term veteran who knew things about war and you could tell by his tone that he was worried for them.

It was nearing daybreak and the moon's pale light was losing its hold. The few men spread out around the wide floor of the terminal were reading or sleeping on benches. Payne checked them in and they dropped their gear near the hangar door. Payne complained his mouth was dry and Willingham gave him a piece of Dubble Bubble. He chewed the gum and smoked a cigarette.

"I gotta go to the head," Payne said. Little knives of gas cut into his bowels.

"The flies," Willingham said easily, smiling. "It's just the waiting."

The latrine was unoccupied and after finishing Payne took a moment to examine his teeth in the mirror; they still looked okay, unyellowed, the gums pink. He studied his eyes under the fluorescent light, giving serious effort to figure out the right one's true color. The color was always changing and he had never been able to call it. Ann thought the true color was gray, not a color at all. In the artificial light both were a no-color gray. The mustache, he decided, was coming off before he went home.

When he came back he took a seat. He felt weak. Willingham sat down beside him.

"I don't know about you," Willingham said, "but my ear's hurting like a motherfucker." He blew a large bubble and sucked it back into his mouth.

"You want a smoke?" Payne lit one for himself.

Too early in the morning for Willingham.

"You going back to law school?" Payne said absently.

"I don't know yet. I may just bum around for a while, try to get my head squared away."

"Yeah, me too."

"Fuck you say, man. You're getting out to go to school. Better take advantage of it. You got a future, an old lady to think about, remember?"

Payne sneered at the thought of Ann. "I used to."

"Don't be so self-pitying. It don't fit on you. If she didn't care about you she wouldn't have done all that work to get you home early. Would she, now?"

Payne brushed the question off.

"The thing that's wrong with you, man, is you just can't figure out your priorities. Do you love her or what?"

"Yeah, sure. I married her didn't I?"

They were silent for a while and then Willingham said, "I had this thing when I was a kid of wanting to be poor and dumb, like an aborigine in Australia, where I would have to work for everything I got. If I wanted to eat, I'd have to kill and butcher an animal for it. If I wanted something to wear in winter, I'd have to skin a deer or a bear. I'd live in a cave and watch the rain pour outside and go play in it. Rain would be free. I'd live alone. But, shit," he said, "I've had everything I wanted all my life. There's hardly anything I didn't get, so I never learned to appreciate it. And now I don't know what the hell I want."

"That's the craziest thing I ever heard," said Payne, looking at him. "Besides, there's no rush to decide what you want to do. You're not exactly over the hill yet."

Willingham chewed his gum and broke out a big grin. "It's six, let's find our chopper."

Payne grinned back; the flies, he noticed, were gone.

Natural light whitewashed the terminal's high windows, awakening the day. They hauled their gear outside. The sky was a brilliant burnt orange across the eastern horizon, a dark gray to the west. A platoon of weary-looking Redcatchers from the 199th marched in formation inside the terminal in front of a lieutenant who seemed to be making a test of his authority, as if he weren't really in charge. Payne caught the deadened eyes of two of the passing infantrymen and stared woodenly; a friendly gesture would only have provoked them.

The chopper pilot had a shaved, shiny head, its golden sheen the product of fastidious attention. The head was too small for his body. He wore a jumpsuit with a jungle of zippered pockets. He was the silent, superior flyboy type; he checked their IDs without a word and the three of them climbed into a Loach and belted in. It was a featherweight chopper, a bubble with a quick lift. The sudden upward surge and forward thrust put lead in Payne's limbs and viscera; he sank in the seat and watched the earth fall away, feeling at once the inexorable sense of power that being up there above it all gives you.

"Where are we headed?" he asked from the backseat, leaning over the console.

The pilot had slipped on his headset and apparently couldn't hear. Payne touched his arm and repeated the question.

"Can't tell you. Orders."

The breaking sun streaked across fog-laden paddy fields and moments later caught the glitter of a wide river traversing the forest like a brown, lazy snake. They seemed to be following the course of the river. The giant red fireball of sun freed itself of the horizon and stayed to the side of them, at three o'clock.

"Looks like the Mekong," Willingham shouted over his shoulder, pointing downward through the bubble glass. The boonie hat drooped over his eyes; Payne thought it was dumb manly hotdogging, the cult of balls, that kept him from wearing a helmet.

The river fell in and out of view under flat patches of fog and seemed to narrow in the thickening jungle. According to the sun they were headed northeast.

The lift took forty-five minutes and then the chopper dropped rapidly, as if falling to earth, into a cleared-out area, an LZ; it had been a long flight that could have delivered them well into Cambodia. Payne hadn't spotted any kind of compound in the descent. The pilot, touching down, yelled, "Here you are. Happy hunting."

"You coming back at three?" Payne asked, getting out behind Willingham.

"Haven't been scheduled to. Get out." He was in a hurry and took off before Payne cleared the wash.

Payne made a dash across the wind-pressed grass to the tree line where a squad of soldiers sat or stood in the casual manner of seasoned troops. The squad leader, a first lieutenant, said they would be escorting the journalists to their destination. His name was Nichols. Payne did not recognize the outfit's patch, the figure of a blood-dripping skull under a half-cocked beret; paratroopers. It was an unauthorized patch, the emblem meant to vaunt the promise of death and decay. The grunts themselves did not wear berets; they wore bush hats like Willingham's. Willingham was over there playing splits with one of the grunts, using the hunting knife he'd used to cut the AVRN's throat.

Payne questioned the lieutenant to find out where they were and where they were headed. The inquiry drew dry, snickering chuckles from the crew of paratroopers, as though he'd said something outlandish.

"You in the boondocks, man," said the RTO, a black man of powerful shoulders. "Headed nowhere yo mama would approve. We gon' escort you fine gentlemen. Not a thing for you to worry bout, though. You with ground-pounding jumpers what make the snake eaters look like Miss Poppins."

Payne gave the huge soldier a look meant to show he knew what he was talking about, that he could dig it.

"Our instructions are to lead you about ten clicks northeast of here," the lieutenant said evenly. "That's all we know. Should be a hamlet or some kind of compound."

"Hell, we don't even know that, Nick," another said. "You

wouldn't want to go and get these guys' hopes up."

"'Sides, who the fuck are they anyhow, man?" said a kid whose fierce, penetrating eyes betrayed his baby face. "Maybe they're leading *us,* maybe into some encounter. Who the fuck are they?"

Payne asked again where they were and the lieutenant said his orders were not to say; it could have been Cambodia.

Willingham had put his knife away and was now slouching against a tree, measuring the men with his impatient smirk as they talked it out. He was being cool, blowing and popping bubbles. He pushed off the tree to address the lieutenant. "It turns out our orders are classified, too," he said. "But you guys got nothing to sweat, just get us where we're going. What are the sitreps on the area?"

"Nothing hot. Okay, let's break," Lieutenant Nichols said, assuming his role. "Waters, take point."

"Aww shit, Nick," Waters complained. Mumbling to himself he sheathed the bayonet he had been throwing at Willingham's feet and quickly taped his pants at the thighs and vanished through a hole in the jungle.

Nichols knuckled the steel pot on Payne's head. "You'll have to get rid of that," he said and snapped a finger at one of his men. "Give, Reese."

The soldier reached into his rucksack and withdrew a boonie hat and gave it to the lieutenant, who handed it to Payne. "Here, wear this. We don't want you stroking on us. Where's your canteen?" He eyed him further, like a tolerant drill sergeant. "Well, try not to lag behind."

The RTO shook his massive black head at this little aside; he displayed a picket fence of white teeth. "Shee-it, where you be all your life? You done been one lucky dude, ain't you, man?"

Nichols tossed Payne's helmet and liner into the thicket and they moved out in single file along an overgrown path. Payne unsnapped the leather and kept his hand on the .45. He stayed alert, straining his eyes for movement in the high brush and treetops.

Yeah, he'd had some luck. But he had been through more shit than most REMFs and he didn't deserve that kind of ridicule. He was here now, wasn't he?

Even with the column taking its time, the effort to breathe air this hot and thick soon became laborious. He wished he'd brought a canteen. Twice he was slapped in the face by branches the man in front released late as if on purpose. The man in front humped with an effort under the weight of his ruck and hand-held ammo canisters. The slung-shouldered M-60 swung back and forth with the grunt's steps like a pendulum, bumping Payne's knee. Payne touched it to stop the swinging and the grunt wheeled around like he was going to strike Payne.

"Hands off my pig, man," he whispered through unmoving lips. "Lay back a ways."

Except for that encounter no one talked on the march. Jungle birds were doing the talking, in squawks and whistles. Their screeching intermingled with the rustling footfalls of the soldiers and the snapping of twigs, the steady chops from machetes up front. For a while the hoarse grunting of a wild boar trailed the column.

Payne kept turning around and looking behind until Willingham offered him the canteen he'd filled with orange juice. It pissed him Willingham hadn't advised him to take a canteen of his own, or given him a reason why he shouldn't wear a helmet.

The column humped up to the crests of hills and walked the ridges when they could because Nichols said the opposition, if it was around, would be in the valleys. "We don't want to invade Charlie's territory any more than he wants to invade ours," he said, explaining to Payne the ABCs in a breach of the silence. "So we stay on the ridges and let them have the lowland. That way we can live in harmony."

Nichols did not let up the pace for two hours. The column trudged quietly through shoulder-high knife grass and up and down hills, across low-grass fields and into contrastingly thick jungle. In places the forest was double-canopied, the top cover reaching a hundred feet above them. High in the tops of the trees, Payne spotted a group of three or four monkeys swinging from vines and branches, moving at the column's pace as if leading them.

Nichols finally stopped and had the squad gather while he checked his map.

He talked to Willingham. "Should be just over this next ridge, down in the valley on the other side," he said. "Looks like some kind of vil but I can't be sure what's there. Maybe you better tell me so I'll know how to approach."

Willingham shrugged his shoulder. "Can't tell you what we don't know."

Nichols didn't like that. "You better damn well tell me, man. I ain't sending my men into someplace I don't know what's going on."

"Listen, sir," said Payne. "It's supposed to be a camp of some kind. Could be a village that's being used as a transfer center for refugees. Our people will be there."

"That right?" Nichols asked Willingham.

Willingham nodded. "Far as I know."

"All right," the lieutenant said with reservation. "But I'll set up flanks anyway. Reese, you and Tommy go off that way," he said, fingering the map. He assigned another two-man detail the other flank and told them to hit it. "The rest of us will approach from the road, or whatever it is," he said and folded the map. Counting Payne and Willingham there were twelve men.

"Might be better if we sweep in three-man groups," Willingham suggested, "just in case the coordinates got screwed up and this is the wrong place. It's been known to happen."

"If I smell anything even remotely close to an ambush, I'm pulling my men back," the lieutenant said. "I don't know who the fuck you are, man, and I ain't about to do somebody I don't know shit about no favors. Savvy?"

"Can't blame you. I'd do the same thing," Willingham said agreeably and walked Nichols away from the group. They exchanged words and came back, the lieutenant appearing satisfied and less worried. He divided up the remaining men, who spread out and climbed the final ridge. Willingham and Payne were with him and his RTO.

A fog obscured the narrow valley below and the descent was slow, Payne taking his cue from the lieutenant and checking the ground in front of him before every step. He imagined tripping a wire, a bouncing betty jumping up and blowing him apart; he wondered if he would feel anything, or if he lived what kind of life it would be.

The fog was high and breaking up and soon they were under it and could make out tiny thatched roofs and sidings of corrugated tin nestled among palm and mango and banyan trees on the valley floor. A dirt road led to the village. In the opposite direction the road stopped at a bridge that had been blown, making vehicular passage impossible.

The lieutenant motioned the flanks to stay in the side growth and took to the road with Payne and Willingham. A high Cyclone fence ran alongside the section of road that passed the village. Farther down, the fence took a sharp cut back into the jungle, appearing to enclose the village. The fence had recently been installed, for vegetation had not yet regrown at its footing.

"What the fuck's that fence for?" Nichols said.

"Could be they got some kind of supplies they want protected," said Willingham. "It looks like there's some Conexes in there." He grinned suddenly as if he were going to say something about sleeping in a Conex at LBJ. It was a quick grin that faded just as quickly.

Nichols shook his head doubtfully. "Never seen a vil perimetered like that before. They usually have some bullshit bamboo, if anything. Must be something they don't want nobody to get at in there."

"Yeah. Or something they don't want out," Willingham said, also looking doubtful.

Payne said, "This is the right place." The other camp where they had been sent, a refugee site, was fenced too.

Closer, the sound of a diesel engine came into earshot and then the familiar noises of human activity. The fog opened to a view of the main yard. Payne saw two U.S. vehicles, a plank-benched six-by and an armored jeep. The bridge had been destroyed after the vehicles arrived or, curiously, behind them. Near the main gate stood a rickety twenty-foot lookout tower, which appeared unmanned.

The lieutenant stopped thirty meters short of the village and had his RTO call in.

"We can take it from here," Willingham said.

Nichols told him to hang on. "Wait till we get word."

The RTO made contact and told the lieutenant, "Cap say to take 'em in, then we can split if everything looks cool."

"Go ahead and split," Willingham said, laying a hand on Nichols's shoulder. "You've done your job. Go on back in the bush."

"Yeah, and thanks for the fucking escort," Payne added resentfully; he was being abandoned, the apprehension of it taking hold. He watched Nichols and his men retreat.

Despite Willingham's company he felt vulnerable, his knees quaking, as they walked toward the gate. "I'd feel a lot fucking better if they went with us," he said, "if you hadn't encouraged 'em to leave."

"They're not going anywhere."

"Didn't you just—"

"Got it worked out with Nichols," said Willingham. "They're going to stay close by for a while. That way, in case anything goes wrong, we get a backup. Gives us the element of surprise."

Payne said with a degree of relief, "I wouldn't have thought of that. What'd you do, promise him a tour's supply of your nose opium?"

Willingham grinned. "Didn't have to. They're ambushers; that's what they like to do."

Two American soldiers who were not MPs stood guard behind the closed gate, both brandishing sixteens. Payne held out his press card and a guard took it and Willingham's through the wire, wanting to know their business.

"Can you believe it," Willingham said with dubious geniality. "They sent us all the way up here from fucking Saigon, man. Just to do a fucking newspaper story on you guys; you must be doing something right."

"Wait here," one of the guards said and went off.

While they waited Willingham talked to the other man behind the fence. He was a tall thin guy with a stiff mustache and gullible bright eyes. He was not wearing a patch but Willingham asked him familiar questions, as if he just assumed the corporal was with the 5th. He wanted to know which outfit in the Forces he was from, where he was stationed, were they still using the Yards on recons.

"Nah, we don't use 'em no more," the corporal said in response. "A bummer too, man. Higher fucked that one, our body counts've been way off ever since. Say, how come you know so much about us anyway, being as you're from Saigon?" He spat out the word Saigon as if it tasted bad.

Willingham grinned at him in an overly friendly way. "Hell, I was with Shell's team for six fucking months. He's here now, ain't he?"

"No shit?" the boy said cheerfully. "Well, fuck me. Come on in." After he opened the gate, he and Willingham went through the knuckle-to-thumb-to-knuckle trick Payne had tried more than once and wasn't going to try again.

"How long you been on this mobile?" Willingham asked.

"Came out last night. We'll pull out today, I guess. Be back at base camp in a week maybe. You was under Shell, huh? Fuck me, man. What's your name?"

Willingham told him and they continued talking like brothers who'd been separated.

An officer wearing the headgear of the Green Berets and camouflage fatigues swaggered ahead of the returning guard, taking long, self-assured steps, his arms swinging, moving swiftly in a mechanical and confident stride. The subdued beret flash was the airborne type. Payne did not have to see his name tag to know he was Shellhammer. When he got close he scowled at the troop who had opened the gate and addressed him.

"Boyd, you had your orders," he said, stopping on a dime. "No one enters this compound without my okay." He turned his attention abruptly to the journalists. "This compound's restricted."

His strut and the commanding force of his voice were strikingly incongruous with the gauzy, androgynous cast of his face; almost the face of a woman, soft-lined and boneless, cherublike. He had wet, twinkling brown eyes that also belonged to a woman. The eyes were pinched very close together, as if his mother had dreaded his birth and had tried to clamp down the walls of her womb. Payne stared disconcertedly at him; he had imagined the opposite of this Green Beret commander; he had expected a man of hewn virile features and great physical stature. It was his reputation that had given Payne that image. The deception could throw you.

His recognition of Willingham revealed little of his thoughts, only that he seemed mildly surprised. "Well, well," he said. "Damned if it's not Willingham. Thought you went home in a box."

Willingham forced his friendliness; Payne knew it was an act. "You kidding, sir? I'm too resilient for that. You didn't know, huh? They transferred me like that," he said, snapping his fingers. "Hear they reassigned you just as quick. Makes you wonder, don't it, sir?"

Shellhammer appeared vaguely dismayed, his soft features showing the slightest tenseness; this was as much of himself as he was going to reveal. He turned abruptly. "Come with me." Payne noticed a slight lisp on the word "with."

As they walked across the muddy yard toward a hut, he pumped Willingham for information about his present duty. Willingham responded with straight answers, that he was with Saigon Support Information and was here to do a story on pacification. If Shellhammer was curious it showed only in his questions and not the deadpan tone he used asking them or the way he responded to Willingham's answers with an easy, "Un huh . . . well, well."

Payne fell behind and took in the layout of the village, searching for places groups of people might be. He furtively snapped off random shots of the surroundings. Except for the high fence and the few Americans hanging around huts, it seemed like any village, tranquil and impoverished. He saw only four ARVN troops, who were grouped together playing cards in front of a hut. He didn't see any civilians. He couldn't tell if the fence enclosed the entire village; farther back the flora was too thick to tell.

Shellhammer directed them inside a large, musky hootch of bamboo and thatch which was divided down the middle by rice sacks stacked four feet high. He was using the hootch as his command quarters. The colonel sat down in a wicker chair, the only one inside. The hut had a single door and no windows.

Payne followed Willingham's lead and stood before Shellhammer in a casual form of attention. Scattered around the plank floor were maps and radio equipment and a cache of piled weapons, mostly AKs and carbines and a few mortar tubes, a single unsheathed machete. There was a bottle of Jack Daniel's on an upended vegetable box next to the chair. A buck sergeant lounged in the doorway wiping down his M-16.

The colonel removed his beret and ran his hand over a white-walled crew cut of stiff brown hair, then wiped his face with a handkerchief and looked at it to see how much he had sweated. He placed a teak stick about the size and shape of a Little League bat across his lap and began whittling it with a hunting knife as he talked. The knife was the kind Willingham had.

"An article, huh. Well, well," he said skeptically. "Those twiddle-asses at MACV haven't been doing their homework correctly. There's no pacification business here. This is simply a hamlet we've commandeered for a field TOC." He looked up at Willingham. "But you don't have to be told our operations are classified."

"Still using the Indians as front mobiles?" Willingham said. "The way it used to be?"

"That's privy information. You know that."

"Intelligence across the border? You running another squad now, a fresh crew?" Willingham went on. His tone was bitter and he grinned coldly. He was going to blow it, Payne thought. He couldn't seem to maintain his composure.

Shellhammer pointed at him with the hunting knife which he was now using to clean under his fingernails. He glanced at Payne and then back at Willingham. "That's no longer your concern, Corporal —or is it? That why you're here?"

Willingham's face had taken on a red heat.

"Sir," Payne blurted, "our orders are simply to get an article on pacification, like he said. It's supposed to just be starting up here. There does seem to be some construction going on, which is the kind of stuff civil affairs wants. We'll just get a little info and some shots and be on our way."

"Let me see those orders."

Payne reluctantly handed over the paper.

Shellhammer was young for a lightbird, close to thirty. He used reading glasses to look over the orders. The orders were vaguely stated, a standing order requesting assistance to Public Information personnel wherever they went in III or IV Corps where the U.S. Army provided matériel or personnel. It did not name a village and did not indicate a specific military unit; Burns had not given Finn specifics.

Shellhammer sighed languidly. "Who are you trying to fool," he said, folding the paper and giving it back to Payne. Removing the glasses he glared sternly at both of them and called out to the buck sergeant in the doorway, "Wallace. Leave us for a minute."

The sergeant nodded and got up.

"Suppose you tell me first who sent you here and then why." The lisp was more pronounced when he spoke in a flat tone.

"Civil affairs," Payne said. He tapped a cigarette on his Zippo, trying to feign casualness and give the impression that he too was confused. "I guess they got their villages mixed up. I've had that problem before. They just screwed up at MACV. We can forget it and split right now."

Shellhammer rolled his eyes; he did not like having his intelligence insulted. He attended Willingham. "Let's have it. Who's behind this?"

Willingham was livid; his chin jutted outward, fiercely working the gum, his eyes set in a wild glower. Payne braced himself for the violence he knew Willingham was capable of, had stored up, and seemed on the verge of letting go.

"You remember a gook ARVN called Su?" Willingham said dangerously. "Know what happened to him?"

Shellhammer half lifted himself out of the chair, his face set hard as Willingham's. His look confirmed he had known Su.

Suddenly the noise of an approaching helicopter broke. Shellhammer frowned.

"Both of you wait here," he said and walked out. A great wind blew through the doorway as the chopper descended outside.

"Give me a clip," Willingham said, shaking an open hand at Payne, his gaze fixed on the door.

"What?"

"Give me a fucking clip, quick."

Willingham stooped over the pile of firearms on the floor and dug out a .45. He slapped the clip into the gun and chambered a bullet, then stuck the automatic in his boot and readjusted the pants leg.

"You fucking blew it, man, saying that about Su," Payne said.

Willingham grunted cynically. "Makes no difference, Payne. He's not about to let us go."

"What the hell can he do?"

"You don't know what he can do. Don't let that sweet face fool you like it did me. I know what he's capable of."

Both Burns and the CIA had said it too: We're dealing with a dangerous man.

The hiss of turbines waned and finally died and Willingham moved to the side of the door, peering out. "A shit-hook," he said, and got an expression on his face of sudden comprehension.

He turned to Payne. "There's no cargo in it, the thing's sitting too light. They're not delivering; they're picking up."

Payne took a look outside. The Chinook's tail ramp was down and Shellhammer stood near it gesturing with his hands and talking to a crewman or the pilot.

"They're probably picking up those Conexes," Payne said.

"Yeah. That's probably where the bodies are kept."

"What bodies?"

Shellhammer trotted back toward the hootch and Willingham

pushed Payne away from the doorway. "We've come at the wrong time, man. Wouldn't you fucking know it. Your fucking CIA people've set us up for this. It's beginning to make sense now."

The buck sergeant entered the hut first behind his rifle, holding it on them. He didn't speak. Shellhammer walked around him.

"Put your weapons over here," he said. "And the camera."

Payne looked nervously from the buck sergeant to Shellhammer and lifted the gun from its holster.

"The belt too," the sergeant said. "Easy. You too." He raked the rifle barrel at Willingham, who laid his bandolier and shotgun on the stack of weapons.

Shellhammer grinned at Willingham. "Afraid I have to take your firepower for the time being, until I can find out who sent you here. You still carry the knife, Willie Boy?" he said and reached carefully around Willingham's back, withdrawing the hunting knife. It was an exact model of the one he used to whittle the bat, a curved four-inch blade serrated on top with a finger guard and leather handle. "Thought so. Now let's have your IDs."

"What's this about, sir?" Payne said, alarmed without faking it. He didn't know what to do with his hands. "If we've come to the wrong camp it's not our fault. A chopper's coming back for us in a little while; maybe he got the wrong information somehow. You'll see when you check us out."

Shellhammer batted his eyelashes as if he meant to express sympathy. He no longer seemed curious or interested in explanations. "Looks like we've got ourselves a situation here. Wallace, show them out."

Wallace led them around the Chinook's aft and across the village to a hut which could be seen from anywhere in the quadrangle. Payne noticed the chopper was empty inside, as Willingham said. Wallace told them not to worry, the CO was just being careful.

"You for real, ain't got nothing to sweat," he said. "But don't go wandering off." Leaving them, he removed a deck of cards from his shirt pocket. "Here you go."

The hut was dark and damp inside and hazy with rice pollen. It was a granary bin. Payne immediately began stomping the ground, searching for a hidden compartment. Willingham chided him silently and stepped outside, sneezing. Payne found only solid earth. In the doorway he sat on his heels. The little knives were in his guts again and he tightened his sphincter on a held breath until the pain subsided. The flies had returned.

"Before he used to go in a tunnel," Willingham said in a soft-spoken voice, "Eyeball always went off by himself and looked at a tree. Didn't matter what kind it was, could have been a hedge. He just stared up at it for a while like he was amazed at how it had grown. The guy loved trees; they were poetry to him. Then he'd strip his gear and go down. You think about it, it takes some kind of dignity to crawl down a black hole looking for death."

He grinned and suddenly reached over and adjusted Payne's boonie hat so that it sat farther back from his eyes.

"What did you mean, they set us up for this? For what?" Payne said. When Willingham didn't answer he added, "I knew it could be tricky, we both did, but I didn't know this was going to happen."

"I know."

"It'll probably work out all right."

"If my guess is right he's expecting us to try to get out of here," Willingham said thoughtfully. He was surveying the village now, studying the proximities of the CQ and guards and fence as if planning how it would be done.

"The village is fenced, he took our weapons," Payne argued. "He doesn't think we're stupid enough that we'd try to leave."

"He's expecting it all right."

"Then you think he wants us to slip out?"

Willingham nodded. "That'd make it convenient, wouldn't it? A couple IO greenhorns buying it from a sniper or booby trap's easy enough to explain off."

"Hey, shit. I can't believe he'd want to have us killed, for Christ's sake."

"Why not," Willingham said, his composure regained. "That's what I'm going to do to him."

Chapter
24

"You planned to kill him all along, didn't you?" Payne said in a singsong voice. He was angry and afraid. He saw it now. The confusion cleared like dispersing fog. How naive and slow-witted he had been not to see it before, see it coming, and now it was too late. Willingham had been waiting for this chance ever since Payne told him about the investigation. He had gotten it into his mind that Shellhammer was the man responsible for the ambush on his squad, that he had authorized it; it didn't stand to reason or make any sense why, but that was what Willingham thought, and he had been biding his time, pretentiously playing the strack soldier, waiting for the opportunity to kill this man. He had deceived Payne and Payne felt betrayed.

It occurred to Payne how right Sterr had been about him; his perceptions had gotten twisted beyond any sense of moral rightness and had turned him into a man whose motives had narrowed to the blind purpose of revenge. It was his sole motivation now, to kill as an act of vindication. It was the war that had done this, wracked him with hatred and it had become a part of his core. Sterr had seen it.

Payne said, "I thought last night meant something special, but you were just fucking me over, stringing me along."

"Last night was me and you, Payne. It was for us. I couldn't tell you. You might have messed up my only chance."

"I'm with you, man," Payne said angrily. "I always was. Why couldn't you have just fucking confided in me?"

Willingham looked him in the eye. His demeanor was calm and thoughtful. "Would *you* have? He's going to pay—he has to pay, and I'm the only one left to see he does."

"You've got the evidence against him. You could have turned it over. I could've helped you nail him."

"You still don't get it, do you?" Willingham said. "They fucking *want* me to do him. They probably made bets you'd tell me what was going on. You think they don't know I wasted Su? Wise up, Payne. Taking him out convinced them I knew Shell set up the squad and they knew if I had the chance I'd go after him too. This way it's a lot neater than if they'd brought me into the picture directly to terminate him. That's the way they do things. They get what they want and keep their hands clean doing it."

"And what happens when they stick you with murder, huh? Don't you care? Does revenge mean so much to you?"

"We were tight, a team. I owe them. Any one of them would do the same as me. That's the only rule in this fucking war that counts, you look out for your buddy."

"Yeah, well, I'm the only buddy you got now." Payne wanted to remind him that his buddies were dead, what good would it do to kill the man? But then, if Willingham was right, Shellhammer was going to get rid of them. So it really came down to who was going to survive here, and Payne dropped any further notion of trying to talk him out of it. He was with him; now they were a team and had to look out for each other.

Willingham retied the lace on the boot that held the gun. "I'm not giving up," he said. "We'll figure a way to get out of this. I owe that to you."

Willingham stood up and waved Boyd over from the gate. The gangly corporal eagerly bounded away from his post, toting his rifle by the carrying handle. "What's happening?" he said innocently. He didn't know what was happening.

"I got some good dew, wanna do some tokes?" the guard said.

Payne kept quiet; this would be Willingham's move. The whole situation was now Willingham's. Payne stooped over, squeezing his knees as the razor blades hacked away at his guts.

"Maybe in a while," Willingham said and asked, "What's the shit-hook doing here?"

Boyd shrugged. "Beats me."

They both looked at Payne swaying on his haunches.

"I have to walk," Payne said grimacing and stumbled off, unable to straighten up. He went around back of the hut in a rush and let the razors out. It left him nauseated and feverish, and he leaned back against the thatch breathing irregular gulps of air, as if he'd been under water too long.

He could hear Willingham talking in his good-buddy tone of voice about Shellhammer, what a privilege it was to be part of his team, and Boyd agreeing. He had the kid's attention.

There was grass and bushes behind the granary tall enough to conceal a man if he wanted to make a run for it. A few hootches dotted the short distance of open ground. Payne saw no villagers and even the fowl seemed unnaturally subdued, as if the roosters had orders not to crow, ducks not to quack. The fence was forty meters off. Lieutenant Nichols's platoon was waiting for them out there. Maybe he could make it.

He waited till the nausea passed, then walked casually in the direction of the fence, checking for a way out.

He stopped short of a hedgerow when he heard low voices, Viets jabbering in that grating tonal quaver. The sound came from a tin-and-lumber structure obscured in the thick-set growth; it was the kind of building Americans erected at refugee camps. As he headed toward it, the voices became clearer, now sounding passive, as though merely rambling. He didn't hear women's voices. The structure was larger than at first it appeared and had strung above it a camouflage netting, a replica of the hidden shed at Xuan Loc where decapitated bodies were strung up, where Willingham had murdered the ARVN. The building was a holding tank. Payne dropped under cover.

Two armed Americans stood in front of the wire-netted door, rapping to each other over the drone of gobbledygook. At an angle to the broad doorway Payne could make out the shadowed figures of the Viets inside. They were standing up and close together, like corralled cattle. There might have been two or more dozen men inside.

Still on his hands Payne started backtracking. Something hard suddenly punched into his back, forcing him flat. A voice behind him spoke nervously. "Who you, why you here? Up."

The Viet soldier kept the muzzle of his rifle pressed against Payne as he turned and stood. He stood rigidly and looked the Viet in the eyes, feeling the rifle tremble in his nervous hands.

"The colonel sent me out," Payne said angrily, frowning down his nose at the small figure. "Take the gun off me," he commanded.

The ARVN looked about, as if unsure what to do. He kept the weapon against Payne's stomach. "Go there," he said, nodding toward the shed.

The grunts took a stance seeing them approach.

"Tell this fucker to take his rifle off me," Payne said, brushing debris off his uniform. His heart pounded in his throat.

One of the grunts smiled menacingly at Payne and waved the Viet off. "Been taking a little stroll? See anything you'd like to write about?" he said. The word had already gotten to them who he and Willingham were. The grunt looked Payne up and down.

The chattering inside the shed trailed off and a few of the faces pressed forward into the sunlight and watched with interest. The prisoners held hands and wrapped fingers over the links in the wire. One of the figures wore a loincloth and kepi; he smiled obliquely at Payne. His teeth were filed down and lacquered.

Payne gave Kroong-the-Warrior a subtle look of recognition and the Indian nodded behind the guards' backs, withdrew, and pushed another of his tribesmen forward. Payne recognized him also from his nights in Paang Dong. This was where they had been sent. This was where Tieng would have brought Payne, to a prison camp that by road would have taken a day or more and was probably inside Cambodia. It would have been an impossible trek.

More fog lifted; it wasn't a coincidence that the Indians were here. It made perfect sense. The CIA had arranged it, moved the Paang Dong survivors to this village where they would be within Shellhammer's reach. They weren't just setting Willingham up; they were setting the colonel up too. Killing two birds with a single stone. Willingham had called it right.

"Hold the fort. I'll take this fucking housecat for a walk," the grunt told the other man and pushed Payne with the barrel of his rifle.

The grunt led him to the command hootch, giving him a shove inside. "Lookie what we found down by the tank, Colonel. The fucking reporter got curious."

Shellhammer raised the corners of his mouth into a delicate grin, appearing unsurprised. "Get the other one," he told the soldier.

Payne noticed his camera on the floor near the cache of weapons, the back open, film canister gone. His ruck had been gone through as well. He stood at parade rest with an absurd sense of military discipline, having removed his hat, and waited like a trained soldier for the colonel to speak. Payne's fatigues were damp and in places soggy; his feverish skin and the palpitations of his heart might have come from malaria or from the flies.

"You seem to be intelligent, a good soldier," Shellhammer said, as if to relax Payne. "I don't know how you got yourself into this mess, but I'm going to give you the chance to walk out of here right now. You're free to return to the comfort of your post." He smiled benignly. "All you have to do is tell me the man's name who sent you."

Payne's hesitation was a mistake. He knew it and Shellhammer knew it.

Shellhammer took a quick drink from the bottle of Jack Daniel's. He breathed a sigh of disappointment. "Now listen to me, son," he said, bringing the wicker chair close and sitting down, keeping Payne on his feet before him. "How much time have you left over here—a few months? Pretty soon you'll be looking back on your tour merely as a small inconvenience in your life. Certainly there's a family that cares about you, that wants to see you return home safely. Think about it."

He offered Payne a smoke and Payne took it without comment.

The colonel stood up and threw a leg over the back of the chair and leaned closer; his disappointment intensified. Payne smelled the whiskey on his breath. "All right. You want to stay mute; that's understandable. You're not sure what you should do. But listen to me, son. You're being used in a game that's way out of your league. The people who put you up to this business are selling you out. They don't give a damn in hell if you make it back or not. The fact is they would prefer if you didn't come back. It would make their job easier if you were out of the way." He spoke matter-of-factly. "I hate to see it when a soldier throws his life away for nothing. Talk to me now; you can trust me. I'm a man who's never gone back on his word."

His words and manner were convincing and Payne could see why Willingham had once prided himself being part of his team.

"What's the alternative?" Payne said, trying to stall him until Willingham came.

"Isn't that evident? Men go on missions and sometimes they

don't return," the colonel said flatly, looking outside. "It's your option, soldier. What's it going to be?"

Payne eyed the pile of weapons, frantically considering his real alternatives. He was reassured Willingham had been right, that they stood no more of a chance of walking out of this village than Kroong-the-Warrior. The clips had been removed from the stack of AKs and carbines; he couldn't tell about the handguns strewn about. The machete was close at hand.

The colonel's move came quick and Payne felt the blunt pain shoot up his shin before the action had fully registered. Shellhammer drew back the teakwood bat as if to strike the other leg as Payne fell to his knees clutching the leg. He cried out.

"You're not as bright as I thought," Shellhammer said, looking down on him with disgust. "Get up. Your leg's not broken; it just feels that way."

Willingham entered the hut in front of the guard. Shellhammer regarded his man. "Thiesman, stick around." Then he said to Willingham, "Your pal here wants to play hero. Maybe you should have a talk with him."

Willingham regarded him stonily and helped Payne to his feet. "What happened?"

The colonel talked. "If I don't get some answers I'll have to let Thiesman turn you over to the cowboys and let them work it out of you. I don't think I need to remind you of their efficiency. Who sent you? What about Major Su?"

"No problem with that, sir," Willingham said easily. "But first you should know that there's a detachment outside this vil coming through the front gate in about ten minutes looking to take us out. One of your own men's out there telling them the situation right now."

"Who?" said the colonel.

"The guy on the gate, Boyd. Don't believe me, just call him in."

Shellhammer rubbed his chin thoughtfully, then barked through the door, "Wallace, find Stick."

"You think we'd be stupid enough to waltz in here without backup?" Willingham said smugly. He exuded self-confidence. "Come on, Colonel. Never move on a vil without backup. You taught me the importance of that yourself."

Willingham was moving around as he talked, animating his arms, scratching low on his leg as if he had a pestering mosquito bite, so that his move for the .45, when it came, would not seem sudden. He already had his leg hiked on a sack of rice. Payne positioned himself between the colonel and his sergeant, ready to lunge at one or the other of them.

Once Willingham caught Payne's eye, confirming his readiness, he leaned forward on a knee and said to Shellhammer, "Tell me about my squad, Colonel. Why did you set us up for the ambush? I'd like to know."

The colonel regarded him with the kind of curious indifference a cat regards a half-dead bird under its paw. "You should know better than to ask that. You think I'd set my own men up, the best team I had?"

He looked at his man Thiesman and smirked. "These troops I have now..." he said, nodding dismally. "That outfit was an unfortunate loss."

"I'll tell you why I ask," Willingham said. "Because I was at Xuan Loc, Su's camp. You probably remember that one. That's where I wasted him. You want to know why I did it?" His voice rose as he talked.

Payne tightened, expecting the move to come at any moment. He tried to keep his nervous system settled despite the adrenaline.

"Humor me, why don't you." Shellhammer didn't change his expression or move, except for the hand he placed on his sidearm.

Willingham's anger spread like a blush across his face. "He was the same motherfucker Lassiter saw in the vil you sent us to right before it happened," he said. "There was one little moment before the ambush when we all knew he'd done it, Su. By then it was too late, everyone was dead."

"Everyone but you," Shellhammer said with curiosity. "All this time I thought it was a total loss. Tell me. How'd you manage to survive it? The hand of God? Or did you run?"

"I had to make it. I had to come and see you about it," Willingham said. He was containing himself; saying this seemed to have a calming effect on him. He wasn't yet going for the gun in his boot.

Payne said to him, "They've got a hootch full of Indians here, Willie. Same as the other camp, but they're alive." He wanted to say they had pictures stashed away of the bodies at Xuan Loc, so Shell-hammer would know. But he didn't; he wasn't sure.

Willingham suddenly grinned. "Supposed to be defectors. Is that it, Shell?"

"That's right, they're ralliers," Shellhammer said boredly. "We're lifting them to division where they'll draw their incentive money and get their Chieu Hoi cards and be relocated. What did you imagine the chopper was for, bringing us supper?"

From just outside the door someone called, "Sir, you want me?"

"It's Stick," Thiesman said.

Shellhammer called loudly, "Boyd, get your butt in here."

Boyd stuck his head in the doorway and Shellhammer coaxed him the rest of the way in. He entered with reluctance, all eyes.

"Did you see any troops outside the gate?" asked the colonel.

"Sir?" Boyd said thoughtlessly, then added, glancing at Willingham, "Oh. You mean *those* guys."

"Never mind," said Shellhammer. "Get back to your post and tell the men to hang loose till I say otherwise. Can you handle that much?"

The colonel turned, offering Willingham a broad grin, a harp-playing angel's grin. "Nice try. You always were pretty quick."

"You gotta try, don't you?" said Willingham. "Now you won't mind telling me what I want to know, since we're going to be casualties anyway. We are going to end up casualties, aren't we, Colonel?"

"That depends on you."

"Like hell it does," said Willingham, scratching his knee again. "Tell me, who's going to waste the dinks, this guy? Does he do the shit work?" He threw a thumb at Thiesman, who grinned as if he had been complimented. He was holding his sixteen on both them, jerking it back and forth. "Shit." The guard seemed impelled to say something; he had the anxious look. "These guys just got off the bus."

"Shut up, Thies," Shellhammer said. "Get your ass over here out of that door."

"What the fuck. No way these dudes going to leave. What the fuck difference it make if they know?"

Shellhammer grinned disconsolately at Willingham. "See what I mean? And Thiesman here's one of my better men. Drop anyone I say, never give it a second thought. I have a great deal of confidence in him." He shrugged as if his were a heavy burden to bear.

"You're going to kill them," Payne said. "Like the ones at Xuan Loc."

"Dude catches on fast for a fucking housecat," said the grunt, lighting a cigarette.

"Why? What good are they dead?" said Payne.

"Fuck a bunch of defectors, man," Thiesman said. "We're talking body count here, a good twenty-five or so, wouldn't you say, Colonel?"

Shellhammer sighed relentingly, as though there was nothing he could do about his man's big mouth and decided what the hell. "I imagine that many. It's a fair haul. Best in weeks."

"Call it Gook Confirm," Thiesman added enthusiastically, as if encouraged by the colonel's concession. "But, hey. Better not quote us in your article." The guard was enjoying himself.

"Tell you what, though," he went on. "Those slopes are gonna help build morale somewhere, ain't it so, Shell?"

The colonel nodded pleasantly at his man and turned to Willingham. "You should have left well enough alone, Corporal. You shouldn't have pushed it. I'm sorry about the team. I want you to know that."

"That doesn't help," Willingham said. He still seemed in control of himself, but he was now resolute and Payne readied himself. The blood sped through him, pounding in his ears.

Shellhammer assumed a rigid military posture. "Now listen to me," he said, letting his eyes go soft. "We're not dealing with conventional warfare here. This war depends on regulating. If you expect to secure peace in this little strip of jungle you've got to regulate it, the population, the economy, the government. We let this backwater country fall and we hurt ourselves, our efforts to maintain a balance elsewhere. That's what it's all about. Winning requires a consistent body count, no matter how it's done."

"What was the deal with Su?" Willingham persisted. "Did you owe him something? Did you think the team knew about your Gook Confirm operations, just what was it?"

Shellhammer was getting bored. He checked his watch. "It wasn't anything personal. I was fond of you men, in fact. It was only business."

"*Business,*" Willingham repeated in a voice that wasn't his own.

"Thies, you'll have to show them out now," Shellhammer said. He sounded sorry and Payne took the order to mean their doom.

Payne said it then: "We've got photographs of the people you had murdered at that camp, Colonel. If we don't get out, they'll go to the CIA."

Shellhammer shrugged. It didn't seem to matter to him. "Thies," he said, gesturing toward the door.

"First tell me this, Shell," Willingham said, leaning closer, scratching low on his leg. "What kind of count did you get for my squad? How much were their lives worth to you?"

As though sensing what was about to happen Shellhammer gave Thiesman a signal with his eyes and made a quick move unsheathing his sidearm. Payne would later be unsure if Willingham shot first or the guard; the moment was rapid and frenzied. And he would doubt that he had done the right thing, that if he had gone for Thiesman, Willingham would not have been hit. Instead Payne went for Shellhammer. It happened too fast to know what to do, which man to throw himself at. But even if he had not acted instinctively, if he had had the time to think it out, he would have done the same thing, tried to stop Shellhammer. He was certain Shellhammer would have shot to kill; he wasn't sure Thiesman would.

In the close confine of the hut the reporting gunfire was deafening. Thiesman sprayed bullets in a wild arc before the sixteen flew out of his grip. He and Willingham seemed to drop at the same time. Even though he was on top of Shellhammer wrestling the pistol from his grip, Payne saw the exchange of fire. He felt amazing strength twisting the gun from the colonel's hand and knocking him down in the same instant. He held the pistol close to Shellhammer's genteel face. His hand did not tremble now, not as it had standing over the young sapper who'd killed Cotton. Now he felt the power of life and death at his fingertip and it would have been easy, even satisfying, to draw his first blood.

Thiesman sat in silence on the hut floor, grimacing as he ripped his pants away from his wounded leg. The slug had torn out a chunk of meat inside his thigh just above the knee and blood spurted despite the pressure his hands now exerted above the wound.

Payne said to Willingham, "God! Fuck, man, is it bad?"

A shard of ivory protruded through the tattered flesh of Willingham's left forearm and his midsection was wet with blood. He was on his feet again with the .45 still in his grip.

"I don't know," he said in an adrenaline-high voice. He was searching his body to find other places he might have been hit, feeling about his head and looking at his legs.

"We got to get you somewhere," Payne said. "This guy too."

Shellhammer made a sudden leap for the door but hit the dirt floor solidly when Payne thrust a foot between his legs. Payne shoved the pistol closer to the front of his head, looking over the stubbed barrel at the man's eyes. He considered doing it; he wanted to do it. But he lowered the gun and turned again to Willingham.

Willingham's left hand was useless. He placed it on the spreading shine of red at his side and tried to pull back the shirt, but the hand would not function. He grunted in amazement.

Picking up the guard's sixteen, Payne ordered Shellhammer into the corner away from the door.

Willingham leaned against the rice sacks, drawing short breaths. He seemed oddly peaceful.

"Let's see it," Payne said and pulled aside the shirt.

Nothing hung out, no guts or other internal parts; he located the dark bleeding hole under the ribs. The bullet had gone through his side and left another tear under the rib cage in his back, about three inches from his side. It might have punctured the spleen or intestines, Payne couldn't tell. But Willingham did not seem to be in much pain or yet in shock.

"I don't know how bad it is, Willie," he said and asked Shellhammer, "You got a medic here?"

The colonel sat cross-legged; he shook his head sideways. "What now?" he said tauntingly. "There's fifteen men out there and you can be assured they'll do what I tell them."

Thiesman said there was no medic. "But, hey, the shit-hook can take us out," he said, his voice panicky.

"The chopper goes on my command," Shellhammer retorted.

"I got an artery here, Shell," the grunt pleaded. He was also sitting, his back against the edge of the door and legs stretched out. "I need a tourniquet."

Shellhammer pointed out the black medical kit in the corner and Payne dug through it, pitching Thiesman a roll of gauze and taking out bandages. There were hypodermics in the bag, and he found some quarter-grain vials of morphine. Payne tediously worked on Willingham, his hands clumsy and tentative, wrapping a long gauze bandage under the shirt and then, more assuredly, bandaging the arm.

There was shouting from outside to know what was going on and Payne, summoning up a voice that sounded threatening, warned to keep clear of the hut. The colonel laughed at him.

"You're a couple of fools," Shellhammer barked. "I've got expert marksmen out there and soon as you show your heads, it's over —when I say."

"You want some morphine?" Payne asked Willingham, who shook his head no. Payne tossed a syringe to the moaning guard.

Thiesman procrastinated with the syringe. "I can't do it to myself, man," he said, on the verge it seemed of crying.

As Payne injected Thiesman's leg he saw Willingham poise the .45 at Shellhammer.

"Don't," he shouted and thrust his hand out, pushing the gun aside. Willingham's face was set with determination. "I'm going to waste this man. Don't try to stop me."

Payne threw his arms out. "Look at us, man. Just fucking look at us. We're shooting each other." His voice went low and beseeching. "Willie, if you shoot him, how are we going to get out? If Nichols and those guys took off, we're going to need him."

"They're there. They heard the fire." Willingham put the gun back on Shellhammer, hammer cocked and ready, but hesitated as though, rather than changing his mind, he was enjoying watching the colonel sweat out his remaining moments.

But Shellhammer wore a poker face; he did not seem worried.

"It's not just us," Payne pleaded, searching for a way to get through to Willingham. "There's all those people in that shed. They're human beings, man. . . . Listen, Willie. They can help us get out. I know one of them; he's from the same village that Saang's from. We can take him," Payne said, indicating Shellhammer. "And you've got the evidence. We can get out of it. Listen to me, man. We can make it."

He added in a somber voice, "If you kill him, you're ruining yourself, any chance of a future. Don't do it. It's not worth it, Willie."

Willingham's color was changing, becoming chalky, and his

breathing had surrendered to short, high-chested gasps. But he was preoccupied weighing the fate of his former commander, not from any pain he had from his wounds.

"I'm going to give you a shot of dope," Payne said, and did.

"Listen to me," Shellhammer said, talking fast, now sensing Willingham really was going to shoot him. "Your buddy here's right. There's no way you'll get out of this vil without me. I know the Agency's behind all this. I can cut a deal with them. Look. The shooting was accidental; accidents happen all the time. Thies here shot himself accidentally. Didn't you, soldier?"

"Fucking clumsy-ass dumb-ass grunt," Thiesman agreed. "Never did know how to handle a fucking handgun."

"Same thing happened to you, an accident," the colonel said to Willingham. "How about it? I'll get you dusted off right now."

Wallace hollered from outside.

"Talk to him," Willingham said, his color returning under the morphine. "Tell him we're all leaving in the bird."

"We've got wounded here," Shellhammer said loudly. "Get the chopper crew ready to leave."

"What about the dinks, Colonel?" Thiesman said casually. "We going to snuff them first?" He didn't seem concerned one way or the other.

"They're going with us," Payne said and called out for Boyd, who answered immediately.

"Come in here," Payne said, backing up to the side of the door. Boyd stepped in slowly.

"Go down to the hootch where those Viets are and get the man that's wearing the French soldier's cap," Payne told him. "His name's Kroong. Bring him back here. You understand?"

Boyd looked questioningly at Shellhammer. The colonel nodded and waved him off. He fixed Payne with a look of disgust. "Those people happen to be VC, the enemy," Shellhammer said in a disdainful, lispy voice. "How in hell's name do you know them? Just where does your allegiance lie, soldier?"

It was a biting, accurate question that Payne had no rational answer for; but he was in charge now and that made it solely his affair how he knew the man, the enemy.

Willingham said, "Don't be fucking stupid, Payne. How the fuck you think we're going to control them and Shell both? You let them loose, no telling what's going to happen. If they're VC they'll turn on us."

"We leave them and they're dead," retorted Payne. "We might as well have killed them ourselves."

Willingham argued reasonably the things that could go wrong attempting to load the helicopter with that number of people, enemy or not. He was right and Payne knew it. They were fighting for their lives now. And he was remembering what Sterr told him, and Willingham was wounded and needed Payne now. But weren't Tieng's people, the ones who were still alive, in some way important to him too? Hadn't he been responsible for what happened to them?

Payne considered the matter of his allegiance, the duality of his position, and it occurred to him how much alike in mind he was, and even Willingham, to Tieng, the man with two faces. There was deception and betrayal everywhere in this convoluted affair. It was wrought of a corruption that was insidious, bred by greed and deception that extended far higher up than right here; where, Payne wondered, was his fucking *country*'s allegiance?

"I'm not going to leave them," Payne said firmly. "That's it."

"Then you're fucked, buddy," said Willingham. "We're not going to make it."

Presently Kroong entered the hut in front of the guard's weapon. Wallace had a stiff-armed hold on the ball of hair at his neck, as though he were touching something dead or diseased. He released the Indian with a forward shove. "What about the detail, sir? Want us to get it on?"

Shellhammer shrugged uncertainly. "I want to hear that helicopter ready to lift off. See to it. And, Wallace, there may be some of our people outside the compound looking to get in. If there are, stall them. Don't let them on the grounds."

Payne said, "Fuck that shit. You see a platoon out there, you let them in and send them here. Understand?"

Wallace left without responding. Payne knew he would do as his commander ordered, but having said it would make the man at least know he was serious; it might help.

Kroong stood motionless with his hands draping his sides, his small rounded dark eyes under the bib of the kepi darting from the stack of weapons to Shellhammer and the others. He looked at Payne with hardened resignation. Payne took it to mean he was resigned to die.

Payne tried to talk to him but he seemed not to understand, and it occurred to Payne that all the time he had been around him he had never heard Kroong speak English. The nights he had spent smoking and drinking in the opium hut Kroong had talked only in his tongue.

"Either of you speak the language?" Payne asked.

Thiesman chuckled indignantly. "Fucking animal talk. Nobody understands that shit."

Willingham said something in Vietnamese and Kroong responded. "I don't know what he's saying," Willingham said.

"Chieu Hoi," Payne blurted at him. "Piaster, goddamn it. You get money, understand? We're getting everybody out of here."

"Okay," Kroong then said and cracked a grin. He understood.

The helicopter's turbines started up.

"Tell your men to get the rest of those people into the chopper," Payne said to the colonel. "Tell them now."

Chapter
25

The waiting did it, got him thinking. It kept going through his mind, the absurdity of their predicament. Two men were already wounded. What was happening seemed unreal. How would he explain it and who would believe him? How had things gotten this far out of hand?

The Chinook's engines purred and the giant rotors chopped insistently at the air, sweeping wind and dust inside the hut. Willingham stood now with his weight half on the stacked rice bags. He and Thiesman were looking at each other and suddenly both of them expelled a kind of mutual self-ridiculing chortle, and then Thiesman threw his hands out as if to demonstrate he too realized the situation was absurd. "Shit, man," he said, "sorry I shot you."

"Me too," said Willingham. The fingers of his useless hand twitched.

Thiesman was fair-skinned and thick-chested, a kid with nondescript, homespun features. Had he been clean-shaven and standing in line at a movie house, you might even have considered him fairly good-looking. Other than his grunt diction his speech was unaccented, suggesting a midwestern rearing, placing him from the heart of America. He was about the same age as Willingham. Maybe he was still a teenager.

Willingham put all his weight on his feet and tested himself, taking a couple of steps and twisting his shoulders. "Hardly feel it at

351

all," he said with an air of toughness. The morphine had them both floating.

"How many in your unit know about these operations?" Willingham said, addressing Thiesman and easing back against the sacks.

"Just me and Wallace and the other guy guarding the tank. I don't know about the chopper crew. How 'bout it, Shell? They're just delivery boys, aren't they?"

Shellhammer glanced at him boredly, keeping to himself now.

"I hate to tell you, man," said Thiesman, "but you guys are going to find yourselves in a world of fucking hurt once we get back. This thing reaches high up division's ass. They need the count and they ain't going to stop the operation. I'm just telling you so you'll know."

Willingham nodded appreciatively. "I think we might get listened to, if we make it back."

Three close shots rang out above the whine of the chopper's warming turbines with a short burst of automatic fire following, and then more firing. Someone outside shouted, "The tank. They're out!"

The chopper suddenly opened up, lifting off, its high-revved throttle and hurricane wind quelling the riotous outside activity. The bamboo walls shook under its turbulence, and the hut quickly filled with dust and flying debris. The quickness of events momentarily stilled the five men inside the hut. Then everyone started to move at once, but it was Kroong who reacted first. His swiftness was an instinct born of a long history at surviving, something jungle training school could not equal, and that gave him the edge. Lunging at the pile of weapons and seizing the machete, he struck, cobralike, the machete descending in a blur of fluid motion.

Payne recoiled, horrified by what seemed a deception to his eyes. Tieng had told him of Kroong's strength with the sword. He'd bragged how Kroong could drop a buffalo's head in one strike, take it off in three. He'd done it in the sacrificial rite on the occasion of his son's advent to manhood.

Shellhammer had gotten only to his knees. The blade caught him at an angle across the shoulder and penetrated deep into his body. For a moment, in the dusty translucence, it appeared Shellhammer was only startled, a little confused. His eyes moved up and down and his chin quivered and dropped in stunned surprise. His body went through a series of twitching muscular and nervous contractions.

Kroong held the colonel's slumped head and retracted the knife from the body. If Kroong was disappointed he hadn't made a clean sweep through the body, he didn't show it. Had it been his bush hook instead of the thicker machete, it might have done the job and swept completely through. When he released the head with a shove, the severed quarter fell heavily aside, followed more slowly by the rest of the body. The blade had sectioned the rib cage and cut through the spinal cord and heart, stopping in the abdomen. A single release of blood hit the floor like an overturned bucket, spattering Thiesman, who was the closest to him, and throwing rivulets on Kroong's dark legs, then draining into the thirsty soil. Payne turned to the wall and heaved a bilious vomit.

The thunder from the chopper became a faint echo of itself before evaporating completely, leaving reports of sporadic fire in its wake. The freed Indians were closing on the hootch, their high-pitched voices a cacophony of excited garble. Two Viets put their heads inside, saw Kroong, and entered, talking rapidly. One had a sixteen; he trained it on Payne, who held the colonel's revolver barrel down at his side.

"Tell them to stop the shooting," Willingham said so forcefully he winced and folded in favor of his side.

They couldn't decide how the Viets had taken over. Thiesman suggested an overlooked tunnel inside the tank, then scrubbed that, saying, "No way." Willingham said they were probably all from a VC regimental battalion and had been trained in escape procedure. "They probably overpowered Boyd," offered Payne.

"Doesn't matter, let's get out of here," Willingham said, moving for the doorway. "We can take the gun jeep. Let them do what they want."

"The bridge is out," Payne said. "I don't know, maybe there's a road the other direction."

"Nichols'll call in a dustoff," Willingham said. "Let's go."

Kroong said something to the Viet with the sixteen, and gestured with the machete toward Thiesman, identifying him. Payne sensed he wanted the man to shoot Thiesman and Payne pointed the revolver at the Indian, but Kroong on a quick upswing knocked the pistol from Payne's hand just as the sixteen clicked. The Indian looked at the weapon, puzzled, unable to comprehend why it hadn't fired.

Payne said, "Kroong, he's wounded, he can't do anything."

Kroong shrugged, waxing indifference. "Go," he said, sweeping the machete in a violent arc to include Willingham. Kroong was in charge now. He grabbed several of the AKs and the other two Indians did likewise, cramming clips in their loincloth diapers. One of the men carried the two radios outside and shot them up.

"You can't leave me," Thiesman said, becoming panicky again. "I'll bleed to death."

Willingham whispered out of Kroong's earshot, "Get to the road after we pull out. You'll be all right, we've got guys out there."

Payne threw up again looking at the side of beef heaped on the floor. But his brain was working; he had enough presence of mind to grab the revolver and take a syringe and a vial of morphine. He stealthily picked up the weapon and concealed it in the back of his fatigues and made an obvious show of taking the medication. Willingham didn't seem to be hurting at the moment, but he would need the morphine later. Kroong had been watching, but Payne was sure he did not see him take the revolver. He gestured them outside again and Payne placed Willingham's good arm across his shoulder and carried most of his weight.

Bodies were strewn about the ground, small and larger lifeless mounds of the disheveled laundry of ARVNs, Americans and civilians. The forms lay twisted in amazingly contorted positions, as though they had been sucked through a wind tunnel and spit out and come to rest where they landed, arms and legs grotesquely splayed like string puppets. As they walked toward the jeep Payne took a count of the bodies—four ARVN who would have been Shellhammer's cowboys lay not far from the hut where they had been playing cards; three Americans, including Wallace, whose bodies were sprawled near each other in the open; and twelve or so of the civilians who were to be part of the colonel's Gook Confirm body count. He left Willingham to wait in the gun jeep and stepped back to take another look at each of the Americans. He wasn't sure if one of the men was dead and he put his nose at the mouth, hoping to detect a breath. The man had taken bullets in the upper chest but not in the head like the other two Americans. He appeared alive, his bright, moist eyes open and fixed as though he had powerful concentration and was working out an impossible problem and this world could go to hell until he had it solved.

A couple of the Indians were under the hood removing the distributor cap and cutting the plug wires. Then they moved quickly to disable the six-by, the only other vehicle. They weren't going to let them go. Payne looked discouragingly at Willingham but said nothing. He only hoped Nichols was still around; but where the hell was he?

He helped Willingham out of the jeep and walked him in the direction of the gate where Boyd had his hands raised high, his eyes bulging with fear under the gun of a Viet. If anyone else in the compound was alive, he was hiding.

"I don't know how they got out, man," Boyd said with his arms still raised. "Maybe I didn't secure the tank. I'm sorry."

"Open the gate," Payne said. "You better come with us."

Boyd had already unlocked the gate and now swung it open. The Viet holding him there laughed.

"Are they taking us prisoner?" asked Boyd. "What about the CO, where's he? What are they going to do to us, man?"

"Be cool," Willingham said with little conviction. "Thies is still in the hut if you want to stay and see to him. I think you should." He looked to Kroong for the okay.

"He needs a tourniquet," said Willingham. "Get going."

Boyd finally dropped his arms. He started tentatively, turning back once and then broke into a run for the hut. Kroong did not seem to care. Payne took his indifference to mean the Indians were interested only in getting to the jungle, their element, and that he was offering assistance to the wounded soldier and Payne out of gratitude for having made possible their release. Perhaps too because he knew Payne from before; maybe he even trusted him.

Outside the village they took to the grooved mud-packed road, Payne glancing about expectantly for their escort platoon, wondering why they had not shown themselves. Willingham faltered, his breathing labored even though the Indians moved slow to accommodate him. It occurred to Payne that Nichols would think they were being taken prisoner and would lay off and wait for the right moment—if they were still out there. Maybe they weren't, maybe with the firefight, Nichols assumed the chopper lifted them out. Thinking this, Payne began nervously to consider just what was going to happen. Willingham would have to be attended to soon. He was weakening, his weight becoming too heavy to carry.

"Kroong," he said, "we've got to make a stretcher. You know," he said, showing him with his hands as best he could, "something to carry him. He can't walk anymore."

Watching Payne's hands, Kroong lifted his brow in comprehension and sent a couple of men off. Payne eased Willingham down and asked if he needed another shot yet. Not yet, he said, he'd wait.

After the Indian walked off, Willingham whispered, "I spotted them. They're over there. They'll be expecting us to react when they make their move. We've got to make sure of what we do from here on out and work it together," he said. "These people aren't your innocent farmers, don't forget that."

Payne nodded. "Yeah, I know." He unscrewed Willingham's canteen and gave him a drink of orange juice.

"They want us for something," Willingham went on. "Otherwise they wouldn't be taking us with them. We would have been finished off back in the vil, at least left there. What do you know about this guy Kroong?"

He didn't appear afraid or nervous or overly concerned that he had two bleeding wounds that could infect or send him into shock from losing so much blood. Willingham was calculating, trying to figure things out logically, as though the twenty-odd Viets, some of whom sure as hell were the enemy, could be figured out.

"He's VC. I know that," Payne said in a low voice. "I don't know if all of them are, if they belong to a unit like you were saying before. I know another one of them, from Paang Dong. Kroong didn't seem to like it when I was there. But I don't know, maybe he's just trying to get us somewhere where we can get some help because we got them out. And because he knows I'm a friend of Tieng's. Tieng is the chief."

"Don't count on it. Let's just hope Nichols doesn't fuck it up. Otherwise I got a feeling we can kiss our asses goodnight."

Payne said quietly, "I got a pistol. He doesn't know it. You want it?"

"No. You keep it—but you fucking better be able to use it if you have to. This ain't no time to get shaky on me."

Payne nodded. "Don't worry."

The Viets milled around in groups of three and four, talking and laughing as though they'd just gotten off work for the day and were making big plans for the night. Kroong broke off and came over. He knelt beside Willingham, grinned, and gently pulled aside his shirt for a look. The bandage was blood-soaked and needed changing. He shook his head up and down as if to indicate there was no problem. Payne could never keep it straight that the Vietnamese shook their heads in reverse, up and down for a negative, ass backward. It was a disorienting thing, like vertigo. Kroong rejoined his men.

Payne made a sling with his handkerchief and the one Willingham wore at his neck and carefully fitted Willingham's injured arm in it. Willingham sat for it without flinching. He was listless, preoccupied.

"Listen, Payne. In case it's only you that makes it out, you've got to tell somebody about his operations. I put the—"

"Don't talk that crap, it doesn't matter now. We're both going to make it."

"Just in case," Willingham said. His eyelids dropped heavily, as though he were passing out. Payne could see his eyeballs rolling behind the lids. "You okay, man? Willie?"

Willingham nodded with his eyes still clamped shut. The birthmark on his temple was a darker red in the hazy jungle light, as if a blood vessel had burst. "How did this ever happen, man," he said in a faint breath, partially opening his eyes and rolling his head to the side.

"It's my fault," said Payne. "It wasn't worth you getting shot. We could've refused to come—*I* could have. If I had, none of this would have happened."

"I mean the whole fucking thing. This," he said and lifted a sluggish finger to indicate the forest about him. "Why didn't I buy it too . . . ? You think they'll give me and Thiesman the PH for shooting each other?" He barked a laugh and grimaced.

"Just think," he continued, as though talking could keep his mind off his grim condition, the situation. "In another year I'll be old enough to go to a bar. Shit, ain't that something."

Then he started to sob. You could see he was trying hard to resist, but his lips and eyes tightened and he whimpered through clenched teeth, slashing his head back and forth.

"We both had something to prove," Payne said.

Willingham wiped his eyes and gauged him. "I don't know. What's there to prove, how do you get so focused down? Listen, Payne. I'm sorry I drug you into this shit. You might not believe this now, but I was going along with you on this crazyass idea you had of helping them. . . . I don't know, man, this fucking war is something else."

Payne could hear Sterr: *It will distort your perceptions of what's right; but that don't matter; it don't matter what's right because there ain't no right; it only matters what is.* And he could hear Tieng: *Tieng-of-the-Two-Face corrupt; a man survive only if corrupt; I love my country Viet Nam; you love you country and you do right you country; all part of war.*

"Yeah, but fuck it," said Payne. "We're going to get through this together and back to the fucking world. Where we belong, man."

Willingham lifted his face, softening it with the hint of a smile. "Yeah. You and me, we'll do it."

The men brought back two cut poles and shredded off the edges of a filthy blanket which were tied to the poles to make the stretcher. And they marched on, taking turns hauling Willingham. It was late afternoon now, the sun already lost below the clustered trees towering on either side of the road that lay ahead of them. The road narrowed up ahead.

Payne walked alongside the stretcher for a while, then joined Kroong at the head of the column. The forest was coming alive with noises. He did not see any sign of the platoon.

"Where are we going?" he asked.

The Viet glanced at him without answering, and Payne tracked along in silence. The best he could figure they were headed in the opposite direction from the way they'd gotten to the village; he did not know what compass direction. Nothing had traveled on this road for a long time; grass grew in high clumps down the middle and thick, ungainly bushes had narrowed the road to no more than four or five feet. Payne offered him a cigarette. He took it.

"Tieng-of-the-Two-Faces is okay, and so is Saang," Payne said. Kroong would not know about the girl, that she had been arrested and beaten. He probably knew Tieng had avoided arrest. "I got her freed from the jail in Saigon and got her to a safe house. She's okay. And I have the truck arranged for. When we get back, I'll see Tieng. It's all arranged where we will meet. I'm going to get your . . . your fallen comrades to Saigon where they can be buried with their ancestors. Tieng will be waiting on me in Saigon."

He thought it wise to say all this, to boast of his accomplishment of freeing Saang and that he was still going to help his chief Tieng.

He felt sure Kroong understood some of what he said, for his attention perked at some of Payne's words, "freed" and "fallen comrades" and "buried." But the Indian said nothing and continued to march in his quick, squat-legged strides.

"Kroong, where is your son now?" Payne thought to ask.

The Indian again ignored him, but in a moment he reached down and picked up a handful of dirt and let it sift through his fingers, then brushed his hands and held them open to show Payne they were empty.

"Was it us, the Americans?"

Kroong nodded sideways, and again Payne was misled. Yes, he was saying, it was the Americans. And Payne remembered that was what Saang had silently told him when he asked her about the fate of her parents; the Americans had killed them too.

The road soon dwindled to a trail that wound around thickets of long-growing bushes and then much older trees with buttresses up to Payne's waist; the thick-trunked trees reached high and wide and had decided a century ago not to crowd one another. The brush was close-knit and impeding and they forded through at a slower pace. The jungle birds here made a quick, high-pitched, echoing noise that sounded eerily like the whine of bullets, causing Payne two or three times to flinch and ready himself in expectation of Nichols's ambush.

The column coursed the jungle like a spine of ants, as if they knew exactly where they were going. And they did. Before night spread its dark fingers through the canopy they arrived at a small outpost of some kind. Kroong sent a man ahead and they waited. A half-dozen palm-thatched lean-tos encircled a few huts on flat land that had been cleared just enough to make room for the huts. One of the larger hootches glowed like a jack-o'-lantern, and voices came from within. There were no outside light or sentries that Payne could see and no vehicles. He stayed close to the stretcher while Kroong waited for his scout. When he returned the group marched into the compound, passing between two lean-tos where men in black uniforms and red armbands ate out of bowls.

"NVA," Willingham mumbled and squeezed Payne's hand. Payne's heart sank with the gesture.

Payne caught the eye of one of the soldiers and held it as he walked by, trying to read him. The man registered surprise, but not hate. Payne tried to convince himself it was a good sign.

They were led to the illuminated hut. Most of the Indians fell off
along the way, and soldiers in black received them like reunited family members. A festive round of hugs and hand-holding ensued.

Payne spotted a row of casket-shaped boxes stacked alongside a
dark unattended hut; his heart sank further, for he knew the outpost
was another field hospital like the one Tieng had taken him to.

The Americans were led inside the main hootch. Under a suspended kerosene lamp, three men stood around a table upon which
were a map, compass, a cigar box, and a framed photograph facing
the other direction. The room filled with moving shadows as they
entered. Kroong took from the ruck of his scout a half-full bottle of
Jack Daniel's and a Topcon camera and displayed the items as offer-
ings, placing them proudly on the table. A short conversation followed, all eyes at intervals turning on Payne and Willingham with
neither friendliness nor contempt.

Two of the men wore tiger-striped uniforms that fit their small
bodies snugly. These two were North Vietnamese Rangers. Neither
wore insignia or rank, but the older one, sporting a Fu Manchu, appeared to be the camp commandant. He took a drink of the whiskey
and shuddered, his low-slanting eyelids lifting almost above the
opaque irises of his eyes. His face was broad and mashed in.

As they chattered, Willingham whispered to Payne, "Some kind
of elitist outfit. Don't say a fucking thing to them."

The older Ranger thoughtfully smoothed his wiry mustache between his forefinger and thumb as he listened to what Kroong had to
say. Then he sat down in the chair behind the desk and gestured with
a brusque nod for the others to leave. His junior stayed. Both had
sidearms in open holsters.

The leader threw a leg on the table and crossed his arms over his
chest and peered down his flat nose with one eye shut, as if lining up
a view directly between the two Americans. It seemed an eccentric
thing. Willingham was standing now, slumping. He was hurting.

"Where you come from?" the commandant said congenially.
Payne and Willingham glanced at each other.

"Yes, English. Many of us speak it, many of us were educated in
your backyard. Where you from?"

Neither spoke.

"United State. No harm saying. I have cousin in one your big
cities, Frisco. City by bay. You know this place?" He started hum-

ming a tune that sounded faintly like the sad Tony Bennett anthem. He was enjoying hearing himself, though he hummed only a few bars and stopped abruptly. "Maybe I want to go there and live with my cousin. Maybe can finish war soon and I can go. This picture my cousin."

He turned the frame around, exposing a photographed portrait of a huge family in front of a temple. It didn't look like San Francisco to Payne. It looked more like Hanoi.

"So this make us like relative and you help me, right?" he said.

Willingham tossed his dog tags on the tabletop. "I guess you can read too."

"Listen, sir," said Payne.

"You call me . . . let me see. You call me Little John, right? I like, good name for me. Little John. Come from English, you know. Little John part of little army that help many poor. I help many poor. Not so you. Maybe you think you help the poor." He smiled and played with his spindly mustache.

Payne went on, "This man needs medical attention. He was shot helping those men get here. We saved their lives."

"Shut up, Payne. I told you."

"Yes, you are both heroes. But you have done me no favor. Now our position has been revealed to your comrades. You see? And I must have your cooperation quickly." He talked dispassionately, the power of his words intensified by the containment of his tone.

"How many of your soldiers are there outside this camp? What is the name of their unit? Who is the ranking officer and do they have radio communication?"

"Fuck you," Willingham said very softly.

"There's nobody. We're on our own. Where'd you get that idea?" said Payne.

"Very well." The man stroked the mustache a little more quickly now. He called out and two men wearing pith helmets came in pointing carbines; the leader said something and they grabbed Willingham by the arms and dragged him toward the door. Willingham did not cry out or let it show the pain he must have felt at their rough handling. He looked silently at Payne and shook his head to tell him to keep his mouth shut and then flashed Payne his horse grin before the darkness swallowed him.

"Why does he smile so when he is going to die?" the commandant said. He seemed truly mystified. He frowned thoughtfully. "You Americans. You value your lives above the cause of your country."

"Tieng-of-the-Two-Faces will vouch for us," Payne said. "I have helped him supply arms and I can do it again. Just ask Kroong. He will tell you we have worked for the Viet Cong. You're damned right about us Americans. We value our lives. And we don't value this war, not the little people like me and my buddy. That's why we're both traitors. We can help you too, whatever you want. We can get you transportation, we can give you the sizes and locations of munition dumps. We are journalists and have access to this kind of information. We can do a lot for your cause. It won't do you any good to kill either one of us."

The commandant appeared only amused and played with his chin. "Yes. We could use such information you speak of. But right now I must know the size and position of the unit outside our present defense. If you do not tell me, we will send your comrade out to greet your unit. And what a surprise that will be for them."

Payne was certain of the terrible thing he meant, that they were going to booby-trap him. It was the kind of warfare Tieng had introduced him to, the kind of warfare that undermined and defied convention and made the enemy untouchable, elusive as a phantom. It was the kind of warfare that gave the enemy control of the war.

"There is no goddamn unit," he said in a rage. "We were dropped off at this village by helicopter and we freed the people who brought us here. That outfit was wiped out there, at the village. That's the truth. Didn't Kroong tell you that?"

The commandant was bored now. He said something to his junior, who drew his pistol on Payne. "You will follow him," the senior officer said. "It is too bad you will not cooperate. The fate of your unit is now your responsibility."

The aide in tiger stripes seized the back of Payne's collar and pressed the point of the gun against his back. Apparently assuming Kroong's men had already searched the GIs, the man made no attempt to frisk him, and Payne twisted sideways so the man would be less likely to brush against the concealed revolver resting against his spine. He collected himself and thought ahead, considering how he could get the gun out quickly enough to use it; he would have the element of surprise. But he was racked with the terrible tension that mixed dread with the glimmer of hope.

The man took measured, cautious steps walking him outside and toward the darkened hut. Payne saw the light of another hut now, smaller, behind the main one, and then he heard a low-throated scream coming from it. Willingham's. The cry came again as the soldier pushed Payne inside the dark hut.

Willingham's tortured screaming turned into a string of incomprehensible words before his ghastly voice was drowned out altogether. Payne knew he was trying to warn him, trying to tell him that he was being rigged with explosives. Payne blocked his mind from imagining what else they were doing to him. He had to act.

In a single sweeping motion he pulled the revolver out of his shirt, wheeled and grabbed the man's shirt at his chest, for the screams had momentarily diverted the aide. Payne fired twice into the center of the body, one of the bullets piercing his own hand. The impact lifted the small man and sent him sprawling into a row of large crates; he had managed to discharge a round which went wild. He slid to the ground as if poured from a vat. Payne took the man's weapon and stuck it in the waistband of his pants and hid behind the stack of coffin-sized boxes. The bullet had gone through the flat of his hand, breaking a bone that rendered the little finger unfunctional. The pain hadn't yet registered.

A commotion erupted in the yard, and he frantically considered what to do before they came for him, his heart pounding like a mallet against his chest.

The gunshots had been Nichols's signal to move; a sudden pop overhead illuminated the yard, casting a swaying, fluorescentlike light through the doorway that exposed Payne and the dead man at his feet. He pulled the body back in the shadows. A succession of four or five quaking explosions went off, the percussive blasts of seventy-nines. This was followed by steady beads of automatic weapons fire that seemed to come from all around and the sporadic violent numbing from concussion grenades. The intense chaos of the explosions shut out human sounds and Payne hesitated inside the hut, stealing looks through the door, considering how he would get to Willingham.

In his haste he knocked the lid off a crate and inside found stick grenades and carbines of various kinds and land mines, bouncing bettys maybe. The contents of the coffins did not surprise him, but he was suddenly struck by a revelation: Tieng's plan was to have him transport similar coffins into Saigon—coffins that would not contain the remains of his tribesmen to be buried in cemeteries there. Payne would have transported weapons into the city. It crossed his mind in a flash that Saang too had been part of it, winning his affections to aid her brother. But what was it she had said to him? *Be careful of Tieng.*

His hand began to throb now; it had started bleeding in a flow. He ignored it and kicked through the rickety straw wall at the rear of the hut. Seeing nobody in the vicinity, he crawled on his stomach in the direction of the hut where Willingham would be, booby-trapped.

Under the sputtering luminescence he spotted Willingham propped against a tree. They had moved him out into the open; they had anticipated the attack. He was resting in an upright slouch against the base of the tree, his bad arm out of the sling and hanging limp on the ground, his head slumped as though he were passed out or dead. He seemed at peace in the midst of the firefight.

Payne began to draw fire, the rounds ricocheting and lifting dust around him. He rolled and sprang to his feet and ran in a zigzag for the cover of a nearby tree. He saw some of the dinks scatter, firing at him as they retreated. He thought he hit one of them but the round that got him might have come from the grunts charging across the yard. The GIs approached spread out in a line, firing barrages to cover one another while closing in on the commandant's hut. The grunts worked as a finely tuned team, two spraying inside the hut on a crouched running pass, the other two diving inside behind them, firing on full automatic. The commandant's mistake was being too slow preparing for the attack; it was a turnabout, the Americans ambushing, and the NVA officer with the Fu Manchu paid for underestimating the grunts. He would not be visiting his cousin in the city by the bay.

They were good at their job. The four grunts moved swiftly in and out of the hut and set it afire, then swept the small hut behind it. Payne exposed himself under the fizzle of drifting light, attempting to get their attention. He didn't think they spotted him. But they spotted Willingham some thirty meters away, seeing that he was wounded and vulnerable in the open. There was a lull in the firing in this part of the camp now, but the noise elsewhere drowned Payne's shouting and the grunts apparently could not hear him saying it was a trap, to stay back. As they started for Willingham, Payne advanced to cut them off. He had seen ten or so dinks vanish in the tree line behind the open area. The grunts were moving into an ambush, they would be cut down or blown up when they got to Willingham. Payne was twice the distance back and when he knew he could not keep them from reaching Willingham, he made his decision and carried it out.

The dinks might have already finished Willingham, but even if he were still alive, what chance did he have of surviving with the enemy waiting in ambush not ten meters away? And was this hope and a prayer worth risking four men's lives for?

In the quickness of the moment Payne thought of it like that; he did not look upon the slumped figure under the tree as a friend he had come to love like a brother, like an extension of himself. He couldn't. Four men were about to die, men no different from those young men in Willingham's lost squad. Straight-leg infantry grunts duty bound, who had faced death and still went on to face it again and again. If Willingham could have said something, perhaps he would have said, "Do it, Payne. This squares it."

The grunts were Sergeant James T. Reese, Corporal Michael Fellows, Private Tommy Lee Jones and Spec 4 Allen Waters. They were from Oak Park, Illinois; Roanoke, Virginia; one from Massachusetts and one from Clearwater, Florida. They had brothers and sisters and other loved ones who prayed for their safety. Three of the men would survive the battle, and those three would describe in their depositions how they saw Payne shoot Corporal Willingham and could neither deny nor confirm that the wounded soldier had been laden with explosives, as Payne claimed. Each would say in his deposition that he saw no reason why Payne would purposely kill a buddy and believed he was convinced the wounded soldier had been booby-trapped and was already dead. They did not think he lied when he claimed he was only trying to save their lives, but they could not prove it. The three soldiers could say only what they saw, and they saw Payne advance, screaming something none of them could make out, and drop to the ground and without hesitation aim and shoot Corporal Willingham.

Payne bolted, racing into the clearing in a straight line. He shouted as loud as he could, bellowing from the bottom of his lungs as he went, "It's a trap, he's rigged to blow!"

Suddenly he twirled and fell in a heap short of his goal; a jack-hammer had smashed into him, somewhere in his lower body.

He tried pulling himself closer by his fingertips, pushing himself with one foot, but it was useless, and he knew it was useless; the grunts were quickly advancing. He uttered in a strained new voice, which was only to himself, "Oh shit, Willie, damn you," and ceased his vain effort to advance and pointed the revolver and squeezed the trigger.

He had aimed for the chest where he reasoned the explosives had been strapped under Willingham's shirt; he estimated that the grunts were still far enough back that the explosion would not cause them serious injury; perhaps concussions or blast burns or hearing loss. But his control was off and the bullet struck the left side of Willingham's head, on or near his only true flaw. The outstretched legs spasmed, but that might have been nerve reflexes.

The flare fizzled out as it had appeared, with a pop, leaving only the burning hootches casting distant light. From the obscured tree line just behind Willingham's body flashes of green tracers announced the hidden enemy. After seeing Payne fire at the body, the GIs had retreated and taken up new positions. Quick whistling lead passed over Payne. He tried but he could not stand up; he belly-crawled, looking for shelter.

Powerful hands clutched him by the blouse and dragged him back and around a burning hut. The firefight continued.

Payne was on someone's shoulders now, the huge RTO's, smelling the grit and fierce odor of a man engaged in battle. Someone had not made it, they were saying, retreating. The sounds turned vague and dreamlike. The bouncing sent sharp wires of pain up his spine and across his back; he felt nothing in one of his legs. The flashing muzzles of rifles and burning debris gave way to darkness, and the close, pounding noise diminished. Then he was let down on vibrating metal. The vibration accentuated the pain in his viscera; a rush of fast wind swept across his face.

The chopper somehow cleared the screaming incoming artillery. The black canvas of forest below was streaked in brilliant Day-Glo hues of yellow and red that licked skyward as if trying to catch the ascending chopper.

There were three casualties, two head wounds and one semiconscious ambulatory, who was Payne. The platoon had taken care of their own and gotten every man out but Willingham. It would have been suicide to try to get the dead man out too, Nichols said, supporting the account his men were giving of the action. No one would know for sure if he had been rigged. Even Payne hadn't known absolutely, and, after time, he would come to question it too.

The cockpit lights bathed the combatants in a soft glow. They were exhausted and breathing hard, their breath intermixing with the whistling port wind. Payne lay with the other casualties, drifting in and out of reality.

"What a fucking trip that was, man," one of the grunts, Kennedy, said ecstatically. "Fuckin, I ain't never felt so high."

"Too bad we can't confirm a count," said another.

"Yeah. Arty's recon personnel will get that glory," said the platoon sergeant, Reese, his voice jumping rat-a-tat-tat with the vibration. "But we still done the job on them. You men done a fine fucking job out there tonight."

"You see that fucker's arm fly off, Sarge, the one that had the machete? Looked like a friggin boomerang, never let go the blade. And then the stupid dink goes after it. Imagine that."

"What? His arm or the hacker?"

"Fuck if I know. Both, I guess. But I didn't let him get to either one."

There was laughter, the kind of laughing that would help them come down from the thrust and intensity and power of combat.

"Man, there's something about rubbing your hands in blood, man, that I fuckin dig, man. Know what I mean, Tommy? Specially when it's still hot and flowin."

"Damn it, Nick, I sure hate it that Waters got lit up," Tommy Lee said. "Look at him. He looks so peaceful. You think Meadows'll make it?" he asked the medic, who shrugged as he gauzed the head like a mummy.

"You guys are going to have to give statements on this man," Lieutenant Nichols said, looking down on Payne. "Just tell it like it was. That's all you can do."

"You think he went bananas, LT?" asked Mickey Fellows. "I mean, his buddy could've been booby-trapped. It happens. Why else would he grease him if he wasn't?"

"I don't know, Mickey. Maybe. They seemed tight. But we'll never know for sure, though. That's a fact."

"He's a head," said the medic. "I found morphine on him. And look at this shit. A fucking earring, piece of wood it looks like. Guy's a weird one. Wonder what his fucking story is. . . ."

Payne heard all this and then he went out again.

He had the orderly move the bed next to the window so he could look out at the city. Listen to it, smell it. Willingham had gotten to know Saigon, that was one thing. Maybe he'd even loved the city more than Payne; perhaps his self-mockery at becoming a Saigon Warrior had only been an expression of his wry, dark sense of humor. He never meant it. He could stand back and laugh at himself, despite himself.

Saigon was a cesspool of corruption and shanties, the largest refugee camp in Southeast Asia with million-dollar villas surrounding it, a historical city of venerable architecture and character diverse as anywhere in the world. Class and slime. Once the Paris of the Orient. Now it was a decayed, dying city clinging to life like a trapped animal. It was the struggle to survive that brought the city to life, gave it its passion and ferocious energy, and that was the thing Willingham had been most attracted to, had loved most of all about Saigon. For the soul of the city was like his own; he too had been a trapped animal whose passion inevitably destroyed him.

The orderly helped Payne onto a gurney and rolled him down the hall to use the phone. He called Lieutenant Finn.

The lieutenant had been notified. He said nothing about his lost camera. "Do you know how bad it is yet?"

"The hip's shattered. It could be worse. I still got my balls."

"I wrote Willie's folks. It's just unbelievable, Payne. I'll come and see you this afternoon."

"That's not why I called."

"What is it?"

"I need you to do something for me."

"Anything. You name it."

"There's an address book, probably in Willie's hootch. I want you to get it and bring it to me. It's important."

Finn sighed into the phone, a whimper expressing his regret: "His articles got taken already. They cleaned his stuff out of the office too. A couple of men from the CIA came and went through everything. What would the CIA want with his belongings?"

Payne was operated on that afternoon and the next day Burns paid him a visit.

"I understand they're moving you to Japan for more surgery. They have some of the finest doctors and facilities there. You should pull through all right." He adjusted Payne's pillow. "I regret things had to work out this way," he added, tapping his pipe on the window casement. "But you must understand that we really have no choice in the matter."

He stood with his back to the bed, blocking Payne's view through the window. He could still hear the city moving.

"Try to see it from our position," Burns continued without Payne's solicitation, as though he had to get it off his chest for his own reasons. "To clarify you were operating on our orders would mean we would have to reveal the nature of the investigation," he said, "and that would get sticky. There would be inquiries and investigations further up, and we can't have that. It has to end here," he said and turned to face Payne.

"It may not be much consolation to you, Specialist, but I want you to know you have done a great service for the army. Under ordinary circumstances, things being different, I'd see to it you got decorated. But our hands are tied. We simply have no other choice," he said, adding, "It's regrettable about Willingham, but it was a high-risk operation."

He did not have to come and say all this, and Payne was in a small way appreciative of it. He had tried not to think about it. He knew they were going to put it off on him, wash their hands of it; Shellhammer had made him see that. Willingham had too.

"Did you count on me telling him?"

Burns didn't answer; he was uncomfortable with the question.

"Tell me. It can't matter to you now."

"Willingham was a hothead," Burns said. "We didn't think it would matter whether you told him or not. We figured he would do the job anyway, when he saw the man. He did the job on Major Su; what was to stop him from putting the colonel away too?"

"I have to tell you something," Payne said nasally. The tubes choked his breathing when he talked. "There were coffins with weapons in them at that place. I think they were going to be sent here to Saigon, to the graveyards, like they were bodies. I saw the same thing at another place. You have to tell somebody about it."

"Of course, I'll see that information gets to the right people," Burns said, looking sadly at him, patronizing him. "But everything was blown all to hell there; they hit it with an arclight."

"But you don't understand," Payne said loudly and went into a fitful cough.

Burns tried to help by adjusting the pillow. "Well, that's just what I've been trying to explain to you," he said with a sad face. "A soldier facing serious criminal charges—who's going to listen?"

Chapter
26

The backgammon board lay open on the straight-back chair between Hansen and Payne, Hansen leaning over it from the edge of the deep chair and Payne on his cot. Hansen had a choice of three or four safe moves, but you could see his mind was set on a riskier one, a move that would better set up his potential but leave him vulnerable. It was the way he liked to play, but it would probably cost him the game.

"You guys were pretty tight, I guess," Hansen said, making his move. He sat back in the deep chair with his legs crossed at the ankles, stretching out as though he were in his own living room reflecting over his own photographs. A glow came over him going through the pictures again.

Payne lay with his legs supported on a pillow, his back against the wall. He took another slug of the cold medicine with ten percent codeine. The bottle was almost empty.

"Say, why'nt you use this picture, man? Shit, you can tell you guys were tight, just looking at it. I can see it."

Cowboy had taken the shot, Payne and Willingham Indian-wrestling, clowning around in the rain.

"Your roll," Hansen said. "Russell?"

He had spent eleven weeks in the hospital. For several days after the next operation they kept him in traction and then put him in a half-body cast for ten more weeks. The left ilium required pins and

371

metal plating. The bullet had passed through him intact; it clipped the prostate and tore up some of the lower intestine and exited through the left hip. The kidney was undamaged; he had been lucky the round did not fragment when it hit bone. They removed the hand cast after a month; he could move the little finger up and down but not sideways. He was attached to IVs and nose and catheter tubes most of his stay.

All the nurses in his sector were Americans and they attended to his needs cheerfully, sponge-bathing and cleaning him routinely, tapping the cast where he itched. They scolded him for using the stretched coat hanger he kept under his pillow, but no one took it away.

"Don't you dare tell who snuck it in when you get caught, you hear?" one nurse, Lorraine, his favorite, would say slipping him an airline bottle of Scotch, as though he would turn her in for it. Whiskey was forbidden in his diet and she knew it could cause him distress but she weighed that against his moods and made the allowance. Lorraine worked graveyard and had extra time to sit by his bed, telling him things about the world, trying to help. She brought outside reading material, paperbacks and newspapers.

In the *Washington Post* he read a sidebar article describing how units of elite Viet Cong sappers had planted themselves in Saigon in preparation for the offensive at Tet. The article said the enemy entered the city disguised as visitors for the holidays and were hidden in prearranged safe houses. Mock funerals were staged at pagodas and churches where the VC armed themselves with weapons that had been packed inside the coffins in the place of bodies. The article quoted a high-ranking U.S. official as saying, "It was an unforeseen and very clever tactic that by all estimations was pulled off in every city in the attack from Can Tho to Hue."

Cholon was destroyed in the offensive. He wondered about the fate of Lai Sin and her family, if there had been an eclipse of the sun to blame for the misfortune brought to her doorstep in this Year of the Monkey. Finn had made a trip out to the hospital when he was in Tokyo putting the magazine to bed. Publication had been postponed after he lost his working staff and again after the Tet attack. He said they were not permitting Viets on post now and he did not know what, if anything, had happened to Lai Sin or her family. She had not contacted the office; Finn seemed visibly upset for having lost Lai Sin and for not knowing what to tell Payne about her.

"Long Binh got hit bad," he told Payne excitedly. "They blew the fucking ammo dump. It was like a fucking atom bomb going off. You should've seen it." He talked like a grunt, fucking this and fucking that. "The gooks that worked on post had been bringing in explosives and plastics for months, preparing for the attack. Every fucking mamasan and papasan the army paid to work there was in on the fucking thing. That night, Payne. Shit, you should've seen it. Everybody was armed and on line, I mean every fucking body, including me. I think I shot one, too. I'm pretty sure I did. The VC were coming in dressed in ARVN uniforms. It was fucking hell, Payne."

He did not mean to say that Lai Sin had participated, smuggled explosives on post; he didn't believe she was VC. Neither did Payne.

There were three new bodies at the IO now, Finn said. "Green. Fucking incompetent." He left him with three copies of the magazine; half the articles were Payne's; the peasant woman with the dead-looking infant between her legs took up the back cover.

At night when Lorraine brought him newspapers, if he couldn't read them for himself, she read to him. She read that the President had announced he would not seek another term in office; the Tet Offensive had turned the war around and the Washington doves used it to make headlines for themselves, basking in their rhetoric as if taking pleasure from the offensive.

Payne tried not to think of what he had been through or where he was headed. But he had hours and days and weeks of solitude. He went over it time and again, trying to piece it all together, considering if he had done the right thing in the end; that was the thing that haunted him. He couldn't get rid of the sound and the smell and the feel of the pistol in his hand, the cylinder rotating, the force of the crack. Executing Willingham. Willingham might not have been dead; he might not have been laden with explosives; the grunts might not have been shot by the enemy lying in wait in the tree line. Yes. They would have, and, yes, Willingham was rigged. He was sure of it. Willingham had tried to tell him something on the way to the NVA encampment; what was it?

Lorraine did her best to discourage him from reading about the war, to talk to her about other things, the world, his family, but Payne was insistent; he wanted to know what was happening. He knew now that his father's death had something to do with wanting to know what was happening. When he was a child it meant nothing to him, and it had taken him five years to get up the courage to find out what really happened. And then he went to the newspaper building downtown and sat at a table and flipped through the pages of a giant volume of bound newspapers. There was a news article about the death on the second page of the June 9, 1957, issue. It was a large headline covering four columns: "Furniture Founder Dies From Gunshot." It referred to Joseph Payne as a prominent businessman who had unsuccessfully run for a seat on the city council the year before. Payne hadn't known that. He did know his father had something to do with the VFW, which then had given him a small sense of pride, seeing his father on occasion dressed in his green uniform. The initial article stated that his father died from a gunshot wound to the head, apparently by the Luger belonging to him. The Luger was found on the floor of the backroom office. The article quoted someone as saying suicide had not been ruled out, but the shooting was under police investigation. He found in the next day's issue that the coroner concluded the shot had been self-inflicted, and that was the official cause stated on the death certificate when Payne later went through the records at the county administration building.

And some years after that he learned from his mother that the Luger was a war souvenir from Korea—a Luger. "Yes," his mother said, "he was real proud of that because no one had ever heard of the North Koreans using that kind of gun." The Luger was a souvenir his father had killed for, and then used to kill himself. Although Payne never understood why his father took his own life, the irony of choosing his souv to do it with now made perfect sense to him.

He didn't have a picture of Willingham in the hospital, but he saw him often, his image a looming specter dropping by in the drug dreams and daydreams. Willingham under the general's palms, not a worry in the world. He would fade, and then reappear up close, as if through a ghost-red starlight scope, and he would flash his ironic grin, wink an eye as if he knew he wasn't real.

But the repeating nightmare was real: Willingham speeding through the smoky, crowded streets of Cholon in the rain, his huge face glistening fearlessly. Willingham showing off in the jeep, swerving on two wheels through the marketplace, dodging motorbikes and pedestrians. The wind's in Payne's face and he has to hang on to Willingham's arm to keep from falling out. He's amazed at Willingham's performance with the jeep and the thrill makes him laugh.

Willingham grinning like a horse, talking crazy, singing. Then Payne sees the earth fall away and they are flying over a range of emerald mountains, close to the sun, wind whistling in his ears. He grasps Willingham with all his might to hold him in, but he can't do it, and when Willingham slips through his hands, falling, Payne cries out.

Lorraine brought a psychologist around who had talked with a number of men broken by the horrors of combat. The psychologist said he would have many recurring dreams of Willingham, that such dreams were normal when someone you had spent a lot of time around was killed. It might go on for years, but that was normal, nothing to make him think he was developing psychosis. The psychologist himself hadn't been in combat and his clinical vocabulary was for the most part distant and unhelpful. He prescribed a drug he said would ease the emotional stress.

Payne remembered Willingham saying his father had never written to him, that it was always his mother, that his father didn't have the time, something like that. Payne received a letter from him; it came shortly before he was to leave Japan. It read:

"It is not easy to write to the person responsible for the death of my son. But I believe it may help you, perhaps in the years to come, to know I do not hold you in contempt for my son's death. Daryll was a boy who always courted danger and I suspect he finally went too far without your or anyone else's help. I am sure from the things he said about you in his letters that whatever the circumstances were on the battlefield you did not act out of malice. He spoke highly of you. He said you had changed his attitude by making him see that the Vietnamese people were not to blame for the loss of his companions who died in ambush. It is evident that you helped him over the loss of his platoon. From that I believe you to be a decent, well-intentioned young man and a good person."

The letter did not end there; Payne wished it had, but it hadn't. "But was there not the slightest possibility my son could have been saved?" the letter went on. "It may be an exaggeration, the speed in which evacuation helicopters can get to the scene, but even if it were a full hour, were the circumstances so critical that you could not have taken the chance and waited? Wasn't even the slightest chance worth taking? I'm sure you followed your conscience under what must have been horrifying circumstances, but where life and death are at stake, who were you to play God?"

The letter was written by a grieving father who might have believed that such was the circumstance of war, that there was not a lack of honor or reason, or even perhaps that there was destiny in his son's death; but the pain of his loss brought out the anguished need for a legitimate reason why his son had to die.

Payne could not give it to him.

And he would have to live out his life trying to answer that question: *Who were you to play God?*

Some day he would go to Huntington Beach, to their ranch home on the suburban hillside, and try to give the father and mother something of their only son they might treasure. Leave some pictures of Willingham in his jungle clothes, say some nice things about their boy. He thought some day he would visit Willingham's grave site. On the anniversary of Tet, and he would hold communion.

He imagined the visit he might make to Cotton's folks. Simple, poor people who had little to show for themselves. Even the ten thousand dollars the government paid for their boy's life would elude them, going instead to Cotton's widow, and their old frame house would still be leaning from years of bitter winter winds, its furniture the same threadbare stuff. They would have pictures of their son on the mantel, boot-camp pictures, and pictures of him with his wife and kid, maybe a snapshot some guy had sent from Vietnam, a buddy. In every picture displayed on the mantel Cotton would be in his marine uniform. Payne wouldn't know what to say to them, how to tell them he had not avenged their son's killer. "How is Grandy?" he would ask, and the father would say, "She passed on. At least she didn't have to know about Junior. We thank God for that. He was more her baby than ours, it seemed. . . . And where are you off to, Rusty? What will you be doing now?"

He imagined driving out to the farm in Moscow, Arkansas; it would now be dilapidated, the windows broken, the screen door he used to slam behind him banging askew on a rusty hinge; hippies would have used the old house as a commune, slept and fornicated in the house and in the barn; he would find the remnants of joints strewn about, in the sink and fireplace, on the floor, everywhere. There would be dried excretion in the corners of the rooms.

The preliminary hearing had been held at Long Binh in his absence. His appointed counsel notified him of the results, that he was being court-martialed and the trial would be conducted in the States. Payne didn't fully understand what was going on, but the lawyer said the change of venue was a break. If Payne had been a seasoned infantryman, the lawyer wrote, an in-country jury would go easier on him, but since he was not, he should consider himself lucky that a Stateside jury would decide the case.

The faceless lawyer forwarded the Purple Heart citation awarded Payne for the wounds he sustained during the firefight. It was the last thing he expected, and seeing the citation put him into a state of painful laughter. "Look at this," he said to Lorraine. "Can you fucking believe this shit."

Lorraine tearfully hugged him when he left. "Keep your chin up, you hear?" she said.

They flew him to Fort Lewis, Washington, and from there to Fort McPherson in Atlanta for the trial.

Captain Lowe gave him a transcript of the preliminary and the material army investigators had amassed; these were the first official papers he had seen.

Among the papers was the official military dossier on Shellhammer, his history up through his last command assignment with the 5th Special Forces. His achievements were impressive—West Point, class of 1961, airborne school, jungle training in Panama, military intelligence training, ranger school, Special Forces school at Fort Bragg, Silver, Valor, and Bronze medals with clusters, a Purple Heart, nothing posthumous included yet. The army hated to lose an officer it had invested that much in.

The dossier was chock-full of citations, letters of recommendation and commendation, previous duty stations; but it was all superfluous information. His operations with the 5th were classified. They had not been included at the preliminary and were omitted for the purposes of the trial. The best Lowe could ascertain as fact was that Shellhammer carried out clandestine counterintelligence missions supported and financed by the CIA. There were no specific missions or operations documented in his records.

The men who had first escorted them and then saved Payne's life were members of an A team from MACV Studies and Operations Group, which Lowe said was a cover title of another clandestine task force connected with the CIA. Nowhere in the transcripted records was it mentioned on whose orders Nichols's platoon had been sent to escort the journalists. The grunts' depositions were fairly sympathetic to Payne, and Lowe saw no reason to subpoena them.

Lowe initially asked for another Article 32 hearing and, failing to get it, motioned for dismissal on the ground Payne had not been adequately represented at the preliminary. The Long Binh lawyer had called only Lieutenant Finn to testify on Payne's behalf, and Lowe imputed the faceless lawyer as an incompetent who had misrepresented Payne rather than defended him. Dismissal was also denied.

The law officer ruled out the CID and CIA investigation into Shellhammer's illegal activities. Any such investigation, he said, was alleged by the defendant and thus hearsay.

So Lowe's only case rested in proving lack of motive, based on friendship. When it was his turn he called as witnesses several combat veterans unknown to Payne who testified to the unlikelihood of a soldier wantonly killing a comrade. He argued against the reliability of witnesses whose assessment of the incident was formed under duress of combat; Nichols's men might have been inaccurate in their account of the shooting, Lowe argued weakly, since they were engaging the enemy at the time and could not be sure of what they had seen.

He thought Payne would make a good impression and put him on the stand. Payne tried to sit up straight, but he soon began to slump, his hands slipping down from the arms of the chair. His demeanor was that of a beaten man trying to be courteous. The law officer at one point asked Payne if he wanted to stand down until he felt better. Payne said no, it was only a chest cold.

Lowe had him draw on a blackboard the physical layout of the village where Shellhammer was killed and then the NVA encampment; he had Payne describe what transpired at both places. Payne thought the jury of officers believed him when he said explosives were planted on Willingham, but the law officer struck the testimony as hearsay. Lowe kept him on the stand for two hours, asking questions that would establish them as friends. Payne answered with a shaky voice, trying to recite instead of remembering.

"Isn't it a matter of record that you and Corporal Willingham routinely took on assignments together and spent many off-duty hours sharing your time together, going into Saigon, doing the normal things buddies do? Wouldn't you say that you were the best of friends?"

Payne nodded and said, "Yes, sir. We were buddies."

"And isn't it true that on one of your assignments off post to-gether Corporal Willingham acted to save your life after you had been shot by a sniper? For which you received your first Purple Heart?" Lowe then read the citation. "And in turn you attempted to protect Corporal Willingham, believing him to be in danger, by advising him that he was under investigation by the CIA? And didn't you do this against orders?"

Payne was not allowed to answer that question.

Much of the questioning was incriminating, but Lowe felt that if he showed the two men had done nothing worse than occasionally smoke marijuana or engage prostitutes, trade once or twice on the black market, he would show them as real men subject to normal behavior in Vietnam, and that it would establish credibility of their friendship. He hoped it would prove to the jury that Payne anguished over having to shoot Willingham.

"Can any of us imagine what we would have done in this man's situation?" Lowe said to the jury, his eyes blinking fiercely. "Having to choose between the life of a man you were tight with, a man who was a close friend, and the lives of four men, virtual strangers, but nonetheless four American soldiers? What a terrible decision for any man to have to make. And imagine this of a soldier who was not trained as an infantryman, a man unfamiliar and inexperienced in the field of battle who suddenly came face to face with a decision even the most battle-tested soldier could easily buckle under. It took more than bravery to save those men's lives; it took moral conscience.

"There was no malice in this unfortunate incident," he said, summarizing. "Instead, this man's actions demonstrates beyond doubt the overriding sense of loyalty you have among men in war. Had it been World War II and not Vietnam, this quality of devotion would have been considered heroic and these charges would never have been brought against this soldier."

The court recessed for the day, and Lowe walked Payne back to the barracks. The lawyer was openly pessimistic. He thought it had gone badly.

"They'll hit you hard tomorrow. Damn. If we only had some kind of hard evidence, I could bring up the investigation," he said. "That would end this thing like that, and you could go on home and start putting your life back together."

He believed Payne; he believed him about Burns and Mr. Fouts and their Machiavellian investigation, that there was an operation called Gook Confirm. Lowe had considered bringing in the press to spell out the implications of such atrocious crimes, emphasizing what it would mean if it were discovered that innocent men were being systematically murdered and sold for body counts, and if left unrevealed the horrendous possibilities it implied. Lowe and Payne and the rest of the world would later learn of the possibilities from the events at a small hamlet called My Lai.

But with no supporting evidence, Lowe said he would have looked like a fool to bring in the press, and that would wash up his military career.

"The CIA went through all his stuff, Captain. There's nothing. . . . What's it like at Leavenworth?"

Lowe's Adam's apple bobbed as he walked; he glanced at Payne and smiled faintly. The sky had turned dark and was rolling in low.

"Tomorrow it will be over. Then we'll talk about that."

But the lawyer would not talk about Leavenworth tomorrow. . . .

Hansen squirmed in the deep chair waiting on Payne to make his move. Payne was standing by the barred window searching the trees in the ebbing daylight. Birds were singing, bluejays or mockingbirds mixed in concert with the trills of sparrows; somewhere a nest of hungry chirpers cried to be fed. He scanned the mulberry tree and then a pine, trying to find where the chorus was coming from, but the elusive birds were invisible in the trees, mere sound.

The singing was melancholy and it reminded him of Saang. Although he would never know for certain her true intentions, he thought of her with a gentle heart, with sadness and reverence, for nothing worse had come of knowing her than the memory he would carry of her painful life. He had asked Lorraine in the hospital to bring him something so he could repierce his earlobe. She said she would but never did.

"You going to roll the dice, man?" Hansen said. It was the first time he had shown impatience with Payne.

Payne eased back to his cot and mindlessly made his play.

Then another MP came in to say that Ann was waiting in the visitors' lounge. She had been to see him the day before yesterday and was supposed to fly back to Dallas the same afternoon; Payne thought she had.

"My wife?"

The guard said, "No. Ann-Margret. Get your butt in gear."

He drained the last of the cold medicine and limped behind the MP in an effort to keep up.

She was wearing tight dark jeans and a black blouse, fitting attire for the black sky outside and the hushed funereal bleakness inside. She greeted him tentatively.

"I thought you went back to Dallas."

"I did. . . . I found something. Rand found it," she said, and turned to the window. "I'm sorry, Russ. He was over yesterday helping me pack."

She turned back to face him but kept her eyes somewhere on his chest. "I guess I didn't tell you. I got the job I've been wanting in New York."

Payne tried to smile, but it came off as a sneer. "Why did you come back? You could have called."

"The rest of your stuff came from over there. There was a gun," she said. "I didn't know they let you bring those things back."

"The AK?"

"A rifle," Ann said. "Rand was taking it apart, cleaning it or something. It fascinated him; I guess he likes guns. Anyway, he found this in it. I knew it would be important and that's why I came."

She dipped into her purse and withdrew an envelope. Payne took it. A wrinkled snip of four 35-mm negatives. He held his breath, turning the film to the overhead light; chill bumps raced across his arms. They were the negatives. Also in the envelope was a sheet of paper the size of an address-book page. It was not in code; Shellhammer's name was on it and some other names, two dates, two villages. It was Willingham's handwriting. He had written on the bottom of the paper: "To Whom It May Concern/These are names and places of missions I was ordered on by Lt. Colonel R. Shellhammer of 5th Special Forces. These missions were for the purpose of collecting data on the male populations of villages which Col. Shellhammer forged as defecting Viet Cong under a program known as Open Arms. Check records against dates and places."

His mind raced back. He couldn't remember Willingham telling him about this; he would have remembered it. Then it came to him. That was what Willingham had tried to tell him on the way to the NVA camp. He had hidden the evidence in the AK; he would have done it while Payne slept on his floor the night before; that was why he made Payne promise not to give his souv away. He'd outsmarted them.

"Those pictures. It's horrible," Ann said, her mouth contorting in disgust. "What in God's name did you do over there?"

Payne hugged her and tried again to smile. Instead he started crying and it came hard. At first she backed off, then she came forward and put her arm across his back where he sat holding his face.

He could not catch enough breath to say anything. He felt her squeeze his shoulder and try to pull him to her, as if she wanted to rock him against her chest. He couldn't stop crying for a long time.

Captain Lowe met early the next day in private session with the law officer. Payne did not have to go back to the courtroom. It was over. In exchange for his freedom he had to give up the evidence; but he kept one of the negatives, and with Lowe's help, or without it, he would take his story to the media. He would be listened to somewhere. He would write Willingham's story himself.

In four days he was let go, all charges dropped. Honorable discharge, back pay and allowances close to a thousand dollars, possible disability pay. He gave Hansen a couple of pictures he seemed especially to like; he grabbed Pruett at the nape of his neck, drew him close and said something private, and left the army compound dressed awkwardly in civilian clothes.

He looked at the shiny, colorful cars passing by, at the crisp spring sky and fought back the terrible urge to cry again.

A kid on a bicycle wheeled up and stopped on the curb close to him. He took off an Atlanta Braves cap to brush the sweat off his face and casually looked Payne up and down. Suddenly he spoke to him in English. "You a soldier, mister?"

The strangeness of the boy's voice startled him. Payne shook his head no.

The kid eyed him skeptically. "You *look* like a soldier."

The kid had buck teeth and freckles. He was a paperboy.

A tractor-trailer screamed by, blowing dust in Payne's eyes, and he saw a small body drawn under the truck's wheels.

He extended his hand and ruffled the boy's long hair.

"Better be careful around these trucks."

About the Author

Ronald Argo was born in Anniston, Alabama. He graduated from the University of Georgia in 1968. After seven years as a newspaper reporter, he returned to receive his M.A. from San Diego State University in 1980, and has for the past eight years been at work in the writing of this novel. His tour in Vietnam, 1970–71, was spent in III and IV Corps as an army journalist. He is a recipient of Sigma Delta Chi's journalism award for investigative reporting. Mr. Argo lives with his wife in San Diego, where he is currently at work on his next novel.